MADELINE

MADELINE

A Novel of Love, Buddhism, and Hoboken

Florence Wetzel

iUniverse, Inc.
New York Lincoln Shanghai

Madeline
A Novel of Love, Buddhism, and Hoboken

iUniverse, Inc.

For information address:
iUniverse, Inc.
2021 Pine Lake Road, Suite 100
Lincoln, NE 68512
www.iuniverse.com

ISBN: 0-595-27631-8

Printed in the United States of America

This book is dedicated to

Beatrice Joy Chute

and

Pema Chödrön

If you wish to move in the One Way
do not dislike even the world of senses and ideas.
Indeed, to accept them fully
is identical with true Enlightenment.

—Verses on the Faith Mind
by Seng-Tsan, the Third Zen Ancestor
Translated by Richard B. Clarke

Contents

Chapter 1   Smoking with Spencer 1
Chapter 2   The Part Spencer Knew 8
Chapter 3   The Part Spencer Didn't Know 25
Chapter 4   Evening at Home 47
Chapter 5   Blind Date 66
Chapter 6   First Date 84
Chapter 7   Second Date 104
Chapter 8   The Gig 128
Chapter 9   Sex 148
Chapter 10   On Call 167
Chapter 11   Brunch from Hell 181
Chapter 12   Living Together 208
Chapter 13   Super Cool 234
Chapter 14   Surprise 255
Chapter 15   Shock 265
Chapter 16   Pain and Knowledge 283
Chapter 17   No Ram Dass 321
Chapter 18   Alison Again 331
Chapter 19   Another Surprise 341
Chapter 20   Happy End 355
About the Author *385*

Acknowledgements

The author would like to thank Daisy Diaz-Granados, Bob Fass, Mihalis Heretakis, George Howard-Heretakis, Margarita Howard-Heretakis, Glynis Jackson, Dan Sugarman, Dorothy Wetzel, and the staff at iUniverse.

Special thanks to Emily Hampton-Manley.

Very special thanks to Doris China.

Very very special thanks to Vicki Clausman.

CHAPTER 1

Smoking with Spencer

Spencer wanted to know everything, and Madeline was just about to tell him when the phone rang.

It was always like that when she visited Spencer: from ringing phones to yells from the street (Spencer had no doorbell) to visits from the downstairs sculptor-drug dealer and upstairs belly dancer, it seemed everyone in Hoboken wanted something from Spencer. Madeline tilted her head against the faded blue velvet couch where she and Spencer were sitting, and half-listened as Spencer made plans for someone to come over.

"That was David Guggenheim," Spencer said after he hung up. "You know David?"

"Mmm—I don't think so."

"But you've heard of Narrow Grave? That's his band."

"I've seen their posters, but I've never gone to hear them."

Spencer raised his eyebrows. "Oh, you should. Big things are happening for them, big things. They're fantastic musicians."

Madeline suppressed a smile. She had learned long ago that Spencer excluded nothing from the word "fantastic": Charlie Parker playing "A Night in Tunisia" was fantastic, but so was a child playing "The Star-Spangled Banner" on a kazoo. Spencer used to run the weekly Jazz Open Mike Night at Maxwell's, and he would let anyone—but anyone—play. Once Madeline was on a date with a local jazz musician, and they had an argument about Spencer: the musician said that creating quality music was more important than making less than competent musicians feel good, but Madeline agreed with Spencer that people needed to express themselves, and so what if the music was not high quality. Madeline had nevertheless passed many painful evenings at the Jazz Open Mike Night, and so she was not convinced by Spencer's assessment of Narrow Grave.

"What big things?" she asked.

"*Big* things. They're in negotiation with—" he named a Big Record Label—"and if everything goes well they'll be signing a contract soon. I've been working with them the last few months, they want a flute on a few of their songs."

"Great."

"Anyway that was David, he plays bass, he and Hanson—that's his partner—are coming by to pick up some smoke."

Madeline widened her eyes. "You're not dealing?"

"No no no. Just Candace had to run into The City and she left the bag with me so David could pick it up. They'll be here in about ten minutes, so don't start your story yet. Speaking of smoke, do you want to get high? Or are you still off pot?"

She waved a hand. "I've renounced renunciation."

"So you'll smoke with me?"

"Sure."

Spencer reached over to the battered wooden end table and picked up a red velvet bag with a black drawstring. He drew out a pipe—a strange little pipe, dark purple and shaped like a spaceship—and a small tin box decorated with corseted Victorian women and curly script. He put the pipe on one knee and the tin box on the other, then opened the tin box and pulled out a green bud so fresh and strong Madeline could smell it from the other end of the couch. As Spencer crumpled the bud into the pipe, Madeline felt a nervous excitement run through her. How long had it been since she last got stoned? A year at least, maybe two.

Spencer lit the pipe, and the rich, dusky scent of strong marijuana filled the air. Madeline looked out the window, worried for a moment: she had been through so much the last five months, what if she smoked and got completely paranoid? I hope I don't freak out, she thought, turning to watch Spencer drag on the pipe. She could usually snap out of a freak out if she caught herself, although there was that one night not long after graduating college when she had gotten high with a Jamaican woman she met at one of her temp jobs. "I got some get high," the woman said. "Wanna smoke after work?" Madeline agreed; she met the woman by the elevator banks, then they walked to the army recruiting office in Times Square and passed a joint in the black evening as commuters hurried by. What was in that pot Madeline never found out, but as they smoked all her synapses realigned, and it had taken every brain cell she had left just to scrape herself off the sidewalk and walk over to Port Authority. Then on the bus ride to Hoboken Madeline had been convinced that two girls from her high school were sitting behind her and talking about her past and all the men she had slept with. Madeline was a trembling mess the entire trip, and when it was at last her stop she turned around to confront the girls, and what did she see but two old ladies huddled over a playbill. Now *that* was a freak out.

"Here," Spencer said, passing her the pipe. "Put your finger there on that little hole, then lift it off at the very end of your inhale."

Madeline took the pipe and did as instructed. The smoke filled her mouth, her throat, her lungs; she closed her mouth and breathed in a little deeper, and suddenly a terrible harshness sheared her throat—she had taken too much, her throat and lungs were on fire. She opened her mouth and let the smoke come out in a rush.

"It's been awhile," she said between coughs.

"Take less."

So she did. A few small puffs, not much but she held them in, and when she passed the pipe to Spencer it was as if an invisible hand had passed over her mind. It was the same room, same Madeline and same Spencer, but it was all different now, a bit looser at the seams, a little more vivid. Well, she thought, I'm stoned.

She looked over at Spencer. He was much older than she was, in his early fifties compared to her twenty-seven. He was medium height, slim and muscular with wire frame glasses, thin grey ponytailed hair and, oddly, beautiful skin, peachy and practically unlined. She met him a few years ago when she moved to Hoboken with her sister and brother-in-law; she approached him after a concert at Church Square Park to tell him she enjoyed his music, and because Spencer was Spencer, he asked her to join him and some other musicians at The Beat'n Path, and so began their friendship. It took awhile before she learned that Spencer was a world-famous jazz musician who had recorded many albums and was in constant demand at festivals in Europe, but by that time their friendship was established and she knew him too well to be in awe of him. He was the funky hippie uncle she never had; he was a genuine article of the Sixties, and she was enthralled by his tales of loft parties and free love and gigs playing background flute for Allen Ginsberg's poetry readings, not to mention his stories of capping parties where a group of people put the latest shipment of Sandoz LSD into capsules, licking their fingers as they went along.

Madeline loved going over to Spencer's apartment and spending the afternoon talking and smoking, although it never happened on a regular basis—sometimes she saw him three times in one week, and then not at all for months. Spencer had his own sense of time, and his own unique way of conducting a friendship.

He handed her the pipe, she took another drag and then a strange noise floated into the room. Someone was yelling; Madeline cocked her ear and the words took shape: "Spen-cer! Spen-cer!"

"It's David," Spencer said. He rose and walked through the apartment—a railroad like most Hoboken apartments, three rooms with no doors in between—and then he disappeared into the hall.

Madeline took the pipe and went over to the window. The window was large and low, with a windowsill just wide enough for her to sit on. She took another hit off the pipe, then looked down onto the sidewalk; she couldn't see the people who had been yelling. Her gaze rose and she looked out onto Washington Street. Despite being Hoboken's main street, Washington Street was quiet and oddly suspended: there were no cars moving on the slice of street in front of her, and the late September sun had laid a white stretch of light on the asphalt. A woman on the opposite sidewalk was strolling her baby, a tall man with black hair had stopped to tie his shoelace, the buildings opposite were brick, the parking meters silver, the parked car dusky blue—and suddenly Madeline was happy. I'm back, she thought. Thank God, I'm back. And I'm here at Spencer's, I'm stoned and I'm not even paranoid. She felt sure, really sure, that the weight and effort of the past five months were finally over.

She did not hear anyone come in, and only when Spencer said, "Madeline?" did she turn and look back into the room. She was framed in the white windowsill, surrounded by apple green walls; her thick dark blonde hair appeared golden against her dark blue sweater, her honey-colored skin was clear, her fullish lips a natural red, and her large grey-green eyes were peaceful. And sitting like that, half-turned with her hands resting on her grey cotton skirt, her small waist looked even smaller, and her full chest even fuller.

And that is how David first saw her.

"Madeline," Spencer said. "Come meet David and Hanson."

She was never good at names, particularly when she was stoned, and so she needed some minutes sitting on the couch listening to Spencer talk before she was able to say with certainty that David was the tall one with dark hair, and Hanson the taller one with long blond hair. Spencer handed David a small plastic bag filled with pot, the pipe was refilled and relit, and the conversation instantly turned to music—Hanson had just bought an old Dexter Gordon album (a picture of a black man in a phone booth, blue and green stripes with white letters proclaiming DEXTER CALLING) and he was eager to listen to it. Although Spencer's furniture was on the point of collapse he did have a decent stereo, and soon music—a dense, multi-colored liquid—poured through the room.

Madeline had taken another turn at the pipe and was now pleasantly stoned. She felt no need to talk, she was far too busy watching the jumping lights on the stereo, and so it took her awhile to notice that David—the dark-haired one on the overstuffed chair closet to her—was staring at her. He was leaning over with his elbows on his knees and his fingers locked, and he was looking straight at her. She was surprised to catch him staring; she blushed, pursed her lips, and looked down. A few moments later she looked up again; he was still staring.

Oh no. Maybe she was mistaken? She looked at the others—Spencer was handing the pipe to Hanson and telling him about a gig he played with Dexter in New York in '62, or was it '63. Madeline let her eyes slowly return to the dark-haired one—David. Yes, he was still staring, his dark brown eyes wide and wandering all over her face. This time he smiled, and Madeline smiled back. He's good-looking, she thought, taking in his dark brown hair cut in bangs, his heavy eyebrows, straight nose, and white skin. Really good-looking, actually.

"I don't think I've ever seen you before," he said. "Did you just move here?"

"Oh no," she answered. "I've lived here for years."

"Strange I never saw you…"

"I don't go to rock clubs all that much. I've seen Antietam and Chris Stamey at Maxwell's, but mostly I go hear Spencer play jazz."

"I'm just getting into jazz myself. Hanson's been really into it for about a year, and now he's got me listening. We're even trying to incorporate a little jazz into our music—Spencer's been a big help."

"Yes, he told me he's playing on some of your songs."

"And you?" he asked, smiling. "What do you do?"

"I'm a writer," she said. "I write short stories."

"A writer! I admire you; I always wanted to write, but I don't have the discipline. Do you write every day?"

She nodded. "Just about."

"That's great."

"Music takes discipline, too."

He smiled. "It's funny, I never think of music that way. With music I'm just—I don't know, I'm just *in* it, I'm in it all the time. It's my whole life."

"And that's how I feel about writing."

They smiled at each other. "So," he said. "Why haven't I seen you at any of Spencer's gigs? We go hear him all the time."

"I've been away. I was living down the shore for five months."

"Do you still live there?"

"No. It was just a temporary thing."

"So now you're back."

"Now I'm back."

"Lucky for Hoboken."

She smiled, then looked away. Hanson passed the pipe to David and called his attention to a change in the music's rhythm. David took a long, hard pull on the pipe, then cocked his head and concentrated on the sounds swirling through the room. He took another hit from the pipe, then held it out for Madeline; and as her hand moved towards the pipe Madeline looked at David, and their eyes locked. She was startled by the intensity of his gaze; he was not smiling, just staring. She frowned slightly, and turned away.

As Madeline held the pipe to her mouth and drew in—a mistake, probably, because how could she possibly speak coherently to Spencer after smoking so much?—Hanson held out his arm and tapped his watch.

"It's quarter to four," he said to David. "We should get going."

David sighed. He looked at Madeline and smiled. "We have a voice lesson at four."

"A voice lesson?" she asked politely.

"Mmm hmm. There's an ex-opera singer who lives over on Hudson Street, she's retired now but she gives lessons. She's really helped us with our harmonies—but have you ever heard our music? We do a lot of different things with our voices, it's a big part of our sound."

"No, I've never heard you guys play."

"We have two albums with—" he named a Small Local Record Label. "You can buy them at Pier Platters. Or come to our next gig, I'll give them to you free."

"Okay," she said, not meaning it.

"David," Hanson said as he rose out of his seat. "We really do have to go."

"Okay." David collected the bag of pot, then stood and looked down at Madeline. "It was really nice meeting you. Hoboken's so small, I'm sure I'll run into you again. And like I said, you should come to our next gig."

She smiled, and said nothing. Hanson collected his Dexter Gordon album, and asked Spencer what night he was free so they could do a little rehearsing. They discussed times, made arrangements to meet, then David handed Spencer money for the pot. Spencer and Hanson started walking to the front door; David was behind them, and as he was about to step from the living room to the middle room, he turned his head and gave Madeline a final, searching look.

Spencer followed them downstairs so he could lock the door, and Madeline was left alone. She leaned back against the couch and looked at the ceiling. She was used to getting attention from men—she seemed to have the kind of looks they liked, something to do with being blonde with high cheekbones and full-ish lips, plus being tall and having a big chest didn't hurt. But in truth the attention embarrassed her, and she did not know how to handle it. Like many attractive women, Madeline's internal image did not correspond to her external facts; men saw her as a tall, good-looking blonde, but inside Madeline still felt like a gangly fifth-grader with cat glasses and, how embarrassing, a chest that sprouted before anyone else's. Over the years many men had told her she was beautiful, but whenever anyone complimented her she always felt they were talking about someone else. So she was not inclined to think about David Guggenheim and his persistent stares; in fact the minute he was out the door, she forgot about him.

Spencer came back and resumed his seat on the couch. He motioned to the pipe on the table. "More?" he asked.

"Oh no," she said, waving a hand. "But you go ahead if you want."

"No, I'm good." He turned himself so he was facing her, then crossed his legs and put his hands on his knees. Spencer always kept perfect posture; even at his most inebriated, his spine was a stick of iron. He once told Madeline that when he was in his thirties he met a rascal guru who had come from India to live in New York. The guru had lived for years in the Himalayas with a radical sect that had no rules; members of the sect roamed the mountains meditating, collecting food and, if necessary, fighting to the death. After leaving India the guru spent several months at the communal Soho loft where Spencer lived, and one day when Spencer was playing the flute the guru came up behind him, put his hands on Spencer's head, and slowly lifted until Spencer's spine was straight. The music that followed was unlike any Spencer had ever played, and later when he asked the guru what happened the guru said, "There is one secret, and one secret only: straight spine."

"So," Spencer said. "I'm ready. Tell me everything."

CHAPTER 2

The Part Spencer Knew

There were two parts to Madeline's story: the part Spencer knew, and the part he didn't know.

The part Spencer knew was this:

Madeline was raised a Presbyterian. She and her family—her parents and her sister Bella—belonged to a solid, undramatic church with a solid, undramatic, and very wealthy congregation. Madeline and Bella attended Sunday school, and their parents usually attended church, but except for church and saying grace before meals, the family was not religious.

Except for Madeline. From a very young age Madeline had strong religious feelings; and whereas her sister Bella complained that church was stupid and Sunday school boring, Madeline always liked church and everything connected to it. She could still recall stepping into her first Sunday school class when she was five years old, could still recall her joy as she looked at the prints on the wall depicting Christ's life: his birth, his youth (wearing a skullcap, carrying scrolls and talking to a rabbi) and of course all the well-known scenes—the miracles, the crucifixion, the rebirth. And she could still recall her feeling of a goodness pervading everything, some kind of shimmering whiteness that filled the room and herself. If Madeline had a gift, then it was a gift of Merger: she had an ability to break through the world of the senses, and feel the connection between herself and her surroundings. Her childhood was full of hours on end of Merger; it was a common enough childhood experience, but unlike most children Madeline felt strongly that this feeling had something to do with Jesus. Christ was extremely real to her—she had him as an imaginary friend as other children might have a clown or a cowboy, and contemplating him gave her a trembly elated feeling, a feeling one might call bliss.

Then puberty hit. The white light pervading everything started to fade, and Madeline entered the most nightmarish years of her life. Junior high was filled with awkwardness, but in high school there was sex and drugs and drinking. Every day was like slamming into a brick wall, and she just kept slamming herself harder and harder, hoping it would stop the pain.

Her sister Bella saved her life. At the beginning of Madeline's senior year in high school, Bella came to the house after years of self-imposed exile. Bella had left the house at age seventeen to begin years of self-destructive rebellion, but recently she had reformed: she was attending Columbia's School of General Studies, and had just moved in with a young Columbia professor. Madeline went into The City frequently to see her sister, but she was not prepared when Bella suddenly showed up at the house and embarked on a screaming fight with their parents. After the fight Bella came into Madeline's room. Madeline, in bed with a hangover, the previous night's makeup still on her face, watched as Bella sat on her bed and in a quiet, calm voice informed Madeline that their parents were crazy, and that was why Bella had been crazy, and that was why Madeline was now crazy.

"I'm not joking," Bella said. "When I say crazy, I mean crazy. I could never see it because I was always in it. They're crazy, Madeline, and they'll try to destroy you just like they tried to destroy me. Look at yourself, Madeline," Bella said, taking Madeline's face in her hands. "You're such a beautiful girl, but all you feel for yourself is contempt. You can't live like this anymore—so as soon as you graduate, you're coming to live with me and Robert."

"But—"

"No, Madeline. There's no choice. And Robert has some friends at Barnard, we want you to apply there. You can get in—your grades aren't great, but your SAT scores are high, and I know they'll be impressed by your writing. One way or another, we'll get you in."

Madeline did move in with Bella and Robert, and she did get accepted at Barnard. The drinking and promiscuity took a few more years to loosen their hold, but gradually she stopped slamming herself into walls. And in senior year, having fulfilled all her requirements as well as most of the courses for her major in English, she took a course called "Introduction to Chinese Thought." And then she had an experience that changed her life.

It was autumn, late November. The Ferris Booth Cafe had just opened that year, and Madeline had gotten into the habit of going there every morning to drink mocha-flavored coffee and eat a chocolate chip muffin. The cafe opened at seven, and Madeline usually arrived a little after. Campus was deserted at that hour; she shared the cafe with one or two professors and a few graduate students, everyone reading quietly or having low earnest conversations. She liked the hiss of the coffee machines, the quiet hum of the staff, the view of campus through the glass windows that ran from floor to ceiling. It was a warm, cozy world, and Madeline appreciated it because it was sane. That was something Bella always said: direct yourself towards sanity.

That day she was reading for her Chinese philosophy class. The class had only one text, *A Sourcebook of Chinese Philosophy* by Wing-Tsit Chan, a thick book with a black binder and light green cover. Madeline loved the book; she carried it with her everywhere, browsing through it at random and underlining the passages she liked, particularly those by Confucius, Mencius, and Chuang Tzu. That morning she was reading in the section on Ch'eng Hao when she came across the following line:

"...human nature does not possess the two aspects of internal and external."

She read the line; she read it again. Then something happened: it was as if something fell and suddenly she was huge—she was all of this, the coffee, the cafe, the students hurrying by outside, Butler Library, the pigeons on the lawn. There was suddenly this enormousness and—what great beauty—a clean, simple peace. She was stunned. She was afraid to move—would it go away? But no, she could still move, still think, still drink coffee; and yet every movement was exactly right, joyous and simple. It was odd, frightening, ecstatic; it was a foreign feeling, and at the same time completely familiar.

She moved through the morning and most of the afternoon in this state. It was the slowest day of her life: every face, every sound, every random shadow was infinitely precious and fascinating. It was like walking through an enormous palace, and yet it was just her ordinary life, just Madeline going to classes. Every so often she reread the line from Ch'eng Hao, as if by reading it she could make this strange blossoming last forever, but slowly the feeling started to fade, and when she stopped at Mama Joy's on her way home and was on line ready to order a sandwich, the feeling disappeared altogether. The magical interconnectedness was gone; she was once again Madeline, and everything else was once again everything else.

But she did not sleep that night. She laid awake half the night thinking, "What *was* that? What *was* it?" There was no one to ask, no one to tell—Bella and Robert were five-senses-only people, and none of Madeline's friends had ever hinted at such an experience. She felt sad that she could not tell anyone, but she knew without a shadow of a doubt that it had been real. And she asked herself: was this feeling the reality, and her every day sense of the world just an illusion? Was it possible to feel this way all the time? She did not know, and she did not know how to find out.

She felt like a person with a secret. She became a silent detective, looking at everyone and wondering if they knew this secret too. Once when she was in line at the cash machine she heard a loud nasal voice behind her proclaim, "Awl dis is just a dream. One day you close yer eyes, and it's awl gone. It's like we're awl dreaming this." Madeline whirled around—she saw a short dumpy woman wearing a red wool coat and a blue wool hat. Her companion, an equally short woman in an equally wooly outfit, nodded and said, "Don't I know it." Madeline studied the women's faces—but no, she saw nothing unusual, nothing at all.

Books were better. She devoured the whole of *The Sourcebook of Chinese Philosophy*, and then when her teacher compared a line by Lao Tzu with a passage from Thoreau, Madeline bought a copy of *Walden*. And yes, Thoreau talked about Merger (as Madeline had come to think of her experience). She reread *Walden* several times, then one day on Broadway she saw someone selling books on the sidewalk, and as she examined the books one caught her eye: *Liberation from the Known* by Krishnamurti. She had never heard of Krishnamurti, but according to the blurb on the back cover it was a work of philosophy, and anyway she liked his picture, liked his big brown eyes and no-nonsense expression. She spent all night reading the book, and the next day she went to Papyrus Books and bought three more Krishnamurti books. By reading and rereading certain passages, she got a hint of Merger. The feeling never came back as strongly, but at least she felt in Merger's presence, like looking at a picture of someone you love.

Her senior year was magical: while others were rushing around pinning down careers and graduate schools, Madeline was reading Thoreau in Riverside Park, coaxing the feeling of Merger. But as graduation approached, Madeline began to think about her future or, more specifically, money. She knew she was going to be a writer, but whether she would ever make money at writing was another matter entirely. She had a long talk with Bella and Robert, and was relieved to learn they had no intention of kicking her out the moment she had her diploma. As a matter of fact, they had recently gone to a brunch in Hoboken, and they were so charmed by the city that they were contemplating buying a brownstone there, a place where the three of them could live in less cramped conditions than on 112th Street. When Madeline asked how much rent they wanted her to pay, they were deeply wounded: they did not want a penny from her. So with rent no longer a problem, Madeline thought she could get away with working part-time; she took a word processing course, and the day after graduation took her first temp assignment at a public relations firm on Fifth Avenue.

She quickly realized that real life was not like college. Although her writing teacher was willing to continue reading Madeline's work, there were no more writing courses, and no more assignments or grades. Now everything depended on Madeline and her discipline, and it seemed best to put her spiritual search on the back burner. If she focused on writing, she would one day be able to write what she liked as she liked, but if she focused on spiritual things—? She did not see the point of it, could not see how it would help achieve her goals. Her searching seemed to have nothing to do with her writing: she was meticulously documenting her childhood via short stories, and writing about her father's hypochondria or her mother's hysteria seemed to have no connection with what she had felt at the Ferris Booth Cafe. So all thoughts of Merger faded into the background; she moved to Hoboken with Bella and Robert, and although she still had her copies of *A Sourcebook of Chinese Philosophy*, *Walden*, and all her Krishnamurti books, she never touched them, preferring instead to concentrate on literature.

Three years passed. Madeline wrote, she read, she dated, she stopped temping and got a steady job working the weekend shift at a law firm. She went to hear Spencer play jazz, visited her writing teacher and other friends in The City, and went occasionally to Connecticut to visit her friend Devon, who was now married with a baby. Sometimes Madeline felt happy, sometimes sad for no reason, but mostly she was just on her course, doing her best at writing, spending time with people she cared about.

And then Michael moved into the apartment above them. Bella and Robert owned the building, but they hated being landlords so they decided to turn the building into a cooperative. They sold the bottom floor to a lawyer, the second to a homosexual couple, the third to a film director, kept the fourth floor for themselves, and sold the fifth floor to Michael, another Columbia professor. From the beginning Michael annoyed Madeline: he was nice to look at—in his late thirties, tall with sandy hair and a calm, handsome face—but he was the slowest person she had ever met. He took forever to say or do the simplest things, and spending time with him drove her crazy. But one evening he was at their apartment playing Scrabble, and when Bella asked him what he was doing that weekend, he said that Saturday morning he was going to Madison Square Garden to hear Krishnamurti. Madeline's eyes lit up: Krishnamurti! Here, in New York! Something inside her woke up; she had to go, she didn't even care if she missed work. She asked Michael if tickets were terribly expensive. "As a matter of fact," Michael said, "they're only five dollars." Madeline blushed and said nothing; then Michael said, "Why don't you come with me? He's an excellent speaker."

So they went. The night before Madeline was so excited she could hardly sleep, and the next morning she woke at seven and started pacing the apartment, waiting for Michael to come. On the bus ride into The City Madeline looked out the window, trying to control her mounting excitement. And when they stepped into Madison Square Garden everything felt magical: they found their seats, waited, talked a little, then Krishnamurti stepped on the stage. He was a small brown man in white pants and a white Nehru jacket; he gingerly sat on a lone chair and began to speak. His main points were that nobody needs a guru, and that we never experience life freshly because our thoughts get in the way. Neither of these ideas changed Madeline's life; she had already encountered them—but not necessarily understood them—in Krishnamurti's books. What affected her was the feeling in that huge room: it was Merger, that feeling of simplicity and peace. How one person could generate that feeling she did not know, but somehow Krishnamurti was doing it. When the talk was over Michael took her out to lunch, and on the bus ride home she was silent with joy.

Her old books came off the shelves. She still read literature, but now most afternoons—silent still afternoons, alone on the couch in the living room—she read from her old books. The books had not changed; they still evoked the same feelings, the same yearnings, but now she was a little older, and she saw that the spiritual search was as essential to her life as writing, and she determined to make time for both.

Her reading expanded, thanks to Spencer and Michael. She and Spencer had always talked about writing, music, and counterculture life, subjects he was expert in, and now for the first time Madeline brought up religion: she timidly told him about Krishnamurti and the feelings that had arisen during his talk. And she saw, to her delight, that this was another one of Spencer's worlds: *of course* he knew about Krishnamurti, in fact he had met him in Switzerland, he was doing a gig and a friend took him to Gstaad. And as for the feeling of Merger, *of course* he knew what she was talking about, that was exactly what he was trying to express in his music. Madeline left that day with a stack of books: *Wisdom and Insecurity* by Alan Watts, *Autobiography of a Yogi* by Paramahansa Yogananda, *Be Here Now* by Ram Dass (which Spencer said originally came with a tab of acid, but Madeline was not sure if she believed him), and *The Center of the Cyclone* by John Lilly. And Michael lent her *Living Time* by Maurice Nicholl, *Memories, Dreams, Reflections* by Carl Jung, *The Crack in the Cosmic Egg* by Joseph Chilton Pierce, and Richard Wilhelm's essays on the I Ching, and on her own she discovered *Who Dies?* by Stephen Levine and *I Am That* by Sri Nisargadatta Maharaj.

She started going with Michael to lectures at Columbia. Michael and several other professors—some like him from the East Asian Studies department, some not—had decided to use their clout as Columbia professors to invite speakers who they wanted to hear. Madeline had usually not heard of the speakers—they ranged from Zen scholars to an advocate for homeless people to a Tibetan lama to a Catholic priest fighting against nuclear weapons—but she always enjoyed the atmosphere, always enjoyed the serious learned people and the important issues raised. Some of the lectures concerned religion, some not, and then one speaker in particular touched Madeline in a sensitive, forgotten place. His name was Lex Hixon; according to Michael he had a radio show and had written several books, but Madeline had never heard of him. She liked him the minute he walked on stage—he had longish blond hair, wore a flowing white caftan, and had a wonderfully quiet way of speaking. His talk encompassed many subjects, but what touched Madeline was his idea that people can rediscover their childhood religion. He said that the gift of faith in childhood is one of the greatest gifts of all, and if we were lucky enough to have been raised in a particular religion we could reacquaint ourselves with that religion, and need not search for something foreign and exotic. Tears sprang to Madeline's eyes; she hardly heard the rest of the talk because she suddenly remembered, for the first time in years, how she had felt in childhood. She had never connected her experience at the Ferris Booth Cafe with her experiences as a child, but now she understood: they were the same. This thought was so exciting, and awoke such feelings of tenderness. She had long ago rejected Christianity—when was it, high school? Yes; smoking a joint with a friend, talking about religion and church when suddenly Madeline realized: the only reason I believe in Christianity is because I was told to believe in it. It was brainwashing, as foolish as believing that America was the greatest country in the world, another idea which had been rammed down her throat from the moment she was born. From then on Madeline was without God and proud of it. And as time went on she could not believe she had ever accepted such foolish ideas. Bella and Robert had similar feelings about religion, and around the apartment it was always acceptable to scorn the Church and all things religious. But now her old feelings were waking up inside her, and she was both ecstatic and terrified.

After the talks Madeline always accompanied Michael and his group of professor friends to The Balcony, a local restaurant. Madeline considered herself extremely intelligent, but these people were on another level entirely: their conversations were fast, sharp, and complex, and they used terms she had never heard of, terms like transpersonal psychology, the Pacific Shift, and the Gaia Theory. Michael always illuminated Madeline afterwards, but during the actual dinners Madeline never uttered a word. She was sure everyone thought she was stupid, but they were always kind to her, and accepted her as Michael's friend—*not* his girlfriend, a fact she hoped was abundantly clear. The night of Lex Hixon's talk she was in a daze; her emotions built to an unbearable pitch, and the scintillating conversation flew right past her. Only at the end when everyone was putting on their coats and leaving did she notice that one of the older men was her Introduction to Chinese Philosophy professor.

"I know you," she said. "I was in one of your classes—but you probably don't remember me."

"On the contrary," he said in a booming voice. "I do remember you. We professors always remember pretty blondes—isn't that right, Michael?"

Madeline started to cry. Michael's eyes widened; he hurried her outside and around the corner to 106th Street. They sat on the steps of a brownstone, and Madeline wept. Michael gave her a handkerchief—he *would* have one, she thought—and waited.

"Madeline," he said finally. "Why are you crying? He paid you a compliment."

"Oh, it has nothing to do with him," she said, blowing her nose. "I think I'm crying because I'm happy." She hesitated a moment, then thought, Well, why not tell him? So as they walked to the subway at 110th Street, waited for the train, rode the Number One to Times Square, walked underground to Port Authority, Madeline told Michael everything: her religious feelings during childhood, her experience at the Ferris Booth Cafe, her feelings during the Krishnamurti talk, the way she felt when Lex Hixon suggested rediscovering one's childhood faith, and how she realized that her experiences in childhood and her experience at the Ferris Booth Cafe were one and the same.

"I feel overwhelmed," she told Michael as they waited for the Red Apple bus to Hoboken. "I feel like I've just discovered something, but I don't know what it is. And don't you dare mention any of this to Bella and Robert."

"Why?"

"They'll make fun of me."

"I won't say anything. And what you've discovered, I think, is called Christian Mysticism. Have you ever read Thomas Merton?"

"No."

"I'll give you one of his books when we get home. He went to Columbia, you know."

Madeline went with Michael to his apartment, watching as he stood before one of his many bookshelves and slowly ran his eyes over the titles. Finally he pulled out a small book, an olive and black paperback with "15 cents" written in the right-hand corner.

The Seven Storey Mountain by Thomas Merton.

"Read it," Michael said. "I think you'll like it."

"What's it about?"

"How he became a Trappist monk."

"But I'm not Catholic."

"Never mind. You'll like it."

The book changed her life in a way no book had before. The closest experience she could recall was in high school when Bella gave her *The Fountainhead*: after she read it Madeline had tried to act like Howard Roark for a week, but without much success. She had learned from books before, had been changed by books before, but *The Seven Storey Mountain* completely transformed her.

The book was a simple, straightforward autobiography. Merton began with his childhood, and Madeline was surprised to find he had not been brought up in any particular religion and, compared to her, did not have much religious feeling as a child. In fact the first half of the book did not really concern religion at all, and Madeline sometimes wondered why Michael had been so sure the book would help her; but the cover said, "The autobiography of a man who led a full and worldly life and then, at the age of 26, entered a Trappist monastery," and that kept her going. She was curious to see how a young man who went on drinking binges, chased girls, and neglected his studies at Cambridge had ever ended up a monk. She read on, not particularly impressed, but when Merton left Cambridge and went to Columbia, Madeline got hooked. The book began to feel very personal, very familiar: she had walked where Merton had walked, had dabbled in the same campus institutions, and at Columbia she had also come to the realization that she needed a spiritual life—more, that there was a spiritual life to be had. As Merton wrote, "The only way to live was to live in a world that was charged with the presence and reality of God." Madeline was on the bus going to work when she read that line, and she had felt a shock of agreement.

That day at work was another special day in her life, a day she would always remember. It was a Saturday; her shift at the Big Law Firm word processing center started at nine, and at ten o'clock one of the partners called and requested her to work with him for the day. She said good-bye to her friends in the center, and carried her bookbag and sweater to the 57th floor. The partner dictated two letters, then received a phone call. "I have to go out," he told Madeline. "I don't know when I'll be back, but you stay here and watch the phones."

He left. Madeline pulled *The Seven Storey Mountain* from her bookbag, tucked her feet under her legs, and started reading. She was sitting at a secretary's desk in a small office; there were no windows, and with the cool from the air conditioning Madeline felt as if she was in a cave. Her excitement mounted as she read; she could not relate to Merton's Catholicism—his ideas about sin and heaven and hell, and all his talk about saints and stations of the cross—but when he wrote about merging into God's love, yes, she could relate to that. And slowly Madeline understood why Michael had given her the book, for every time Merton wrote about "resting in Christ" and merging into God's love, was he not describing her experiences as a child? Had she not lived that way for years and years? As a child, completely non-intellectually, she had understood and lived in another kind of consciousness. And she saw that this other kind of consciousness had never really left her; it had always been waiting. The incident at the Ferris Booth Cafe was a kick in the pants, just a friendly reminder of something as easy and intimate as her own name.

At twelve-thirty someone came to replace her so she could go to lunch; she went to the cafeteria and spent an hour talking and joking with the other word processors, then went back to the cool cave of the secretary's office. She continued reading, and came across a line that hit her like a slap: "It was God alone I was supposed to live for, God that was supposed to be the center of my life and of all that I did." She read the line twice, then put the book down; she picked it up again, and read the line once more. And a few pages later she read a scene that literally raised the hairs on the back of her neck. Merton was talking to Lax, his best friend and fellow Columbia undergraduate; Lax had asked Merton what he wanted to be, and Merton replied,

"I don't know. I guess what I want to be is a good Catholic."

"What do you mean, you want to be a good Catholic?"

The explanation I gave was lame enough, and expressed my confusion, and betrayed how little I had really thought about it at all.

Lax did not accept it.

"What you should say—" he told me—"what you should say is that you want to be a saint."

A saint! The thought struck me as a little weird. I said: "How do you expect me to become a saint?"

"By wanting to," said Lax, simply.

And on the following page:

The next day I told Mark Van Doren:

"Lax is going around saying that all a man needs to be a saint is to want to be one."

"Of course," Mark said.

Madeline finished the book that afternoon. As she walked out of the building onto Chambers Street, the world felt completely different—less solid, but extremely vivid. She felt as if she was composed of air: there she was, an airy person drifting into an airy subway station, putting a token of air into a turnstile of air, sitting in an airy subway car with airy people, floating through Port Authority and onto the Red Apple bus. She was so happy; she had been feeling this urge towards—well, towards God, she might as well call it—for a long, long time, but she had always been ashamed to speak of it. Even as a child she had never let anyone catch her reading the Bible, and had never told anyone how much she enjoyed church and Sunday school. And now after reading *The Seven Storey Mountain* she no longer felt ashamed. Merton had put so many of her own thoughts and feelings on paper, and she saw that the things she had been ashamed of were in fact things to be proud of. And best of all, the most compelling part of Merton's story: he had been like anyone else, just a normal person without much religious feeling, a person flawed and confused and over-opinionated, and he had evolved into a person who devoted his life to God.

And if he had done it, why couldn't she?

That night as she laid in bed, she could not think of anything else. Could she really set her sights so high? Could a person really decide such a thing?

According to Lax and Merton, one could. She did not know how or if she could change her life so radically, but she could not stop thinking about that one line: "It was God alone I was supposed to live for, God that was supposed to be at the center of my life and of all that I did."

The next day after work she went to Coliseum Books on 57th and Broadway and bought her own copy of *The Seven Storey Mountain*. She spent the next week slowly rereading, carefully marking important passages with a red felt-tip pen. One night when Michael came over to play Scrabble she gave him back his copy of the book. He asked her if she had liked it; she blushed, nodded, but did not speak. Later she saw him notice her copy of the book facedown in the TV room, but he said nothing.

Madeline's state of rapture continued for several days, but it slowly faded as problems arose. The first problem was Bella, and Madeline's friends. How could she tell them about this? Would they ever understand a desire to put God at the center of one's life? Madeline was on the brink of an enormous change, and she felt frightened: Was she going to end up in a monastery like Merton? Was she going to have to stop masturbating and smoking pot and eating ice cream and watching television? Was she going to become some weird little pious person who no one could stand? She wanted God, but did not know if she could reconcile God with modern life.

She solved the problem by becoming what she thought of as a closet spiritual person. "I'm in the closet," she would think as she hid her Bible under the bed when Bella knocked, or snuck off in the mornings to attend mass at a local church ("Where were you off to so early this morning?" Bella always asked, and Madeline would reply, "Oh, I felt like taking a walk..."). Luckily many of the changes she made were unobservable—she had started praying again, she memorized passages from the Bible and repeated them to herself over and over, and as much as she could whenever she could she brought the image of Christ to mind, and concentrated on Him. And all those things were invisible.

The second problem was writing. From early childhood Madeline's greatest passion was books, and from a very young age, reading Jane Austen, Charles Dickens, and the Nancy Drew mysteries, she knew she wanted to write. What a wonderful way to spend one's life; she could not imagine anything finer. But now she had to ask herself: If she put God at the center of her life, what about writing? If she became increasingly involved in religion, would writing be in the way? She could not live without writing; it was unthinkable.

The solution came when Madeline was wandering in the fiction section of Coliseum Books and the name Flannery O'Connor caught her eye. I should read her, Madeline thought. She had read a few of Flannery O'Connor's short stories in collections, but she did not know her work very well. She bought a novel called *Wise Blood* and a collection of short stories entitled *Everything that Rises Must Converge* (whatever *that* meant). She began with the novel. It was difficult to get into the book; Madeline was not sure she really liked it, but in no time she was reading at a frantic pace, and she finished the book in two days. It was a crazy book, she did not claim to understand it, but it was—no other term for it—a religious novel. Flannery O'Connor was trying to say something with all her ministers and symbols and The Holy Church of Christ without Christ, and Madeline was impressed. Then she read the short stories, and all of them, overtly or covertly, concerned religion. Madeline bought the rest of Flannery's fiction as well as her collected letters and her essay collection *Mystery and Manners*, and while reading the letters and essays everything became clear: Flannery had been a devout Catholic (another one, Madeline sighed—why no Presbyterians?) and while confined to her mother's house, slowly crippled by lupus, surrounded by her beloved peacocks, Flannery read tomes of Catholic mysticism and tried to write literature that expressed the living reality of God.

Discovering Flannery's work was another joyous time for Madeline, another season of possibility and growth: she saw that writing and God were not incompatible, and she decided that if Flannery had done it, so could she. And in another bookstore Madeline found a postcard of Flannery. At first glance Flannery looked like the nerdiest square in the world with her cat glasses, marcelled hair, and old-fashioned dress, but there was a quiet dignity in the way she stood with her leg braces and crutches, and the peacock strutting in front of her added a touch of wildness. As Madeline stared at the picture she was moved to tears of love and gratitude. What a strong, beautiful woman! Madeline bought the postcard and had it framed, and except for her copy of *The Seven Storey Mountain* it was her most valued and inspiring possession.

Madeline did change. She took Merton's statement about putting God at the center of one's life very seriously, and gradually everything—family, friends, food, literary success, entertainment—began to come second. She found herself drawn to asceticism; she began to believe that her body and five senses were getting in the way of Merger with God. If only she could break her attachment to the sensory world! Then surely Merger would come, and be permanent. She began reading Hindu mysticism (supplied by Spencer) and more Christian mysticism—St. Theresa of Avila, St. John of the Cross, *The Pilgrim's*

Progress, Joan of Arc's biography. She read accounts of fasting, celibacy, and self-flagellation, and while some of it horrified her, the basic premise made sense: the time and energy you devote to your body could instead be devoted to God. She and Michael went to The Himalayan Institute to hear a talk on vegetarianism, and the man giving the talk made the same point: he said if you overeat or combine your food wrong or do anything that makes digestion difficult, your body uses more energy, and that's energy you could be devoting to spiritual practice. From that day on Madeline began to change her diet, and began trying to break her attachment to food. She went often to The Hoboken Farmboy, Hoboken's lone health food store, and spent hours sitting on the olive oil canisters, sipping carrot juice and reading about fasting, food combining, macrobiotics, and raw foods. The upshot of her reading was that she no longer ate anything solid before noon, and gradually she gave up coffee, black tea, chocolate, ice cream, and meat. She would have given up food altogether if she could have, but Bella drew the line and told Madeline that a glass of beet juice was not a proper dinner. All these dietary changes seemed to have an effect—Madeline had an increasing sense of the world being less than solid, and she often felt strange trembles of energy running through her. Most times it was because she was light-headed from lack of food, but other times she really seemed on her way to a higher level of consciousness.

Then there was celibacy. In the early years of college, after the dark days of high school, Madeline had made a firm resolve: No more casual sex. Ever. After college she had a relationship with a lawyer, and after she broke up with him she occasionally had sex with an old boyfriend, but otherwise she never slept with any of the men she dated. She was amused to see that she had traveled from one kind of reputation to another: once she went on a date with a sculptor from Hoboken, and after he had spent an hour trying to rest his hands on various parts of her body, he shook his head and said, "Any man who wants to sleep with you needs a crowbar." So giving up sex was no real hardship—there was nothing to give up.

And as for self-flagellation, she simply was not interested.

She also became intrigued by the idea of silence. Merton had written a great deal about silence, and Madeline found herself reading more eagerly whenever the subject arose. Michael lent her a magazine published by a Zen monastery in upstate New York, and one of the articles concerned Morita therapy, a Japanese form of therapy that involved isolating people for a week or more. You were given a room in a hospital and your meals were provided, but you spoke to no one and had no phone calls, letters, books, television or radio. The idea was to take away all distractions so you would have time to think and feel. Madeline was enchanted by the idea—she did not consider herself in need of therapy, but she could imagine doing something similar with a religious purpose. Silence worked on the same principle as food: the time and energy you devoted to talking and socializing could instead be devoted to God. Madeline started craving silence, and to her surprise it was hard to come by. She was alone in the house during the day, but even so Bella and Robert usually called, Bella because she wanted to talk, Robert because he wanted to know what bills had arrived; and her own friends called, and the UPS man came—it was impossible to get any real peace. And in the evenings forget it because Michael came down to talk to Robert and play Scrabble, and then on weekends Madeline worked. Nevertheless, she spent as much time silent as she could, and the more she did so the more she enjoyed it.

Slowly she began to feel that she was suited for another kind of life, a solitary, perhaps monastic life; and she began to feel sure that if she could eliminate all distractions, something would fall away and her fleeting feelings of Merger would become permanent. Yet she had no desire to join any organizations—Madeline was not the type to take orders from anyone. She thought about going to the Zen monastery in upstate New York, but they had a strict schedule and she did not see how she could fit her two hours of daily writing alongside hours of meditation and work practice. If only she could have that kind of life, but with her own schedule. And one day while taking a walk on the Stevens Institute of Technology campus, she thought: Why don't I just do it? After years of not paying rent she had saved a great deal of money—she could just take her savings and go. And she even knew the place: two years before she had shared a summer house with some artists from Hoboken in a tiny seaside community called Swan's Cove, a calm little town with Victorian houses and a beautiful boardwalk and park. She could go there; she *would* go there. She decided that six months was a decent amount of time—it was long enough to see if she really wanted a solitary lifestyle, but not so long that she would be stuck if she did not like it. She was sure, of course, that she would like it, but it was always best to be cautious, and besides she did not want to exhaust her savings. So in mid-March, without telling anyone, she took the bus to Swan's Cove, and after just two hours of knocking on doors she found the perfect place, a tiny apartment on the second floor of a rickety old stable. The furniture was old and tacky and unmatched, the ceiling low and in some places sloping, but the windows looked out onto the bay and the stable was set behind a Victorian house in an overgrown rose garden. Her landlords—a couple, both visual artists, sweet and eccentric—lived in the Victorian house, and were easy about everything: she did not have to pay a security deposit, she could use their phone, and they had an old bike she could take whenever she liked. And rent was only $300 a month.

Madeline returned to Hoboken elated, but also scared: now she would have to tell Bella. But how could Madeline tell Bella what she was doing without Bella thinking she was crazy? Madeline said nothing during dinner and Scrabble, but when Michael rose to leave at the end of the evening she asked him if she could come up and borrow some books. They walked up to his apartment and went into his book-lined living room. Madeline sat on the couch and looked up at him.

"Actually," she said. "I don't want any books. I need to talk."

She told him about renting the stable and her plans to move to Swan's Cove. He listened carefully, and when she was done he said it sounded like an excellent idea.

"It will certainly help you if you can live without distraction for awhile," he told her. "Probably that's something everyone should try at least once."

"So you've done it?" she asked.

"Yes. And the fact is, Madeline, it wouldn't hurt you to live on your own for awhile. You never have, have you? Your sister has always taken care of you; some time alone might help you grow up."

"Are you saying I'm spoiled?" she flared. "And are you saying I'm immature?"

"Well—you said those things, just now."

Michael was so annoying; but she trusted him, and she needed him. They discussed what she should say to Bella. Michael felt that Madeline could tell the truth and simply leave God out of it. "Because Bella won't understand," Michael said. "And it really won't help if you tell her."

"Will you come with me?" Madeline asked. "If I go down now and ask her, will you come?"

"Of course. Let's go."

It was a scene, complete with tears and anger and wails of betrayal. All Bella's, of course; Madeline was interested to see that Robert was not in the least upset. But what did she expect? Except for the first few months of their marriage Bella and Robert had never lived alone. For nine years Robert had—patiently, it must be said—shared his home with his sister-in-law, and maybe now he was ready to be alone with his wife. Probably he had always been ready. So if Robert agreed then eventually Bella would too. Madeline appealed to Robert, Robert appealed to Bella, Michael supplied explanations at awkward moments, and finally Bella relented. So it was all set: Madeline would give notice at work, then in two weeks Robert would rent a car and the three of them would install Madeline in her new—"but only temporary," Bella insisted—home.

CHAPTER 3

The Part Spencer Didn't Know

Madeline moved to Swan's Cove on April 2. She did not bring much with her, just her clothes, typewriter, kitchen supplies, groceries, *The Seven Storey Mountain*, and her picture of Flannery O'Connor. Except for *The Seven Storey Mountain* she brought no books—Swan's Cove was tiny, but it was only a twenty-minute bike ride from Tom's River, which had an enormous library. In fact after Madeline arranged her things at the stable she drove with Bella, Robert, and Michael to Tom's River to apply for her library card. Afterwards they ate lunch at a small pizzeria; Bella cried the whole time, and as much as Madeline loved her sister it was all she could do not to throttle her. Finally they drove back to the stable and everyone kissed Madeline good-bye, even Michael—and Michael also handed her a shopping bag with a gift inside. Madeline stood in front of the Victorian house and waved good-bye. She did not cry, and when the car pulled away all she felt was relief.

Back in the stable she fixed a cup of herb tea, then sat in a black vinyl chair and looked out the window. Peace, she thought. At last I have peace. She sat in silence for at least an hour, then her eyes rested on the shopping bag. She may have been trying to detach herself from material things, but she still loved presents. She brought the shopping bag over to the chair and carefully unwrapped the gold ribbon and the gold and maroon paper. It was a beautiful hardcover book with pictures and testimonials by people who had known Thomas Merton. There was the Dalai Lama, Mark Van Doren, and yes, even Lax. In fact Lax discussed, modestly, the famous "saint" conversation that had changed Merton's life. Lax had a kind face, and he seemed like such a good, intelligent man—Madeline wanted to frame him and put him next to Flannery, but she dare not disfigure the book. She put the book on her bedside table under her copy of *The Seven Storey Mountain*.

"Well, Flannery," she said, looking up at the picture hanging over the bureau. "We really did it; we're actually here."

The next two months were like a dream. Madeline was free to do exactly what she wanted, and what she wanted was to devote herself to her spiritual life. She drew up a schedule and stuck to it: rise at seven, fix carrot juice for breakfast, read the Bible or some other religious text, take a walk on the board-walk, shop at the corner store, then be home at nine to begin writing. Write for two to three hours, eat lunch, then ride her bike to Tom's River and spend the afternoon reading in the library. Come home, nap or clean or sit in the garden, eat dinner at six and afterwards read in bed until ten. Sundays were free days, but she always attended the eleven o'clock service at the local Presbyterian church.

She felt she was making progress; in any event, she was happy. Everything felt fresh and new, even on days when it rained and she could not go out except to make a dash to the corner store. She was politely friendly to her landlords and the people in town, but she always evaded questions and invitations, say-ing only that she was a writer working on a special project and so needed to be alone. A few times a week her landlord or his wife popped their head out the back door of their house and called, "Madeline! Telephone!" It was usually Bella, although Michael, Devon, and Rose also phoned regularly. Sometimes she was glad to hear from them, but mostly she felt they were interrupting her. Bella was especially annoying—she always wanted to visit, and always cried when Madeline said no. Madeline also received letters; like everyone else in town she had a box at the small post office next to the bay, but as she was not particularly interested in human contact she only went there once a week.

A few times she felt lonely, but that was rare. The only odd, unexpected feel-ing was fear. In all Madeline's life she had never lived alone: she had gone from her parents' house to Bella and Robert's apartment, and except when Bella and Robert were on vacation, Madeline was never alone at night—and even then she wasn't really alone, because Michael was always right above her. But here it was different, and Madeline was afraid. She would feel fine all evening, but when she went to bed she was often gripped by the fear that someone was out-side trying to get in. It was a ridiculous fear: Swan's Cove was a tiny town with no crime to speak of, and while the stable was not directly on the main street it was surrounded by houses, and even the most fainthearted scream would awaken half the town. Nevertheless, she was terrified. She would talk to herself for hours, trying to calm down and be reasonable, and thus she passed some very difficult nights. Waking at seven after such a night was never easy, but she was determined to keep to her schedule, and so she always rose at seven even when her body begged for a few more hours of sleep.

But never mind. She was sure she was on the verge of a break-through—something would fall away, and the feeling of Merger would become permanent. She would become Enlightened, as the Buddhists put it; she could hardly wait for that day. She continued reading accounts of saints and mystics, and was especially touched by Swami Rama's book *Living with the Himalayan Masters*. Swami Rama described men and women who had become Enlightened and spent their lives meditating in caves and monasteries. Madeline was slowly becoming convinced that she could be one of these people, and she was encouraged by anything she read about "normal" people who abandoned everything for the spiritual search.

June came. The little town began filling up as families moved in for the summer; school let out, the bay opened for swimming, an ice cream stand opened up on the boardwalk—and Madeline was oblivious to all of it. As she walked through the town it felt like a shimmering dream, a strange world completely unconnected with the life she was leading. She began to yearn more and more for a complete break from the sensory world, and to that end she decided to start meditating. Every morning and every evening for twenty minutes Madeline sat down, crossed her legs, and focused on her breathing. When thoughts came she looked at them briefly, then let them go. Results came quickly: after so many hours spent in silence it was easy to sit quietly, and the occasional moments when all her bodily sensations dropped away convinced her she was on the right track. She had days when she was sure she was about to break through, and on those days she would think of her old life in Hoboken and shake her head. How could she ever have enjoyed a life with so much activity and so many material things? Thank goodness she had broken away from all that; thank goodness she had her new life at Swan's Cove.

And then it all started to unravel.

One morning she was sitting cross-legged on a towel on the floor, meditating. It was a sunny day with a mild breeze—the heavy scent of roses lazed through the window, she could hear the snip snip of clippers as a neighbor trimmed his hedge. She had extended her meditation periods to thirty minutes, and was about a third of the way through when, out of nowhere, a memory popped into her mind: herself in college sophomore year, sitting at a desk checking IDs at one of the dormitories, lowering her head in shame as a group of students walked by. And sitting and meditating eight years after the fact, she felt that shame again. She knew what this little memory referred to, and no part of her wanted to replay the full story. No, no, she told herself. I don't want to think about that. She pushed the memory away and went back to focusing on her breath, then a few minutes later the memory came back. I don't *think* so, she told it. Go away! She went back to her breath, but the memory once again popped up, and she felt herself fill with hot, humiliating shame, a scorching sensation that started from her chest and rolled up her neck and down into her stomach. She went back to her breath, determined to keep meditating. That part of my life is over, she told herself firmly; there was no need to think about it, not now or ever.

The rest of the day did not go well. She managed to complete her meditation, but during her two hours of writing the memory and the feeling of shame flashed through her several times. The moment she finished writing she got on her bike and rode furiously to Tom's River. She went to a restaurant and had a large meal, then went to the library to read. She could not concentrate; she wandered around the stacks, unable to find anything that held her interest. She rode furiously back to Swan's Cove, furiously cleaned the kitchen, furiously swept the floor, furiously refolded all her clothes—but it was no good, the memory was still waiting for her. At last she stopped, and laid down on the ugly red vinyl couch. She could not fight it anymore, she just had to let it come.

Of all the memories she could have had it was certainly not the worst. She could even see the humor in it, and in fact it was a story she sometimes told to make people laugh. It began freshman year: she and Devon were out for a night of drinking and dancing at The Pub, Columbia's famous den of iniquity in the basement of the John Jay dormitory. Madeline spent so much time at The Pub she might as well have set up a bed and slept there: she got in free because she knew the bouncers, she drank free because she knew the bartenders, and she ate free because she knew the boys who worked the snack bar. It was her second home. That night she and Devon arrived, drunk on whiskey and high on pot or speed or amyl nitrate or whatever substance they were into that week. They walked in the door and as they stood surveying the noisy drunken gyrating scene, Madeline grabbed Devon's arm and declared, "Devon, I want a man."

"Oh no," Devon said. "I don't like the look in your eye."

"I want a man, and I'm going to find one."

Thus far Madeline had been careful at Columbia. She knew how fast a reputation could spread, so except for kissing someone at a fraternity party she had not had any sexual contact with the boys across the street. But physical frustration was beginning to gnaw at her, and that night something snapped—she could not hold out any longer, never mind the consequences. She surveyed the scene with a critical eye. She knew most of the boys, and she dismissed them for various reasons: one was in her Spanish class, another had slept with one of her friends, another was fat…there was no one suitable. Then a tall boy she did not recognize struck up a conversation with her. He said he did not go to Columbia, he was from some godforsaken suburb in northern Iowa and was visiting as a recruit for the basketball team. A senior in high school, in other words. Madeline questioned him carefully about his grades and SAT scores. He screwed up his big toothy face; he could not recall his grade point average, and his combined SAT score was 850. He'll never get in here, she thought. And the next day he would go back to his hometown in Iowa, never to return again.

Pay dirt: the perfect one night stand.

Next thing she knew she had told Devon good-bye, and was outside with the recruit, kissing passionately by the tennis courts. Where can we go? she thought as his big hands moved over her breasts. He was sharing a room in Carmen with three other recruits, so that was out, and no way could she bring him to Bella and Robert's. Careening drunkenly through campus, she brought him to the BHR dormitory lounge, where she shut all the doors and turned out the lights. Never mind that she had to kick out a few people; she was so drunk she hardly saw their faces. Certainly, though, they remembered her… Anyway, she had sex with the basketball recruit right on the couch in the BHR lounge. How they left things, how she got back to her apartment—these were things she could not remember.

The next day Madeline and Devon ate lunch in the McIntosh commuter center, and Madeline told Devon everything.

"Oh, Madeline!" Devon said, shaking her head. "A recruit. *A recruit.* He's not even out of high school!"

"It's perfect," Madeline said, sitting with folded hands and a big smile on her face. "I'll never see him again, and no one will ever know. And don't you dare breathe a word of this to anyone."

"You could not have sunk lower."

"I know, and I don't care. By now he's back in Iowa, and he'll probably never come east of Chicago again."

But one day that fall, when Madeline and Devon were sharing a bottle of wine on the Columbia steps, Devon passed Madeline the latest issue of *The Columbia Spectator*.

"Excuse me, Madeline," Devon said, pointing to a picture on the sports page. "Isn't this your little friend?"

Oh no—it wasn't true. It couldn't be. But there he was, Billy Ray Bonner of Hofalouka, Iowa, smiling a smile that showed every one of his big teeth. Madeline read the article in horror: it seemed that Billy Ray had been All-State throughout high school, and he had not only led his team to the State Championship junior and senior year, but he had set a new all-time Midwest Division scoring record. All the top schools had wooed him, but his heart was set on Columbia. "I chose Columbia because I want to live in a big city," Billy Ray was quoted as saying. "And when I came out here to visit, people were real friendly."

"Oh my God," Madeline said.

"So, Madeline," Devon said. "Maybe the athletic department should hire you as a recruiter."

"Oh, shut up. Well," she sighed. "Never mind. I'll never see him."

Wrong. Because one day, sitting behind a desk at her new and easy job checking IDs at the East Campus dormitory, Madeline became aware of laughing voices. She looked up from her book and saw a flock of tall freshmen heading her way. She watched them flash their IDs, and then she saw that one of them was looking at her intently. Her throat clutched: it was him, Billy Ray Bonner. She looked down and pretended she did not recognize him. The group passed into the dorm but then they stopped and huddled in a circle. "It's *her*," she heard a voice insisting. "I'm telling you, it's *her*." Because of course he had told them everything, she thought, her face turning bright red as she willed herself not to crawl into a desk drawer. What a big score for him, coming as a recruit and getting laid. Madeline was in agony: she could hear the other boys encouraging Billy Ray to talk to her, she heard Billy Ray's murmured protests, then she heard one of his friends exclaim, "But she *slept* with you!" Madeline kept her eyes glued to her book, and only after the voices had subsided did she dare look up. They were gone.

When her replacement came at the end of her shift, Madeline grabbed her books and fled. She punched her time card at the security office in Low Library and then went to see her boss, a short black man with glasses and an odd, high-pitched voice.

"Lieutenant Marshal," she said. "I would prefer not to work at East Campus anymore. Is there another dorm where you can put me?"

"I'm sorry, Miss Boot," he said. "But East Campus is our only opening. If it weren't for East Campus you wouldn't have a job. Is there a problem?"

"No, not exactly. Just—I don't know, I think it'll be cold in winter."

"Oh, don't you worry, Miss Boot. We have space heaters; we won't let you freeze."

She would have quit, but she desperately needed the money, and it was a job where she could do her homework. So she stayed, reliving that excruciating embarrassment again and again. Billy Ray never got up the nerve to approach her, thank goodness, but he still passed by with his friends, and being sexually ogled by the freshmen basketball team three times a week was more than Madeline could bear. But, as it turned out, Billy Ray was the reason why Madeline cleaned up her act: she vowed never again to have casual sex, and her residency at The Pub was soon a thing of the past.

Remembering made her cry; she was sad all evening, but in the morning she felt relief. She meditated, wrote, then rode her bicycle to Tom's River, all the while thinking that remembering had helped. She felt lighter now, and she could once again see the humor of the situation. But it bothered her that the memory had come up at all: she had moved to Swan's Cove to put God at the center of her life, not to think about Billy Ray Bonner.

The next few days went well. Madeline kept to her schedule faithfully, and she was sure she was back on track. But then one afternoon as she was raking leaves and grass from the rose garden, another slice of memory flashed through her mind: herself in high school, half-naked in someone's garage, on her hands and knees throwing up semen and Southern Comfort. She stopped raking, and closed her eyes. No, she told herself. No. She continued raking, but the next thing she knew she was sitting on a stone bench, holding her stomach and crying. No, no, no! Not all of that, not now! She had stopped doing such things, and she did not need to remember them, not now and not ever.

Nevertheless, the memories came. Sometimes at random moments, but most often while she was meditating. The Billy Ray Bonner memory was nothing compared to what was coming now—and she saw that Billy Ray had come first because he was the least painful. Here they came, one by one, every single degrading sexual encounter she had ever had. Nothing in her life was as painful as the last two years in high school, nothing. But—high school? Surely none of that mattered now; surely the past was not relevant to meditating at Swan's Cove. Yet here was high school all over again, a moment by moment replay.

And worst of all, she suddenly understood things she had not understood then: like the time she and some friends had cut school to have a drinking party (and I slept with someone then, too, she recalled) and at four o'clock in the afternoon she had decided to go to school to see how the sophomores were doing editing their first issue of the literary magazine. Madeline was editor of the magazine, and it was her responsibility to make sure the sophomores had help. Laying on the vinyl couch one night, remembering this incident, Madeline suddenly realized: I was completely drunk when I went there! I must have smelt of alcohol, must have stumbled and slurred my words because, let's face it, I was always a sloppy drunk. The poor sophomores must have known—and had they said something to the literary magazine's advisor, a nice middle-aged woman who was sure Madeline was the next Edith Wharton? Shame, deep and dark and red, flooded Madeline's body as she laid on the couch and remembered.

Dozens and dozens of memories came back. At first they all involved sex, but then they expanded to include things she had done to other people, as well as to herself. The hardest, most painful memories arose during meditation; every time Madeline sat cross-legged on the floor, she braced herself for the latest installment. There were many people in the world who Madeline would have crossed the street to avoid, and meditation was like walking in a narrow alley with all those people walking towards her one by one. Worse, they all wanted to stop and talk. And if she turned around to flee, there was a brick wall; and if she tried to climb the wall and leave the alley, the people were leaning over the roofs, waiting for her. There was no escape: they wanted her to look at them, and the pain of trying to escape was just as bad as the pain of sitting down and remembering.

Her fear of being alone at night escalated until it was almost unbearable. She was convinced that someone outside wanted to come in and do her harm, and she was afraid to fall asleep lest she wake to the sight of a masked face holding a knife to her throat. She considered buying sleeping pills, but then maybe she wouldn't wake up when someone started turning the doorknob or prying open the window. She took to pushing the black vinyl chair in front of the door each night, and she also covered the windowsills with glasses, hoping for a little warning if someone came through the windows—at least that way she could scream and attract her landlords or one of her neighbors. Swan's Cove was flooded with people now, especially on weekends—who knew who they were? And if they saw her, and asked about her, and learned where she lived? It was all she could do not to run to her landlords and beg them not to tell anyone anything about her; it was all she could do not to go whimpering to their house and sleep on their doorstep every night. And the worst thing about these sleepless nights was that the memories often came then. So there she was night after night, exhausted but too afraid to sleep, tossing and turning in bed while humiliating scenes from her past marched through her mind. By four-thirty, five o'clock, she finally fell asleep, and then she would sleep until noon or even later.

Needless to say, her schedule—her lovely, disciplined schedule—fell apart completely. She tried to continue meditating, not because she thought it would help but because she was still clinging to the idea of herself as some kind of special spiritual person. Her whole identity was tied up with this notion of herself, and it was not easy to watch it go. But go it did: she watched helplessly as all the elements of her spiritual life—prayer, meditation, intensive study, church—fell away because she did not have the mental or physical strength to continue with them. She was extremely frustrated by this turn of events; her aim in coming to Swan's Cove had been to eliminate all distraction so she could break through to a constant state of Merger, so why were her past and her psychological problems—things that were separate from Merger—coming up now? She did not want to think about them, and yet there they were, taking over her life and ruining her retreat.

In early July she got a crazy idea: she decided to do a three-day water fast. From all her reading about saints she knew that many had breakthroughs while fasting, and maybe that would happen to her. She thought she was ready; she had done short juice fasts, after all, and for a long time her diet had been mostly juices. She used up all her food, bought thirty bottles of water, and then she started. The first day went well; she drank water all day and felt no real change. But by the afternoon of the second day she was so weak she could not move off the couch. I need to eat, she thought. I must eat, and I must eat now. She literally crawled across the floor to the door, then sat on the top of the stairs and bumped down the steps one by one. She was sitting on the bottom step, weak and faint and wondering how she would ever make it to the store, when she realized that she had left her money upstairs. She started crying, and was sitting and sobbing quite awhile before her landlady happened to drive up.

"Why, Madeline," her landlady said, kneeling before her. "What's wrong? Are you sick?"

Madeline did not know what to say. She did not want to explain that she was fasting, so she told her landlady she had low blood pressure and sometimes felt faint. All she needed was to eat something, and here she was so weak she could not even make it to the store.

"I'll go for you," her landlady said. "I'll buy whatever you want. You just sit here—and why don't I get you a little something from the house to tide you over."

"My money—it's upstairs."

"Never mind. You can pay me back later."

Her landlady went into the Victorian house and came out with two slices of whole wheat bread and a thick wedge of cheddar cheese. As her landlady walked off to the store, Madeline sat on the stoop nibbling the cheese. She was wearing a sleeveless flowered dress with a short skirt, and as she sat nibbling she looked at her legs. Thin, very thin. And her arms, like pretzel sticks. How much weight had she lost these last months? And when was the last time she had looked at herself in a full-length mirror? Sitting and staring at her bony kneecaps it suddenly occurred to Madeline: I am having a nervous breakdown.

Her landlady returned with a grocery bag full of food—an eggplant parmesan sub, potato chips, yogurt, cottage cheese, bananas, apple juice. She wanted to help Madeline upstairs but Madeline said no, she was much better now; in truth she did not want her landlady to see the bottles of water, the glasses lined up on the windowsills, or any other indications of instability.

Madeline ate, and felt better. She decided to go for a walk; she needed to get out, breathe fresh air, see human beings. The sun had set but there were still many hours of light ahead, the cool summer evenings with the multi-colored sky that she remembered so well from her first summer in Swan's Cove. She put on a light sweater and took her post office box key so she could get her mail. Walking the long way to the post office, past families barbecuing, mothers hanging swimsuits on clotheslines, teenagers on porches smoking cigarettes, Madeline breathed in the tangy sea air and once again thought: I am having a nervous breakdown.

She needed to speak to someone. But to whom? Bella was her best friend, but if she told Bella she was having problems Bella would insist Madeline return to Hoboken. But maybe it was time to tell Bella everything, time to explain about Thomas Merton and meditation and putting God at the center of her life. No, I can't tell Bella, she thought as she opened her mailbox. Bella will think I'm crazy if I tell her the truth. She sighed deeply, and took out her mail. A postcard from Devon from her vacation home in Maine, a rejection letter from a literary magazine, a chain letter sent by Rose's sister (Rose had called to warn Madeline), and a letter from Michael in Japan where he was spending the summer working on a sutra translation. She read everything quickly, then stuffed the letters in the pocket of her dress.

As she was walking home she suddenly thought: Michael. Of course—I'll write to Michael. He knew the truth about why she was here, and if she could tell him what was going on, if she could just get it all down on paper, she knew she would feel better. Or Spencer, she could write to Spencer…but he was in Germany playing at a music festival, after that he had gigs in Holland and France and she was not sure how to reach him. No, she would write to Michael; she knew that he meditated every morning so maybe he would understand. And so when she arrived at the stable she took the cover off her typewriter and wrote a fifteen page single-spaced letter explaining everything she was going through and basically asking him whether or not she was crazy. Michael was, as Bella always said, the sanest man she knew other than Robert, so he would certainly be able to judge if Madeline was teetering on the edge. After she typed the last words—"Please write me soon! Take care, Madeline"—she felt cleansed, like someone whose fever had broken. That night she slept well for the first time in weeks; and as soon as she woke the next morning she walked to the post office and mailed the letter.

Madeline spent the next two weeks walking on eggshells. She felt like a pinball machine on the verge of tilting; she was afraid to do anything, afraid she might lose her mental balance completely. She did not meditate or pray or read anything spiritual; she limited herself to reading Patricia Highsmith novels and taking long walks on the boardwalk. And she was miserable: all her dreams, all her ideas about who she was and the direction of her life—it was all gone. And the memories were still coming; she accepted them wearily, and accepted the crying after. What else could she do? She felt as if she were trapped in a body that was nothing but pain, and she had to somehow keep dragging this body around, keep dressing and feeding it until—until what? Until she went completely insane or until she somehow, some day, felt better. She thought about packing up and leaving, just going back to Hoboken, but she was too stubborn and proud to admit defeat.

One morning as she was sitting on the top step of the stairs outside her apartment, wondering what on earth to do that day, she saw a Federal Express truck pull up in front of the house. Something for her landlords, no doubt. Chin in hands, she watched the man jump out of his truck and walk purposefully towards the Victorian house, a flat package in his hand.

But a minute later he was again in view, this time walking purposely towards her. It's for me, she realized. It was about her writing, it had to be; an editor had read one of her stories and was so impressed he was sending his congratulations express. She had always been enchanted by the story of Dostoyevsky's first glimpse of success: friends had come to visit while he was asleep, and on their way out they noticed one of his short stories on the table. They read it and then woke him up, demanding to know how he could sleep when he was such a great writer with such a great future. So maybe Madeline's moment had come. She flew down the steps and signed for the package. It was flat and rectangular—a letter, no doubt about it. But when she examined the label she was crushed to see that it was from Michael.

"You look like you don't want it," the Federal Express man said, laughing. "Should I take it back?"

"No, no… It's just I thought it was something else."

With a heavy heart she went back upstairs to her apartment. She fell into the black vinyl chair and opened the packet; it held a cream colored envelope with a thick letter inside. Michael's handwriting was clear and neat, although his capital I curled in a most peculiar way. It was a long letter, and as she finished reading it for the second time, she decided that Bella was right: Michael was really a very sensible person. The letter was soothing and kind, and had some good suggestions as well. He began by telling her that most people have painful memories during meditation, especially at the beginning, and this was completely natural: "We're always talking to ourselves; we do so for many reasons, but one of the chief reasons is in order to suppress pain. So of course when we stop talking to ourselves all the pain comes up. But this is not something bad, or something to be avoided: now that the painful things have come up, you can deal with them one by one and move on. And when meditation is no longer chiefly concerned with the past, it begins to get very interesting." He encouraged her not to run away from the pain; he said that it was full of richness and knowledge, and perhaps contained insights that could change her life. "I don't want to say that you should be masochistic," he wrote. "It's just that this pain is valuable, and you shouldn't try to make it go away. I do think, however, that it is very hard for anyone to do this sort of work alone, and I strongly suggest you get some help. By 'help' I mean some kind of non-traditional therapy, whether it be massage therapy, rolfing, or rebirthing; in other words, someone who can help you, but someone with a—I hesitate to use this word, but it's the best I can find—'spiritual' orientation. And if you can't find anyone like that where you are, if there are only analysts, at least let it be a Jungian analyst." He also recommended she return to a normal diet, which was something she had anyway been considering, and he said she should stop meditating altogether if it was really more painful than she could bear. The rest of the letter was a pep talk, nice things to raise her self-esteem, and even though it was all from Michael she appreciated it; she needed to know she was a good, sensible person, and not, as she feared, a misguided religious fanatic. Michael closed by saying he would be back at the end of August, and would call her as soon as he returned.

A therapist: it was a good idea. She needed someone—anyone—to talk to. In the lobby of the Tom's River library there was a large bulletin board with business cards; Madeline had glanced at it a few times, and she was sure she remembered seeing cards for therapists and New Age-y activities. Although it was close to eleven and boiling hot outside, Madeline got on her bike and rode to Tom's River, arriving at the library hot, sweaty, and full of hope.

The upshot of her library visit was an appointment with Rebecca Smythe, a rebirther. She had called several people, but Rebecca seemed the most down-to-earth, and she was also accessible by bike. So the next day Madeline rode her bike to an address close to downtown Tom's River, a beige split-level house with a baby blue pick-up in the driveway. Madeline leaned her bike against the side of the house, then went to the front door and rang the bell. Rebecca herself answered the door. She was as tall as Madeline, and had brown doe-like eyes and straight brown hair pulled back into a ponytail. She was extremely thin—her hipbones jutted against her maroon sweatpants, and her collarbone was so prominent it made Madeline squeamish. But she had a kind, open face, and her voice was creamy as she said hello and asked Madeline to leave her bookbag in the hall closet. She guided Madeline downstairs to her office, and on the way down Madeline glimpsed a messy kitchen and a hairy husband fixing a toaster.

Rebecca's office was like a separate planet. A quiet womb of a room, it was decorated in white and pastel and natural woods, and had crystals of all colors on the windowsills and even hanging from the ceilings. Oh no, Madeline thought. Crystals. Was this going to get New Age-y? They sat on a comfortable couch made of light wood and big white pillows, and despite Madeline's doubts about the crystals she was soon clutching a big purple one and telling Rebecca an abridged version of her story. Rebecca listened carefully, her doe eyes never leaving Madeline's face. When Madeline was done and crying into the wad of tissues Rebecca had gently pressed into her hand, Rebecca asked Madeline what she knew about rebirthing.

"My friend Spencer did it," Madeline sniffed. "And another friend recommended I do it. It's a breathing thing, right? And the idea is that the birth you had affects your whole life, especially if it was traumatic."

"That's right. Each session is two hours long, an hour for talking like we just did, then about forty-five minutes for breathing, then another fifteen minutes or so to discuss what happened. Plus I'll be giving you affirmations at the end of each session; I want you to write them out fifty times each day. And you can practice the breathing every day as well. Ten sessions is the minimum, but if you like we'll do more. Now, tell me—do you know anything about your birth? Did your parents ever tell you anything?"

They hadn't, but Madeline knew the whole story from Bella. Madeline's birth had been a humdinger; it was, as Bella said, an insane introduction to an insane family. The bare facts were that Madeline's mother Polly started having contractions in the morning. Her water broke, the contractions grew closer, but instead of going to the hospital she decided to wait for her husband Spam (his name was Thaddeus, but everyone called him Spam) to return from work. Bella was nine at the time, and when she got home from school she begged Polly to go to the hospital. But no—Polly said Spam had not been there for Bella's birth, and she wanted to be sure he did not once again shirk his responsibilities. Spam arrived home at five, by which time Polly's contractions were two minutes apart and she was screaming in pain. As for Bella, she was huddled in a corner, crying hysterically. "Why she was waiting for Dad I had no idea," Bella told Madeline. "I was only nine years old, but I knew he'd fuck everything up." Polly was a hysterical, overdramatic person to begin with, but in pain she was completely out of control—Bella said her ears rang for days from all the screaming. So with Polly stretched out on the backseat screaming and Bella hunched at her feet crying, Spam drove to the hospital.

And then Madeline started coming out.

"The baby's coming!" Bella cried. "I can see hair, and blood!"

"Blood?" Spam said. "Not on my new seat covers! Polly, you are not having that baby in this car."

"But Daddy!" Bella protested. "The baby's coming!"

"Then hold it in, Goddammit!" To emphasize his point, he threw back a hand and split Bella's lip. And so Bella, only nine years old, hysterical and dealing with hysterical parents, put one hand on her bleeding mouth and the other against Madeline's head. And every time a contraction started pushing Madeline out, Bella pushed her back in.

Finally they arrived at the hospital; and as the two attendants lifted Polly onto a stretcher, Madeline popped out, free at last.

"And that's my birth," Madeline said.

Rebecca's face was dead white.

"Rebecca…?"

"I'm sorry. Just—I need to get this straight: your father didn't want you born in the car because he didn't want you to mess up his new seat covers?"

"That's right."

"You're not exaggerating?"

"Not at all."

"My God—you could have died! And your poor mother, she must have been in agony. Tell me, was this sort of behavior commonplace in your family?"

"Rebecca, the story I told you is just the tip of the iceberg."

"Good Christ. Listen, why don't you stretch out on the floor and we'll do some breathing."

Rebecca lay two fluffy white towels on the gold carpet. She told Madeline how to breathe—it was a simple technique, just breathing through her mouth into her chest—and then she sat at Madeline's side, quietly watching. Madeline breathed and breathed and breathed. She was bored, but what else could she do? She breathed in earnest until Rebecca's creamy voice broke in and said, "That's enough for now."

They returned to the couch and settled amongst the white cushions. "Well?" Rebecca asked, smiling.

"Well—nothing. I didn't feel anything in particular, just a little sleepy is all."

Rebecca nodded. "That's fine. So, shall we get together at the same time next week? And if you feel anything odd in the next few days, give me a call. Day or night." She reached over to a side table and handed Madeline a business card, yellow with a raised gold sun and raised gold letters that proclaimed "REBECCA SMYTHE—REBIRTHER."

Riding home on her bike, Madeline felt disappointed. Sixty dollars for *that*? The talking had been nice, and Rebecca certainly was a sympathetic presence, but the breathing technique seemed mild and ineffective. Still, she would keep seeing Rebecca, if only because it was nice to have someone in Swan's Cove to talk to. She spent the rest of the afternoon reading, and in the evening went to sit on the boardwalk where she had a nice conversation with an elderly couple. She went to bed feeling much better, and slept through the night without any thought of intruders.

But in the morning when Madeline woke, she was astonished to find herself crying. Was I crying in my sleep? she asked herself. She had never done that before; and the way she felt, as if a mountain had landed on her chest. Oh my God, she thought. What's happening to me, what's happening? She literally could not get out of bed; all she could do was cry, and feel the mountain of sadness pressing down on her. I *am* having a nervous breakdown, she thought. I am, I truly am.

There was nothing to do but cry. She dragged herself out of bed, crying; took a shower, crying; made carrot juice, crying. The pain was not the sharp pain that accompanied the memories, it was rather a thick, heavy sadness. I want to die, she thought as she laid on the couch and stared at the wall. I want this tacky vinyl couch to open up and swallow me whole. Then she remembered Rebecca and the yellow business card. I'll call Rebecca, she thought. I'll call her, and maybe I can go to her house and she can rebirth me out of this.

It took nearly an hour, but Madeline got dressed and dragged herself down to the pay phone on the boardwalk. Rebecca's hairy husband answered the phone, and for one awful moment Madeline thought Rebecca was not home; but then the hairy husband told Madeline to wait, and after a few minutes Madeline heard Rebecca's creamy, "Hello?"

"Oh, Rebecca, thank God you're home. It's me, Madeline, and I'm totally freaking out."

Madeline explained about the mountain, and Rebecca said soothingly, "That's from what we did yesterday."

"Really? Just from that breathing?"

"It's all in your chest, right? The breathing really loosened things up in there. Don't worry; it's actually a good sign."

Rebecca told Madeline that she didn't need to come in again, and suggested they get together next week as planned. Madeline hung up unconvinced, but at least she knew she was not crazy. Rebecca did not think so, in any case.

The mountain slowly dissipated, and the rest of the week Madeline felt a bit better. She was still too shaky to write or meditate, so she spent most of her time sitting on the boardwalk, thinking and watching people go by. She felt so groundless without her schedule and her religious reading and her goal of being a saint, and she clung to Rebecca and rebirthing as her last hope for Merger. Every day she practiced the breathing, and every day she took out a pad of paper and wrote out the affirmations Rebecca had given her: "It is safe for me to breathe" and "It is safe for me to receive love." She was not sure if the affirmations were effective, but she did them with a vengeance, writing them out a hundred times each day even though Rebecca had said fifty times was enough.

Madeline had two more sessions with Rebecca. The mountain of sadness came back, and at the end of the third session a new emotion reared its head: panic. Rebecca was explaining to Madeline that later on they would do a "wet" rebirth where Madeline would submerge herself in the bathtub and do the breathing technique with a snorkel. Panic slammed into Madeline's chest—she told Rebecca she could not do that. Rebecca asked why, and Madeline said, "Because I'll die." Rebecca calmly explained that of course Madeline felt scared: during her birth she had been forced to stay in her mother's body, so naturally the idea of recreating the womb was terrifying.

"I'm sure you had a full-blown panic attack when your sister was holding you in. You had an extremely traumatic experience, Madeline. Tell me, are you claustrophobic? I bet you are."

"I'm not," Madeline said, although she was a little.

"And I bet you have a lot of trouble letting men get close to you."

"Not really," she lied again.

It was the first time she had lied to Rebecca, and she did not feel good about it. But this wet rebirth! No, no, no—Madeline was not going to put on a snorkel and lay in Rebecca's bathtub. No way. And the next day as Madeline laid in bed thinking, she remembered something that seemed like an omen: Thomas Merton had died in a bathtub! Well, not exactly: Michael had told her the story, he said Merton was traveling through the East and while in Bangkok took a shower or bath, then touched an electric fan and died instantly. As far as Madeline was concerned, that clinched it: no wet rebirthing. She was strictly a towel on the floor woman.

Then a few days later on a bright, sunny morning, Madeline was writing out affirmations. The affirmations for the week were "I forgive my mother" and "I forgive my father." She had just written "I forgive my father" for about the fortieth time, was feeling anger and pain and panic and not the tiniest bit of forgiveness, when suddenly she put down the pen and said, quietly, "No." No. No more. She did not forgive her father, she did not forgive her mother, she was tired of wallowing in the past and was tired of trying to be a saint. No. No more.

She pushed her chair away from the table and swept the paper and pen onto the floor. "What am I doing to myself?" she asked aloud. "No one else is doing anything like this, they're just going about leading their normal lives."

A normal life—she wanted a normal life. She wanted to eat breakfast, she wanted to have sex, she wanted to watch television while eating a pint of ice cream, she wanted to get high and go listen to jazz. No more asceticism, no more God at the center, no more rebirthing—she wanted life, just plain ordinary life.

Well, Madeline, she told herself. If that's what you want, then go ahead.

The relief was tremendous. She cried, but this time from joy, joy and exhaustion. I can leave all this, she thought. I can give up all my plans and schemes and just go back to Hoboken. And she would not have to wait long; Bella, Robert, and Michael were coming to visit in a week, she could just go back with them. She rose and began pacing the little apartment, her mind working furiously. Should she call up the Big Law Firm and get her old job back? No, she shouldn't work on weekends anymore—no one else worked weekends. She would sign up with a temporary agency and work two days a week. Yes, that's what she would do. As for everything else, it was already in place waiting for her: her room at Bella and Robert's, her writing, her friends, Hoboken—nothing had changed, except now she would appreciate it. Only eight days, only eight days and she could go.

Her last days at Swan's Cove were devoted to decadence. She slept late every morning, then cycled to the diner in Tom's River where she ordered enormous breakfasts, her first breakfasts in over a year: pancakes, omelets, French toast, fried eggs, home fries, blueberry muffins—she ate whatever she wanted. I love breakfast, she would think as the waitress set down yet another mouthwatering dish; and she vowed never to drink carrot juice again. After breakfast she went to the library and sat for hours reading back issues of gossip and beauty magazines. Even these magazines had their share of articles about the spiritual journey, and Madeline skipped over each one. No more, she would tell herself as she slipped past an article on how meditation enhances beauty. No more.

She ate lunch at one of the local restaurants, then went back to the library for more light reading. Once as she was locking her bike she spied Rebecca across the street talking to an overweight woman. Oh no—what would she tell Rebecca? The truth, of course; she had nothing to be ashamed of. And after days of eating well and sleeping late and not taxing her mind with anything more difficult than articles like "Ten Ways to Improve Your Skin Tone," Madeline felt so strong and confident she was sure she did not need any more rebirthing—probably she had never needed it at all.

So on the last Wednesday of August, two days before the others were coming to take her away, Madeline went to Rebecca's house. They sat on the white and wood couch, Rebecca asked Madeline how her week had gone, and Madeline told her everything. Rebecca listened patiently, her brown eyes moist and sympathetic.

"So," Madeline concluded, "I'm going home. On Saturday. Which means this is our last session, and if you don't mind I'd rather not do any breathing."

Rebecca nodded. "Okay. But before we make any decisions, can I tell you what I think?"

"Sure."

"I think it's no accident that you stopped just when you were writing those affirmations for your parents. And I think that if you muster up the courage to unlock all the pain you feel about them, I think you'll experience life in a totally new way. The same with the wet rebirth—I think you need that more than anything."

Madeline's heart sank. "But Rebecca, remembering all that stuff from high school was bad enough. If I start dealing with my *parents*—oh my God, I'll be crying for years. I can't do it. I don't know—I can write short stories about them, but I somehow can't let myself feel about them."

"You know," Rebecca said softly. "I remember when I first started doing this work—when I was being rebirthed, that is, before I became a rebirther. I remember I was sad—really, really sad, depressed and crying—for a full four months. But after that I was never sad in the same way."

Madeline eyed Rebecca carefully. Rebecca was so cool and collected, so thin and together in her sweat suit and hair band—what had happened to Rebecca that deserved four months of crying?

"Rebecca," Madeline said, taking her hand. "You're much braver than I am. But you have to trust me on this: I cannot go on. I cannot do any more of this work. And anyway I'm leaving on Saturday—my sister, my landlords, everyone is expecting me to go."

"Okay," Rebecca said. "I understand. But I want to tell you: the day will come when all these feelings will come up again. I don't say this to scare you, but I can tell you that one day something will happen—some loss, some disappointment—and you're going to feel it a thousand times worse because of these unresolved issues in your life."

"Yes, well…"

"And when that day comes, you can find another rebirther in New York, and you can finish what you started here."

Madeline nodded, but said nothing. They talked a little longer, then Rebecca brought Madeline upstairs and made them tea. The hairy husband joined them, and after half an hour Madeline rose and said it was time to leave.

"Don't forget what I said," Rebecca told her as she walked Madeline to her bike. "And you can always call me, anytime."

"Thanks," Madeline said. She gave Rebecca a quick hug, then got on her bike and rode off without a backward glance.

Two days later she packed. Her typewriter sat by the door, and her suitcase was open on the bed, filled with her clothes. She took her picture of Flannery O'Connor off the wall and rested it carefully between two sweaters, then put in her copy of *The Seven Storey Mountain* and the book Michael had given her. She hesitated a moment, then leafed through Michael's book until she found the picture of Lax.

"Thanks a lot, Lax," she told him. "You got me in quite a mess."

She put the book inside, shut the suitcase, and locked it. She was ready to leave.

❦   ❦   ❦

"Well, my dearest," Spencer said. "That's quite a story."

Madeline looked out the window: it was dark, and the streetlights were turned on. She had been speaking over an hour, and Spencer had sat through it all, listening carefully, his posture erect.

"Thank you, Spencer," she said, her eyes filling with tears. "Thanks for listening."

"You don't have to thank me."

"But I do—you don't know what a relief it is to talk about all this."

"You don't have to cry, Madeline. And don't be so hard on yourself—what you did was very brave."

"What I did was *crazy*. I was convinced I could be a saint, that I could be as great as Thomas Merton. I don't say that was stupid, it was just out of my grasp." She smiled sadly. "It's like a regular old musician wanting to play like Charlie Parker—you're either Charlie Parker or you're not. And you're either Thomas Merton or you're not."

"But both of them worked very hard, they weren't just born that way."

"Yes, but—I don't know. Anyway, all that's behind me now."

"So what's next?"

"What's next is that I am what I always was—a writer. And just a person living her life. It's not so horrible, I suppose, being ordinary."

Spencer laughed. "No, it's not."

"And if I ever have a quasi-religious experience again, I'll ignore it."

"Like they say, 'If you see the Buddha on the road, kill the Buddha.'"

"Exactly," Madeline agreed, although she did not know what Spencer meant.

"But—if I can say something?"

"Go ahead."

"The revulsion you feel towards anything spiritual? It's just a phase; it'll pass."

She sighed. "That's what Michael said."

"And maybe it's a little extreme for you to cut all that out of your life."

"Michael said that, too. But no, Spencer—no. It was so hard, and I was so lonely. I'm not made for the spiritual life."

"But the spiritual life is everywhere."

"Spencer, my mind is so tired I can't even talk about it. The truth is, I just want to be normal."

"Do you have the time?"

"To be normal?"

"I mean, do you know what time it is?"

"No. Do you have to be somewhere?"

"Yes, at six-thirty, but the batteries on my clock are dead and I have no idea what time it is."

"Call on the phone—it's 976-1616."

"Ooh, good idea."

Spencer called, and Madeline watched him nearly jump out of his skin. "Oh my God, it's five to six. I have to be at The Angry Squire in half an hour." He rose and started pacing. "I need to take a shower, I have to roll a joint—where's my flute?"

"Forget the shower, take your pot and pipe as they are, and isn't that your flute case next to the stereo?"

"Yes—yes. It's a good thing you're here, Madeline."

Madeline found Spencer's coat and gave it to him, then she tucked the velvet bag in his coat pocket and put the flute case in his hand. Spencer turned out the lights, and they walked down the brownstone's creaking steps and went out into the street. The street lights, lit-up shop windows and rushing people jumped at Madeline with an odd vivacity, and she knew she was still stoned.

She and Spencer practically ran the four blocks to the end of Washington Street; they turned onto Newark Street at flying speed, crossed Hudson Street, and ran down to the PATH station.

"Bye, Madeline," Spencer called, hardly looking at her as he ran down the steps.

"Bye. Thanks!" she called, but he did not turn around.

She walked slowly over to Washington Street. She did not feel like going home, not yet, so she called and left a message on the machine telling Bella not to expect her for dinner. She wandered over to the cash machine next to the pharmacy and withdrew forty dollars, then went into the pharmacy and bought a copy of *Vanity Fair*. She crossed the street and went into Kobe, the sushi restaurant between the travel agency and the realty office.

The restaurant was not crowded; she was able to sit in one of the booths made semi-private by cloth pictures of flying carp. She gave her order, then sipped green tea and read in peace.

CHAPTER 4

Evening at Home

Madeline unlocked the door and entered the apartment. All the lights were on, and the rich garlicky smell of Italian cooking hung in the air. She heard Robert and Michael talking in the living room, and the off-key singing and banging of pots in the kitchen told her where to look for Bella. She hung up her jacket in the hall closet and headed for the kitchen.

"Hi," she called out as she walked into the small, warm room. "Something smells good."

"Manicotti," Bella said. "There's still some left, it's in the refrigerator. What did you eat?"

"Sushi."

"Ooh, ooh, lucky you. You've got some mail—over there on the counter, next to the radio."

Madeline hopped up on one of the wooden stools and reached for the two envelopes. One was a manila envelope, and Madeline knew what that meant: a literary magazine had returned one of her stories. She carefully opened the envelope and pulled out a letter and her story.

"'Dear Ms. Boot,'" she read aloud to Bella. "'Thank you for the enclosed submission. Unfortunately, it does not suit the current needs of our magazine. Best of luck placing this elsewhere. Sincerely, blah blah blah.' And then here under the signature the lady wrote 'This is a *fascinating* story!' She even underlined fascinating and used an exclamation point." Madeline threw the letter and story on the counter. "If it was so fascinating underline exclamation point, then why didn't they accept it?"

"Sorry," Bella said. She leaned against the sink, gnawing a slice of carrot she had plucked from the remains of the salad. "Which story was it?"

"The one about Dad and the paint can."

"Oh yes," Bella said wryly. "Dad and the paint can. It is pretty fascinating, I suppose."

The other letter was from Oriana, a friend from college who lived in Berkeley, California. Madeline read with great concentration about Oriana's job, her new boyfriend, and the books she was reading. Madeline reread the letter, then made a mental note to write a reply on the weekend. She put the letter back in the envelope and idly watched as Bella cleaned up the last of the dinner dishes. Even after all these years it was still a novelty to see Bella doing housework; in the old days Bella was lucky to be conscious, never mind domestic. One time when Madeline was in eighth grade Bella had invited her to dinner at her apartment; when Madeline arrived Bella was sitting on the living room floor with her friends, getting high and drinking a bottle of wine. Madeline reminded Bella of her invitation; Bella motioned Madeline into the kitchen where Madeline watched a very drunk and stoned Bella wrestle with a can opener and a can of chili. Bella dumped the chili in the pot and they returned to the living room where Bella and her friends got Madeline high for the first time. A half hour later Bella remembered the chili, and presented Madeline with a blackened mess on a not very clean plate. But the worst part was, Madeline had been so stoned she ate very bite. And that was Bella on one of her good days... But now here was Bella in her beautiful apartment, in her well-equipped kitchen, carefully tucking plastic wrap over an expensive cut glass salad bowl. In her jeans, Columbia sweatshirt, and red moccasins, Bella was the model of sane, reasonable living. Which was not to say that the old Bella was entirely gone—Bella still had a spark of mischief in her eyes, and an air of barely contained wildness. As one of Madeline's dates had said, "Your sister strikes me as the kind of woman who would skinny-dip at the drop of a hat." And the past had left its mark on Bella in other ways: she was only thirty-six, but her face was deeply lined, particularly around the eyes and mouth. She and Madeline had the same large grey-green eyes, but Bella's features were pointier, and instead of Madeline's long blonde hair Bella's was jet black and cut short with bangs. She was a little taller than Madeline, a little less curvy, and she had an energy level that Madeline could not muster on her best days.

"So!" Bella announced after putting the salad in the refrigerator and giving the counter a final wipe. "Michael's here, and I've got good news for him."

"What?"

"I've finally found a woman for him."

"Bella, you find a woman for Michael every week."

"But this one's different. She's funny, she's smart, and more than that she's *sexy*. She's the kind of woman who'll grab him by the hair and drag him into the bedroom. Maybe that's what he needed all along, and I just never saw it."

"How do you know her?"

"It's my friend Patty, the one I always talk about. You know—she works in the advertising department. She got divorced a year ago, but I never fixed her up with Michael because I thought she'd be too much of a pistol for him. But then today it hit me—they'd be perfect together."

"Hmpf."

"And what do you mean, 'Hmpf?'"

"Bella, you've been setting Michael up for years and it's never worked. He's never interested in the women you introduce him to." She paused. "Have you ever considered that Michael might be gay?"

"Michael—gay? Are you crazy? He's the least gay man I've ever met. As a woman, can't you feel that?"

"No," Madeline said stubbornly.

"Then you must be dead from the waist down. Gay! I don't think so, Maddy. First of all, that would mean he was lying to us all these years, and you know Michael never lies, or acts mysteriously. And second, don't forget he was married."

"As if that means anything."

"I'm sorry, Maddy, but you're way off-base on this one. Michael's very masculine, and he's very sexy. He's like—I don't know, he's like a big cat. If I wasn't with Robert, I would have jumped Michael's bones years ago."

"I just don't see him that way, Bella. He's handsome, okay, and he's smart and he's nice, but otherwise he's so annoying. You know—his slowness."

Bella clicked her tongue. "The only reason he annoys you is because he doesn't slobber all over you like every other man. In fact, I would say he's not interested in you at all—sexually, that is."

"Which is fine, because I'm not interested in him."

"So you'll help me? He's so tired of getting set up, but if you and I both work on him—"

"I'm not getting involved in your schemes, Bella. Anyway, I have to go to my room for a little while, I need to send out this *fascinating* short story again."

"Gay!" Bella snorted as she turned out the kitchen lights. "Michael is *not* gay."

"You never know," Madeline replied. Actually, Madeline was sure Michael was not gay: he once told her that when he was a teenager he wanted to be a Franciscan monk, and when Madeline asked him what happened he replied, "I discovered women." But Madeline did not tell Bella this.

The brownstone used to be a complete house, but at some point—in the forties, Robert thought—someone decided to create discrete apartments by putting dividing walls next to the staircase. This meant each apartment had a long, skinny hall where two adults could not walk side by side or pass comfortably, a situation exacerbated in Bella and Robert's apartment by bookshelves. Madeline walked in front of Bella, past the bathroom, the hall closet, the TV room, the dining room, and the living room. She could not see Robert and Michael but she could hear their voices as she passed: "…should have gotten tenure last year, but there was that mix-up." "Yes, I remember…" At the end of the hall, facing Washington Street, was Madeline's room. It was a small room, too small for her, actually: she always kept the door open at least a crack or she felt she was in a submarine, particularly when the lone shade was down. The room was just large enough for a single bed, a wall-to-wall bookcase, her typewriter on a stand, one closet, and one window. That was all. The rich ruby carpeting, dark blue walls, and pile of pillows on a flower-patterned comforter all gave the room a warm feeling, as if it were a good place to snuggle up and read, which in fact it was. It was also a good place to write; Madeline always wrote in bed, sitting cross-legged and using a lapdesk she had bought in a stationery store years before.

She pulled down the shade, took off her shoes, sweater, skirt, and stockings, then changed into dark blue sweatpants, a white T-shirt, and a dark blue V-neck sweater that Robert, clearly ignorant of its fashion value, was about to throw out when Madeline rescued it. She hung up her clothes and put her shoes in their place on the closet floor—the room was so small everything had its place, and Madeline had changed from semi-sloppy to orderly just by virtue of wanting a place to sit. Then she took her writing submission notebook from the bottom shelf of the bookcase; she sat on the bed, opened the notebook, and frowned. Her teacher at Barnard had a notebook exactly like Madeline's, and Madeline still remembered the first time her teacher had shown her the notebook: twenty pages flew by before a check mark appeared in the "Accepted" column. Madeline had been stunned: her teacher had published four novels, five books of short stories, and had even had a Broadway musical made out of one of her novels; Madeline had assumed her teacher had always been successful, but apparently not. So when Madeline was ready to send out her first short story she went to a stationers in The City and paid twenty dollars for this hard-cover, blue marbled notebook. Madeline had been sending out short stories for four years; eight pages of the notebook were filled, and in the Accepted column there were three checks. Her teacher had a great deal to do with those check marks; she always suggested magazines to Madeline, and always told Madeline to mention her name. "I know the editor," she would say modestly. And even if the story was rejected the editor always wrote a few words: "Much regrets" or "Give my love to Faith." When her teacher died—at the thought Madeline's eyes instantly filled with tears—Madeline was alone, without help, and so it was a great moment some months later when a well-known literary magazine accepted one of her stories, a story submitted without her teacher's gentle assistance. But gentle assistance or not, Madeline missed her teacher. She wanted her back so she could once again go to her teacher's apartment on 63rd Street between First and York, watch the doorman pick up the phone and announce "A Miss Madeline Boot to see you," then ride the elevator to the tenth floor and see her teacher standing at the end of the hall, old and thin but always smiling, always upright and dignified. They would eat her teacher's homemade cookies, then sit on the couch where her teacher would go through the story Madeline had brought. In the beginning, in college and the first year after, her teacher filled the margins with pencil checks. "This isn't quite clear," her teacher would say; or "I think you can find a better word here." Towards the end there were less and less checks, and one day her teacher looked at her and said, "You're going to be quite a writer." That was one of the best days of Madeline's life; and even now, years later, she repeated her teacher's words to herself, trying to give herself courage in the face of this latest rejection. Three published stories were better than nothing, but as Madeline saw people her age or younger publishing short story collections, she could not help but feel despair.

But she hated despair—it never got you anywhere. If her teacher had gone so many years without publishing and had never given up, well, then Madeline would not give up either. So there. She paged through the notebook—she currently had seven stories roaming the country, and she found the one she had just gotten back: "The Paint Can." She put a check under the column "Denied" (her teacher said that was a friendlier word than "Rejected"), then pulled out her copy of *The Literary Marketplace* to find another magazine. Then she sat down at her typewriter and quickly typed:

Dear Editor:

Enclosed please find my short story "The Paint Can" and a SASE.

I am a graduate of Barnard College. I studied writing with Faith X and have had short stories published in *The Big Literary Magazine*, *The Semi-Big Magazine*, and *The Obscure Literary Magazine*.

I look forward to hearing from you.

Sincerely, Madeline Boot

She typed out labels for the envelopes, ruffled through the story to make sure it did not have coffee cup stains, then tucked the letter, the story, and the self-addressed stamped envelope into another envelope. Tomorrow she would go to the post office and mail it.

From her room she could hear Bella quietly playing the piano, and Robert and Michael still talking. She knew without a doubt that Robert and Michael wanted her to play Scrabble, but it was possible their Columbia-professor-departmental-restructuring conversation would go on for some time, so she grabbed the book she was reading, turned off the light, and headed into the living room.

The living room was not large, and was even less large given that Bella's piano took up a third of it. One wall had two long windows overlooking Washington Street, the flanking walls had overflowing wall-to-wall bookshelves, and in lieu of a fourth wall there was an archway with molding that connected the living room with the dining room. There were two big soft flower-patterned couches at right angles; one couch had its back to the archway, and just by turning around someone on the couch could have a discussion with someone in the dining room. A large oak coffee table covered with oversized books and a beautiful silver bowl sat in the center of the room, and there were small oak tables on either side of the couch, also piled high with books.

Robert and Michael were sitting on one of the couches, talking intently. "Don't let me bother you," Madeline said as she flopped onto the other couch. "I can read until you're done."

"What are you reading?" Robert asked.

She showed him the cover: *The Joke* by Milan Kundera. Robert grimaced. "Come on, Robert," Madeline teased. "Take the plunge and join the rest of us in the twentieth century."

"No thank you."

Madeline smiled and shook her head. She read a few pages, but she was not really in the mood so she put the book down on the table with a deliberate thud, hoping the men would get the hint. She followed their conversation for a few minutes and saw it was not a conversation at all, it was just Robert obsessively worrying and Michael listening calmly, now and then offering advice which Robert completely ignored. Several times Michael looked at Madeline and smiled as if to say "Be patient"; once Madeline rolled her eyes at Michael, hoping to make him laugh, but he—of course—did not bat an eye.

"...don't know what to do, I've done everything I can but..."

Poor Robert. He was the oldest of twelve children, and had never outgrown the childhood pattern of looking after the little ones. He had gotten tenure five years before at age thirty-seven, and now seemed to feel it was his personal duty that everyone below him also got tenure, which was of course impossible. Robert's field was the Victorians, and his specialty—his obsession—was George Eliot. Robert's idea of modern literature was Henry James, and beyond that he would not go. Madeline remembered a man at one of Bella and Robert's parties literally getting down on his knees and begging Robert to read Thomas Pynchon's *The Crying of Lot 49*, but Robert had refused, saying that like a fish he would die if removed from his element. His devotion to Victorian literature and George Eliot was so complete that he even hung a large drawing of George Eliot in the bathroom, a move Bella and Madeline could have lived without. What was particularly odd about all this was that Robert was an Italian from Brooklyn with a tongue twister last name and a Brooklyn accent that became more pronounced when he got angry. He was about five-nine with black hair, a trim black beard and mustache, close-set dark brown eyes, and an intensity in his gaze and manners. As Bella had said to Madeline when she first described Robert, "He looks like someone who orders around guys with piano wire in their pockets." He was, in other words, about as far from an English gentleman as one could possibly imagine.

Michael, on the other hand, was just that: an English gentleman. Or rather a half-English gentleman; his father was English, and his mother had been American. And although Michael had grown up in Cambridge, Massachusetts and did not have an English accent, he exuded a graceful dignity that was distinctly un-American. He was calm but not boring, precise but not fussy, elegant without seeming effeminate, considerate but not tentative, good-humored and witty but never, ever vulgar. And all this drove Madeline crazy: she could not stand his measured, unflappable calm, she wanted him to blurt out an unforgivable faux pas or get roaring drunk and swing from the light fixtures. But he never did.

She remembered the first time she met him. Bella and Robert had shown Michael the upstairs apartment, and afterwards they invited him in to discuss terms over coffee. Madeline had been curled up on the couch in the TV room reading, and she saw him before he saw her. Her first thought was that Michael was quite handsome, and wouldn't it be nice to have such a good-looking upstairs neighbor. He was tall, over six-foot, long legged and thin; his hair was sandy, almost brown, his features were regular and his cheekbones sharp. His best feature, however, was his eyes. They were large and green, still and penetrating; and at the corners there was a webbing of fine wrinkles that seemed to indicate time spent in a sunny, foreign land. My goodness, Madeline thought. Our new neighbor.

Then he turned to look into the den, and he saw her. He looked at her, and something about that look—what was it? To this day she did not know, but she suddenly decided that she did not like him. And when Bella beckoned Madeline to join them and Madeline listened as Bella plied Michael with questions, Madeline knew why she did not like him: he was a snob. His father was a Harvard professor, he himself went to Harvard for his B.A., M.A., and Ph.D., and all that Harvard could add up to only one thing: a snob. Madeline clung to this opinion for several weeks, but as it became obvious that Michael was not in the least bit snobby—nor conceited, boring, or any of the other adjectives Madeline tried to pin on him—she finally found a criticism that even Bella and Robert could not deny: Michael was slow. Everything he did, he did slowly, whether it was eating, turning the pages of a book, telling a story, or putting Scrabble letters on the board. Slow, the slowest person Madeline had ever met; and every time Bella tried to fix him up—every time they sat through yet another brunch or dinner with the latest candidate—Madeline was sure that whatever charms Michael possessed, the woman would run out of the room screaming once she saw how slow he was.

Nevertheless, Madeline and Michael were friends. Family, practically, because from the beginning Michael was often at the apartment, and when he proved willing to play Scrabble—a game Bella loathed—he was as welcome as Christ's second coming. Robert loved Michael for his half-Englishness, and respected him for his translation work, which included translations of *The Flower Garland Sutra*, *The Platform Sutra*, and *The Diamond Sutra*. Apparently the sutra translations had been well-received, and Michael had gotten tenure after publishing the second. Michael loved Robert as well—they traveled to work together, read each others' manuscripts, constantly exchanged books and ideas. On rare evenings when Michael did not come to the apartment Robert paced impatiently, saying, "But where's Michael? Should I call him? Oh, that's right—he has plans. But maybe he'll come back early…" Bella was equally fond of Michael, and her only regret was that she had been unable to find him the woman of his dreams.

Madeline snapped out of her musings—had she detected a pause? Yes, finally: Bella was still playing piano, but the human voices had ceased. She looked over at the men; Robert was staring morosely at a pillow, and Michael was waiting patiently to see if Robert would resume talking. Madeline caught Michael's eye and made a hand gesture as if to say, "Hurry up and say something!"

"So, Madeline," Michael said, turning slightly to face her. He had one elbow resting on the back of the couch, and his intermeshed fingers rested on his hip bone. "How was work today?"

"Great. I was on call all morning, and no one called so they sent me home at eleven thirty."

Robert shook his head. "I can't believe they pay you for doing nothing."

"Well, last week when I was on call the agency sent me to The Big Cigarette Company; I guess it behooves them to have people at their office in case someone phones in sick at the last minute."

"And they pay you how much when you sit around?"

Madeline widened her eyes and smiled. "Seventeen-fifty an hour, buddy."

Robert sighed. "I'm going to give up teaching and become a word processor."

"Don't be silly," Madeline said. Robert always worried about money even though he had no need to: as a tenured professor he made $65,000 a year, plus there was Bella's salary as assistant editor of *Psychology Now*. Not to mention the small fortune they made when the building went co-op. "From what I hear you professors do pretty well for yourselves."

"Yes, but with taxes it's not as much as it sounds."

"And so, Madeline," Michael said, veering the conversation from one of Robert's gloomy monologues on taxable income, "what did you do after that?"

"I went to a cafe in the Village and wrote for a few hours, then I wandered around a little, then I came to Hoboken and dropped in on Spencer."

"And how's Spencer?"

"Fine. We had a nice talk." She raised her eyebrows as if to say, "A talk about you-know-what." She was still unwilling to tell Bella and Robert about her—as she now mentally dubbed it—religious phase, and was grateful that Michael had kept her secret.

"Good. Well," he said, moving slightly forward in his seat. "Shall we go play Scrabble?"

They moved to the dining room, and the ritual began. Madeline and Michael cleared the oval antique table, putting the salt and pepper shakers, place mats, and stray silverware on the equally antique sideboard. From the top of the cupboard Robert brought down the Scrabble box, a Scrabble dictionary, a small clock, a notebook, and a square of green felt. He shook out the felt, then positioned it in the exact center of the table; he picked off lint, then opened the Scrabble box and put the board in the center of the felt. He placed the wooden letter holders on the felt, put the bag of letters in the center of the board, then lay the notebook, dictionary, and clock on the exposed half-moon of wood. Then, and only then, did Madeline and Michael sit down; they sat next to each other on one side of the table, and Robert sat across from them. Madeline used to sit next to Robert, but one evening he told her that her breathing disturbed his concentration, and he insisted she sit next to Michael. After an indignant explosion Madeline took up her new place on Michael's side of the table where her breathing, Michael said, did not bother him at all.

The dictionary was especially for Scrabble, and they were not allowed to consult it unless a word was in dispute. The notebook was for keeping score as well as keeping track of games won. And the clock— Well, the clock was not as innocent as it looked. Michael was, as has been noted, slow, and if not prodded could spend an inordinate amount of time searching for a word. Madeline had also been known to take a long time during her turn, and so one day when they sat down to play Robert brought out a timer.

"You're joking," Madeline said.

"I'm not. Everyone gets five minutes."

They played for half an hour, and after half an hour of chafing under the sound of Robert re-setting the timer, Madeline burst out, "Robert, I'm going to kill you or that timer. Take your pick."

"We need it," Robert said huffily. "You two slow everything down."

"Excuse me, but last I heard this was just a game; I didn't realize we were in such a hurry."

"Well, *you* certainly aren't."

All Michael's efforts to interrupt went unheard, and the argument grew so fierce Bella stopped playing and tried to intervene. Madeline had a temper and was stubborn—a bad combination—and as a Sicilian Robert was always ready to fight to the death. The fight ended only because Robert, in one of his impassioned speeches, slipped into heavy Brooklyneese and said, "Youse guys take too lawng." Madeline burst into laughter, and the tension broke. Michael took the opportunity to suggest that they use a clock: it was much less intrusive, and Robert could keep a silent eye on it whenever Michael or Madeline had their turn. Madeline was given the task of buying the clock, an assignment she carried out under protest. She went to Casey's and bought a $1.99 Mickey Mouse alarm clock, and was quite pleased when Robert not only did not like the colors, but could not bear the hesitant ticks. So Robert bought a clock, but the ticks were sharp and loud, and Madeline felt as if she were about to be blown up by a bomb. Finally Michael bought what they all agreed was the perfect clock: red, round, and silent.

All of this was why Bella refused to play Scrabble: she said games brought out all of Robert's neuroses, and if she joined them her marriage would be over in a week. Besides she had better things to do, like play piano. Madeline was not particularly fond of Robert's neuroses either, but in an odd way she respected him for his precision, and she appreciated his sense of ceremony. She did not even mind that he was hypercompetitive; actually she found it funny, and suspected Michael did too although he was too polite to let on. Madeline and Michael never discussed these things when they found themselves alone; Robert's quirks were simply not important because his good qualities—his honesty, his loyalty, his warmth and intelligence—far outweighed his tendency to be intense over things that did not deserve the least bit of intensity. Besides, Robert's moods were laughably mild compared to Spam's, and from the occasional stories Michael told about his mother he was also no stranger to the bizarre and illogical. So the evenings of Scrabble went on: Robert was happy when he won, devastated when he lost; Madeline enjoyed winning because when she won Robert lost; and as for Michael, he did not react either way. And Bella, as always, stayed above the fray, wrapped in the private world of her piano.

Tonight the game went quickly, although Michael often reached the ceiling of the five-minute limit. At one point as Madeline watched Michael put a word on the board—watched him slowly pick up a letter, slowly bring it to the board, slowly put it in place, then slowly retract his hand for the next letter—she looked at Robert and asked, "Does Michael's five minutes include the time it takes him to put the word on the board? I think he should get only three minutes to look for a word since it takes him two minutes just to transfer his letters."

Michael laughed. "Don't give Robert any ideas," he said, and continued putting his letters on the board just as slowly as before.

Madeline sighed. He would not hurry, no matter how much she goaded him. Once the word was finally in place she was pleased to see it gave her access to one of the coveted red-triple-word-score squares. Quickly she put down ZONED, and did nothing to hide her smile of triumph.

"Michael," Robert said.

"What?"

"I don't want to have the same argument with you."

"What?"

"You could have put that word over here, you didn't have to put it there and give Madeline access to the triple word score. Here," he said, pointing to the right-hand corner of the board. "See what I mean?"

"Oh—you're right. Oh well."

"'Oh well'? She just scored over thirty points, that's what's 'Oh well.' At least tomorrow night we'll play counterclockwise, that way I'll have half a chance."

This was another one of Robert's pet peeves: he claimed that Michael was not competitive enough, and never made things hard for Madeline. Robert even calculated that Madeline always had a higher score when Michael's turn came before hers. Madeline's Scrabble pride had been hurt, and only after great persuasion did she agree to Robert's system of playing counterclockwise every other night. There was a certain truth to what Robert said: Michael often gave Madeline access to triple-word-score squares, and Robert would have died if he knew something else Michael did, which was glance over Madeline's letters and suggest words anytime Robert went to the phone. Michael was an excellent player, and he often suggested obscure words which Robert would eye suspiciously on his return.

"'Tantric,'" he'd say. "Interesting, Madeline, very interesting."

Close to nine o'clock the piano music suddenly stopped, and Bella called out, "Who wants ice cream?"

"Would you get it, sweetheart?" Robert asked. "I'm in the middle of my turn."

Bella came over and wrapped her arms around Robert's neck. "For you, my dearest husband, anything."

Michael kept them supplied in ice cream; he said it was the least he could do to repay their hospitality. Tonight he had brought a pint of Ben and Jerry's Cookies and Cream as well as a pint of Coffee Heath Bar Crunch, which was Madeline's favorite. They moved into the living room to eat; Bella and Madeline sat on one couch, Robert and Michael on the other. The conversation meandered from subject to subject—Bella's boss, Robert's athlete's foot, the benefits of hypnosis—then Bella leaned forward and said coyly, "So Michael, I have good news for you."

Michael raised an eyebrow. "And what's that?"

"I've found the perfect woman for you. I mean it—she's perfect."

He sighed.

"No, don't sigh, Michael. This one is different; this time I'm sure you'll really like her. And we'll do it very casually, we'll have a brunch or dinner or maybe a party. It's been awhile since we had a party—isn't there some holiday soon?"

"Halloween," Madeline supplied.

"Halloween! We'll have a Halloween party! But no, actually, better not. And you know why? Because this woman is so beautiful and sexy and intelligent that if I gave a party you wouldn't even get a chance to get close to her because she'd be so busy fighting off admirers."

"If she's so busy fighting off admirers," Michael said, "then why does she need to be fixed up with me?"

"Don't get smart with me, Michael. She's always out on dates, she's always seeing men, but she was divorced a year ago and it's been a little hard for her to meet the right person. *You* know how it is."

"And so what do you want me to do?"

"I want you to give me your permission to invite her here, and I want your word that you'll show up with an open mind and a willingness to meet someone fabulous."

"Bella, you can invite anyone you want to your house, you don't need my permission. And you know if you ask me to brunch or dinner, I'll be here."

"Michael. That's not enough. You have to be willing to be fixed up."

He said nothing.

"Michael," Bella said, putting her ice cream bowl on a stack of coffee-table books. "I've known you over two years now, and you've never had a girlfriend. I don't believe you've even had a date. I mean—don't you *want* a girlfriend? Don't you *want* to fall in love and get married and have children?"

"Of course I do," he said calmly. "I want very much to get married and have children. I just don't go chasing after it."

"You don't have to," Madeline said. "My sister does it for you."

Michael smiled at her. "She certainly does, doesn't she."

"It's my small attempt to help my fellow man," Bella said. "You don't know what it's like out there, Michael. Women are lonely, they're dying of loneliness, and a man like you—! You're smart, you're handsome, you have a great job, you're sane, you're funny, you have a nice apartment, you're not gay—" Here she shot a look at Madeline, as if daring her to disagree. "The point is, Michael, I can't bear to see you single. *I can't bear it.* I know so many wonderful women, and I can't believe you can't have a relationship with one of them."

"And I can't believe you have anyone left to fix him up with," Robert said. "You've tried everyone."

This was true. All Bella's friends from the past, all her friends from Columbia General studies, all the single women at *Psychology Now*, two of Robert's sisters, a friend of the third floor neighbor's, even a woman Bella met while buying mozzarella at Lisa's Delicatessen—all the available woman in the center and on the periphery of Bella's life had passed through the doors of the apartment, and each one had passed out again without the slightest interest on Michael's part.

"What you don't understand, Bella," Michael said, "is that we have different philosophies about this. I think it's better if things happen naturally, without force."

"I'm not talking about *force*," Bella said. "I'm just interested in creating serendipitous circumstances."

"Robert got Bella by force," Madeline said.

"That he did, Madeline, that he did." Bella leaned forward and planted a loud kiss on Robert's cheek. Robert grimaced and rolled his eyes. "Oh, come on, Robert," she said. "You know it's true."

And it was. Bella told the story again, although Madeline and Michael knew it by heart: Robert had been a junior faculty member teaching a course on the Victorians for General Studies, and Bella was one of his students. He had managed to contain himself until the end of the semester, then the moment Bella handed in her final exam Robert whispered, "Can I take you out to dinner?"

"No," Bella whispered back. She picked up her books and coat and walked out of the exam room. She was putting on her coat in the hall when Robert, in violation of university rules not to mention common sense, left the exam room unattended and followed her into the hall.

"Why won't you go out with me?"

"Because you and I are utterly, completely different. Bye."

She walked down the hall; he chased after her. "You have to say yes," he said. "The moment you walked into my classroom I knew I had to go out with you."

"Excuse me," Bella said, "but I don't *have* to do anything." And she walked into the stairwell, slamming the door behind her.

The next morning when Bella came out of her apartment building, Robert was on the front stoop waiting for her.

"Are you some kind of maniac?" she asked. "Or maybe you're just deaf. In case you don't remember, I said no."

"At least give me a chance," he said. "At least let me buy you coffee and you can explain why you won't go out with me."

"You want me to go out with you so I can explain why I won't go out with you? Fine. I'll let you buy me a cup of coffee, then I want you to go away and leave me alone."

Over coffee and corn muffins at Tom's Restaurant, Bella did her best to dissuade Robert from loving her. She told him that although she looked pulled together, it was a relatively new phenomenon. Hoping to scare him away, she gave him some highlights from her past: she told him about her senior year in high school when she got arrested at her supermarket job because she was running a scam ringing up twenty dollar steaks for one dollar; she told him about her stint as a drug dealer, which led to arrest number two; and she told him about her years following the Grateful Dead, during which time she had more lovers than she could count, and mostly she couldn't count because she had been so drunk and stoned and high she could hardly remember faces much less names.

"And that's just the tip of the iceberg," she said. "Do you want me to go on?"

"I don't care," Robert said. "I don't care about any of it."

"Professor Dellasandandrio! Don't you hear what I'm saying? I have a criminal record, I've fucked countless men, and I've tried every drug in existence. Look at you—you're a professor at Columbia, you don't want to get involved with someone like me."

"Yes, I do."

"Okay then, let me tell you something else: I've had five abortions. You're an Italian-Catholic—aren't you horrified?"

"A little. But I still want to go out with you."

"Well, how about this: I didn't particularly like your class. And I don't like George Eliot."

"You'll learn to like her. Let me take you out."

Eight months later they were married.

"Madeline's right," Robert said. "I did get Bella by force."

"So, Michael," Bella said, "is it all right if I speak to my friend? We work together; I can tell her tomorrow."

"Bella," Michael said. "You can do whatever you like."

The phone rang. Robert put his ice cream bowl on the table and hurried to the kitchen. Usually the calls were for him, either students working on papers or someone from his extensive family tree. But a moment later he called out, "Madeline, it's for you."

Madeline put down her bowl and went into the hall, Robert stepping into the bathroom so she could pass. She went into the kitchen, grabbed one of the wooden stools and brought it over to the phone.

"Hello?"

"Hey Madeline, it's me, Rose. Guess what?"

"Hi, Rose. What?"

"I've got a man for you."

"Really? That was quick."

Rose was a friend from Madeline's old word processing job at The Big Law Firm. The same age as Madeline, Rose was a beautiful Puerto Rican woman with thick black hair, large brown eyes, and a wide smiling mouth. The night before during a long phone conversation Madeline had declared herself willing to date, and Rose had promised to sniff out any available men.

"Listen, when I say I'm going to fix you up, I don't fool around. I have to speak quickly, he's waiting for me to call him back."

"So what's the deal?"

"Okay: his name is Frank, and he's a friend of my sister's boyfriend. He's white, he works with computers, and he's cute—he's got blond hair and wears glasses and has a good sense of humor. And he's single, of course."

"Well—all right. I'll go out with him."

"How's Thursday night?"

"So soon? That's only two nights away."

"What are you waiting for? This could be the man of your dreams."

"Okay. Thursday night's fine."

"Great. Listen, I'll call him back and then he'll call you."

"Okay."

"Then you call me and tell me what he said, okay?"

Madeline laughed. "Okay. Bye, Rose—and thanks."

"No problem."

Madeline sat on the stool, waiting. How long had it been since she had had a date? Forget that—the real question was, how long had it been since she had

had sex? A year, two years? She calculated a moment and realized with a shock that it had been *two and a half years.* Two and a half years without sex! It was time to get back to business, time to be a woman and not a saint.

The phone rang. Madeline let it ring for three rings and would have let it ring longer except for Robert anxiously calling out, "Madeline! Get the phone!"

"Hello?" she said.

"Hello," a not very deep male voice replied. "Is this Madeline?"

"It is."

"Well, hi. I'm Frank. Rose's friend."

"Hi, Frank."

"Hi. Listen, Rose said you're free Thursday night?"

"I am."

"Me too. So—you're in Hoboken?"

"Mmm hmm."

"And I'm in Queens. Look, why don't I come out there? I work in The City, I can just jump on the PATH train."

"Okay."

"We can go out to dinner. I'll take you to dinner," he corrected himself. "Where would you suggest?"

"Maxwell's has good food."

"Okay. So let's say Maxwell's at seven?"

"Okay. And a friend of mine is playing at a local club that night, we can stop by after dinner."

"Sounds great. See you then."

"See you."

"Wait—Madeline? How will I recognize you?"

"I'm tall with dark blonde hair."

"And I have blond hair, glasses, and I'm not very tall. Good enough. See you Thursday."

Madeline called Rose and told her the plan.

"Great," Rose said. "He's a really nice guy, Madeline; I'm sure you'll like each other."

"We'll see."

"Oh, don't pretend like you're all indifferent. You need a man worse than anyone I know."

They talked a little longer, then Madeline went back to the living room. Bella was reading a book, and Robert and Michael had returned to the dining room.

"We can't start playing yet," Madeline protested. "I haven't finished my ice cream."

"Scrabble waits for no one," Robert said.

"Fine. I'll eat while I play."

"Oh no you don't. As you know you're not the world's neatest eater, and I don't want you getting ice cream on the felt. And it's your turn, by the way." He looked at the clock. "Five minutes and counting."

She quickly put down a word, then went back to the living room. Bella put down her book—*Ladies' Man* by Richard Price—and asked, "Who was that?"

"Rose. And then a guy she's fixing me up with."

Bella raised her eyebrows. "You have a date?"

"Yep."

"Finally! You were getting as bad as Michael. You hear that, Michael?" Bella said, leaning her head back against the couch and looking at Michael upside down. "Even Madeline is willing to get set up."

Michael said nothing.

"Aren't you a little old for blind dates?" Robert asked.

"Shut up, Robert," Bella replied. "So!" she turned eagerly to Madeline. "Who is he?"

"A friend of Rose's sister's boyfriend. He has glasses and is into computers—not really my type."

"You never know. I never thought I'd end up married to an Italian with a George Eliot fetish."

"I don't have a fetish," Robert said.

"Fine, then let's say obsession. So when's the big date?"

"Thursday. We're having dinner at Maxwell's."

"Nice, very nice. He's paying, I hope?"

"He made noises to that effect."

"That's a good sign."

"Well, we'll see what happens. Robert, is it my turn yet?" Madeline asked.

"It's Michael's turn," Robert said. "He has four minutes and fifteen seconds left."

"Which means I can take my time."

"Don't mind them, Michael," Bella said, again leaning her head back against the couch. "They're of a lower evolutionary species and are unable to appreciate you."

Again, Michael said nothing.

CHAPTER 5

Blind Date

Madeline pushed open the door to Maxwell's at seven-twenty. The dining room—a large, airy room with a long wooden bar—was almost empty. The jukebox was playing the Bongos' song "Barbarella," and from the dark cave-like room in back she heard guitars being tuned, the sound check for that night's band.

Madeline looked around the room. There—a blond man with glasses was sitting by one of the big front windows that faced Washington Street. As there were no other single men and as he matched his own description, well, it had to be Frank. Here goes, she thought, and started walking across the room. She saw that Frank had spotted her as well and was clearly giving her the once over. She could not blame him, but it annoyed her; she set her face into an indifferent mask and did not look at him. Her biggest dread was appearing eager.

"You must be Madeline," he said, rising and extending his hand. "I'm Frank."

"Hi Frank," she said, taking his hand and giving it a firm, brief squeeze. He's cute, she thought as he helped her take off her jacket. On the delicate side and not tall, but no shorter than her five-foot seven. He had even features, dark blue eyes behind wire-frame glasses, and blond hair cut short in a style that was almost punk. The hair was a puzzler; she wondered if he was involved in the alternative music scene, or maybe the military. But his clothes—neat jeans, white oxford shirt, dark blue sweater—were strictly conservative, and she reminded herself that he worked with computers. Oh no: could it be that Frank was a computer nerd? Keep an open mind, Madeline, she told herself.

Look at Bella and Robert, they're as different as can be, and after nine years of marriage they still carry on like newlyweds.

Madeline sat down and folded her hands in front of her. She smiled slightly, and looked at Frank without looking at him. I hate blind dates, she thought; but she trusted Rose, and she had to agree with Rose's pronouncement that she needed a man. And beneath all the awkwardness, Madeline felt a ripple of excitement. The truth was, she had spent the better part of the past two days fantasizing that Frank might be The One. And who could say? Maybe he was, maybe her search would end tonight. At this point anything could happen; the evening was wide open, with no strikes on either side.

"Well," he said. "Rose said you were pretty, and you are."

Madeline half-smiled, half-grimaced. "So," she said. "Did you have any trouble getting here?"

"No, not at all. I know Hoboken pretty well; I come here a lot with my high school buddies to go to the Clam Broth House."

"I love the Clam Broth House," Madeline said. "Every time I feel a cold coming on I stop in there and drink some clam broth from the big vat by the bar."

"It's a great place. I love the calamari."

"I like calamari too, but only when it's just the round circle things. I hate when they give you the whole calamari and you see the eyeballs and everything and it makes that weird crunching sound when you bite into it."

Madeline! she scolded herself. *Calm down*—don't talk about crunching calamari eyeballs. She took a sip of water to hide her distress.

"I know what you mean," Frank said. "Well, speaking of food, how's the food here?"

"It's good. I used to come here just to hear music, but one night I came here with some friends to hear a band and we were early so we ate here and it was really good. And reasonable prices, too."

"Don't *you* worry about prices," he said, smiling. "This is my treat."

"If you say so," she smiled back.

The waitress came over and gave them menus, then reeled off the specials of the day. After she left, Madeline and Frank opened their menus and studied them intently.

"Hmm," Frank said. "I don't know—what do you think?"

"The angel hair pasta with shrimp is good—I had it once, maybe I'll order it."

"You should never order the same thing twice from a restaurant," he said. "Have something else."

Madeline hated being told what to do. "No," she said, putting the menu a decisive distance from her table setting. "I'll have the angel hair pasta."

"I'll have the steak with wine and mushroom sauce," he said. Not a vegetarian, she noted. Not great, but she could deal with it.

"So," Frank said, rubbing his hands together and leaning forward. "What do you say we get a bottle of the best wine in the house?"

"Actually, Frank, I don't drink."

His face fell. "You don't?"

"No."

"Not at all? Never?"

"No."

"Oh. Wow—I'm disappointed."

"You're disappointed because I don't drink?"

"Well—a little."

"And why is that?"

"Well—it's fun to go out and have a few drinks."

"A few drinks, yes. But I was never the kind of person who had only a few drinks."

"Oh, so you did drink."

"Yes. Too much."

"Too bad I didn't know you then."

Strike one. Absolutely and unequivocally, strike one. Quitting drinking was one of Madeline's greatest achievements, and now this Frank regretted that he didn't know her when she was a roaring crazy drunk? Madeline did not move, but mentally and emotionally she took one step back.

The waitress took their order. Frank ordered a bottle of wine anyway, which only deepened the magnitude of his first strike. A whole bottle of wine, she thought. Well, well; let's see if he gets through it.

"So," he said, again leaning forward, his blue eyes and glasses fixed on her face. "Rose tells me you're a writer."

"That's right."

"What do you write?"

"Short stories."

He shook his head. "You should write novels; you'll never make any money with short stories."

"We-ll Frank," she said. "I'm not exactly writing to get rich. And actually short stories are back in vogue. Which is not why I write them," she said hurriedly. "I would write them anyway, they're what I like to write. But there are lots of short story collections out now, in fact one of the best American writers writes only short stories. Raymond Carver—have you read him?"

"Don't know him."

"He's wonderful. And then there's Flannery O'Connor, she's great too. She's dead, of course, but she's one of the best writers of this century."

"Still," he said. "If you wrote a novel and made some money, you wouldn't have to work as a secretary."

"I'm a word processor, not a secretary." Immediately she bit her lip—what a snobby little distinction *that* was! As if she had never photocopied anything in her life. "What's wrong with being a secretary?" she asked.

"Nothing," he said. "It's just that Rose said you went to Barnard; I'm sure you could get a better job."

What the fuck was wrong with this guy? Would he be ashamed to go out with her because she worked as a secretary? Her writing teacher had worked for years as a secretary; as she always told Madeline, "Writing is a habit, and it's a habit you have to support." Madeline had long ago decided that a high-powered job would interfere with her writing, and everyone in her life understood and supported her decision. Until now.

Strike two. Most definitely, strike two.

The waitress brought Frank's bottle of wine and Madeline's glass of mineral water. "And what about your job, Frank?" Madeline asked. "Rose says you're a computer programmer."

"That's right. I work for The Big Computer Company."

"Sounds like a good job."

"It is. I've been there three years and already I make $50,000 a year. And I'm only twenty-five, you know." He took a healthy sip of wine. "And because I still live at home you can imagine how much I save."

"A lot?"

"A whole lot. And my salary isn't the whole story—I also get bonuses and stock options. See, I know it's unusual for a guy at twenty-five to still be living at home, but I want to save up money for when I get married. I want my wife and I to be able to buy a house right away; I want us to start big immediately."

"Really."

"And I'm not one of those commitment-shy guys, either. I know what I want: I want to get married and have kids. It's just a matter of finding the right woman."

And then he gave her a look that made her want to reach across the table and slap him. He had been leaning forward on his elbows, talking intently while looking into her eyes, and then after declaring his desire to get married his eyes left her face and slowly, slowly traveled down her neck and rested on her chest. It was horribly insulting, as if he was checking out her body for its breeding ability. Then his eyes rose slowly until they met her gaze, and he smiled approvingly as if to say, "You're got large breasts—you'll do."

Strike three. He was out.

"Will you excuse me?" Madeline said coldly. "I have to go to the ladies' room."

"Sure. Go ahead."

She pushed back her chair, rose and walked to the bathroom, trying hard not to stalk across the room. As she passed the bar she saw a painter she knew, and she waved and said hello. The ladies' room was next to the dark back room; she went inside and locked the door with a small hook. She peed, then put her chin on her fists and proceeded to fume. I'm going to kill Rose, she thought. Mr. Frank the Computer Programmer was not her type at all. He was wife shopping, which was not such a terrible thing, but he was so smug about his good job and big salary—he did not have the slightest idea what it meant to be an artist. And he seemed hell-bent on changing her; he probably couldn't wait to see her in an apron or, more likely, working at some soulless job she hated so she could bring home a big paycheck and help him buy a couch. Or microwave oven. And checking out her breasts like that! What a pig.

Can I leave? she thought. Or spend all night in the bathroom? But the truth was, she was hungry—and from what she remembered the angel hair pasta was awfully good. Madeline knew she had a temper, and she was willing to accept—just barely—that maybe Frank was not as bad as she thought. Give the guy a break, she told herself. It's your first date, and even worse it's a blind date. People say dumb things on blind dates; look at you, going on about calamari eyeballs. And Rose would never set you up with a loser, she knows you too well. So calm down, splash cold water on your face, and try to get through the evening with a little dignity.

She returned to the table greatly subdued. She must have been gone longer than she thought because Frank's bottle of wine was almost empty.

"Everything okay?" he asked.

"Everything's fine," she said, managing a smile.

"So tell me about this friend of yours who plays music. The one we're going to see tonight."

Oh God—she had forgotten about Spencer's gig. The evening was going to be longer than she thought. "Spencer," she said. "His name is Spencer Simon. Have you heard of him?"

"No."

"He plays the flute. He's really well-known, more so in Europe than here, but he's played with a lot of really great musicians. And he's a wonderful person as well."

"Was he ever your boyfriend?"

"Spencer? No—he's much older than me, he's in his fifties."

"But I bet he wanted to be your boyfriend." And to emphasize his point, Frank reached out two fingers and poked Madeline's shoulder.

Did he really do that? Madeline asked herself. Did he really just *poke* me? She decided to let it pass—it was first date jitters, just a poke born of first date jitters.

"No," she said firmly. "Spencer and I are just friends."

By the time the food had arrived, Frank had polished off all the wine; and as the waitress was leaving he asked for yet another bottle. Madeline could not believe her ears—Frank was not a large man, he was going to get completely drunk. And yet he remained in control: his words did not slur, his eyes were not bloodshot, his coordination seemed fine—his fork always made it to his mouth, in any case. No, the only change in his behavior was that annoying poking. Whenever he wanted to tease Madeline or emphasize a point, those two fingers shot across the table and jabbed her shoulder. With each jab Madeline's blood rose a little higher, and finally she could take it no more. Frank made some comment about pretty blondes and then those two fingers started coming at her again. Madeline dropped her fork and caught Frank's hand mid-poke. She squeezed his fingers as hard as she could and said, "Frank, if you poke me one more time I swear to God I'll rip your hand off."

Well. That certainly put a damper on the evening.

"I'm sorry," he said. "Did I do something?"

"Frank, for the last half hour you've been poking me. Or are you so drunk you didn't notice?"

"I'm sorry," he said. "I guess it's because—I'm nervous. I like you; you're a nice girl."

"Woman," she corrected him.

"A nice woman. And, Madeline? Could you let go of my hand?"

After that Frank really tried. He stopped drinking, and he dropped his aggressive-go-getter-write-novels-and-make-more-money personality. He lowered his voice and started telling her how difficult it was for him at work, how it was so cutthroat competitive and how he didn't like that but if you wanted to move up you had to play hard ball; and he had problems at home, his parents fighting all the time, and his little sister dating "a black," as he put it. It was a new Frank, a softer, non-poking Frank. Madeline finished her angel hair pasta in silence. If only he had been like this from the start they might have had a nice evening, maybe even could have started dating…but no. Better she saw from the start that Frank—or one side of him, at least—was a bully, not to mention a lush.

She was ready to leave the moment she took her last bite of pasta, but Frank persuaded her to order dessert. As she worked her way through a mound of pecan pie, vanilla ice cream, and fresh whipped cream, taking occasional sips of tea, Madeline listened to Frank: he was lonely, it was hard to meet women, he and his friend had met Rose's sister at the same time and Frank had liked her too but his parents would have hit the roof if he brought a Puerto Rican home (a fact Madeline could not tell Rose or Rose would skin Frank alive) and so he had been happy when he heard that Rose had a nice blonde friend who went to Barnard and was a writer and he thought, well, you never know, maybe he and Madeline would hit it off and—

"You do want to get married, don't you?" he asked her. "You do want to have kids?"

"One day," Madeline replied. "Not now."

"Well, how many years do you need? I mean, I think this is something we should clear up from the start."

The start? The start of what? Obviously Frank was under the impression that they had a future, and obviously it was Madeline's job to convince him otherwise.

"Frank," she said gently, pushing away her empty plate. "I don't think we're destined to be a couple."

"No? Why not?"

"We're just completely different people."

"I don't think so—I don't think so at all."

He called for the check. Madeline sat with chin in hand and watched Frank take out his credit card, watched the waitress negotiate the little credit card machine, watched Frank sign the receipt and rip up the carbon copies. The minute he was done Madeline was out of her seat, putting on her jacket and walking towards the exit.

Frank followed her, his jacket half-on as they emerged onto Eleventh Street. Madeline had decided to send him off to the PATH station, then wait a few minutes and walk to the club; but then Frank clapped his hands and said, "So—where's your friend playing?"

"You still want to go?"

"Sure, don't you? That was our plan."

She sighed. "Okay. It's all the way down by the PATH station."

"Let's go."

Madeline led Frank one block over to Hudson Street, a quiet street with some of Hoboken's most beautiful brownstones. It was a late September night, cold enough for a jacket but beautifully still with a full moon and no wind.

Although the street was quiet, Frank was not. He had somehow seized upon the misguided notion that Madeline wanted to hear about his job, and he proceeded to explain it to her in excruciating detail. Madeline felt horribly depressed; a few times she even raised her hand and wiped away tears. As much as she tried to be cool and indifferent, the truth was that she wanted a boyfriend, and had pinned her hopes on Frank. And now it was clear she had no future with Frank, so what next? She could not bear more years of loneliness; she wanted a boyfriend, and she wanted one now.

In all her twenty-seven years Madeline had never had a genuinely serious relationship with a man. Not in high school, not in college, and not after college—well, there had been someone after college, but Madeline was never sure how to count him. He was a lawyer from one of her temp jobs; he was young and good-looking, and had just moved to New York after three years at Duke Law School. Madeline went out with him several times and after two weeks—on her initiative—they slept together. After that he seemed to assume they were engaged; he started prefacing sentences with statements such as "When we get married—" or "I think our first child—" Madeline thought he was joking; she certainly had no such intentions with him, in fact from the start she was sure the relationship could not last. She knew she was in trouble when she told him a story about birth control, and afterwards he said, "So I guess you weren't a virgin with me." Madeline laughed and said, "Of course not! And what a ridiculous double standard—you certainly weren't a virgin." He looked at her with great seriousness and said, "I never said that." Madeline's heart flipped—he had been a virgin! Oh no. It was hard to believe a man of twenty-five—and a lawyer at that—could be so innocent, but there he was. A week later Madeline broke up with him. He cried like a baby, said he couldn't believe she was doing this to him, and as she was walking out the door he said, pitifully, "Call me if you change your mind." He tried repeatedly to win her back, but she would not budge: she was reading a great deal of Anaïs Nin in those days, and being married to a lawyer had nothing to do with the romantic bohemian life she envisioned for herself. Finally he moved to Seattle, but if Madeline thought that was the end of him she was wrong, because every month he sent her a letter. The letters were carefully written and painfully neat—he even used Wite-Out to correct mistakes, a fact that made Madeline and Bella scream with laughter. "Wite-Out!" Bella said. "Why doesn't he cross out like everyone else?" Madeline never answered the letters, and gradually they stopped coming.

After the lawyer Madeline never got serious with anyone. It was always the same pattern: she would meet a local artist (painter, musician, sculptor, poet), they would go on a few dates, the men would get serious, and she would break up with them. Over and over and over, every time the same. And she never slept with any of them: every six months or so she had sex with an old flame from high school, thus relieving the worst of her sexual tension, but after The Virgin (as she and Bella referred to the lawyer) Madeline was careful not to leap into a sexual relationship. But why, she asked herself as she and Frank walked down Hudson Street, why did you never get serious with any of those guys? She thought a little, and decided it was because none of them had seemed good enough for her. Not good enough, and not smart enough. They were struggling artists with seedy apartments and seedy jobs, and it had bothered her that she was always better educated than they were. And in truth, it had always been too easy: they all wanted her from the start, there was never any sense of challenge. She remembered a date she had with a local painter: while they were waiting to be seated at East LA he suddenly turned to her and said, "You know, you'd make a good wife." It drove her crazy—here she was trying to be artistic and free, a sort of low-key Anaïs Nin, and instead men took one look at her and imagined cozy domestic scenes. She never went out with the painter again although, looking back, he had been a nice guy, very sweet and attentive. You blew it, Madeline, she told herself. Over and over again, you blew it. She had been so snobby about the men's lives and apartments, but the only reason she lived in a beautiful place was because of Bella and Robert. And as for education, so what? Most of the men she went to college with had ended up on Wall Street, and that certainly didn't fit in with her idea of herself. No, the artists she had dated had been nice, nothing like horrible Frank the Poker.

You'll meet nice guys again, she told herself. You've been out of circulation awhile, but there are still nice guys around.

Frank was still blab blabbing away when they reached Signore's Lounge, a small Italian restaurant in a brownstone on Hudson Street between First and Second. Madeline had never heard Spencer play there before, and she suspected that Signore's had never had jazz before. But this was just an example of Spencer's gift of getting the unlikeliest people and places involved in his music; if someone had a stage where Saturday nights a middle-aged man with a tuxedo and blue frilly shirt played synthesizer and sang Frank Sinatra, Spencer would go in and convince the owners to book an evening of jazz. He spread the music everywhere, and even got people like herself interested. So now he was playing at Signore's... Good for you, Spencer, she thought as she stood outside with Frank and studied the placard that read: TONITE AT 9—JAZZ WITH SPENCER SIMON.

"Well," Madeline said. "Let's go in."

"Okay."

They walked down four steps and entered the dark, low-ceilinged restaurant. At the far end of the room—and not on a stage, because there was no stage—Spencer, a saxophonist, a bassist and a drummer were blaring jazz. Standing by the bar was a big Italian man with waxy black hair and large forearms crossed over his chest—the owner, Madeline assumed. He rushed over to Madeline and Frank and escorted them to a large table in front of the musicians. A group of people were at the other end of the table; Madeline recognized them and said hello, then waved to a couple sitting at a smaller table by the wall. Mr. Signore bent over them and shouted something about drinks; Madeline shouted back that she wanted club soda, and Frank ordered the same.

The drinks came. Madeline glanced at Frank—he looked a little green. Too much wine and too much poking, she thought.

"You don't look too good," she shouted. "You don't have to stay if you don't want."

"I'm okay," he shouted back.

"Do you like jazz?" she shouted.

"I hate it."

"Is it a long trip back to Queens?"

"Yes."

"Do you have to get up early for work tomorrow?"

"Yes."

Madeline paused; she hoped the facts would jump together and Frank would draw the obvious conclusion. But maybe he was concerned about leaving her alone; maybe he would not leave until she did.

"It's okay for me to be here alone," she shouted. "I generally come to these things by myself."

He nodded. She fell silent, a little ashamed of being so rude. They sat and listened, and as time passed Madeline grew so fidgety she wanted to haul Frank out of Signore's chair and all. She was so desperate she started devising a scheme: she would say she had a headache, they would leave, Frank would offer to walk her home and she would say no, why bother, they were so close to the PATH station he might as well just go. They would part ways, but instead of going home she would duck around the corner, wait a few minutes and then return to Signore's. A good plan, she decided; and she was just about to open her mouth when the empty chair next to her moved. She looked up and saw—what was his name?—David. Yes, David, David and his friend Hanson.

David leaned over and shouted, "Is anyone sitting here?"

"No," Madeline said.

He took off his jacket and placed it on the back of the chair. Mr. Signore rushed over, David shouted that they wanted two Heinekens. Madeline looked at David's hands on the table, then looked up at his face. He was staring at her and smiling.

"It's really nice that you're here," he shouted.

She did not know how to reply, so she smiled and said nothing.

"I was hoping you'd be here," David went on.

He moved his chair so he was facing her, his back almost entirely turned to Hanson, who was already absorbed in the music. Obviously David had not realized that the man on Madeline's left was in any way connected with her, and it was with a sinking heart that she indicated Frank.

"This is Frank," she shouted.

David rose slightly out of his chair and leaned forward to shake Frank's hand. "Nice to meet you, Frank," he shouted.

"Same here," Frank shouted back.

David shot Madeline a smile, then turned his attention to the music. What bad luck! she thought. And it would be terribly rude to do what she wanted, which was to move *her* chair slightly so that her back was to Frank and she was facing David. As the band played on—a free jazz composition that squeaked and squawked—Madeline took several full glances at David. He was very handsome and was, as Bella would say, a hotty. It was his eyes, she decided:

they were a rich dark brown and slightly oriental at the corners. Very sexy; and his eyebrows were heavy and almost met in the middle, giving him an intense, serious expression. He had a nice straight nose, nice not too full lips, and clear white skin. And, from what she could gather from her fact-finding glances, he had a nice body, slim but solid and healthy looking. And his hands were beautiful—his fingers were long and tapering, his fingernails clean and well cut. Madeline sighed; she wished she was on a date with him, not Frank.

The band stopped for a break. Mr. Signore turned up the lights slightly, and the room shifted as everyone changed from a posture of listening to a posture of socializing.

Frank clapped his hands together. "Well, Madeline, I'd better go."

"Really?" Madeline said, trying to keep the joy out of her voice.

"Will you walk me to the door?"

"Sure."

They rose. David turned away from his conversation with Hanson and asked, "Are you leaving?"

"Frank is," she said. "I'll be back in a moment."

"I won't let anyone take your seat."

"Thanks."

Frank put on his jacket, Madeline left hers on the back of her chair. She walked with Frank out onto the sidewalk, then stopped.

"So," she said. "Thank you for dinner."

"When can we do this again?" he asked. "I'm free both nights this weekend."

"Frank," she said in a voice she hoped was both kind and firm. "It's not going to work between us. It was nice of you to take me out to dinner, but I think that's as far as we're going to go."

He cocked his head and frowned. "You're sure?"

"I'm sure."

"Well, I'll call you in a few days anyway, maybe you'll have changed your mind." He leaned over and kissed her cheek. "Bye, blondie."

Blondie! she repeated as he walked away. *Blondie.* Oh my God—what had Rose been thinking, fixing Madeline up with a man who used words like blondie? But it's over now, she thought as she watched Frank walk jauntily down Hudson Street. It's all over.

❦   ❦   ❦

When Madeline walked into Signore's she saw David turned in his chair and looking towards the door. His face lit up when she walked in, and when she reached the table he stood and held out her chair.

"Thank you," she said. She felt self-conscious, but deliciously so.

"Hanson, you remember Madeline," David said. "We met her at Spencer's the other day."

"Sure," Hanson said. "Nice to see you again."

Hanson was the kind of man you wanted to pat on the head and bring a warm sweater. There was something fragile and pained about him, something vulnerable and raw. He was taller than David, and thinner; he had long blond hair, delicate cheekbones, a hawkish nose and large light brown eyes. Between his eyebrows was a deep furrow, as if he were constantly worrying. He was not sexy like David, but he was handsome in an ascetic Jesus Christ sort of way; not Madeline's type, but she could imagine women really falling for him.

"So," David said. "Are you enjoying the music?"

"Oh, of course. I love hearing Spencer play. I can't claim to know much about jazz, but I like listening to it."

"Madeline's a writer," David told Hanson. "Are you published?"

"Slightly." She told him about The Big, Semi-Big, and Obscure Literary Magazines that had published her stories.

"That's great," David said. "You're really on your way."

"I hope so. And you guys, too—Spencer said something about a record contract?"

David beamed. "That's right. With The Big Record Label."

Hanson winced. "Dave…"

"Hanson doesn't think we should mention anything before the contract is signed, but I don't agree, I think it creates a good buzz. Alison thinks so too."

"Alison?" Madeline asked, trying to keep her voice casual.

"Hanson's girlfriend. She's our unofficial manager. Anyway, it doesn't matter what I say; everyone already knows, you can't keep a secret in Hoboken. Every time we play The Big Record Label's A&R men come, and it's no mystery what they're doing."

"Still," Hanson said. "It might not come through."

"If it doesn't come through with them, it'll come through with someone else. So don't worry so much."

Madeline felt a hand on her shoulder: Spencer. He exchanged a few words with her, then pulled over a chair and sat next to Hanson. Spencer wore a red and gold vest studded with mirrors, plus a fez of the same material; he said hello to Hanson and David, then clapped his hands and said, "Yea!" Madeline and David leaned over and listened as Spencer and Hanson spoke, but then Hanson asked Spencer a technical question; Spencer began talking about syncopation and modulation, and Madeline was completely lost. David saw her expression and smiled.

"Pretty technical, hmm?" he said.

"Well, I'm not a musician, so it doesn't make any sense to me. But you understand them, of course."

"I do, but we've just been rehearsing and talking about our own songs for four hours, and the last thing I want to do now is get into another heavy conversation about music. So," he said, turning his back to the others and lowering his voice, "tell me about your friend Frank."

"He's *not* my friend. That was just—" She was going to say, just a blind date, but blind dates sounded desperate. "That was the first time we ever went out on a date."

"How'd you meet him?"

"Through a friend."

"Mmm hmm." He nodded, his eyes looking deeply into hers, his expression teasing. "So if you two were on a date that means you don't have a boyfriend."

She blushed. "Not at the moment, no."

"It's hard to believe someone as pretty as you is single."

She blushed deeper.

"I'm really glad you're here tonight," he went on. "I was hoping you'd be. And if you weren't I was planning on asking Spencer for your number."

Suddenly Madeline felt a sensation deep in her belly, a warm, heavy ripple that spread lazy waves into her stomach and thighs. She was surprised; very few men set off that feeling in her. She blushed again, a different sort of blush this time.

David was about to say something else, but then Spencer called out his name and asked him a question. As David was answering, the drummer came to their table and told Spencer it was time to begin the next set.

The blaring music made conversation impossible, and Madeline was grateful for the chance to think. She was very aware of David sitting next to her; the space between them was by no means empty. She was still shocked by the sexual current that had run through her. The feeling scared her; it was stronger than logic, and it always, always meant trouble. Or it used to, she told herself. I'm older now, so I know that just because I'm attracted to him doesn't mean I have to run off and sleep with him. Anyway I hardly know this guy, she thought, sneaking a look at his handsome profile and those beautiful hands lightly tapping the table. I know Frank the Poker better than I know this David the Budding Rock Star. And so with an effort of will she extinguished the feeling: Go away, she told it. This man is a stranger, so don't even think about sleeping with him.

At the end of the set the lights again rose a little. Spencer put down his flute and immediately came over to their table; Hanson whispered something to David, then David turned to Madeline and said, "We're going outside to get high, would you like to come?"

"Sure."

Now why did I say that? Madeline wondered as she put on her jacket. It was almost eleven o'clock, she would be going home soon, and if she got high now she would be up half the night eating ice cream and thinking nonstop. Which meant she would wake up late the next day, which meant her writing would be thrown off schedule. Nevertheless, there she was, walking next to David, going outside to get high.

Without anyone saying anything, they all started walking towards Court Street. This was Madeline's favorite street in Hoboken; it was an alley between Washington and Hudson that ran from Newark Street to Seventh Street, and was the former back road for servants and horses. Even after all these years Court Street was still paved in cobblestone and still had a few original stables, and despite occasional piles of garbage and dog feces, it retained a beautiful, old-fashioned feeling. It was also a good place to get high; very few cars came through Court Street, and most of the foot traffic stayed on Washington and Hudson. Madeline and Spencer had gotten high there countless times, and as usual they went to Spencer's favorite smoking place, the back doorway of The Beat'n Path. The door was only used for moving in band equipment, and since a band was now playing no one would bother them.

They stood in a circle, Madeline with David on one side and Spencer on the other. As Hanson filled up the pipe, David leaned toward the door and listened.

"It's Who's Your Daddy," he said. "Do you like their music?" he asked Madeline.

"I've never heard them," she said. "But I've seen their posters around town. Are they good?"

"Oh, they're very good. And they have a great name."

"Where did you guys get your name?"

"From The Doors' song 'The Soft Parade.'"

"Well," she said. "I like The Doors, but I don't know that song."

"David and I both wanted to be Jim Morrison when we were growing up," Hanson said. He took a long drag from the pipe, then passed it to Spencer.

"Hmm," Madeline said. "Do you think he's a good person to model yourself after? I mean, it's like when actresses say they want to be like Marilyn Monroe—it kind of makes me wonder."

Hanson exhaled, then said, "Other than his self-destructiveness, I think he's the *only* person to model yourself after. If you play rock 'n' roll, that is."

"Tell me why," Madeline said. "Because I don't quite see it."

"You need to read *Nobody Gets Out of Here Alive*."

"That's our Bible," David said, smiling at Madeline.

"You see," Hanson said, looking handsome and serious and Jesus Christ ascetic as he spoke. "Morrison was a poet. He was a very sensitive man who thought deeply about love and death and pain and human frailty. And he saw the hypocrisy of the conventional dead-end suburban lifestyle. He had no interest in living that way, which is something David and I both feel very strongly about."

Spencer passed the pipe to Madeline. He was rocking back and forth on his heels with a little grin on his face, totally uninvolved with the conversation. Madeline smiled at him as she took the pipe; he raised his eyebrows but said nothing. Spencer's body is on Court Street, Madeline thought, but his mind is still on stage playing music.

"I'll have to read that book," Madeline said. "I always had this image of him as just some wild self-destructive musician."

"He was that, too," David said. "But it's his music and ideas that inspire us, not his lifestyle. I certainly have no intention of dying in a bathtub, and neither does Hanson. Anyway that would never happen to us; we have each other, whereas Morrison had no one."

"But he had his bandmates, and he had a girlfriend, didn't he?"

"She was a junkie, she was no real support for him. Whereas we have Alison, who is the most organized, non-junkie person you could ever meet."

Madeline put the pipe to her mouth and took a quick, superficial puff. She held the smoke in her mouth, blew it out, and then took another superficial puff. Her sight shifted slightly and her heart beat faster, but that was all; at this rate she would not get very high, and would have no trouble writing the next morning.

She handed the pipe to David and watched as he took a long, strong hit. He held his breath some moments, and as he did he turned to look at Madeline. She was embarrassed to be caught staring; she quickly looked at the ground, again aware of that not-empty space between them. If that not-empty space had a color it would be purple, a dark swirling purple with flashes of light. Although invisible to the others, that purple color connected her to him as surely as if they were handcuffed.

David and Hanson continued talking about Jim Morrison, and as they spoke Madeline saw how respectful they were to each other. It touched her the way each listened so carefully whenever the other spoke; and once David corrected one of Hanson's facts, and he did it so gently he was almost apologetic. And Madeline saw that, although it was subtle, David deferred to Hanson more than Hanson deferred to David. David listened carefully to Hanson's exposition on Jim Morrison's theories on death, love, fame, and the role of mass entertainment; and though David added his own articulate comments it seemed to Madeline that he was in the secondary role. Hanson struck her as some kind of prodigy; he was a person like Spencer, a person whose mind was always rolling, always picking up facts and ideas, always thinking and creating. Madeline enjoyed thinking and learning and creating as well, but she could take time out for things like Scrabble and ice cream and *Vanity Fair*—and at Swan's Cove she had seen what happened when she did not. She suspected that David was more like her; she remembered his comment about not wanting to discuss music again after having talked about it for four hours. Spencer and Hanson were possessed; she and David were not. And maybe in the long run it was healthier not to be: maybe Spencer sometimes drank too much and said crazy things because it was his only way of jumping out of this possession; and as for Hanson, you just had to look at him to see that he was bowed under by his gift. But luckily Hanson had David, David who was strong and healthy, his posture good, his white skin glowing, his eyes clear despite the pot. Hanson needed David's strength, and thank goodness he had it.

And suddenly Madeline understood something else about them. She had just finished another superficial turn at the pipe and was handing it to David when she realized: They're going to make it. *Really* make it. She knew it without ever having heard a note of their music. There was a glow about the two of them; it was part confidence, part determination, but mostly it was the obvious fact that David and Hanson were a perfect fit. They looked right together, somehow; you could imagine them on the cover of *Rolling Stone,* or being interviewed on MTV. My goodness, Madeline thought. My-y goodness.

This on-the-verge-of-making-it had a power that Madeline was not immune to, and as they walked back to Signore's her attraction to David deepened. He was handsome and intelligent and a serious artist; he was good to his friend Hanson, he knew Spencer, and like her he was not interested in a conventional suburban lifestyle. I've never met anyone like him, she thought, sneaking a glance at his handsome profile. And best of all, David was clearly interested in her: he held the door for her, pulled out her chair, ordered her another club soda, and all through the next set kept looking at her and smiling. The attention excited her, but it also scared her. Trouble, she thought as the sensation in her belly returned. I'm in trouble. She decided to leave as soon as the set was over—the last thing she wanted was to seem available.

So when the lights went up again, Madeline pushed back her chair, took her jacket on her lap and announced, "Well, I better go."

David widened his eyes. "You can't go! It's so early."

"It's close to midnight," she laughed. "Is that early?"

"For us it is, we're on such an odd schedule." Madeline rose to put on her jacket, and David stood also. He looked her in the eye and said, "Listen, can I take you out? I'd really like to."

"Well—okay."

"So why don't you give me your number and I'll call you."

He took a pen and small spiral notebook from the inside of his jacket and handed them to her. She leaned onto the table and wrote "Madeline 792-8978." She handed him the notebook and pen, and smiled shyly.

"So I'll call you," he said. "Okay?"

"Okay."

She said good-bye to Hanson, found Spencer and told him it had been great. Walking towards the door she sent David a farewell smile and then, it is safe to say, walked home without her feet once touching the ground.

CHAPTER 6

First Date

He called the next day.

It was ten-thirty in the morning, and Madeline was in the kitchen making tea. She had just finished writing, and as always after writing she was decompressing, feeling a little foggy after hours immersed in her own thoughts. As she was wrapping her tea bag around a spoon and squeezing it, the phone rang; she picked up the receiver absentmindedly and said, "Hi, Bella."

"Hello—Madeline? This is David. From last night?"

"Oh—hi—sorry." She brought her teacup over to the phone, her hand shaking. "I thought you were my sister, she usually calls about now. How are you?"

"Good. Listen, I know it's kind of last minute, but are you free tonight?"

"Well, as a matter of fact I am. The friend I had plans with left a message last night, she has the flu."

"That's great. Well—I thought we could maybe go out for a bite to eat."

"Okay."

"It'll have to be late, though—we rehearse from six to ten. Is that a problem?"

"Um—no. No problem."

"So why don't we meet at, say, quarter after ten at Leo's Grandevous? You know Leo's?"

"Of course. Frank Sinatra land."

He laughed. "Right. See you then."

"See you then."

Madeline hung up the phone and gave a whoop of joy. She danced around the kitchen singing, "I have a date with David the Rock Star, I have a date with David the Rock Star…" She whirled up the narrow hall, took a turn around the living room, then whirled back down to the kitchen where she spun a few more times before settling down to her tea.

She was happy all day. After her tea she showered and went into The City to buy something to wear. It was a glorious September day, crisp and a little cold with a smell of autumn that all the exhaust in the world couldn't hide. She wandered around the East Village, and in a little store on First Avenue she found a beautiful black cashmere cardigan for twenty dollars. The sweater had fake pearl buttons down the front and came just below her waist; she would wear it with her charcoal gray pants that, according to Bella, made her butt look good. Perfect. She also bought earrings, books, pens, and a late sushi lunch. After eating she still had energy, so she took a bus up to Coliseum Books at 57th Street and Broadway and bought a few more books. By the time she arrived home it was six-thirty, and Bella and Robert were in the dining room eating pizza. Madeline flew into the dining room, kissed Bella on the cheek, kissed Robert on the cheek, then flew into her room where she dropped all her packages on the bed.

"What's come over you?" Bella asked as Madeline sat down at the dining room table. "Your date must have gone really well—I tried calling around noon to get all the dish but you weren't home, then when I called at three Robert said you weren't here."

"I was in The City, shopping."

"So, how was the date? Have some pizza."

"No, no, I had a late lunch. It was *horrible*. A sheer, unmitigated disaster. He poked me."

"He *poked* you?"

Robert sighed. "If you two are going to start talking dirty, tell me in advance so I can leave."

Madeline laughed. "Oh, Robert—I mean he *poked* me. Like this." She jabbed Robert's shoulder. "He did it over and over again, so finally I grabbed his hand and told him that if he did it one more time I'd rip his hand off."

"Good for you," Bella said.

Robert stared at Madeline in horror. "Women like you," he said slowly, "are the reason why men are so terrified. You're just like your sister."

"But Robert," Madeline said. "He was so obnoxious, what was I supposed to do? And he was drunk, and he was ogling my breasts, and he told me I should write novels not short stories or I'd never make any money—"

"Which is true," Robert said.

Madeline stuck her tongue out at him, then went on: "And so after I threatened him his personality totally changed, he told me how unhappy he was and how he wanted to get married and how he hoped I wanted to have children soon."

"Sounds like a psycho," Bella said. "So why are you so happy?"

"Because after dinner we went to Signore's—you know, the place next to Laemmel's—and after Mr. Poker left I hung out with this other guy who I met the other day at Spencer's, and then this morning he called me and asked me to go out, so I'm meeting him tonight for dinner."

"I can't keep up with you," Robert said. "I wish you'd just get married, it'd be easier for all of us."

"That's great, Maddy," Bella said. "So who is this guy?"

"He's a musician. He's in the group Narrow Grave."

Bella rolled her eyes. "Dumb name."

"Oh, so says the woman who followed The Grateful Dead half her life. For your information David and his band are on the verge of signing a record contract with The Big Record Label, and they already have two albums with The Small Record Label. So there."

"Is he cute?"

"Very. Extremely. And he's smart and funny and charming—I really like him."

"You hardly know him," Robert said. "I want you to be careful, Madeline; musicians are always slimy."

"Oh, so says the man of the world," Bella scoffed. "What do you know about musicians?"

"I know the kind of guys that kept showing up the first few years we were together—they were all musicians, and they were all slimy. So excuse me."

"Anyway, Bella," Madeline said. "I need you to do my hair. The thing with the braids on the side?"

"Sure. We don't have any plans for tonight."

"Madeline," Robert said. "Michael is coming over any minute for Scrabble. Are you telling me you can't play?"

"Oh, Robert, relax—I can still play, I'm not meeting David until ten-fifteen."

"So late?"

"He rehearses until ten."

"I can't wait to meet him," Bella said. "I promise to be on my best behavior."

"As if that's supposed to reassure me. But he's not coming here—we're meeting at Leo's Grandevous."

"He should pick you up," Robert said. "I don't like him already."

Someone knocked. Slowly. "Come in, Michael," Robert called.

The door opened and shut, slowly, then Michael appeared in the doorway. He was wearing, as always, khakis and a white Oxford shirt and he looked, as always, calm and handsome. "Sorry," he said. "I didn't know you were still eating."

"We're done," Bella said. "We're just talking about Madeline's date. Or should I say, dates. You should hear the adventure she had."

Michael did not look particularly interested, so Madeline said nothing. Bella, however, could not resist a good story, and told Michael all about the poking and the threatening and the mid-evening switch to another man. "So tonight," Bella concluded, "Madeline is going out with Mr. Soon-to-be-Famous Rock Star."

"So no Scrabble?" Michael asked.

"Mr. Rock Star will not be free until ten, so your Scrabble game is still on."

"He's not picking her up," Robert said.

"He's not?" Michael said. "He should."

"Oh, stop it, you two!" Madeline said. "You're both so conservative. Let's clear off the table and play. Bella, would you do my hair during the ice cream break? You can eat later, if you don't mind."

"Anything for my little Madeline," Bella said, leaning over and kissing the top of Madeline's head.

After a quick game of Scrabble where Madeline was soundly trounced ("You're not paying attention," Robert scolded her; "And I don't care," she replied), they adjourned to the living room and ate ice cream while Bella stood at Madeline's side, braiding her thick blonde hair.

"I meet such *in*-teresting monsters with such *in*-teresting hairdos," Bella sang out.

"Thank you, Bugs Bunny," Madeline laughed.

"You should leave your hair free," Robert said, scowling at them. "He's just a musician; you don't want to look like you went to a lot of trouble for him."

Madeline looked up at Bella, Bella looked down at Madeline, then they both rolled their eyes. "Robert," Bella said. "When I need fashion advice, I never come to you. And do you know why? Because, as usual, you are completely wrong. Madeline looks really sexy with her hair free, and if she wears her hair like that Mr. Rock Star will think she intends to sleep with him. Which she doesn't—right, Madeline?"

"Right."

"I don't have to tell you, Maddy," Bella said, her nimble fingers braiding, "that you should never, ever sleep with a man on the first date."

"You're right, you don't have to tell me. And coming from you, Bella, I find that advice a little ironic."

"I'm a reformed slut, you should listen to me."

"Well, I'm a reformed slut, too, so don't worry."

"My little sister," Bella said, throwing an arm around Madeline's neck and hugging her. "I'm so proud. Do you know that one of her dates told her that anyone who wants to sleep with her needs a crowbar to open her legs?"

"I can't take any more of this," Robert said. "Come on, Michael, let's go to the TV room."

"Oh, Robert. Okay—we're done." Bella held up a mirror so Madeline could see. As usual, Bella had done a lovely job: six small braids swept along each side of Madeline's head, then all the braids came together in the back where they were tied together with two more small braids. "You like?" Bella asked. "Michael, you're a man, tell us what you think: should Madeline leave her hair free, or is it better like this?"

"I think Madeline looks very pretty either way," Michael said. "But one thing bothers me."

"You think the braids are too thin?"

Michael looked at Madeline. "Why isn't he picking you up?"

"Oh, Michael!" Madeline sighed. "He rehearses downtown, we're eating downtown, so why should he come up here? It's easier this way."

"Easier for him."

"Oh, *please*. All this picking up stuff, it's so old-fashioned. Maybe not in *your* youth," Madeline said, looking at Michael slyly, "but times have changed."

"In Michael's youth!" Bella laughed. "In Michael's youth he had hair down to his waist and was living in Nepal. Isn't that right, Michael?"

"Something like that."

"I agree with Michael," Robert said. "He should pick you up."

"Oh, what do you know, Robert?" Bella said. "You never really dated; I'm the first girlfriend you ever had. When everyone else was out discovering free love, you were locked in your bedroom reading *The Mill on the Floss*."

"You're not my first girlfriend," Robert said stoutly.

"The ninth-grade prom doesn't count. And neither does George Eliot."

Robert sighed, and looked at the ceiling. Bella put down the mirror, went to the sofa where she sat down and threw her arms around Robert. "My husband," she said, ruffling his hair. "Isn't he cute?"

"Anyway," Madeline said. "I didn't hear anyone complaining last night when Mr. Poker didn't pick me up."

"That was different," Robert said. "It was a blind date, you didn't know him."

"Well, excuse me!" Madeline burst out. "And have any of you ever considered that maybe I don't want him to come here and be judged by all of you? Have you ever considered that?"

"Oh no," Bella said. "Madeline's getting angry." She stood and held out her hand. "Come on, Maddy, let's go to your room and you can show me what you're going to wear."

❧   ❧   ❧

He was late.

She was late, on purpose, but he was later still. She walked into Leo's Grandevous at ten-thirty; she saw Leo behind the bar and waved to him, then ran her eyes along the male backs at the bar. No David. And no David at one of the tables lining the walls, and no David in the small dining room. Well, she thought. Well, well.

She took a seat at the bar, then took off her jacket and lay it on her lap. Leo asked how she was doing; she told him she was fine, she was just waiting for a friend—and could she please have a club soda with lemon? Leo nodded sagely, and said no more. Leo knew her because once she and a date had talked to him for two solid hours about Hoboken in the old days, which meant, of course, Leo's childhood friendship with Frank Sinatra. And the friendship continued to this day: about once a year Frank would call at three in the morning and ask Leo to open up the restaurant and fix him calamari, and of course whenever Frank was singing locally he sent two tickets "for me and da wife," as Leo put it. The restaurant itself was a shrine to Frank: the walls were covered with black and white stills from his movies, and the jukebox was entirely given over to his songs. Leo lived in his own Frank Sinatra world and it was, he told Madeline and her date, a good life: "I have my restaurant, da wife, my friends—who could ask for maw?"

So Madeline sat, drinking her club soda and waiting. And when the clock behind the bar read ten forty-five, when she had listened to "The Lady is a Tramp" for the third time, it occurred to her that she was being stood up. The thought made her furious, so furious she slapped two dollars on the bar and was halfway to the door putting on her coat when the door swung open and David walked in.

"Where are you going?" he laughed, grabbing her hand and stopping her flight.

"I thought you weren't coming."

"Wasn't coming? Are you kidding? I was held up at rehearsal, that's all." His brown eyes were wide and incredulous. "I would never make a date and then not show up. So tell me, are you hungry?"

"A little."

"So come on, let's go sit down." He squeezed her fingers and, still holding her hand, led her into the dining room. Madeline trailed behind him, her anger confused with the pleasure of his warm hand.

The only free table was a table for four next to the wall, so they put their coats on the empty chairs and sat down. On each place mat there was a battered brown menu; Madeline picked hers up and opened it, hoping to hide her fluster. What bad luck that he caught her when she was so angry! But a half hour late was really too much—she still wasn't sure if she should forgive him.

"I like your hair like that."

Madeline looked up from her menu. David was sitting with his elbows on the table and his hands folded; he was looking at her intently, his menu untouched in front of him.

"Oh," she said, putting a hand to her head. "My sister Bella did it."

"Is she a hairdresser?"

Madeline laughed. "She was, in a previous incarnation. She used to do hair at Dead shows."

"Really? Cool. I used to be really into The Dead; I went to a lot of their shows."

"Well, she's a lot older than me, she's thirty-six, so she probably wasn't around when you were going. But she was quite well-known, apparently; there's even a picture of her in a sort of coffee-table book on The Dead. It's her claim to fame."

"And how about you?" he asked, looking deeply into her eyes. "Were you a Deadhead?"

"I went to a couple concerts here and there, but I never threw myself into it like Bella did."

"So tell me more about your sister—does she still follow The Dead?"

Madeline laughed. "Oh no, not at all. Those days are long gone. She's an assistant editor at *Psychology Now*—you know, the pop psychology magazine."

"I've seen it, but I've never read it."

"Well, it's okay. My brother-in-law—Bella's husband, his name is Robert—he thinks it's trash. Only he told me that privately, he would never say it in front of Bella because it would hurt her feelings and he would never do that because he really loves her and she thinks it's the greatest magazine in the world although—"

Then the waitress came, thank God. Madeline took a deep breath; she did not hear a word about the specials of the day, she was just thankful she had been cut off in the midst of one of her calamari eyeball rambles.

"Cheese ravioli," she said. "With tomato sauce—no meat in the sauce."

"And to drink?" the waitress asked.

"Club soda," she said. The waitress said thank you, and walked towards the kitchen.

"You don't drink?" David asked. "I noticed last night that you only had club soda."

"No, I don't drink at all."

"And why's that?"

"Mmm—it's kind of a long story. Let's just say one too many nights dancing on the table with a lampshade on my head." Or one too many times dodging Billy Ray Bonner, but she was not about to tell him *that*.

"It's better not to drink," he said. "I never have more than one beer a night."

"And why's that?"

"Well—it makes you fat, for one thing. And it's not healthy generally. And I think there's nothing more repulsive then going to hear a band and seeing the lead singer too drunk to perform. Drinking has ruined a lot of good musicians—writers, too," he said smiling.

"That's true."

"Hanson and I have been playing the club scene for about ten years now, and you wouldn't believe some of the things we've seen. I mean, I've seen guys throw up on stage, I saw one guy throw up in a guitar case—" The waitress set down David's beer and Madeline's club soda. "Horrible stuff. I don't think real professionals do that kind of thing."

Madeline immediately thought of Spencer, and as if reading her mind David said, "Which is why I had my doubts about working with Spencer."

"Spencer has cleaned up his act," Madeline said quickly. "He's much better now; he's looking after his health, he's trying to be more organized—I think it's hard for him."

"What do you mean?"

"I mean—well, he's so gifted. He's in another world, it's hard for him to be practical. But he's come a long way."

"You really care about him, don't you?"

"Of course. He's my friend."

"Were you and he ever—?"

"Me and Spencer? No; never."

"Hmm." David paused, smiled, then went on, "Well, I have to say I think you're right. He's been great with us; he's never missed a rehearsal or showed up drunk. I needed some time to accept him, but Hanson took to him right away."

"Yes, I noticed they seemed quite close."

The waitress brought a basket of hard rolls and a little plate with frozen pats of butter. From nervousness Madeline grabbed a roll and proceeded to shred it into pieces.

"Spencer knows an awful lot about music," David said. "We've both learned a lot from him. But he can be a little, you know, far out."

"And how would you define 'far out?'"

"Oh, you know—spiritual, always talking about spiritual stuff. Like he's always saying how music is Cosmic Love expressing itself—that kind of thing."

"But that's what I like about him," Madeline said.

David raised an eyebrow and gave her a look half-doubtful, half-flirtatious. "You're not one of those New Age people, are you?"

"Me? Oh no—no, not at all."

And I'm not, she told herself stoutly. Not anymore, anyway.

"So tell me about you," David said, looking at her carefully. "Tell me about your writing."

"Well, what do you want to know?"

"About your work, about how you write—that kind of thing."

"Well—I write short stories. I'm working on one now, it's about a father who destroys his daughter's piano. I've been working on it for a few months; I'm on about the fifteenth draft now."

"Do you always write so many drafts?"

"Always. I write tons and tons of drafts; in fact it's very difficult for me to let go of my stories. It's the only way I know how to work—it's how my teacher taught me."

"And who is your teacher?"

"Well, she died, unfortunately, so she's not my teacher anymore. Her name was Faith X, you've never heard of her but in the forties and fifties she was quite famous for her short stories." Tears came to Madeline's eyes. "I really miss her."

"You're very sensitive, aren't you?"

Madeline shrugged. She looked down at her place mat, a red and green map of Italy with the heads of famous Italian-Americans (Frank included, of course) floating around the borders. Oh fuck, she thought as she dabbed a napkin to her eyes. I can't believe I'm crying.

"So now who do you show your work to?"

"To my sister and my brother-in-law and our upstairs neighbor—he's sort of part of the family. And then I send my stories out—and then I get my stories back."

"That's hard."

"It is. The other day I got one back. I try not to let it get to me, but you can't help it."

"And what was that story about?"

"It's called 'The Paint Can,' and it's about a man who has a morbid fear of the sun, and one day he borrows paint from a neighbor and he holds it up to the side of his head so he doesn't get hit by the sun, but then the paint spills all over his face and it turns into this bizarre family drama."

"Sounds great. Where on earth did you get the idea for that?"

"Well, actually, it happened to my own father. And my sister and I tried to clean him with turpentine which got into his eyes and he accused us of trying to blind him—you get the picture."

"Your father—"

"—is crazy," she said, smiling.

"Well, I was going to say, he sounds a little odd. Was he really so afraid of the sun?"

"He was, and he is. And now they live in Arizona for my mother's asthma and he barely leaves the house."

"You're not at all like a person who has a crazy family. I mean, you seem so calm."

"Well, I had my time—but no, now everything is fine. I live with my sister and brother-in-law and we try to be as non-crazy as possible. And your family?" she said quickly. "What are they like?"

"Nice. Normal. A bit boring, actually. My father is a high school principal."

"That's so weird—my father was too."

David smiled. "Ah ha, so that's why I was instantly attracted to you." Madeline blushed. "It's horrible, isn't it?" he went on. "I mean, you always have to be on your best behavior, and you can't even go to your locker without seeing your dad."

"Oh, my father wasn't principal in my high school. Thank God."

"You're lucky. I was so relieved to go to college, it was my first chance to really break loose."

"Where did you go to college?"

"I went to Berklee School of Music in Boston. Where did you go?"

"Columbia. Barnard, actually—that's the woman's part."

"Really. But I'm not surprised; the first time I saw you I could tell you were intelligent."

"So, what was Berklee like?"

The waitress arrived with their food. "Who's got the ravioli?" she demanded.

"Me," said Madeline.

"And eggplant parmesan for you?" she asked David.

"That's right."

As soon as the waitress left a young couple stepped up to the table. Madeline had noticed them lurking behind the waitress, and now she understood that the couple had been waiting to speak with David.

"Excuse me," the young man said. He had a bush of black hair and large, watery blue eyes. "Excuse me, but aren't you David Guggenheim from Narrow Grave?"

David looked at the young man encouragingly and said, "That's right."

The young man was beside himself—he grinned, coughed, took a step back and slapped his hand on his thigh. The woman, a small thin redhead in a Rastafarian skullcap, clutched her boyfriend's arm and bit her lip.

"Man—I knew it was you," the young man said. "And I had to come up and tell you that, like, we go to all your shows, we listen to your albums all the time—you guys are great."

"Thank you," David said easily.

"No, I mean it, man. You guys are the best. And I hear that The Big Record Label is interested in you?"

"They've been hanging around our shows. We'll see what happens."

"You'll be at The Beat'n Path, right, in two weeks?"

"That's right."

"We'll be there, man, we will definitely be there."

"Why don't you give me your name," David said smoothly, "and I'll put you on the guest list. You and your friend," he said, directing a smile at the red-headed girlfriend.

"Seriously? Oh man, that would be awesome." He ran his hands frantically over his leather jacket. "I don't have a pen."

"I do," David said. He reached into the inside pocket of his jacket and pulled out his pen and small spiral notebook. With trembling hands, the young man leaned close to Madeline's ravioli and wrote in abrupt letters "Colin O'Brien and Jasmine."

"Great," David said, pocketing the pen and notebook. "So we'll see you in two weeks?"

"Two weeks. Great." The young man was smiling so hard Madeline thought he would cry. He stepped back from the table, again slapping his thigh; he bumped into the waitress, but did not notice her angry glare. "Enjoy your food!" he called out, then grabbed his girlfriend's hand and went out the side door.

"So," David said, turning back to Madeline. "Where were we?"

"That was nice of you," she said.

"Anyone loyal enough to buy both our albums and come to all our shows deserves free tickets. Alison goes crazy when I do that, but I think it's important."

"Why does she go crazy?" Madeline asked as she speared a steaming ravioli.

"Well, because clubs want you to play if you make them money, and Alison says that the more free tickets we give out, the less money the club makes, so there's less chance of us being asked back. But I say our days of worrying about being asked back are over; we're always asked back, and lately we've been turning people down. How's your food?"

"Good. Yours?"

"Very good."

"So," she said, dipping a wedge of bread into her tomato sauce. "Why are you guys turning people down?"

"Well, right now we're focusing on writing new songs. It really looks like The Big Record Label is going to come through, and when it does we want to go into the studio and cut an album right away. So now we're busy rehearsing, you know, hammering out all the kinks in our songs. We have about five we're really happy with, about, mmm, three that need just a little work, and about seven that we really have to get moving on."

"How many songs do you need for an album?"

"About ten to twelve, if they're regular length songs. Want to try my eggplant?"

Madeline hated trying other people's food in restaurants; she thought it was vulgar. "Okay," she said. She pushed her plate forward, but instead of putting the food on her plate David speared a square of eggplant on his fork and held it out for her to take with her mouth. His eyes never left her mouth as her lips closed upon the food and drew it off the tongs. "It's good," she said, blushing. "So, how often do you rehearse?"

"Every day Monday through Friday, from six to ten. Or sometimes later," he said, looking up and catching her eye. "As you know."

"And weekends?"

"Weekends we reserve for songwriting and listening to new music. If we don't have a gig, that is."

"What do you mean, listening to new music?"

"Well, Hanson is always buying records, anything from Tibetan bells to Buddy Holly to hard-core German punk bands. He sorts it all out, then he plays me what he thinks is the best stuff and what would maybe work with some of our songs. And we compare ideas; I show him things I've written, he shows me what he's written—like that."

"You guys are a real team. And it sounds like you work really hard."

"You have to work hard if you're going to make it."

"How did you meet Hanson?"

"At Berklee. It was weird—it was the first day of the semester freshman year, I happened to be sitting next to him in Music Theory class and someone walked by and said, 'Look, Lennon and McCartney.' You know, because of how we look, him with long blond hair and me with short brown hair. So we laughed, and we started talking—and we laughed even more when we found out that he played guitar and I played bass."

"Like Lennon and McCartney."

"Right. And, I don't know, it's like that guy put an idea in our heads. After class we went back to Hanson's place to jam and—I don't know. It worked. Just like that."

"Hanson strikes me as being extremely intelligent."

"Oh, he is. He's a walking encyclopedia of music. And he has a great voice, and he's a great guitar player—he even plays classical guitar, he's really excellent. And he's a great guy; he's my best friend. But he's—well, he's kind of fragile. If he didn't have Alison propping him up I don't know what he'd do."

"How does she prop him up?"

"Well, for one thing, he doesn't work. She has a really good job and she pays for everything—rent, food, clothes, all of it. I mean, we make some money with our gigs and our albums, but we put it all back into the band."

"So you work? You have a job?"

He raised an eyebrow and eyed her flirtatiously. "What, you thought I was a shiftless musician? Yes, I have a job; I wait tables at Maxwell's. At lunch time."

"Maxwell's!" she laughed.

"Is that funny?"

"No, it's just that I ate dinner there last night."

"With Frank."

"With Frank," she said, meeting his eye.

"Poor Frank," David said, his gaze wandering from Madeline's eyes to her mouth to her eyes again. "I don't think you'll be going out with him again."

"And why's that?"

"Because now you're going out with me."

"Oh," she said, and blushed. She grabbed a piece of bread and started mopping up tomato sauce.

David reached out his hand and clasped it around her wrist. "Look at me," he said softly. She looked up: his brown eyes were fixed on her face. He softened his hold on her wrist. "You're really shy, aren't you?"

"A little," she said. "Well—no, not really."

"You're shy with me."

She shrugged. He let go of her wrist, but continued staring at her. Madeline felt her lower belly fill with heat.

"You hardly know me," she said.

"That's not true. Last night Spencer and I had a long talk about you."

"Oh really?"

"Umm hmm. And he said you're a great girl. And he said you don't sleep around."

Madeline stared down at the pool of tomato sauce on her plate. She could not look at David—she felt happy, but she also felt scared.

"Will you excuse me?" she said, glancing up quickly. "I have to go to the ladies' room."

She rose and walked in what she hoped was a dignified manner to the small toilet by the kitchen. Her head was humming one moment, roaring the next. She went into the tiny room—just a toilet, with a sink so close to the toilet she could have rested her chin on it. She sat on the toilet, and lay her flushed face in her cold hands.

She peed, stood up, and splashed cold water on her face. She looked in the mirror and saw, to her immeasurable horror, a piece of oregano the size of Rhode Island clinging to one of her front teeth. Oh fuck, she thought as she wiped it off. How long had it been there? She pictured herself smiling at David with that big green splotch on her tooth. "Very sexy, Madeline," she told herself. "Very, very sexy."

If it had been anyone else she would have made a joke about the oregano, but when she sat down again she said nothing. David smiled at her warmly and said, "I ordered coffee. Do you want some?"

"I'll have tea. And dessert—they have great desserts here."

"I think I detect a sweet tooth."

"Oh, I *love* sweets. Don't you?"

"I do, but I have to be careful—too many and I'll get fat."

Weird for a man to worry about getting fat, she thought. But that certainly was not cause for a strike—in fact, David had managed to get through the entire dinner without a single black mark.

"And I was thinking," he said, "that maybe after coffee we could go back to my place. You know, smoke a joint, hang out."

"Ah—I don't think so," Madeline said. "It's kind of late, isn't it? My sister will be going to bed soon, and if I come in late I'll wake her up."

"As an ex-Deadhead I'm sure your sister doesn't go to bed so early."

"The key word there is *ex*-Deadhead. And besides, there's my brother-in-law—he's kind of overprotective."

"Okay," he said simply. "No problem. Another time."

"Another time," she echoed.

During dessert David asked her what she did to earn money, and she told him she worked as a temporary word processor/secretary. She told him all about the temp agency, about being on call and sitting silently with the other temps while the obnoxious receptionist called her friends and rattled on and on about soap operas and her diet and how she knew the words to each and every Billy Joel song; and how thus far Madeline had only worked with one company, The Big Cigarette Company, and how it was a surreal experience because everyone was in denial about the dangers of smoking, instead of non-smoking signs there were signs that proclaimed "Enjoy Smoking," and how everyone smoked at their desks and got a free carton of cigarettes every week and how on the bulletin board in one of the employee lounges she had read no less than four notices of people who were in the hospital and where you could send them flowers and how even though the word CANCER was never mentioned you just *knew* they all had cancer and it was from the smoking, of course, not to mention inhaling all that secondhand smoke, and how maybe it was unethical for Madeline to work there but the offices were beautiful and there were great works of art scattered about—she went on and on, aware of her color rising, aware that if she said just one little sentence, one small, "Well, why don't we go back to your place and smoke a joint?", they would be in bed. Naked. Making love. In less than an hour, probably.

David listened, and was really quite tolerant considering Madeline did not once pause for breath in fifteen minutes. She knew she was unstoppable when she got going like this: Michael called her "Stream of Consciousness Madeline," and said her long rambles were charming, whereas Bella and Robert squirmed and sighed and did everything but plug their ears and writhe on the floor in pain. David looked amused, charmed even, so maybe Michael was right.

Madeline's monologue was cut off by the waitress handing David the bill. He paid, helped put on her jacket, then walked her out into the chilly night.

"I'll walk you home," he said, and Madeline mentally stuck her tongue out at Robert and Michael.

"You know," he said as they walked down Grand Street, "you told me about your writing but you didn't tell me about your dreams for your writing."

"You want to know?"

"Sure."

"Well—for starters I'd like to get published in literary magazines, and then publish a collection of short stories. And have everyone praise it to the skies, I suppose, and then get grants and lots of royalties so I don't have to work anymore. But more than all that—I don't know, I guess I'd like to help people. I mean, I've read so many books that helped me, it would be nice if I could do that. Help others, that is, with my stories."

"I'd love to read something you wrote. Will you let me?"

"Sure, if you want to."

They reached the corner of Fourth and Willow. Madeline started to turn right, then David lay his hand on her arm.

"My apartment is only two blocks away. In case you changed your mind."

She looked up at him. He's so handsome, she thought, her gaze running over his dark brown eyes, his heavy eyebrows, his high cheekbones. And he was tall, and had nice skin, and held himself so well. My goodness, she thought. My-y goodness. She felt a heavy soreness in her belly; she wanted so much to say yes, to just go and have a night of great sex (because it would be great, of that she was sure). But—no.

"No," she said, smiling a little. "I just can't."

"You're very sweet," he said, running a finger along her cheek. "You're one of the sweetest girls I've ever met. I like you."

"I like you, too," she said, looking at the ground. "But I don't really know you."

"So you don't want to come with me."

"It's not a matter of not wanting to, it's a matter of—well, of not knowing you."

"It might be a good way to get to know me."

"And it might be a good way to get hurt."

"I would never hurt you, Madeline. I like you."

Although mild, his persistence was beginning to annoy her. "I have to go," she said abruptly. "You don't have to walk me if you don't want to."

"Of course I'll walk you—I said I would, and I will."

They turned onto Fourth Street, walked a block then crossed the street to Church Square Park. A couple wearing Hoboken High jackets was sitting on a bench kissing furiously, and a few people were in the dog run, talking quietly while their animals romped.

"So," David said as they left the park. "Are you busy tomorrow night?"

She was not, and she hated to admit it. "Tomorrow's Saturday; hmm, I have tentative plans with someone, so I don't know. Maybe."

"Because there's an opening at a gallery; the girlfriend of someone we know is a painter and she has an exhibit. But you say your plans are only tentative?"

"That's right."

"Well, why don't I call you tomorrow? When do you think you'll know?"

"Oh—by noon, I suppose. Or one."

"Okay; I'll call you at one to find out. And if you can't come, we can make plans for another night. If you want to, that is," he said quickly. "Do you?"

"Sure," she replied, hoping she sounded casual.

They reached Washington Street, then made a left. They passed a group of drunk Stevens students, a few couples, a retarded Chinese girl who Madeline saw every day, and a musician that David knew and said hello to. David was in the midst of explaining why the musician's band had broken up when Madeline stopped in front of 821 Washington Street.

"This is it," she said.

David looked up. "Nice building. Does your brother-in-law own it?"

"He did, then he made the building a co-op."

"What did you say he does for a living?"

"He's a professor at Columbia. But they moved here before the real estate market got crazy."

"Good for him. Well—" He moved his head a little to one side, his eyes pouring over her face.

"Yes, well—" She turned and raced up the stoop, putting distance between herself and any good night kiss he might be planning. "So I'll speak to you tomorrow?" she asked, looking down at him on the sidewalk.

"That's right," he said. "After one."

"Okay. Good night. And thank you for dinner."

"Good night, Madeline."

She let herself inside, and in the tiny foyer she turned around and looked out one of the narrow windows set in the door. David was still there, standing on the sidewalk with an amused look on his face. Safe, she thought as she waved at him. Now I'm safe.

She walked up three flights of stairs and quietly let herself in. The apartment was dark except for a light in the TV room; Madeline hung up her coat and went into the TV room where she found Bella on the couch reading *Ladies' Man*, her feet propped up against the wall in what she called her "sperm assistance posture." For years Bella and Robert had wanted to start a family; Bella had gotten pregnant twice, but she miscarried both times. Her doctor assured her that she could carry a baby to term, so she and Robert were still hopeful, and still trying.

"Hi," Bella said quietly, lying her book on her stomach. "How'd it go?"

"Good. Robert's asleep?"

"Yep. So tell me all the dish."

Madeline fell into an oversized green armchair. "Well—he was late, first of all. But then he finally came and, I don't know, we talked about ourselves and our lives and his music and my writing. It was nice."

"But—? Because I hear something funny in your voice."

"Well—I think he really likes me. Or would really like to sleep with me."

"Of course he wants to sleep with you—he wouldn't have asked you out otherwise."

"He asked me to go back to his place with him. Is that a little forward for a first date, or is it just me?"

"It's just you. Lots of people sleep together on the first date—you just happen to be smarter than that."

"Maybe it would have been okay," Madeline said thoughtfully. "I mean, Devon slept with Joe on their first date, and in the morning he brought her breakfast in bed and asked her when she wanted to get married. And they did get married."

"And I know about a million women who had sex on the first date and then never even got a phone call. You know better, Madeline—a real relationship takes time. Assuming, of course, that you want a real relationship."

"I do—but it's hard, all this waiting."

"I know, honey. You haven't had a boyfriend in ages. But it's your own fault; you were always so hard on all the guys you went out with."

"I wasn't ready then. But now I am, now I really want someone."

"So if this guy likes you, he'll wait until you're ready. But you should be careful—I mean, at the risk of sounding like Robert, you hardly know him. Spencer knows him, right? He could maybe tell you about him, if he's a good guy or not."

"Well, I could ask him, but you know Spencer, he likes everyone."

"Well, time will tell if he's a slime or not." Bella looked at Madeline knowingly. "You really like him, don't you?"

"Well—I'm attracted to him. He's really interesting. And he's, I don't know, he's really alive and busy and he's into what he does and he's apparently quite successful. And he asked me about my writing, which was nice. I think he really wanted to find out who I am."

"I hope it works out for you, Maddy, I really do. My biggest dream is for you to find someone who'll make you as happy as Robert makes me. And if the guy lives in Hoboken, so much the better. So tell me, how did you leave things?"

"He asked me out for tomorrow night. I said I had tentative plans so he's going to call me tomorrow to see."

"What are your tentative plans?"

"Nothing."

Bella clicked her tongue and shook her head. "You always do things like that. You shouldn't."

"I don't want him to think I'm too available."

"Well, since you didn't fuck him I imagine he got the message."

"I guess so," Madeline said. She rose and stretched. "I better get to bed. How about you?"

"I'm going to hang out here for awhile. Robert's sperm need all the help they can get."

Madeline leaned over and kissed Bella good night. "He liked my hair, by the way. And he's into The Dead."

"A fellow Deadhead, hmm? Better not tell Robert that."

"I wasn't planning to. Good night."

"'Night, Maddy. See you tomorrow."

CHAPTER 7

Second Date

Madeline knocked on the door.

She was at 413 Jefferson Street, at Hanson and Alison's apartment. David had called at one o'clock on the dot and asked her if she would be free that evening. She said that her tentative plans had been canceled, he said he was glad to hear it, then asked her to meet him at Hanson's at eight. And all day long, every time Robert asked Madeline what time Mr. Rock Star was picking her up, she shot him the dirtiest look she could muster.

So here she was in an old, sagging brownstone. Hanson and Alison lived on the third floor, and on the way up the stairs Madeline saw, in the corner of one of the landings, a melted stick of butter. It had obviously been there a long time, long enough to melt anyway, and the butter combined with a general smell of rancid cooking oil made Madeline a little nauseous. Well, she told herself as she knocked, you wanted to live an interesting, artistic life. Still, Anaïs Nin had never mentioned dodging decaying food products...

The door opened, and Madeline was hit by two strong forces: a cloud of marijuana smoke, and the intense gaze of a woman with glasses and long dark hair. The first word that came to Madeline's mind was: dumpy. A dumpy woman. A little short, a little fat with unflattering loose dark clothes, and hair pulled back in a tangled ponytail.

"I'm Alison," the woman said. "You must be Marilyn."

"Madeline."

"Come on in."

The woman opened the door and Madeline stepped into the apartment. Or into the kitchen, rather, because there was no hall or entranceway; Madeline was standing in a small room jammed with a stove, refrigerator, counters, a wooden table and, in makeshift shelves above the table, a stereo system and hundreds of albums. There were also stacks of albums on the floor, plus a few guitars and some small amplifiers. David was sitting at the table rolling a joint, and Hanson was sitting with his head thrown back, holding a tissue to his nose and taking a hit off a joint.

"Here she is," David said. He stood and kissed Madeline's cheek. He looked handsome—he wore a chocolate brown corduroy shirt, off-white jeans, and broken-in hiking boots; and as he leaned over to kiss her she smelt after-shave, which she normally hated but for some reason not tonight.

"How are you?" he asked. "Here, I'll help you with your coat—and don't mind Hanson, he's got a nosebleed."

"Hi Madeline," Hanson said. "Sorry I can't look at you when I say that. Here, have a smoke."

He waved his hand; David plucked out the joint and gave it to Madeline. She was thankful to have something to do to cover her shock, because now that she was inside she saw that the apartment was a filthy mess. It was a railroad like most Hoboken apartments; looking through the doorway she could see a string of small rooms, like a rabbit warren. But surely even rabbits lived better than this. The rooms were jam-packed with albums, stacks of magazines, guitars, headphones, old TVs, speakers, and amplifiers in every size from small to massive. And in addition to the sheer volume of things, Madeline had the distinct impression that nothing was clean, nor had been for a very long time. The kitchen was particularly grimy: it was a dark, airless room with horrible wallpaper, yellow flowers on a brown background that surely had not always been brown; and all the appliances had a weird sheen which made her think that anything she touched would be sticky. The smoke, the dark colors, the smell of cooking, Hanson's bloody tissues piled up on the table—she longed to ask someone to crack a window, but that would be rude considering she just walked in. She took a deep breath, and sat at the head of the table with David on her right and Hanson on her left. At least when she was sitting she didn't feel so dizzy.

"So, Madeline," Alison said, standing by the table with her hands on her hips. "What would you like to drink, beer or red wine?"

"Madeline doesn't drink," David said, smiling and putting his hand on Madeline's.

"Actually," Madeline said, "if it's not too much trouble, I'd like some tea."

"It's not a problem."

David squeezed Madeline's hand. "You okay?"

"Actually—could we maybe open a window?"

"All the smoke, huh? Alison," he called, "Can you open a window? Madeline's not a professional smoker like we are."

Alison opened a window that led out to the fire escape, and Madeline could actually see the smoke being sucked out of the room. She took another deep breath.

"Better?" David asked.

"Better," she smiled.

From where Madeline sat she could see Alison preparing her tea. She watched as Alison filled up a chipped blue kettle and put it on the stove, watched as Alison lit a match and held it to the gas burner, watched Alison take a mug from a cabinet and wipe it with a paper towel. And then, from somewhere on the counter, Alison picked up a small black thing and put it in the cup. It was a used tea bag. Madeline looked at the shelves above the stove and saw, clear as day, a glass container full of fresh, dry, never-used tea bags. Madeline felt as if someone had slapped her in the face; it was the rudest, cheapest act she had ever witnessed.

"Sugar?" Alison called out.

"A little," Madeline replied. Then Hanson waved a joint in her general direction—she grabbed it and took a short hit. She was about to pass the joint to David, but he was lighting a fresh one. He gestured to Alison; Madeline rose, walked over to Alison, and held out the joint.

"Bless you," Alison said. She grabbed the joint and took a long, strong hit. "Do you want milk?"

"No," Madeline said, taking a quick peek at the shriveled tea bag in the bottom of her mug. "Just sugar."

Madeline sat down again, and David took her hand.

"You look pretty," he said. "Did your sister do your hair?"

"Yes. Do you like it?" She put her hand on her hair and turned her head a little. Bella had braided her hair into an elegant style they called Defying Gravity: Madeline's hair was pulled up and back, then braided in such a way that the end of the braid was tucked in and did not show. Madeline could never figure out how Bella did it, but Bella insisted it was simple.

"What does it look like?" Hanson asked.

"Well," David said, "It's braided in back but it's cool, you can't see the ends." She felt his fingers touch her hair, then gently brush the nape of her neck. Her whole body jolted: for some unknown reason, the back of her neck was as sensitive as her nipples; she could still remember the first time someone touched her there, a boy in high school had kissed the back of her neck and she saw stars. And—oh no but oh yes—David once again brushed his fingers there, and it was all Madeline could do not to whimper. She turned away quickly, her cheeks bright red.

"So Hanson," she said. "Do you often get nosebleeds?"

"All the time," Alison said, putting Madeline's tea on the table and taking a seat next to Hanson. She passed the remains of the joint to Madeline, but as it was just a roach Madeline took a quick puff and stubbed it out in the ashtray. "Ever since we met. In fact that's how we met: I was at a Clash concert and Hanson happened to be standing next to me, and next thing I knew he was bleeding all over me."

Madeline took a sip of her tea which was, not surprisingly, quite weak. "What actually causes nosebleeds?" she asked.

"High blood pressure, stress, too much coke. In Hanson's case it's just nerves. My honey is awfully sensitive," Alison said, leaning over and kissing Hanson's shoulder. "But that's what happens when you're a genius."

That's a strong word to throw around, Madeline thought. She looked at David—he was watching her and smiling. "Will he be able to go out tonight?" Madeline asked, using the third person because obviously Hanson was not talking for himself.

"Oh, sure," Alison said. "This isn't a bad one, and as you can see by all the tissues, the worst is definitely over. You see how the tissues have less and less blood, and the one he's holding now has none at all—but I always have him stay like that a half hour after the bleeding stops, just to make sure."

"How much time do I have?" Hanson asked.

"Twenty more minutes, baby."

"You know a lot about this," Madeline asked. "Are you a nurse?"

Alison laughed and took a sip from a glass of red wine. "God, no. But I'm an expert on nosebleeds because of Hanson."

"David said you had a good job, so I didn't know…"

"Well, I'm the office manager at a graphic design firm, but that's just to pay the bills. Really I'm a painter—and a nurse too, I guess," she said, patting Hanson's knee. "Hanson's nurse. And David said you're a word processor and a writer?"

Madeline laughed. "Yes, but not necessarily in that order." David passed her a joint; she took a small hit and gave it to Alison.

"And you've published a few things, David said."

"A few short stories, yes."

"She's on her way to being rich and famous," David said, winking at Madeline.

"Aren't we all," Alison replied. "Aren't we all." She took a long, noisy hit off the joint, but instead of passing it to Hanson she kept it in her hand. "Hanson and David, first of all. It's only a matter of time now, right guys?"

"Don't be too sure," Hanson said.

Alison rolled her eyes at David. "Mr. Gloom and Doom."

"Isn't there a joint around here?" Hanson asked. "Or is Alison holding onto it as usual."

"Sorry, my love," Alison said. She took a quick hit then passed it to him. "Speaking of being famous, Madeline, I'm sure David was too modest to tell you, but tomorrow afternoon they're being interviewed on the radio."

Madeline turned to David. "Really?" she asked. "That's great."

David shrugged. "It's Bing Wallace's show. He's had us on a couple times before."

"He's had you on *six* times before," Alison corrected. "Bing loves Narrow Grave, he plays their music all the time."

"I didn't know you guys got radio play," Madeline said, again to David.

"Are you kidding?" Alison said. "Three cuts off their last album were on constant rotation on all the indie stations. I suppose you don't know about *Rolling Stone* either?"

Madeline shook her head no.

"Alison," David said. "Not now."

"Oh, David!" Alison said. She stood, hands on hips. "Wait a moment, I'll get it." She went into the next room and came back with an old copy of the magazine. "Page forty-seven. In New Faces."

Sure enough, there they were, David and Hanson, looking very serious and—in David's case at least—very handsome. There was a short blurb underneath saying how Narrow Grave had just released its second album on The Small Record Label, and how it was only a matter of time before "the strong songwriting and imaginative harmonies of Reginald Hanson and David Guggenheim will be snatched up by one of the major labels. We'll be watching you, guys."

Wow, Madeline thought. She looked up at Alison. "And this was published when?"

"Nine months ago. Isn't it fabulous?"

David sighed. Madeline turned and saw him shaking his head.

"Alison's a one-woman publicity machine," he said. "She doesn't know when to stop."

"How much time do I have?" Hanson asked.

"Fifteen minutes, my love."

"Actually," David said, "the way the whole *Rolling Stone* thing came about was very funny. Hanson and I were hanging out at my place and—"

He proceeded to tell a long story involving journalists and missed appointments and one of Hanson's nosebleeds. After that he told a story about their first time being interviewed on the radio, which reminded Hanson of one of their early gigs in Boston, and he asked David to tell the story about the guy who wanted to be their manager. Madeline's discomfort in the dark crowded apartment slowly disappeared as she was drawn in by David's charm. All that existed for her was the sight of him pushed back from the table, his lovely hands playing with the plastic bag of marijuana as he spoke; and as he spoke he looked mostly at her, his eyes bright and lively. She gazed at his well-formed mouth, his high cheekbones, his dark hair, his good posture, his nice corduroy shirt—and if she inhaled deeply she could smell his after-shave, a rich, musky scent. Again she felt that heat between them; and although Hanson and Alison were sitting with them, Madeline felt as if she and David were enclosed in a cocoon, and swirling all around them was that dark purple with flashes of light. Her whole body felt warm, as if it were humming. He was lovely, she thought, just lovely; and so funny and articulate and although quite confident also genuinely modest about Narrow Grave's success. This man is a catch, she thought. A serious catch.

"Oh God," Alison said. "Look at the time, it's nine-thirty."

"What time did the opening begin?" David asked.

"Seven. It goes from seven to ten."

"Which means it won't end till twelve. But we should probably get going. You okay, Hanson?"

Hanson, sitting normally at last, nodded. "I don't think I'll be bleeding again tonight."

Madeline touched Alison's arm. "Where is your bathroom?"

"All the way in back—come on, I'll show you."

David gave Madeline a warm smile as she rose from the table. She followed Alison through two small rabbit warren rooms, threading her way along a path that allowed them—barely—to pass.

"Hanson's a pack rat," Alison said over her shoulder. "As you've probably guessed."

They passed into the bedroom, a larger room with windows looking out onto Jefferson Street. Madeline saw an unmade bed, more guitars and, balanced on top of a box of tissues on the bedside table, Alison's diaphragm. There was another door on the left-hand side of the room; they passed through the door into a room that was surprisingly clean—a nice blue and red oriental carpet covered the floor, and there was, all neat and lined up against the wall, an upright piano, a small set of drums, four guitar cases, and several amplifiers. In the corner there was a small refrigerator, and on top of the refrigerator a small plastic skeleton.

"Hanson and David practice here. When they don't practice at the studio."

"What studio?"

"They rent space at one of the recording studios in town. That's where they practice every night. And these rooms," she said, opening a door, "are *my* studio."

Just as there were two little rooms on the other side of the apartment, there were two little rooms on this side. Alison flipped on lights in both rooms, and suddenly there was so much color and clutter Madeline did not know where to look first. The walls were crammed with posters, thumbtacked for the most part, many fading or half-fallen; Madeline saw Munch, Picasso, Buffet, Watteau, Monet, Stella, Degas, Manet, Rothko and, her favorite, Kandinsky. She went to the wall and touched a finger to the Kandinsky poster.

"I love Kandinsky," she said as she gazed at the explosion of dancing colors. "He's the best."

"So you know something about art?"

"I don't know a thing about music but yes, I love art. I took a lot of courses at college."

"Well, I've got a mountain of books here if you ever want to borrow one."

And mountain was no exaggeration: stacks of books towered everywhere, on top of tables, on the floor, on an easy chair—it seemed that no one had told Alison about bookshelves. Strewn over and next to the books were brushes, rags, tubes of paint, cans of turpentine, and pieces of wood dabbed with colors, and behind and beside all that were stacks of canvases, all turned over or faced to the wall. In the second room there was actually a spot where Alison appeared to work—there was an easel in the corner, and a canvas covered by a sheet.

"Your latest painting?" Madeline asked.

"Yep. You want to see it?"

"Sure."

Alison took off the sheet and Madeline found herself staring at one of the oddest paintings she had ever seen. The words "Pretty freaky" jumped to mind, but of course she did not say that. She stepped back a little to get a better look: the canvas was painted so that it appeared to be a window, and peering from behind the window were three people—children, maybe, but Madeline could not be sure. The people were crowding up against the window, their hands pressed flat and their faces imploring. The colors were opaque and startling—one person had a purple face and red hands, another an orange face and blue hands; and in between the people was a solid, heavy gray, as if they were trapped in a horrible choking fog and were pressing at the window looking at—looking at what?

Madeline turned to Alison. "What are they looking at?"

Alison eyed Madeline shrewdly. "Do you know, you're the first person who asked that? Not that many people have seen it, but still…"

"And what is it? What do they see?"

"Well," Alison said, squinting at the canvas. "They're looking at a perfect world. And they can't get in."

Madeline stared at Alison. I could like this woman, she thought. Despite the tea bag, I could like her.

"They remind me of characters from Dickens," Madeline said. "You know, Fagin's urchins or something."

"I was sort of hoping for that effect," Alison said. She sighed, and covered the picture with the sheet. "I still have a lot to do, it's not anywhere near finished. I should stay home tonight and work but I don't want Hanson out all alone after one of his nosebleeds. Besides, we have to go tonight, it's business."

"Business? How?"

"The artist having the exhibit is the girlfriend of a drummer who used to play with Narrow Grave. He played on their first album, but he wasn't up to snuff so they had to let him go. It was kind of a sensitive thing for awhile—anyway, he's in another band now. But we have to go and show support; you know, keep everyone lubricated."

Lubricated? Madeline imagined Alison rubbing people with motor oil.

"The bathroom is through there," Alison said. "On the left."

❦   ❦   ❦

On the way to the art gallery Madeline and David walked behind Hanson and Alison. It was a beautifully cool night, the streets empty and peaceful. David held Madeline's hand in a warm grip, and she felt happy.

"You look so pretty tonight," he said. "I love your hair."

"I guess my sister learned a thing or two at all those Dead concerts."

"I don't just mean the style, I mean the color. It's like honey—it's blonde but brown too."

"Mmm—thanks."

"'Mmm—thanks,'" he mocked her gently.

"What?" she said, laughing.

"I don't know—you're funny. You're really shy. And you're completely unable to accept compliments."

She rolled her eyes; he squeezed her hand.

"Alison showed me her studio," she changed the subject. "And her latest painting."

David sighed. "She's been working on that painting for six months."

"Is that a long time? I mean, I have no idea how long it takes to do a painting."

"It's a long time, but that's because she never works. Or rather, never works at her art—she's at her job all day long, and then she spends the rest of her time doing stuff for us."

"Like what?"

"Well, we don't have a manager, but then we don't have to because we have Alison. She's amazing—she arranges our gigs, she does all the publicity, she negotiates with The Small Record Label. And she does all kinds of things that we'd never think of—like you know that radio show tomorrow? She found out when Bing Wallace's birthday was, and she sent him flowers from us. It's a little thing, but it really helped fix us in his mind. I mean, he loves our music, but he'd rather have people he likes on his show, so it helps that he likes us personally. And, I don't know, Alison makes cassettes and sends them to people, she organized our tour down South, she's still in touch with the guy from *Rolling Stone* who wrote that blurb about us... The only problem is, she doesn't know when to stop. I'm sorry she inundated you tonight."

"Oh no, I didn't mind. I want to know about your band, I want to learn what you've done."

"Oh you do?" he said teasingly. "And why's that?"

"Because—I don't know, because it's the most important thing in your life."

"I see. So I guess that means you like me," he said, swinging her hand.

She blushed. "Mmm."

"'Mmm'—which means?"

"Which means yes. But I don't really know you," she added hastily.

"Yes, I remember you saying that last night. Well, if you want to get to know me you're just going to have to spend more time with me. Is that what you want?"

"I'd like that," she said, looking at him and smiling.

"I'd like that too. You're not dating anyone else, are you? I mean, other than Frank."

"I was never dating Frank and no, I'm not dating anyone else. Are you?" she asked timidly.

"Me? No one. I broke up with someone three months ago, and since then you're the first girl I've dated. Or I should say, the first girl I've wanted to date. Are we dating?" he asked.

"I think so. I hope so."

"Well, then, let's say we are. Because I haven't met anyone like you in a long, long time, and I don't want to let you get away from me."

It was almost ten o'clock at night, but Madeline felt like the sun had just come out and she was laying on her back in a field of alpine flowers, a fresh breeze caressing her face.

❧   ❧   ❧

Hanson and Alison stopped in front of a well-lit storefront, waiting for Madeline and David to catch up. Madeline had occasionally gone to exhibits with Spencer, but this was her first time at—what was it called? A little sign in the lower left-hand corner of the window said "Magic Gallery."

David peered through the window. "Looks packed. Well," he said, turning to the others, "Are we stoned enough to face all those people or should we smoke another joint?"

"We're late as it is," Alison said. "And I think you should save something so we can smoke with Raller; I think that would be a nice gesture."

David pushed open the door, and with a sweep of his hand indicated that the others should enter. Madeline went first, and found herself in a long rectangular room full of lights and smoke and running trills of conversation and laughter. It's too crowded in here, she thought. She turned around, and David was behind her; he put his hand on the small of her back and gently nudged her forward. And then something strange happened: there was a sudden hush in their part of the room, and people backed up a little to let them through. Madeline felt like Moses parting the Red Sea; she was about to make a joke to David when she noticed there was a genuine stillness, and people were staring at them. Are they staring at me? Madeline wondered. Her hairstyle was interesting, but not that interesting. And then she heard a man on her left murmur to someone "…from Narrow Grave." So all this was for David and Hanson? She looked at David: his face was calm, and he was smiling slightly. Hanson was looking at the ground, and Alison was clutching his arm, her round face beaming. So it is for them, Madeline thought. How odd.

"Well, well! Here they are!" a voice boomed. "I was wondering if you guys would make it."

A tall rangy man—about thirty-five, maybe older—stepped in front of them. He had narrow blue eyes, a hooked nose, high cheekbones and full, mobile lips that were set in a smile that was more like a sneer. His brown hair was long and curly, and he wore a loud yellow shirt, black jeans, and black boots; he had a pair of sunglasses propped on his head, and an open beer in his hand. Instinctively Madeline did not like him; she moved a bit behind David as if to protect herself.

"Raller," David said, raising his hand and meeting Raller's in a gesture half-high five, half-handshake. "Of course we're here, we wouldn't miss it."

Raller turned to Madeline. "And who's the pretty blonde? The accessory no rock star should be without."

The sweet sourness of his breath hit Madeline in the face. He's drunk, she thought. And I hate him.

"This," David said, "is Madeline." And he turned to look at her with something in his eyes that said "I'm sorry—please bear with this asshole."

"Ma-de-line!" Raller said. "How do you do, Ma-de-line?"

"Fine," she said, accepting Raller's outstretched hand and shaking it briefly.

"And Hanson, my man!" Raller clapped Hanson on the shoulder, making Hanson wince. "Good to see you. And I see you brought the old ball and chain, as usual."

"Nice to see you too, Raller," Alison said sweetly.

The tension was thick; Madeline saw that although David was smiling, his jaw was taut. What had Alison said about the prehistory to all this? That Raller used to play with Narrow Grave but was kicked out because he was not up to snuff. I'm glad I'm a writer, she thought. I don't need anyone else, I can do it all myself.

"So," Raller said. "What's new?" He took a chug of beer, and narrowed his eyes.

"Not much," David said. "You know—rehearsing, writing, the usual."

"Oh, come on, Dave, don't be coy with me. Everyone knows you're about to sign with The Big Record Label. Don't worry, you can tell me, I'm not going to beg you guys to take me on again. I've been unhitched from your rising star, I'm used to it by now."

The worst thing was that people were standing around them listening. But David was impressive: he did not lose his nerve or look guilty; he stayed calm, and radiated a quiet power. He stared Raller in the eye and asked, "And how's No Mercy doing? I saw you guys had a gig at The Dirt Club."

"Yeah, it was all right. We're okay. We'll never make it, but we have a good time. Remember when we played The Dirt Club? Long time ago, huh?" He turned to Madeline. "In case you don't know, Ma-de-line, I am one of the founding members of Narrow Grave. Left my home in Boston and followed these guys down here to find fame and fortune."

"Really," Madeline said. "And what instrument do you play?"

"Drums. Are you a groupie?"

"I beg your pardon?" Madeline said icily.

"Madeline's a writer," David said, putting his arm around her. "A published writer."

"Nice, nice, very nice. But then David always has nice girlfriends. Hanson! You're awfully quiet, what's up?"

"I see Spencer over there," Madeline whispered to David. "I'm going to go say hi."

"Okay," he said. He took her hand and squeezed it, again giving her a look that said I'm sorry.

"It's okay," she whispered.

She released his hand and began making her way toward Spencer, who was standing near the back talking to a tall woman with short purple hair. "Pardon me," Madeline said to a tall laughing man with pierced ears. "Excuse me," to a small animated blonde. "Passing through," to an arguing couple.

"Madeline!" Spencer said, giving her a kiss on the lips. "Isn't this great? Do you know Kaitlin?"

"No," Madeline said, smiling at the purple haired woman whose face, Madeline saw, was wall-to-wall freckles. "Nice to meet you."

"Kaitlin's a dancer," Spencer said. He was in a good mood—he was rocking back and forth so spiritedly he was practically bouncing. "She founded her own company here in Hoboken, they're having a recital next month and I'll be playing."

"Great."

"Are you an artist?" Kaitlin asked.

"I'm a writer."

"Madeline's a fantastic writer. So, did you come alone?"

"Actually, I'm here with David Guggenheim. I met him at your place, remember?"

Spencer widened his eyes and lifted his eyebrows. "David! David is a fantastic musician. And now you two are—?"

"Well," she said, smiling broadly. "Dating, I guess. It's only our second time out."

"Perfect," Spencer said. "You two are the perfect couple."

It seemed like a good time to drag Spencer off into a corner and pump him for information about David, but just as she was about to ask Spencer if she could speak to him alone she noticed that Kaitlin's hand was on his thigh. Oh well—another time.

"I think I'll take a look at the paintings. If I can fight my way through the crowd."

"Do," Spencer said. "They're fantastic."

Too much smoke, too much noise. And I'm stoned, Madeline thought as she moved away from Spencer. And I'm not sure if I should be upset by that remark "David always has nice girlfriends." But Madeline, she told herself. Be realistic. David is a handsome thirty-year-old man; of course he's had other relationships. It would be weird if he hadn't. So calm down.

Seeing the pictures was actually not as difficult as she had imagined. The crowd had left a margin of about two feet in front of the walls, and people were slowly making their way around the room, stopping and looking at the artwork. Madeline inserted herself in this space; she moved over a little, and found herself in front of a picture. Oh my God, she thought, feeling at once scared and shocked. She was standing in front of a black ink drawing of a naked woman. The woman was on her back with her legs spread; her face was turned to one side, and her eyes were closed as if she were in pain. But most disturbing of all, the woman's vulva and nipples were covered with splashes of orange, a weird translucent reddish-orange. Madeline stood still with her hand to her mouth. It was so raw, so revealing—how had the artist found the courage to paint such a thing? It was painful to look at, but Madeline could not stop looking.

She stared at the picture a long time, then heard a gentle murmur to her right: a couple was standing there, smiling at Madeline and obviously ready to move into her place. "Sorry," Madeline said, and quickly moved to her left. Oh God—another one. Another naked woman, again with orange splashes, only this time the woman was sitting on her haunches and staring at the ground. And as Madeline slowly moved around the room she saw that all the paintings were the same: the women were different, the poses were different, but the women were always naked, and always had those painful orange splashes. Madeline no longer heard the hum and buzz of conversation, and she forgot she was here on a hot date with a sexy man—all she could see were those pictures. Raw, she kept thinking. They are absolutely, completely raw. This painter knew something that Madeline knew: she knew about a woman's sexual wounds. And although anyone seeing Madeline, anyone seeing the tall young woman with the composed expression and honey-blonde hair (and what an interesting hairdo!)—if anyone saw her looking at the pictures, they would never guess that she was looking into a mirror. Because that was exactly how she felt: here was her psyche on the wall, here was picture after picture of her most hidden self. This was how she felt at Swan's Cove when she remembered her past, and this must be how she felt in the past, only she was always so drunk and wild and out of control she never really knew what she was feeling. This was why she had not slept with anyone in years, and this was why she was afraid to sleep with David.

And this woman, this sensitive woman who had drawn all these pictures—this woman was dating that big obnoxious Raller? Oh no, she thought. No, no, no.

"Excuse me," Madeline said, turning to the couple on her right. "Could you tell me where the artist is?"

"That's her, over there sitting in back. The one with the hat."

"Thanks."

Madeline made her way to the back of the room. There was a row of folding chairs against the wall, and in one of the chairs sat a small woman wearing a black coat and a black pillbox hat decorated with shards of mirror. She had a delicate face, but her skin was pale and puffy and her hair, Madeline saw with surprise, was dyed the same odd orange as the splashes in the paintings. The woman was holding a cup of wine and looking at the floor as an older man with a long grey ponytail talked at her earnestly.

"I'm sorry to interrupt," Madeline said. The woman and man looked up at her. The man looked impatient, but Madeline had come this far and was not to be deterred. She sat on her haunches in front of the woman, her back to the impatient man.

"I just had to tell you," Madeline said, looking the woman in the eye, "that I really, really like your work."

"Thank you," the woman said hoarsely.

"It's very—it's very female. So I understand it. Do you know what I mean?" She gave the woman what she hoped was a meaningful look.

"Thanks," the woman said. "Thanks a lot."

Madeline paused. What she really wanted to do was invite this woman home so Bella could meet her and fix pasta and they could all have a heart-to-heart talk; what she really wanted to do was take this woman in her arms and tell her that she understood. I know what you know, Madeline wanted to say; I've been in the backseat of one too many cars, just like you. But it was not appropriate to say any of that, so Madeline reiterated her praise, then rose and walked away.

The crowd had thinned, but those who remained were still making a great deal of noise, still generating clouds of smoke. It's so odd, Madeline thought as she worked her way up front. The walls are full of bleeding women, and everyone is standing around chatting and laughing. She returned to the spot where she had left the others, but all she found was Alison peering out the front window, a cup of wine in her hand.

"Hi," Madeline said.

"Hi. Having a good time?"

"Umm—I suppose. The paintings are pretty disturbing, don't you think?"

"Really? I hardly noticed, I'm so worried about Hanson. Did he look okay to you?"

"A little pale, maybe—but that's normal, isn't it, after losing blood?"

"Hanson is so sensitive, and now tonight with Raller…"

"Where are they all, anyway?"

"Outside smoking a joint. You were way in the back so David asked me to wait here for you."

Good, Madeline thought. He's attentive.

Alison sighed. "So now they're out there and I don't know what's going on and I'm kind of worried."

"Why?"

"Oh, Raller still tries to make them feel guilty for kicking him out of the band. And Hanson still worries about it—sometimes he gets so obsessed about the whole situation it's all David and I can do to calm him down."

"Really? But I'm sure they wouldn't have done something like that unless they had a good reason."

"They had an excellent reason: Raller is an alcoholic. He's a good drummer, but he has no idea about stage presence. Do you know he sometimes threw up on stage? And he showed up drunk at the studio when they were cutting their first album. He's just a totally self-destructive person."

"Strange that someone like him is going out with the woman who painted all these pictures," Madeline said, gesturing at the walls.

"Oh, she's a total nutcase too. Listen, I can't bear this anymore, let's go out and join them. Raller plays such weird mind games; David can handle it, but Hanson can't. Come on," Alison said, putting down her wine and grabbing Madeline's wrist. "Let's go."

They pushed open the door. Madison Street was silent; a few brownstones had lights, but most windows were dark.

"Over there," Alison said. "On that stoop."

A few buildings over Hanson and Raller were sitting on the stoop of a condemned building, Raller with his long legs stretched out on the sidewalk, Hanson with his bony body practically curled up in a ball. David was standing in front of them, one hand in his coat pocket, the other holding a joint to his mouth.

"It's the girls," Raller cried. "Come on, girls, come smoke with us."

Madeline stood next to David, and Alison curled up next to Hanson, putting his head on her shoulder and stroking his long blond hair. "How's my baby?" she cooed. "How's your nosebleed?"

"Hey Alison," Raller said. "Have you ever thought that maybe you're the reason for Hanson's nosebleeds?"

"Since he's been getting them since he was a child, no, I never thought that." Alison's voice was terribly sweet, and Madeline decided that this meant danger.

"What I mean is, you coddle him too much. You always have."

"And you're too hard on him. As you know."

Madeline felt terribly uncomfortable. David held out the joint to her; she shook her head no.

"So," Raller said, looking Madeline up and down. "Here she is, David's new girlfriend. What can you tell us about yourself, David's new girlfriend?"

Red, raw anger rose up within her—she could feel its thick sting as it forced its way into her chest. Oh no, she thought. Don't say anything, Madeline; this is not your scene, not your problem. But her temper got the better of her: her mouth opened, and she found herself saying, "I think, Raller, that it would be far more interesting to talk about *your* girlfriend."

"My girlfriend?" he laughed. "And why's that?"

"Because anyone who paints the kind of pictures she paints must be terribly unhappy. And if she's so terribly unhappy, I have to wonder who's making her that way."

Raller's eyes narrowed; David cleared his throat. Oh, Madeline! she told herself. You big dummy. But she could not help herself—she wanted to stand up for that poor woman.

After that there was silence. Lots of it, yards and yards of it. The joint was passed to Alison, and the air filled with the sound of her noisy inhaling. Madeline set her face into a mask and stared at the boarded-up windows in front of her. Alison passed the joint—now just a roach—to Hanson; he took a quick hit then flicked the roach into the street.

"Well," David said. "I guess we better get going."

"Yeah, I better be heading inside," Raller said. "Thanks for showing, guys. See you around. Bye, Alison." He rose up on his long legs and walked right by Madeline without even glancing at her.

They waited silently, watching as Raller walked down the street and entered the Magic Gallery.

"Well, well, Madeline!" Alison said as soon as the door shut. "You're pretty feisty, aren't you?"

"I'm sorry," Madeline said, turning to David. "I lost my temper. I didn't mean to cause any problems."

But David was smiling. "Oh no, don't apologize. That was perfect; you struck him right in his Achilles' heel."

"But I meant it," she said. "Those pictures—she seems much too sensitive to be going out with someone like him."

"It's a lo-ong story," David said. "I'll tell you on the way."

"On the way where?"

He widened his eyes. "To the Malibu Diner, of course. That's our second home."

David put his arm around her waist, and as they made their way up to Fourteenth Street and Willow he told her a lengthy complicated story about Raller and his girlfriend Deneen that involved multiple breakups, restraining orders, hysterical scenes, Deneen's battles with heroin, Raller's trouble with alcohol—your basic horror story love-hate relationship. Alison chimed in with the occasional frightful anecdote, and by the time they reached the diner Madeline was a whirl of emotions: she felt sad and angry and stoned, but she was also floating in a humming bliss caused by the pressure of David's arm around her waist.

They sat in a booth, and Alison grabbed the oversized menus tucked behind the mini-jukebox. She gave one to Hanson and one to David; David propped the menu on the table, and they were hidden behind the large fake leather cover.

"Have whatever you want," David said to Madeline. "My treat." He leaned over and kissed her on the nose, then he pulled away and looked at her, his gaze running over her face and hair. He reached out his hand and softly stroked her nose with his finger. Madeline melted into a puddle on the floor; she collected herself, then turned her attention to the menu.

"I have the worst munchies," Alison said. "I wish I could order dessert first."

"They have coconut cake," Madeline said, lowering their menu to the table so she could see Alison. "I saw it as I came in, it was enormous."

"Oh, I've had it—it's awesome."

David looked at Hanson and winked. "Oh no, Hanson—now we've got two of them."

"Women and food," Hanson said. He turned to Alison and looked her up and down. "I thought you were on a diet."

Madeline tensed; she would never let anyone talk to her that way. But Alison just looked at Hanson pleadingly and said, "I know, honey. But you know how I get when I'm stoned—if I don't eat, I'll die."

"Yes, but you get stoned every day so you eat too much every day." Hanson turned to Madeline. "Alison used to be fat."

"That's right," Alison said. "I was a fat kid."

"And a fat adult. Last year she lost twenty pounds, but she gained it all back."

"Because I was tired of being addicted to diet pills, that's why."

Madeline looked at David—he was so cute, studying the menu, his eyebrows drawn in concentration. Even his ear was cute, the lobe pink from the cold, his slightly long hair laying over it like a feather.

"So, Madeline," Alison said. "What do you think?"

Madeline folded her hands on the table and announced, "I want a basket of onion rings, a coffee ice cream milkshake, and for dessert tea and a piece of coconut cake."

"You don't want a hamburger or something?" David asked.

"I don't eat meat."

"I love meat," he said. "Will it bother you if I order a cheeseburger?"

"No." She smiled at him, and he smiled back.

They ordered, and then the conversation returned to Raller. Alison worked herself into a state of righteous indignation and was busy justifying David and Hanson's decision to kick Raller out of the band, was going on and on at great length, when Madeline suddenly noticed a line of blood trickling from Hanson's nose.

"Hanson," she said quickly. "Your nose."

"Oh God," Alison said. She thrust a napkin in Hanson's face. "Head back. At once."

"Don't talk about Raller anymore," David said. "It upsets him."

The food came. Alison forbade Hanson to lower his head and eat, but he said he was starving so, to Madeline's stoned amazement, Alison cut up Hanson's food and fed him. Madeline snuck a glance at David—he was eating his cheeseburger, and seemed unfazed. I suppose he's used to them, she thought.

Madeline ate with gusto—everything tasted wonderful. Occasionally images of the pictures arose, but she decided to postpone thinking about them until she was home. Madeline loved laying in bed and thinking—she loved being warm and snug under the covers and presenting herself with a problem or question and just letting her mind knit thoughts, draw conclusions. Certain experiences demanded reflection, and tonight's pictures were one of them. But that could wait until later.

David was silent as they ate, but when he finished he leaned back and put his arm on the back of the seat and let his fingers rest on Madeline's shoulder. She was not sure how the evening would end—would there be another verbal tussle about going back to his place?—but when everyone was done eating (and done being fed) Alison insisted Hanson needed to go home, and David suggested they call a taxi.

"We can drop you off at your place, Madeline," he told her. "Is that okay?"

"That's fine."

Alison went to call a taxi, and David picked up the check and paid. Hoboken being Hoboken, the taxi was waiting for them in the parking lot when they stepped out the door. In three minutes they were at 821 Washington; David got out with Madeline and walked her to the door.

"So," he said. "Tomorrow I have that radio thing and then we'll probably hang out afterwards with Bing, but why don't I call you tomorrow night and we can make plans for Monday?"

"Actually Tuesday night is better; I work Tuesday, and if I go out Monday night I'll be tired."

"You're going to make me wait that long?" he laughed. "Okay—Tuesday."

"I had a nice time tonight."

"Me too. A really nice time."

"David!" Alison called from the taxi. "Hanson's nose is bleeding again, hurry up."

"All right, all right!" he called. He put a hand on Madeline's shoulder, leaned over and softly kissed her on the mouth. "I'll talk to you tomorrow, okay?"

"Okay. Good night."

"Good night."

🍁   🍁   🍁

Once again Bella was in the TV room, reading on the couch in the sperm assistance posture.

"My, my!" Madeline said as she flopped into the green armchair. "You and Robert are really going at it."

Bella put down her book. "Well, I'm ovulating—not that it's ever difficult to convince Robert to have sex. So, how was it?"

"Good. We had a really nice time."

"Tell me everything," Bella said. And she meant it: one of the things Madeline loved about Bella was that she was interested in everything. She loved meeting new people and having new experiences, and if she was not the one having the experiences that was okay, she still wanted to hear about it. Madeline often said that Bella should be a psychiatrist, but Bella always replied that she had spent the first seventeen years of her life with crazy people and that was enough, thank you very much.

So Madeline told Bella about the grimy apartment and Hanson's nosebleed and Alison and the used tea bag ("That is *shocking*," Bella said) and smoking joints and David's funny stories and Alison's painting and the Magic Gallery and meeting Raller and the strange unsettling pictures.

"Those pictures affected me so much, Bella. It was like, there were all these sexually wounded women all over the walls. And it was like looking in a mirror, somehow, because I guess I feel like that. You know, from high school."

"I know what you mean."

"Do you feel bad, Bella? You know, about the old days?"

Bella folded her arms across her chest and sighed. "I do. I mean, I know I joke about it, but it still hurts. It's not even that I slept with so many people, that's not what bothers me, it's more that it wasn't, you know, joyful. Not joyful sexuality. It was aggressive, wild, angry, self-destructive, but never joyful. And I blame Polly and Spam for that, I blame them one hundred percent. Because you remember how it was, you remember her locking him out of their room and him outside, banging on the door and pleading with her to let him in and let him sleep with her. That was horrible."

Madeline nodded, all her insides wincing.

"So that fucked me up," Bella said. "Or rather, fucked you and me up. And I think that because Polly never wanted it, fucking around was sort of the ultimate rebellion—you know, flinging sex in their faces. And I also blame them for not giving us enough physical attention. They never *touched* us, Madeline—can you remember any hugs or kisses or pats on the head? No, because they never did those things; it was like they never really wanted us. I can remember when you were a baby, they would just let you lay in your crib and scream. If it wasn't for me taking care of you, I don't like to think what would have happened to you. You would have ended up like me," Bella sighed. "A complete fuck-up."

"Don't be so hard on yourself, Bella. You haven't been a fuck-up in years."

"I know, but I wasted my twenties. My early twenties, anyway. Just—gone," she said, snapping her fingers. "Years of life just gone, and I can never get them back. If I had known then what I know now, I could have really done something with myself."

"But you did, finally. You went back to school, you got a good job—and you met Robert."

"Thank God for Robert, Madeline. Thank God for Robert. And you know, I didn't want him at first. I was so scared of him—he was the first man who treated me decently, and all I wanted to do was run away from him. Luckily he persisted, though Lord knows he suffered. I didn't let him touch me for six months—I didn't even let him hold my hand."

Madeline smiled. "I know."

"I was scared. I was scared because I just couldn't believe he loved me. I thought all he wanted was to sleep with me, but what I didn't understand was that he wanted to sleep with me *because* he loved me. It's such a huge difference, you can't imagine. And I remember the first time we slept together it was like, I don't know, it was just an amazing experience. Not that Robert is any Casanova, that's not it, it's that he *loves* me. When we make love—I don't know, he just *loves* me. And I can't believe I ever settled for less than that," she said, tears in her eyes. "And I guess that's why I'm always on your case about not fucking around—I don't want you to settle for less either."

"I don't know, Bella. I'm so confused about all this. I mean—I know what you mean, I feel like I've never had a normal, healthy sex life. And I want to, I need to, but I'm just so petrified. Petrified of men, I guess, and of sex. I mean, on the one hand I want it so much, I want to be touched so badly it drives me crazy, but on the other hand I feel like if someone touches me I'm going to break into little pieces."

"And so with this David?"

"With David—Bella, I'm so attracted to him. Not just his looks, but everything he does—how he speaks, how he lives his life, the way he's so devoted to his music. He's a great guy. And his looks attract me too, I guess, and just the way he is with me. He's a very sensual person; he doesn't seem at all inhibited."

"Did he ask you to go back to his place again tonight?"

"No. We went to the Malibu Diner after the exhibit and then we all took a taxi and they dropped me off. But he was very affectionate with me—you know, holding my hand, putting his arm around me. He even kissed my nose."

"He kissed your nose. Wow."

"In the diner. Behind a menu."

"He sounds like a hotty. But if you'll take a little advice from your big sister—wait. Just wait. Because some men are interested in who you are, and some men pretend to be interested in who you are so they can sleep with you. David may be totally enchanted with you, but it may not last."

"Oh, don't say that, Bella."

"Or he may be falling madly in love with you. Maybe you'll even marry this guy, I don't know. All I'm saying is, take your time and see who he really is. And if you like who he really is, if he treats you well, if he's stable and trustworthy—then go ahead and sleep with him." Bella looked at Madeline affectionately. "What you need, Maddy, is to find a Robert. You know, someone who really loves you. Maybe this David is the one—I hope so."

"Me too. You know, it's so weird, when I was at Swan's Cove I was sure I was finished with all this men stuff. But I guess that's just because I was scared."

"Madeline," Bella said. "Can I ask you something? What were you doing down at Swan's Cove? I mean, what were you *really* doing?"

"It's a long story."

"I'm not going anywhere. And tomorrow's Sunday, we can sleep in."

"If I tell you, you'll laugh at me."

"I swear to God I won't laugh. Please tell me."

"Well, if you really want to know…" And so Madeline gave an abridged version of her spiritual journey gone awry. Bella listened carefully, and when Madeline was done she said, "I knew it was something like that. I mean, I didn't know you were meditating and having mystical experiences, but I saw the books you were reading, and I saw you and Michael having deep conversations—and I remember once I found a church program in your coat pocket." She paused. "You could have told me."

"No, I couldn't have. You would have made fun of me."

"That's not true. Well, maybe it is true. But I would have stopped when I saw you were serious. I mean, I don't make fun of Michael, do I? And he's the most religious person I know."

"Michael?"

"Yes, Michael. Don't you think so?"

"I think it's all kind of intellectual for him, don't you? I mean, he never talks about devotion or mystical experiences or anything like that."

"That's because you never ask him. Michael is not a person to go on and on about himself, you know that. But if you look at him, if you look at who he is and everything he does, I'd say he's figured something out. He didn't translate all those sutras just to get tenure, you know. He's really trying to contribute something—and he couldn't do that if he didn't have anything to contribute."

"Well—he's so slow."

"Oh God—tonight he was going into The City to meet some friends and he stopped here on his way out to tell Robert something, and like a complete idiot Robert asked Michael to glance over something he wrote. I mean, you know Michael can't just glance at something—I finally had to rip the paper out of his hands and kick him out. Anyway," Bella said, stretching and yawning. "So when will you see Mr. Rock Star again?"

"Tuesday night. Tomorrow he's busy, he's going to be interviewed on the radio. And do you know he and Hanson were in *Rolling Stone*? It was just a blurb but still, *Rolling Stone*."

"God, I haven't looked at *Rolling Stone* in years. That's pretty impressive."

"*He's* pretty impressive."

"So when do we meet him?"

"I'm not too anxious to bring him here what with Robert being so negative."

"Robert's just protective of you. And I am too. You should be glad people are looking after you, Madeline."

"I suppose…"

"Well," Bella said, rising off the couch. "I'm glad I finally solved the mystery of why you went away by yourself for so long. I thought you were tired of us."

"Oh, Bella," Madeline said. She leapt up and put her arms around her sister. "As if I could ever get tired of you."

CHAPTER 8

The Gig

Madeline stood in front of The Beat'n Path, staring at the placard on the sidewalk. Magenta letters on a black background proclaimed: NARROW GRAVE 10 P.M., and attached at a diagonal was a white piece of paper with red letters: SOLD OUT.

Shit, Madeline thought. What do I do now? David said she should come at ten, and it was now ten exactly. But from what she could see through the front window, the club could not fit another living soul. On the sidewalk clusters of people were standing around discussing where else they could go.

"The Cucumbers are at Maxwell's," someone said.

"No, that was last week. This week it's Strange Cave."

"So let's go."

"Or we could just get a drink at Fabian's."

Madeline felt so frustrated she wanted to cry. She had been looking forward to this gig all week, she could hardly wait to see David on stage. And he was excited, too; he said that he and Narrow Grave were inseparable, so if Madeline wanted to get to know him, she had to see him play.

"Madeline!"

Madeline turned towards the door. It was Alison, wearing a black sweater over black leggings, her hair in a bun and her eyelids covered with a peculiar sparkly purple substance.

"What are you doing?" Alison asked. "Come on in."

"But it says sold out."

"Not for you it isn't. Come on."

Alison grabbed Madeline's wrist and pulled her inside. There was a tiny foyer, then another door that led into the club. A podium was set up next to the door, and standing behind it was a tall muscular man with curly blond hair.

"It's okay," Alison said to the man, shouting to make herself heard over the jukebox and chattering crowd. "She's David's girlfriend, she's on the list. Madeline Boot."

The man ran a thick finger along a piece of paper taped to the podium. "Okay," he shouted. "But that's it—any more people and we're in violation of fire regulations."

"Don't even *say* the word fire!" Alison laughed. She led Madeline over to the side of the podium, then put her arm around Madeline and gave her a squeeze. Madeline was surprised; in the two weeks she had been dating David, Alison's behavior had ranged from slightly rude to slightly friendly. But warm and huggy? Never.

"Isn't this great?" Alison shouted. "And we've made tons of money. I always stand up front and keep track, that's how I saw you moping around outside."

"I thought I was going to miss it."

"David would have died if you didn't get in."

"Where is he?"

"They're upstairs in the green room smoking their brains out. It's better if we stay here; they need someone to look after the place."

"Okay."

"Do you want a drink? Oh, that's right, you don't drink."

"A club soda would be nice, but—" Madeline motioned towards the bar and the crowd of people three deep waving money and shouting orders at the harassed bartenders. The room was long and thin; at the far end was a divider with lozenges of thick smoked glass, and beyond that was the room with the stage. There was dark paneling, a high tin ceiling painted black, and strings of tiny colored lights on the molding and the big mirror behind the bar. It was noisy and smoky and packed with people, which reminded Madeline why she never got into the club scene—she found it boring and exhausting, and not much fun if you didn't drink. But tonight was different: tonight she was here to see David.

Alison somehow found stools for them, and they sat next to the little counter that was attached to the front window.

"See that girl over there?" Alison shouted. "The one with the short blonde hair and the crab earrings? In the green dress?"

"Who is she?"

"David's old girlfriend."

"Oh—Carrie?"

"No, the one before Carrie. Or the one before the one before Carrie—I can never keep track."

You are such a bitch, Madeline thought. But she was not upset; things were going well between David and her, and she knew she did not have anything to fear from his old girlfriends. And she knew about all of them: one night Madeline and David ate dinner at Helmers', and afterwards they sat in the dark wooden booth until one in the morning as David told Madeline his history with women. Since coming to Hoboken six years ago he had had about twelve short relationships, and none of them had worked out. The reasons varied: one woman was bulimic, another was jealous of his success, one did too much coke, another fell in love with Hanson, one cried all the time, another wasn't bright enough—none of them were right for him. He told Madeline this, then said, "You, on the other hand—you're perfect for me."

"Oh really?" she laughed. "And why's that?"

He crossed his arms on the table and looked deep into her eyes. "You're pretty, you're smart, you're an artist, you have a good sense of humor. And you're extremely sweet and sensitive and nice and—I don't know, you're ladylike."

Ladylike? That was a first: Madeline had a quick flash of herself at the Columbia Pub, wearing a pink jumpsuit and dancing on a table with three men. Well, she thought, no need to disillusion him.

"And I think I've met you at the perfect time," he went on. "I mean, here we are about to sign a contract with The Big Record Label, and it's just so wonderful for me to have someone to share it with." Then he reached across the table, took her hand, and brought it to his mouth. He kissed the back of her hand, then turned it over and covered her palm with tiny, gentle kisses. Madeline was already happily agitated by David's words, but when he kissed her like that she felt something in her chest start to soar, start to fly, and the most incredible tender joy filled her whole body. Which is when she knew she loved him.

He was so good to her. They went out every night except Sunday and Monday, and on those nights he always called her. He paid for all their dinners, and he often brought her little gifts—a rose, a candy bar, a coupon for a pint of ice cream at Ben and Jerry's. And he was always attentive to her—always held the door, always took her coat, always wondered if she was too cold or too hot or maybe the room was too smoky or maybe she hadn't gotten enough to eat.

And he asked questions about her life and her ideas and her daily routine, and always seemed genuinely interested in her replies. She hated men who didn't listen, but David was a listener; he was curious about who she was, and she told him everything. Well, not quite. She never told him about her past experiences with men, nor about her involvement with mysticism; she did not want to scare him away, and it probably wasn't necessary to tell him all that anyway. But everything else—her crazy parents, her love for Bella, her writing, her reading, her friends—everything else she told him over long dinners and walks. Nothing made her happier than walking down Hudson Street late at night with David's arm wrapped around her, his face turned towards her and his eyes watching her steadily while she spoke about who she was and how she felt and what it was like being Madeline.

Best of all, he no longer pressed her about sex. He touched her a great deal and was always affectionate, but he never again asked her to come to his apartment. Every night he walked her home, kissed her cheek, stroked her hair, then left. She began to feel safe with him; he wouldn't press her, and they could do things at her speed. But even that was changing: Madeline found herself thinking about him almost all the time, and a good deal of those thoughts were sexual fantasies. One night after he walked her home she laid in bed and let herself imagine what it would be like to make love with him. Soon her body was so aroused, her lower belly so congested and hot, that she had to masturbate for relief. Afterwards she went into the bathroom and looked at her reflection in the mirror—her cheeks were red, her lips full, and her eyes glazed. She wanted him; she really wanted him. And she loved him. Going to work, riding the Red Apple bus into The City, she lay her head back and closed her eyes and let herself remember all his small touches and kisses. Once she was so deeply engrossed in her fantasies she did not realize that the bus had arrived at Port Authority until the bus driver called out "Miss? Miss?" Madeline still wrote, still word processed, but she was terrible at Scrabble and following conversations and walking down the street without knocking into someone. And once during an ice cream break she absentmindedly picked up Bella's dish and started eating from it. "Madeline!" Bella said. "You are so useless these days, what's wrong with you?"

She wanted him, and she loved him, and she did not think she could hold out much longer. And she did not think she should: they had a lovely relationship, and thus far David had no strikes. Which was not to say there weren't a few tiny things that bothered her. First and foremost, it really did seem that maybe David smoked a lot of pot. Okay, yes: he *did* smoke a lot of pot. He had once made a comment about needing to smoke before he played music, which she interpreted to mean that he smoked before and probably during rehearsal. And he always smoked at least once during their dates: if they were going out with Hanson and Alison they always met at the apartment first and smoked, and if they went out to eat he lit up a joint as soon as they left the restaurant. Madeline did not feel that smoking pot was in any way morally wrong—of course not—but she had to wonder: Why did David need to smoke so much? What was it about his normal every day waking reality that made him want to change the channel? He did not seem neurotic, and did not strike her as unhappy or unconfident, so why? What was wrong? She told herself that he was simply different from her: when Madeline got high all she wanted to do was drift around and eat a lot of food, but others felt that pot sharpened their perceptions. Bella was like that—no matter how stoned she was, she could always execute the most complicated hairstyles. And whereas Madeline could not even add up a check when she was stoned, she knew someone from college who got stoned every morning then went to work on Wall Street as a trader. So everyone was different, and she mustn't judge David by her standards.

Another small thing was his schedule. He said he rehearsed from six to ten, but it was usually ten-thirty, and now and then eleven. In a way this was good—Madeline never missed a night of Scrabble, and so did not feel her relationship with David interfered with her peaceful evenings at home. But Madeline was not a night owl—she did not like staying up late, and she hated waking up feeling sleepy and sour. How could she write if her mind was not clear? At first she woke at seven as usual, but gradually she started waking up at nine, even ten. She felt all right as long as she got eight hours of sleep, but she missed those clear early morning hours, missed the smell of brewing coffee, the sounds of Bella and Robert preparing for work, the peace that descended when they shut the door and left. She and David never went out on Sunday or Monday nights because she was afraid it would affect her performance at work, and David accepted this. Thank goodness she only worked two days a week—she could not imagine how Alison did it. One night when the four of them were walking back from the Malibu Diner at two in the morning on a Wednesday night, Madeline asked Alison how she was able to keep such hours and then show up at work at nine a.m. "Caffeine," Alison said. "Lots of caffeine. Plus I'm always tired. But I like living this way, it's exciting." Madeline only wished she could say the same.

The last of the tiny small things was that David was not incorporated into her life at 821 Washington. It would be so nice, she often mused, if he could play Scrabble with them. She pictured him coming over and sitting at the dining room table, joking with Robert and Michael, then all of them eating ice cream together. She enjoyed her family so much, and it would be nice to have David share that. She once asked him if he liked to play Scrabble; he said he thought it was boring, and Madeline never mentioned it again. But most of all, it bothered her that in the two weeks they had been dating he had never once picked her up. He kept saying he wanted to meet Bella, but he never did much about it. Madeline could no longer bear Robert's comments every night as she was putting on her coat: "Still not picking you up, hmm? Doesn't have very good manners, does he?" Michael, thankfully, never said a word after her first date with David, but whenever Robert said such things Madeline always felt Michael watching her carefully.

But other than those hardly worth mentioning minor irritations, everything was fine. Perfect, even.

Alison sighed. "I'll be so thankful when they've moved beyond clubs like this," she shouted into Madeline's ear. "When they played The Bottom Line it was so huge and well-run, it was heaven."

"They played The Bottom Line?"

"They were the opening act for The Replacements. Didn't you know? David isn't very good at generating publicity, is he. Anyway, Narrow Grave is much too big to play at dinky clubs like this. They need to develop exclusiveness, allure."

"David told me they're always turning down gigs."

"And they should have turned down this one. These local places are nowhere."

"But Bruce Springsteen still plays The Stone Pony."

Alison rolled her eyes. "Bruce Springsteen? Madeline, please—Hanson and David are artists."

So it probably wasn't a good moment to tell Alison about the time she and Bella parked for hours outside Springsteen's house, hoping to catch a glimpse of him. "I was born and raised in New Jersey," Madeline said by way of explanation.

"That's not your fault," Alison shouted back.

Madeline sighed. She was not sure if she and Alison could ever be friends.

"I like your hairdo," Alison shouted. "Did your sister do it?"

"That's right." Bella had really outdone herself—in the morning she stood in front of Madeline and proclaimed, "You're going to be the best-looking woman there." Bella started off by giving Madeline a hot olive oil hair treatment, then she washed out the oil and separated Madeline's hair into about twenty braids. Madeline walked around in braids all day, then Bella undid them and brushed them out. Madeline's thick hair was subtly rippled, and even Robert admitted she looked good. Then Bella dug up an old dress she had bought at a thrift shop, black and silk and sleeveless with an hourglass waist; Bella combined the dress with black stockings and low black heels and over-sized gold hoop earrings. "You're with the band," Bella said. "You have to look good."

Alison grabbed Madeline's arm and gestured towards the door with her eyes. Three men, all wearing button-down shirts and expensive leather jackets, were talking with the bouncer.

"I have to take care of this," Alison told Madeline. "It's the A&R men from The Big Record Company." Alison moved over to the door, said hello to the nicely dressed men, then grabbed the bouncer and told him she didn't care if he had to kick people out, these men needed a table. While Alison and the bouncer debated, Madeline studied the men. They were obviously not part of the Hoboken music scene: their clothes were better than anyone else's, and their expressions were sharp, almost haughty. Unlike everyone else they were not here for a good time—this was business. Strange to think that these men held David and Hanson's future in their hands, but so it was.

"We're going in," Alison shouted at Madeline, as if it was a war. "You stay here and don't let anyone pass through the doors. If someone gives you a hard time, just get vicious—I saw you with Raller, I know you can do it."

So Alison, the bouncer, and the three important men moved off, and there was Madeline behind the podium. And who should come in but the couple from Leo's two weeks before.

"Hey," the young man said. "What's up? It says sold out but—I remember you, you were with David Guggenheim at Leo's. So you remember us," he said, bringing his tiny redheaded girlfriend up to the podium. "We're on the list."

"Go on in," Madeline said. "And have a good time."

"Oh, we will. And tell David thanks again."

Good thing Alison's not here, Madeline thought. Then two other hard luck cases showed up, and Madeline let them in as well. What else could she do? She was just not bouncer material.

Alison and the bouncer came back with four young women who, like Madeline, were wearing black dresses. They gathered around the podium and wrote their names and addresses on a piece of paper. "I promise we'll send you free tickets for the next two local gigs," Alison shouted. "Thanks a lot, you really did us a big favor." The young women did not look happy, but Alison had them out the door in no time.

"Groupies," Alison shouted. "We don't need 'em going after our men."

"So the A&R men have a table?"

"And drinks on the house and two joints courtesy of Narrow Grave. And if they asked for blow jobs I'd give them that, too. The VP is here, you know—he was the really tall one. He's never come before, so I think this might be it."

"What do you mean?"

"Well, he's the one who decides whether or not to make Narrow Grave an offer, and he only shows at gigs if he means business. I know he listened to their tapes and liked the music, so now he wants to see the band live and see if they have what it takes. You know, if they're good performers."

"So it's a big deal."

"Very. I'd like to find David and tell him—I can't tell Hanson, though, he'd get too nervous. And we'll all be hanging out in the green room afterwards. You know how to behave, don't you?"

"I'm not going to make a fool out of myself, if that's what you mean."

"Well, it's probably best if you don't say too much." Alison stepped back a little and eyed Madeline from head to toe. "You look good—and that's good, they'll like that. And don't be afraid to flirt and show a little leg—they eat that stuff up." Madeline rolled her eyes. "I'm serious, Madeline—you never know what tips the balance on these things. We have to do all we can to help Hanson and David."

Madeline saw that Alison was sincere, not to mention anxious and over-wrought. "I'll be good," Madeline promised. "But I'm not showing any body parts."

"Hey, hey, here's my girls!"

Madeline turned around. Oh no—Jessie, Narrow Grave's other guitarist, a man so perpetually flirtatious Madeline could not take him seriously. Jessie was forty-two, older than the others; he was tall and lean with a shock of grey hair, bright green eyes, and a bony, handsome face. A nice looking man, but somewhere along the line he had decided he was sexually irresistible. David told Madeline that Jessie was a good guy, but a little screwed up about women.

"Hi sweeties," Jessie shouted, putting an arm around Alison and winking at Madeline. "You two look good enough to eat."

Alison sighed. "What do you want, Jessie?"

"I wanted to see how my favorite girls are doing."

"We're fine. Listen, the A&R men are here with the VP."

"Yikes. Better not tell Hanson."

"Don't you dare."

"What'll you give me for keeping my mouth shut?"

Alison pushed him away. "Stop pawing me and go find a twenty-year-old. And leave Madeline alone—she'll bite your head off."

"Oh, Madeline's too sweet for that."

"Try me," Madeline said.

"You know I'd like to, but David would kill me. Why oh why didn't I meet you first?"

"Go away, Jessie," Alison shouted. "Don't you have an instrument to play?"

"You two are bad for my ego."

"Go. Leave."

He blew them kisses, then walked into the crowd. Madeline and Alison exchanged looks. "The man is a walking erection," Alison shouted.

"Does he really think women respond to that kind of talk?"

"They must, because he gets laid all the time."

"Really? But who would—?"

A roar went up from the crowd. Madeline stood on tiptoes and saw David and Hanson stepping through a door at the far end of the room. Madeline felt a rush of love as she watched David work his way through the crowd, reaching out to shake hands, turning this way and that to acknowledge everyone who was acknowledging him.

"Come on," Alison shouted. "It's time."

She grabbed Madeline by the wrist and plunged into the crowd, elbowing and shoving and pushing their way through the wall of people. Alison, Madeline thought as she sent apologetic glances to the people Alison had injured, would be a good person to have in your platoon if you were, say, fighting a war in Vietnam.

They reached the divider with the lozenges of smoked glass. From far away the dividers appeared to be one wall, but the middle divider was actually about two feet in front of the side dividers; Alison whipped through the optical illusion, bringing Madeline with her. The room was jam-packed; tables were set up in front of the long built-in benches, and each small table had a huddle of four to six people. Everyone else was standing, smashed into one another. Help, Madeline thought. Because it was smoky and beery and loud, and if she did not love David so much she would have turned around and gone home.

Alison created space against the wall next to the bathroom, about fifteen feet from the stage. Madeline stood on tiptoe and yes, now she could see the stage, and David. He looked good, very good: he wore slightly baggy white pants, a black leather belt, and a long sleeved button-down shirt with a funky swirling pattern of red, yellow, green, and purple. Not many men could get away with such a shirt, but David was so solid and handsome it somehow suited him. It's a flashy shirt, she thought. Flashy, but not obnoxious. Hanson wore jeans and a white button-down shirt that already had large damp patches in the armpits. Then there was Jessie, and Plug, the drummer. Plug was a wild man, short and wiry with a fierce expression and hyperactive eyes. "He's exactly what a drummer should be," David had told Madeline. "A complete lunatic."

Madeline feasted her eyes on David as he played a few chords on his bass, joked with Jessie, whispered something in Hanson's ear. David looked comfortable and not the least bit high, although Madeline was quite sure he was stoned out of his mind. She stood higher on her tiptoes and glanced around the room—she saw Raller, Spencer, the couple from Leo's, a poet she had dated, the table with the A&R men, the blonde with the crab earrings. It seemed all of Hoboken had come out to see Narrow Grave.

Then the band members had their instruments in place; David took a quick look around the stage and said, "One, two, three, four." The music burst out, and Madeline felt a slight shock. She had not listened to the tapes David had given her, and that was at his request: "You have to hear us live first," he said. "Recorded music never captures all the colors." Well, she did not know how the tapes sounded, but she felt a shock because the music was beautiful. Like most everyone else, Madeline grew up listening to rock 'n' roll, had bought records and gone to a few concerts, but she could not read a note of music, and had no idea about composition. But Bella always told Madeline she had good taste, and so Madeline trusted the thrill running through her, trusted her sure certain belief that Narrow Grave was an excellent band. She had heard a few other Hoboken bands, but the music she was hearing now was far richer than any of the other groups. It was a rich swirling mix of color, but behind all that was something—well, logical. The music made sense, if one could talk about music that way.

As Narrow Grave continued playing, Madeline's belief only strengthened. Unlike many bands, Narrow Grave's songs did not all sound alike: some featured David, some Hanson, some they sung together; and some songs were hard, some soft, some sad, some ironic. And the band was extremely professional—everyone was on the beat and in tune, David's stage patter was brief and funny and confident, and even Hanson did not seem so weak and misera-

ble. It was clear the band had worked hard, and it was clear they were organized and mature. The A&R men had to be impressed, Madeline thought. She
looked over at their table and saw them listening, bobbing their heads, the tall
VP taking a hit off a joint.

The band played for almost an hour, and Madeline never got bored. This
was unusual, because usually in clubs she faded after half an hour, and just put
in time until her companions wanted to leave. It helped that the band played a
few covers: "The Kids are Alright" by The Who, "And Your Bird Can Sing" by
The Beatles, and "Ripple" by The Dead. Spencer played along on the last few
songs, and the very last song they played was an original composition that was
apparently well-known because when David played the opening chords the
audience practically wet their collective pants. After the song a grinning sweaty
David thanked the audience, thanked the club, and invited everyone to sign
their mailing list on the way out. The stage lights dimmed and that was it, the
gig was over.

Madeline turned to Alison and smiled. "That was amazing," she said.

Alison had her arms folded, and was thinking. "They could have cut out a
few songs. And had one less cover. And the lighting was lousy. But otherwise—yeah, it was pretty good."

"And now?"

"Now I go up front and help Hanson. He's always a physical wreck after he
plays, and I don't want him to get a nosebleed in front of the A&R men. It
wouldn't look good."

"I'll wait here."

"Suit yourself. We'll swing by and grab you on the way to the green room."

Alison and her elbows disappeared into the crowd. Madeline pressed herself
into the wall; she did not want to go up and join the crowd fawning over
David, she could not bear to lower herself that way. She stood with her hands
behind her back, watching as half the crowd left and the other half pressed
around the band. The couple from Leo's waved at her on their way out, and she
waved at Spencer but he was on the other side of the room and did not see her.
The A&R men had not moved; they sat at their table with their heads close
together, talking.

At least now Madeline could breathe a little. There were less people and
someone, thank God, had opened the back door and let in a slice of cool air.
Madeline was absentmindedly looking up at the lights when she overheard a
snatch of female conversation.

"The drummer is cute."

"If you like short intense types."

"Which I do."

"And the bassist is cute."

"Nah. I talked to him once, he's a conceited asshole."

Madeline felt as if someone had punched her in the stomach. How could anyone possibly say that about David? She glanced after the two women, but all she could see were two black dresses, frizzy brown hair, and ear-length black hair.

"There you are, hiding in a corner."

She turned around: David. He was soaked in sweat, and with his bangs slicked off to one side he looked like a little boy. He was so cute and handsome and happy she wanted to throw her arms around him and kiss him, but instead she smiled and said, "It was beautiful, David, just beautiful."

"You're the one who's beautiful," he said, leaning forward and kissing her cheek. "Follow me, we're going up to the green room. Grab onto my arm, that way I won't lose you."

He held out one sweaty multi-colored arm, and she grabbed onto him with both hands. They slowly moved through the crowd, David smiling, slapping hands, saying something polite to everyone who stopped him. Madeline stared at the floor, embarrassed. Finally they were next to the jukebox, in front of a closed door. "'Night, everybody," David said, then pushed open the door.

They went up a small spiral staircase that led to a musty, dimly lit hall. One door led to a front room, another to a back room.

"This is the green room," David said, pointing to the front room. "Have you ever been up here before?"

"No, never."

"Well, it's the secret party room. You know, we're all alone up here, which means I can kiss you."

He leaned forward and kissed her on the lips. Even his sweat smelled good, salty and masculine.

Madeline pulled away from him. "Alison said the A&R men are coming up. The VP is here, did you notice?"

"I saw them when we were tuning up."

"Alison also said I shouldn't say very much."

"Well, Alison is full of shit—you can say whatever you want. These guys don't bite. Anyway, we have something they want."

"And they have something you want."

"There's lots of record companies, but only one Narrow Grave." The door to the stairwell opened; David put a finger to his lips.

The green room was more like a red room—there were red walls, red cushions on the floor, and red Venetian blinds on the two large windows facing Washington Street. The walls were lined with ancient psychedelic posters (a green rose on a black background, Jimi Hendrix with a multi-colored afro); in one corner there was a well-stocked bar, and in another a stereo system with careless stacks of albums and cassettes. Madeline's tight dress gave her trouble as she tried to sit—she would be showing a lot more than leg if she wasn't careful. Finally she stepped out of her shoes, hiked up her dress, and sank awkwardly onto a cushion.

Hanson and Alison had come up with Jessie and the A&R men, then the club owner and a few of his friends joined them as well. Plug popped in for a moment to say hello and good-bye; he lived in Brooklyn, and had to catch the PATH to The City. Soon everyone had a beer, and Alison had *London Calling* on her lap and was rolling joints as fast as she could. David was next to Madeline, his hand resting on her knee as he listened attentively to something the VP was saying. Madeline sipped her Perrier, trying to gauge the atmosphere in the room. Something peculiar was going on, and when she figured out what it was she wanted to laugh. It was the A&R men: they were sitting on pillows, were drinking and smoking like everyone else, but they radiated the most supercilious, snobby air. Madeline wished Bella was here so they could laugh at them; Bella would take one look at their haughty expressions and say, "Oh, I see—they're Super Cool." It was just like high school, how a certain group was popular and if you weren't you couldn't even hope one of them might nod at you in the hall. Madeline had encountered similar scenes in college, but in the real world it always seemed that everyone had grown out of that, and you could just be whoever you were. But not these men—they might as well have had neon signs on their foreheads that said "We're better than you." And as Madeline took a hit off a joint, observing the A&R men through the smoke, she decided that either they had been Super Cool in high school or, what was more likely, had not been Super Cool at all and were making up for it now. Why couldn't they just act human and available? Why did the one have to curl his lip slightly every time Alison let out a peal of raucous laughter? Why did they have to make little in-jokes and leave David with an uneasy smile on his lips? It was all so ridiculous. Despite what David had said these men had all the power, and they knew it. The VP was the best of the lot: he was leaning forward on his cushion, listening respectfully as David explained a chord pattern in one of their songs, but even he had an air about him, as if he were behind a glass wall. Madeline felt herself getting angry—who did these people think they were?—but she swallowed her feelings. She could not ruin David's future with an untimely rude remark.

David, she was proud to observe, was handling it all beautifully. He was confident but not arrogant, respectful but not ass-kissing. Hanson was silent as a tomb; he was leaning against Alison, sweaty and pale. Jessie, like Madeline, was watching everything warily. And Alison—well, Alison could have taken a little of her own advice. She was blab blabbing away to one of the A&R men, the one with the short brown hair, big nose, and cold eyes, the one Madeline considered the worst of the three. And Alison had rolled and lit so many joints practically everyone had one; the little room was choked with smoke. Well, Madeline thought, if it's too risky for me to say anything I'll just get stoned. And listen.

"...a wonderful variety," the VP was saying in his bass voice. "I recognized most of the songs from your tapes, but there were quite a few new ones as well."

"Five, actually," David said. "We have a lot more new songs, of course, but we wanted to play the old songs that the crowd knows."

"Was that the first time you played those new songs live?"

"It was the first time for three of them, yes."

"Well, you could have fooled me, because they all came off without a hitch. In fact, the entire set never sagged—you showed good judgment in your selection. Because, as you know, if you play too much new stuff you risk losing your crowd."

"And if you play too much old stuff," David said, "you risk just going through the motions."

"Exactly. It's a tricky balance." The VP took a lengthy hit off a joint. "I'll never forget, once I went to see Joe Jackson at The Beacon, and about midway through the set he played 'Is She Really Going Out with Him?'—you know, one of his biggest hits—and afterwards he said to the audience, 'Thank God that's over with.'"

Everyone laughed, but Alison and the other two A&R men acted as if the VP had just told the joke to end all jokes. Which reminded Madeline of the Monty Python sketch where a joke was so funny that everyone who heard it died from laughter, and so the military used it as a weapon, holding up German translations of the joke in order to kill the enemy. Madeline gave a bark of laughter; and this was long after everyone else had stopped. Alison gave her a warning look—oh, fuck you Alison, Madeline thought—but the VP winked at her, then took out a joint and passed it to her.

"As the prettiest woman in the club tonight I think you should have the honor of lighting this. It's Thai stick."

Madeline smiled at the VP, and gingerly took the joint from his outstretched hand. She put the joint in her mouth and David lit it for her. My goodness, she thought as she inhaled. It was nice, but strong; she felt as if she were floating two feet above the cushion. Which was disorienting, so she looked down at her legs to make sure no one could see up her dress. She was fine. And when she looked up David was looking at her and smiling, and for the first time she noticed three deep lines across his forehead.

Then, as if a signal had been given, the club owner and his friends left the room, and the VP started talking business. Madeline listened carefully as the VP told David, Hanson, and Jessie the step-by-step process of cutting a record; and as Madeline watched David's happy nods, saw Alison's beaming face, she understood that the VP was as good as promising Narrow Grave a contract. And in a subtle shift, David, Hanson, Jessie, Alison, and herself were no longer outside the charmed Super Cool circle; the two A&R men were suddenly solicitous and friendly and—a major shift—respectful. It was as if the VP had handed them all something, and that something was power. Power, and fame, and money. And then Madeline thought, Why are you including yourself and Alison? This is David and Hanson and Jessie's band, they're the ones being invited in. But it was so seductive sitting there and basking in the power-fame-money, because even though it was the men's band, flecks of good fortune flew off them and stuck to those around them—stuck to her, stuck to Alison.

And suddenly Madeline understood Alison's obsession with the band: Alison was not getting success from her own work, but via Narrow Grave she at least got to be around it, and perhaps even delude herself that it was hers. And maybe that was why Alison was the one constantly touting the band: David did not have to because it was all happening to him, and Hanson—well, Hanson was in some odd kind of denial, as if he did not think he deserved success. But Alison had to keep puffing the band because that's where she derived her importance; and since it was secondhand importance she had to work even harder at it. In Madeline's days of learning about nutrition she had been struck by the fact that after a meal of junk food your body wants to eat more because although you're full, you're not nourished. And that was Alison: full with Narrow Grave's success, but not nourished by it. And how could she be? It was not hers.

Madeline sat awhile inwardly scorning Alison, but then a little voice inside her asked, And what about you? How does David's success make you feel? Well, she said to herself. It makes me feel important. As if I'm in the center of things. But it also made her feel off-balance: David's success seemed so big, and her work so little. And she saw how one person's success could make another person's efforts seem—well, feeble. Writing every morning was not bringing the same results as David's music; certainly no one was coming up to *her* in Leo's Grandevous. But so what? Madeline thought, her anger flaring. So what? Her work was just as important as David's, and published or not it was still the same hard daily effort. And that moment, sitting on a red cushion in the green room, Madeline promised herself that she would not fall into the same trap as Alison. Obviously Narrow Grave was at the start of a wild, glamorous ride—she pictured them all on a roller coaster, their compartment just beginning to glide from its resting spot—but if she kept her head she would not confuse David and David's success with herself. If she kept her head, she would not eat food that did not nourish.

So maybe it was okay to be silent, maybe silence could be a sign of self-respect. Alison, on the other hand, was in the thick of the discussion, asking questions about what expenses The Big Record Label would incur—would they pay for voice lessons, for rehearsal space, for rent while the band was on tour? The VP answered, Alison asked something else—she's lost, Madeline thought, just completely lost. Madeline remembered Alison's unfinished painting, those ghoulish urchins staring through the window, and she felt sad, as sad as if one of her short stories was laying about neglected. And she felt angry at Hanson—why did he let Alison neglect her work? Was it so impossible for both of them to have full creative lives? I don't want a man like that, Madeline thought. I want a man like—well, like those paradigms of supportive mates, Virginia Woolf's husband Leonard, and George Eliot's companion George Henry Lewes. Those men had their own literary work, but they also stood by their women—so it was not true that one member of a couple always had to go under. Alison did not have to do what she was doing, and Hanson did not have to let her do it.

And David? He was very interested in Madeline's writing, and when he asked again to see her work she printed out copies of the seven stories she was sending around, and photocopied the three that had been published. He thanked her, but that was a week ago and he had not said anything since. Well, he had been busy preparing for the gig, she could not expect him to drop everything for her. But she was sure he would read them soon.

"…a million miles away. Madeline?"

She looked up. Everyone was staring at her; David had a hand on her knee and was smiling. "Hi," he said. "You okay?"

"That Thai stick is pretty strong," the VP said sympathetically.

"I'm fine," Madeline said, drawing her legs together tightly. "I was just thinking."

"About?" David asked.

"Oh…" She waved a hand in the air.

David laughed. "Madeline's a writer," he explained. "She was probably composing her next masterpiece."

"Are you published?" the VP asked.

"A few short stories."

"Good for you. It's a hard business."

"Harder than rock 'n' roll?"

He laughed. "Nothing is as hard as rock 'n' roll. Nothing. Well," he said, slapping his hands on his long thighs. "We better get going. So why don't we leave things like this: we have a few things to talk over with our number crunchers, then I'll be calling you guys. We'll have another informal meeting, then we'll start putting things on paper. Do you guys have a lawyer?"

David and Hanson exchanged looks. "No," David said.

"You need one. And a manager too—I don't know how you've survived so long without one. Well, we'll talk about all that next time."

He stood, and everyone else stood as well, although Madeline needed some assistance from David. Everyone shook hands, and as the VP shook Madeline's he winked at her and said, "Good luck with your writing. And take good care of David—he's about to make us a lot of money."

Madeline's mouth opened, and she found herself saying, "I think David can take care of himself."

The VP laughed. "You're probably right about that," he said.

They left the room. Alison grabbed Hanson and puffed her cheeks out as if she were about to scream; David put a finger to his lips. The door to the stairwell opened and closed, then Jessie ran to one of the front windows and opened the red Venetian blinds.

"The door's opening," Jessie said. "Now they're walking out…They stopped, they're stoned and can't remember where they parked…They're going right. Okay," he said, turning to the others. "They're out of earshot."

Whereupon Alison opened her mouth and let loose a scream of joy, and David picked up Madeline and swirled her around the room. "We did it!" he said. "It's really going to happen."

Madeline kicked her legs and pounded David's back. "Let go of me," she laughed. "Let go, I'm getting dizzy."

He dropped her in front of him, put a hand on either side of her head and gave her a big kiss on the lips. "We did it, Madeline," he said. "We did it."

"Congratulations," she said, running a hand over his sweaty hair. "You deserve it."

David kissed her again, then let her go. "Hanson," he said, clasping an arm around Hanson and giving him a hug. "We're on our way."

"Well," Hanson said, scratching his head. "Don't be too hasty; we haven't signed anything yet." But even he was smiling, Madeline saw; yes, even he was smiling.

❦   ❦   ❦

They left the Malibu Diner around three-thirty a.m. Alison had called a taxi, but David said he was keyed up and needed fresh air and would Madeline mind if he walked her home?

They were silent as they walked. Washington Street was empty; an occasional car passed, but there were no people, only streetlights and quiet brownstones. There was no breeze, and the bitter smell of coffee from the Maxwell House factory lingered in the air. Madeline walked with her arms wrapped tightly around her chest. It was a cold night, and her thin dress and thin wool coat offered no insulation against the chill. But she did not mind: she was happy and exhausted and only mildly stoned now that hours had passed and she had eaten well at the diner. She looked forward to the peace of her bed, looked forward to thinking over the night's events.

When they stopped in front of 821 Madeline expected David to peck her on the cheek and say good night, but instead he put his arms around her and lay her head on his shoulder, one hand moving lazily up and down her back.

"Tired?" he asked softly.

"Umm."

"I always keep you out so late. Does your sister mind?"

"My sister doesn't mind," she said. "But my brother-in-law is another story."

"He's protective of you."

"Very. He's Italian. Worse, Sicilian."

"I see."

She closed her eyes, and sank her nose into the scratchy black wool of his coat. His hand moved up her spine and came to the nape of her neck; he took two fingers and softly stroked his nails over her skin. She gave an involuntary murmur of pleasure.

"You're really sensitive here, aren't you?" he whispered next to her ear. "I remember that night at Hanson's, you nearly jumped out of your skin when I touched you here."

"Mmm."

Falling, falling, falling. He pressed her tighter to him, kissed her ear, and kept up that slow, hypnotizing scratching. She put her arms around his waist and snuggled her face deeper into his coat. I love him so much, she thought. He's so good and kind and I love him so much. She sank into that dark purple swirl, and it was just how she felt when she was on the bus fantasizing about him, only now she was in his arms, now she touched him and smelt him and the intensity was so strong she almost could not bear it.

"Madeline?"

"Hmm?"

"Can I tell you something?"

"What?"

"I want so badly to be inside you. When are you going to let me, hmm? When are you going to let me inside you?"

She felt something hot burst in her groin.

"I think about you all the time," he went on. "All the time, hmm? I can hardly play music, I can hardly work, all I do is think about you." He paused. "Do you think about me?"

"Mmm hmm."

"I thought you did. I knew you did. We're very attracted to each other, aren't we? Hmm, aren't we?"

She lifted her head and looked up at his face. "Yes," she whispered.

"So, look: tonight it's late, but tomorrow, why don't you come to my apartment? You've never been there."

"Tomorrow?"

"Why don't you come around one, that way we'll have gotten enough sleep. I live at 10 Willow Terrace, between Sixth and Seventh Street. Can you remember that?" She nodded. "Well, if you forget, I'm in the phone book."

"David?"

"What?"

"I'm just—I'm just glad I met you."

"I feel the same way. So you'll come tomorrow? I can expect you?"

"I'll be there. At one."

"Good."

He bent forward and kissed her on the mouth, then softly withdrew.

"You better go in," he said. "I don't want your brother-in-law coming after me with a knife."

"Okay," she laughed.

They said good night. He waited for her to go in; she waved at him from the foyer, and he walked away. And later, in her room laying on the bed, pressing her pillow against her chest and stomach, Madeline thought about David and all the pleasure he was about to bring her. Pleasure, not pain.

CHAPTER 9

Sex

Madeline opened her eyes.

Sunlight filled her little room—or rather, was trying to: brightness pressed up against the shade, throwing a muted yellow rectangle on the ruby red carpet. She could hear cars on Washington Street, but everyone was driving in a Sunday morning way, without horns, without screeching brakes.

She looked at the clock: a little after ten. Bella and Robert were not home; they were spending the day in Brooklyn with Robert's family, and had left before nine. Thank God they're not here, Madeline thought, because otherwise Bella would ask about last night, and ask when she was seeing David again.

"Today. At one," Madeline would say, avoiding Bella's eyes.

"Oh. Do you have any special plans? Because if not he can come over here."

"Actually we were planning on hanging out at his place."

"Hanging out at his place. I see." Pause. "It's too soon, Maddy. You've only been dating him two weeks, it's much too soon to sleep with him."

But I want to! Madeline said to herself, rolling over in bed and staring at her bookshelves. I want to. Talking isn't the only way of getting to know someone. And besides, we have been talking; for two weeks that's all we've been doing. She rose to a sitting position and hugged her knees. Well, it was too late now: it was going to happen, and that was that. Bella was much too suspicious of men, but it was her own fault: the only men Bella had slept with were Deadheads, and what could you possibly expect from men like that? Bella's one semi-stable relationship had been with a guy who made and sold beaded necklaces; for awhile they had joined forces at Dead shows, then Bella got bored with him and slept with his best friend. Then when Bella stopped traveling with the Dead she became the most ferociously celibate person on the face of the earth; finally she met Robert, but she only slept with him after months of intense scrutiny. And now Bella wanted Madeline to do the same with David. But I'm not you, Bella, Madeline pleaded. I'm not you, and I don't have to do to David what you did to Robert.

Okay. Time for strategy. First a shower, because her hair and skin smelt like old party. Then a hot steamy bath to relax her muscles and clear her head, which was still foggy from last night's Thai stick. Then get dressed, drink tea. And dig up her diaphragm—it was in her room somewhere, probably rusted from lack of use. And what should she wear? Nothing fancy, just jeans, a T-shirt, and sweater. She closed her eyes, remembering David and what he had said last night, how she had felt in his arms... What a powerful force this attraction was, and what a relief to finally, finally give in to it.

She got out of bed, went to the bathroom, and took a hot shower. She washed every inch of her body three times and washed her hair twice, afterwards using Bella's expensive papaya conditioner which Bella usually hid but today foolishly left in the bathroom. Then she wrapped her hair in a towel and drew a hot bath, so hot it hurt when she sat, but after a minute the hot seeped into her bones and she felt great. Bella kept a small bottle of olive oil for bath oil; Madeline poured a little in the water, then lay her head back and thought about David.

After her bath she went into Bella and Robert's room and blow-dried her hair in front of their big mirrored bureau. As an afterthought she dropped her towel and stood naked in front of the mirror. Well, not bad; her breasts were nobody's definition of perky, but Bella always said don't worry, big breasts never go out of style. And otherwise she was slender, no longer the stick figure she was at Swan's Cove. Suddenly she remembered all that: the meditation, the prayer, the fasting; Thomas Merton, carrot juice, rebirthing. "What was I *doing*?" she asked her reflection. "What on earth was I *thinking*?" She was planets away from that mentality now; hard to believe it was only a month since she had returned from Swan's Cove, but so it was.

She went into her room and, naked on her bed, negotiated the very tricky business of trimming her pubic hair. Then she dressed in jeans, a dark blue T-shirt, and an oversized grey sweater she had permanently borrowed from Robert. Then she rummaged in her closet and found, nestled amongst canceled checks and old jewelry, her diaphragm and a tube of spermicide. She checked the expiration date on the spermicide—still a few months to go, thank God. She looked at the clock: twenty minutes past eleven.

She sat at the kitchen counter and drank a cup of tea. She debated calling Rose or Devon, but it was still early and anyway it seemed rather childish to call them and get all giggly about the fact that she was two hours away from being naked in bed with David. She went to her room and tried to read, but after five minutes jumped up and went into the living room. She sat at Bella's piano and idly banged out a few chords, then she went into the TV room and turned on the TV. She jumped from channel to channel, then turned off the set; she went to her room, made her bed, dusted her bookshelves, put her dirty clothes in the bathroom hamper. She moved to the kitchen and ate a piece of Italian bread. She looked at the clock: noon. On the dot.

She went into the TV room and threw herself on the couch. Should she leave now and walk around town until it was time? No—she'd get sweaty, and perhaps be tempted to stop in somewhere and get something to eat, and she hated having sex on a full stomach. Should she try to read again? No, she was too worked up to concentrate. She sighed, and crossed her arms over her chest. This was ridiculous—she had to calm down. She closed her eyes and made herself think about the story she was writing, but somehow the story made her think of David. Okay, she thought. You win. So she closed her eyes and thought of him, thought of what it would be like to make love with him.

At twelve-thirty she realized that her diaphragm and the big tube of spermicide would not fit in the little black handbag she used for work. And her bookbag was too big, which meant she had nothing else. She considered stuffing everything in her coat pockets but what if, horror of horrors, something fell out when she was walking down the street, or when David was hanging up her coat? She went to the small storage room next to Bella and Robert's bedroom, searching for something to use. There was a knapsack, but it was too bulky and anyway she was not going camping. There was a pink plastic shopping bag, big and tacky—forget it. And there was what could only have been Bella's purse during her hippie days, a leather bag shaped like a teardrop, with a thick shoulder strap and multi-colored beads sewn on the seams. It was appalling but, who knew, perhaps it was so out-of-date it was back in style. She brought the purse into her room and put in her plastic diaphragm case, the spermicide, the little plastic spermicide inserter in case they had sex more than once in six hours (she should be so lucky) and, as an afterthought, a fresh pair of underwear—because sex, for females at least, was often a messy business.

Twelve forty-five. She could leave now if she walked slowly. She went into the bathroom and brushed her hair, then grabbed her coat and the hideous bag and let herself out. She had just finished locking the second lock when she heard above her, "Hello, Madeline."

Oh no—Michael. He was walking down the stairs wearing a dark blue wool coat, obviously on his way out. Oh God, he was the last person she wanted to see!

"Hi Michael."

"Going out?"

"Yep. You too?"

"I'm meeting some friends in The City. Professor Tummel—you remember him, you met him at one of the lectures. He's the one with the limp."

"Right, I remember."

"And you?" he asked as they walked down the stairs. "Where are you off to?"

"To see David."

He nodded.

Michael opened the front door and they walked down the stoop. It was a fresh, blustery day, both sunny and windy.

"You're walking downtown?" Michael asked. "Because I am too."

"You're not taking the bus?"

"They live in Soho, so I'm taking the PATH." He smiled. "If you prefer I can cross the street and walk on the other side."

"Oh, don't be ridiculous. Come on."

She stalked off down Washington Street. They were across the street from Vito's Deli when Michael said, "Madeline, what on earth is wrong with you?"

"What do you mean, what's wrong with me?"

"You're acting very strange."

"I am not."

"Yes, you are. You're not only carrying that horrible leather purse, but you're clutching it as if someone wants to steal it. Which no one does, I can assure you. And you have this stricken look on your face, like a deer caught in headlights."

From his tone of voice she knew he was teasing her, but she was not in the mood to be teased. "Stop it, Michael," she barked. "And if you want to walk with me, hurry up."

"Are you in a hurry?"

"Not particularly."

"So why should we hurry?"

"Because you're so slow."

"I see. That makes sense."

"You know, Michael, no one else alive is as slow as you. I can't believe you're even able to function in the modern world. Aren't you afraid of getting hit by a car, or a bus?"

"I'm more afraid of getting hit by that purse of yours, the way you're swinging it. What on earth do you have in there, anyway?"

"Nothing."

"Oh, I see. You must be carrying it because it's so fashionable."

She stopped. "Michael, you are making me so pissed off. And stop smiling."

"I can't help it. You're very funny this morning."

"It's not morning."

"Sorry—you're very funny this early afternoon."

She sighed, and continued walking.

"How is the writing coming along?" he asked.

"Pretty well. I'm almost done with my new story. You know, the one about the father destroying the piano."

"Good. When will you be ready to read it to us?"

"Mmm, maybe a month. A month and a half. And you? What's going on with your sutra?"

"I'm about midway through the third draft. I've been having trouble with one section but yesterday I had a breakthrough. So things are going well."

"You're so lucky. I mean, you write something, and you know it'll get published."

"That's only because I've published before. It wasn't like that when I started, believe me. And besides, I'm forty. You're only twenty-seven; your day will come."

"You think so?"

"I know so. So don't worry."

They reached Seventh and Washington. "I go right here," she said.

"And I go straight. I'll see you tomorrow night then, for Scrabble?"

"Of course. And get some Rainforest Crunch, that's my new favorite flavor."

"All right. Good-bye, Madeline."

"Bye."

She turned right onto Seventh Street, walking by well-kept brownstones and small stores, but she was so caught up in nervous excitement she did not see anything. Her mind was racing with disjointed thoughts—she thought about Rainforest Crunch, then about rainforests, then about a picture of Sting standing next to Amazon natives with big plates in their lower lips, she wondered if that hurt, of course it did, did they ever take the plates out and if so what did their lips look like, it must hurt, the waitress at East LA with the pierced nose, does it hurt to get your nose pierced?, if it hurts to get your ear pierced of course it hurts to get your nose pierced, I forgot to wear earrings, never mind...

She was in front of David's building. A small brownstone with a tiny front yard with flowers and, oh no but oh yes, two plastic elves. It was funny that David should live on this weird little side street, a place Madeline imagined inhabited by elderly Irish women and retired cops. She walked to the door and saw two doorbells: BRIDGET HARRIGAN (so I was right, she thought) and D. GUGGENHEIM. She pushed David's doorbell, and waited.

She heard a door open and shut, heard feet running down the stairs, then the door opened and there he was. His eyes were puffy as if he had just woken up, but his hair was clean and he was wearing jeans and a dark red button-down shirt. He motioned Madeline inside. To the right was a door with a big cardboard shamrock, and in front a short staircase. They went up the staircase; there was a tiny landing, then the stairs turned left and at the top of the stairs was a door.

"My place," David said.

He opened the door. It was a small apartment: you walked directly into the living room, and to the right was a kitchen separated from the living room by a counter with stools, and to the left there was a closed door which Madeline assumed led to the bedroom. The apartment was surprisingly simple and airy and—given that David was a man—shockingly neat. It was beautiful, even. There was a dark grey carpet that was not cheap, a plush blue couch with matching armchairs, a round coffee table made of good, solid wood. And there were pillows on the couch, plump cream pillows with blue, grey, and purple stripes. The walls were white and unmarred by handprints and anonymous stains, and there were carefully hung framed posters: a poster of a shirtless Jim Morrison with the caption "AN AMERICAN POET," a poster from a Bowie concert in Germany, another from a Clash concert in Cleveland, and several of those funky psychedelic posters done in the sixties in San Francisco—Madeline had seen pictures of them in one of Bella's books on the Dead. The coffee table had a few dust-free knickknacks—a blue box with gold stars and moons, a black onyx ashtray, a magic eight ball, and one of those triangular wooden puzzles with nine holes and eight pegs. And look at that kitchen, she thought as David helped take off her jacket. It was clean. There were dark grey hand towels hanging on pegs. The stools were covered with a pretty dark blue cloth with purple circles. And he had appliances, good ones; at that very moment the coffeemaker was gurgling, sending the bracing scent of coffee throughout the apartment.

Madeline looked at David suspiciously: this did not look like a man's apartment.

"Well," he said, taking her hand. "Do you like it?"

"Like it? It's beautiful. And it's so clean."

"I try."

"Did your mother help you do all this?"

"My mother?" He laughed. "Of course not. I did it myself, it was easy." He reached out and tweaked her nose. "You look surprised."

"Well, it's just—I mean, after seeing Hanson and Alison's place…"

"Oh God, I could never live like that. Come over to the couch, sit. Do you want something to drink? Some tea?"

"Tea would be nice."

He went over to the kitchen, filled a kettle, and put it on the stove. Madeline nearly fainted when he opened a cabinet and pulled out matching blue mugs. He's a—he's a *housewife*, she thought. It was such a shock for her: she had expected grime and slime and rock 'n' roll indifference, and instead to find a man, an artist, living like this—it was different. It was nice. The only other men she knew who lived in such nice places were Robert and Michael, but Robert had Bella and Michael was Michael, so they hardly counted. But come to think of it, David was a very clean person: his clothes were always neat and pressed, and his hair always freshly washed. He's a serious person, she thought, watching him watch the coffeemaker. He takes himself seriously, and he lives like an adult. And for a moment she felt a little ashamed of herself, ashamed of her small room and the fact that besides living in Swan's Cove she had never had her own place.

David brought the mugs over to the table—on a tray, with a white ceramic sugar bowl and a matching milk pitcher! Then he went over to the stereo system that was neatly enclosed in low bookshelves; he flicked a few switches, put in a cassette—Neil Young's *After the Gold Rush*—then sat next to her.

"I only had black tea," he said. "Maybe you would have preferred herbal?"

"This is fine."

She watched as he measured off a careful teaspoon of sugar and put it in his coffee. He took a long sip, then reached for the blue box with the gold stars and moons. He opened the box, and her heart sank when she saw an ounce of pot, rolling paper, and other smoking paraphernalia. I cannot get high, she thought. No way, no how, not now. But she said nothing.

"So," he said, taking out the rolling paper and pot. "Any problems with your brother-in-law last night?"

"No, not at all."

He turned to her and smiled. "I don't want to be a bad influence on you."

"You don't have to take it personally. Robert never likes it when I go on dates. I don't know why—maybe it's an Italian thing. He used to be okay about it, but the last few years he's really been overbearing."

"I picture this big hairy guy in a white tank top chasing you into your room and locking the door."

She laughed, her eyes on David's hands as he rolled the joint. "No, no, you're completely wrong. Robert's an English professor at Columbia. He's extremely Italian, but Italian in the wiry intense way; you know, DeNiro-ish. And how about you? Did you get any sleep last night or were you so excited you couldn't sleep? Excited about the record deal, I mean."

"You know, Hanson called about an hour ago. He said both he and Alison were so stoned last night that they woke up today and thought maybe they had dreamed it all, so I had to assure them it really happened. But I don't know—it may sound odd, or arrogant, but I always knew this would happen. From the beginning, from the moment I first picked up my bass—do you know what I mean?"

"Umm—sort of."

"I mean, I'm happy. I'm really happy. But I expected it."

"So when the VP said an informal meeting, what did he mean?"

"I don't know. It's odd, these guys have their own vocabulary; they might know exactly what they mean by an informal meeting, but I have no clue."

"He told me you were going to make a lot of money for them."

"That's pretty typical of the kind of things they say. But the VP's a good guy; I like him."

"The other guys—" Madeline wrinkled her nose.

"Bastards. Stuck-up snobs with nothing to be stuck-up about. Is that what you mean?"

"Something like that."

He shook his head. "I can't stand them, but I can't let on."

"Oh no, you were great with them. I was impressed."

"Oh, you were?" he said teasingly. He lit the joint, took two deep puffs, and passed it to her. "Well, if I impressed you, then it was worth it."

She took the joint, and hesitated. Devon always said that whenever she got high all she wanted to do was have sex, whereas when Madeline got high sex was the last thing on her mind. But if it's good pot, she thought as she brought the joint to her lips, it should be okay, right? She took a hit, blew it out quickly, took a smaller hit and held it in.

They smoked without speaking. As Madeline got stoned, the music seemed more poignant and liquid, and the clean little room appeared—well, beautiful. There was a rhythm and grace to the colors; they were pleasing, strong but not jarring, and all the different accents—the maroon in the Bowie poster, the bright yellow of the kettle—stood out like splashes of colored light.

"This room," she said to David, her voice sounding strange and far away, "this room is exactly like one of your songs."

He looked at her. "What do you—no, I know what you mean. Thank you."

She smiled at him. He stubbed out the roach in the ashtray, then turned to face her, moving one knee onto the couch. He reached out a hand and stroked her hair.

"No hairstyle today, hmm? But your hair is nice down like this."

Madeline looked at the ashtray. David moved his hand to the back of her neck, then he leaned forward and kissed the side of her face. She did not move. He took her chin in his hand and turned her face so she was looking at him.

"You," he whispered, gazing into her eyes, "are very shy, and very difficult. Don't you want me to kiss you?"

"I do."

"Well, then you have to kiss me back. Unless you don't want to."

"No, I do."

Still holding her chin, he leaned forward and put his lips on hers. She inhaled sharply, and the smell of him—so clean and fresh, from soap, shampoo, his clothes, she didn't know what—made her dizzy, intoxicated. He kissed her again, this time putting his tongue in her mouth. He moved a hand to her lower back and pressed her towards him. She kissed him back, and the pleasure was so sharp it was all she could do not to whimper. She put her hands on his shoulder blades, and as their kissing deepened she tightened her hold and pressed against him. Then her hands started wandering: she touched his arms, his hair, his face—he was delicious, so masculine and hard and clean, with a nice smell and such fine white skin.

He pulled back a little. "Should we go into the bedroom?" he asked.

She nodded. But instead of moving they fell into kissing, and this time he leaned forward against her until she was laying back on the couch. He moved his body on top of hers, and she felt his hard penis against her groin. Her whole body jolted with the shock, and it was as if a wildness released within her. She pressed against him and kissed him passionately, wildly, one hand deep in his hair, the other pulling out his shirt, then moving under his shirt to scratch his back. He responded just as passionately, deepening his kisses, moving his hands over her breasts, her hips, her rear. As they kissed he pushed his penis against her; she moved one leg up and around his back, arching herself against him.

"So maybe you're not so shy, hmm?" he whispered in her ear. "I guess I should have known, hmm? You're so beautiful, Madeline, you're so beautiful… Let me take you into the bedroom, hmm? Let me make love to you."

She nodded. David rose and held out his hand to her; she took it, and he pulled her until she was standing. He moved to the bedroom door, trailing her behind him, and as he touched the doorknob she put her arms around his waist, leaned forward and gently bit the back of his neck. He turned around and grabbed her; he pulled up one of her legs and held it as he pressed his penis against her. He put his other hand on the back of her head and brought her face close to his; he kissed her passionately, roughly, his tongue deep in her mouth. She put her hands on his shoulders and pressed against him, moving up and down against his penis. He put his hands on either side of her head and held her slightly away from him. His eyes were wild and intense, and he was breathing so hard he was almost panting.

"You want me," he said, his groin moving against hers. "You want me, don't you? Hmm, don't you?"

"I do," she said weakly. "I do."

"You're really something, you know that? You're not shy at all, are you?"

She shook her head no.

He brought her face close to his, then put his mouth on her ear and kissed it, bit it. "I'm not letting you out of my sight. You're with me from now on, okay?"

"Okay."

His hand fumbled for the doorknob, he found it and opened the door. Madeline had a few brief impressions of the room—light pouring through two large windows, a bed with a dark blue cover, a bookcase—but she did not care about any of that, she just found her way to the bed, never taking her eyes off David as he pulled the curtains closed. It seemed an eternity until he was next to her again, until she was wrapped once more in that clean warm hardness, but—finally, here he was, he sat next to her on the bed and pulled her into his arms. They wrapped their arms around each other, kissing furiously; he kicked off his shoes, then pulled her onto the bed and lay himself on top of her. She had one hand in his hair—that beautiful thick brown hair—and with the other she began unbuttoning his shirt. He had one hand on her waist and with the other he was tugging her sweater, then her T-shirt, up and over her head. He had trouble with her bra, so she reached back and unhooked it for him. He took off his shirt, and the feel of his naked chest on hers was wonderful, delicious. She ran her hands up and down his back—he was solid and strong, firm without being muscle-bound. His skin was fine and white, silky and healthy and warm. He's gorgeous, she thought, just completely gorgeous.

He lifted his lips from hers and moved back. "I want to look at you," he said. He reached out his hands and moved her arms above her head, holding her wrists in one hand. He ran his free hand over her breasts, ribs, and waist, then looked her in the eye and smiled. "You're beautiful," he whispered. He lowered his head and put his mouth on her nipple; his free hand ran over her other breast, then traveled down between her legs. He moved his mouth to her other nipple, and the pleasure was so intense she dug her nails into his back and wrapped her legs around his waist.

He lifted his head. "I don't think we can wait any longer," he said. He moved towards the head of the bed and reached over to the bedside table, opened a drawer and fumbled around until he found a condom.

"Oh no," Madeline said. "I brought something—my diaphragm."

"But we can use these."

"Sometimes they break."

"Okay." He kissed her nose. "Why don't you go put it in?"

"All right."

She could not leave him that easily; they kissed awhile longer, then he whispered in her ear, "Go."

Shy to walk in front of him barechested, Madeline grabbed her sweater from the floor and held it to her breasts, then rose and went into the living room. She took her leather purse from the couch, then stopped. She could not imagine sailing back into the bedroom, throwing off her pants, spreading her legs, and inserting her diaphragm right in front of him. Maybe later, but not now. She went into the bathroom which was, not surprisingly, scrupulously clean. The walls were crimson, the floor black and white tile, and there were black, white, and crimson checked towels hung neatly on a brass towel rack. Madeline peed, then lay a towel on the floor and sat down. She took out the white plastic container, flicked it open with her thumb, then took out her diaphragm. Balancing it on her knee, she put the plastic container back in her purse and took out the spermicide. She squeezed spermicide into the diaphragm until there was a healthy dollop in the center. Oh fuck, she thought. I should have taken my pants off first, now I'll get spermicide on everything. She put the diaphragm on her sweater, then took off her jeans. Laying on her back, she picked up her diaphragm and spread the spermicide around the edges; then she spread her legs, pinched the diaphragm so it folded, and with a swift movement sent it along its way. She put a finger in her vagina to make sure the diaphragm was covering her cervix, and that was that.

She was ready.

She stood up to wash her hands, and when she glimpsed herself in the mirror she hardly recognized herself: her hair was a sexy mess, her eyes burned, and her lips appeared about twice their normal size. She put on her pants, put all birth control paraphernalia back in her purse, hung up the towel. Again with the sweater to her chest she left the bathroom; she dropped her purse on the couch, then walked through the living room and into the bedroom.

David was laying on the bed naked, his hands behind his head. Madeline sat on the bed, and everything happened quickly: her sweater was on the floor, her pants thrown in a corner, she was on her back with her legs spread and he was above her, leaning on his elbows, his eyes burning into hers. He put his hand on his penis and was guiding it into her, when suddenly she was gripped by a horrible thought:

This man is a stranger.

She was scared; she did not want to have sex. Going to the bathroom and dealing with the practicalities of birth control had broken the fever of her passion, and now she was just Madeline, just naked and scared. But before she could open her mouth and tell him to stop, he thrust inside her; her body snapped back with the pain. Then he was moving, moving inside her; he pressed his mouth to her ear and started a steady stream of talk—she was beautiful, she was so wet, she was so sweet, so hot; she was perfect for him, she was just what he liked, all he wanted was to be inside her, to be inside her like this, wasn't it beautiful, wasn't it sweet... She turned her head to the wall and closed her eyes. Her hips were moving, her fingers were digging into his back, but she was in the grip of an almost hysterical panic. Some women were tough enough—or bold enough, free enough, whatever it was—to have sex just for the sake of sex, but Madeline was not like that. She was too wounded, too sensitive and afraid. She knew what it was like to be touched by men who did not love her; it was a horrible, empty feeling, and she never wanted to feel that way again. So what was she doing? Why was she here with this David? A sob escaped her, but he must have thought it was from pleasure: "…you like it, don't you? You want this, don't you? You're beautiful, Madeline, you're so beautiful to make love to. And you're so hot inside, how come you're so hot…" The pictures from the Magic Gallery flashed into her mind, and it all seemed so wrong, so terribly wrong. She hardly knew David, and he hardly knew her—he didn't even know Bella, for God's sake, and he hadn't even read any of her stories. And then, thank God, he stopped: he shuddered a long minute, his eyes closed, his head thrown back. Then he collapsed on top of her, his face buried in her shoulder. Madeline opened her eyes and looked at the wall. Well, she thought. It's over. I'll wait a few minutes, then get up and go home. Bella will be back soon, I'll just hold on till then.

"Madeline?"

She turned towards him. He had lifted his face, and was looking at her.

"Hi," he said, tweaking her nose.

"Hi."

He kissed her shoulder, then raised himself onto his elbows. "You okay?" he asked.

"Mmm."

"I feel great." He reached out his hand and stroked her hair. "You're so beautiful. I love you."

"What did you say?"

"I said I love you."

A flicker of hope. "You love me?"

"Of course I love you. You're such a beautiful girl. And you're intelligent and you're sensitive and you're funny. I love you."

"Oh, David," she said, putting out her hand and touching his face. "I love you too. Do you really love me?"

He laughed. "I wouldn't say it if I didn't."

A tender happiness spread through her. Maybe things would be okay after all; maybe this would work out. She smiled, and buried her face in his chest.

"So tell me," he said, kissing the crown of her head. "When did you realize you loved me? Just now?"

"Oh no," she said, raising herself up so she could meet his eye. "It was that night at Helmers' when you kissed my palm. That's when I knew."

"I knew the moment I saw you. I remember Hanson and I walked into Spencer's apartment, I saw you sitting on the windowsill and I thought, 'I have to have her.'" He kissed her nose.

"But you must meet tons of women all the time. I mean, like at last night's gig, there were so many women."

"Yes, but they're not women I'd like to be with. I don't sleep with groupies; I don't like women who've passed through a lot of hands."

Oh well, she thought. Guess I won't be telling him about my past anytime soon.

"Not that I want to go out with a virgin," he went on. "It's just that a lot of women who hang out at the gigs—well, they've kind of been around. Alison was like that."

Madeline widened her eyes. "Alison?"

"Alison was one of the biggest groupies in Boston. I'm probably the only musician who never slept with her."

"And Hanson?"

David sighed. "Hanson needed someone. His family is pretty fucked-up, he's always been lonely. Then Alison just kind of came into his life and took over. She stopped sleeping around, but we're forever playing double bills with her ex-lovers. It's pretty hard on Hanson."

"I can imagine."

"You, on the other hand," he said, kissing her. "There's something very pure about you."

"Well, I think it's a mistake to think I'm inexperienced, David."

"No, I know that. I don't know—maybe it's more emotional than physical. There's something very ladylike about you. But you're not ladylike in bed, which is good. Speaking of which," he said, moving her a little so she could feel his hard penis. "If you're not too tired…"

"I'm not tired."

"I love you, Madeline," he said, looking her straight in the eyes. "I am completely, totally in love with you."

"I feel the same way about you."

"So let's make love again."

❧   ❧   ❧

Hours later Madeline laid under the bedcovers, her head resting on David's chest, on the soft spot under his collarbone. She felt happy, very happy; she knew now that everything was going to work out just fine.

She looked up at David's face. Still sleeping. But she could not sleep; she was too excited by the good fortune that had upended her life. He loves me, she thought. He really loves me. And I love him, too. He's different from the other guys I've met in Hoboken—he's serious, he's on his way career-wise, he's organized and hard-working. Not to mention intelligent, funny, interesting, kind, attentive. He's a good person. She smiled, and rubbed her nose into his chest. All of that, and now there was also the miracle of physical contact. What sweet relief to be in a man's arms after so many years of loneliness. True, she had occasionally slept with her old high school flame, but sex once every six months or so could never give her the reassuring feeling she had now. Only a person who has lived years without physical contact could imagine the ache and need that had built up in her. And behind that ache and need were the sexual wounds from high school, and behind those wounds were the years in Spam and Polly's sick sphere, years without touch, years without affection. How have I survived all this time? she wondered. And actually the answers were simple: Bella's love, and the security of life in the apartment; and on a physical level masturbation, and an ability to subjugate her sexuality. But now there was no need to hold back her sexual feelings, now there was no need to live in that strange, neutered state—because now she had David.

They had made love how many times? Five, six, seven? She had lost count. David was not a man who lasted a long time, but he had amazing powers of recovery, and over the course of a few hours they had gone through half a tube of spermicide. He was very intense during sex—either he talked in her ear without pause, or he held himself above her and stared into her eyes. She would even venture to say he was a little rough; he moved inside her quickly, forcefully, and it was only during the third or fourth time that she understood he was hitting exactly the right spot. She raised herself up to meet him, feeling small waves of pleasure each time he thrust into her—thrust after thrust, the waves growing and growing and then, what sweetness when that first orgasm flowed up and through her. She threw back her head and let her body melt away. And another time as she was coming David said, "Look at me, open your eyes and look at me," and she had stared into his eyes, holding onto his shoulders as her body buckled beneath him. It was an incredibly intimate moment; afterwards she felt shy, and had turned away from him and buried her face in a pillow. He pressed himself against her back and started kissing her neck and shoulders, stroking her hair and whispering in her ear about how she made him feel, about how much he wanted her, on and on until she was once again on her back and he was inside her. Then he had fallen asleep, but she did not mind; her body was a little shocked by all the action, she could already feel a tight soreness in her vagina—another round of sex might have proved painful.

She looked at the clock on the bedside table. A few minutes after six. Outside there was still a little light; the bedroom glowed a strange grey-yellow from the sunset seeping in through the curtains. She ran her eyes around the room. The walls were papered a rich eggplant purple, and the carpet was navy blue. The wall to the right of the bed had a large built-in closet, the wall opposite had a bureau, the door to the living room, a carefully placed bass and an electric blue amplifier. The wall on the left of the bed had a low bookshelf; Madeline peered through the half-light to read the titles of the books. In any new house she always went straight to the bookshelves—she remembered the first time she and Bella and Robert had gone to Michael's apartment, she had walked around for half an hour with her head tilted to the side, reading book spines. David had about three hundred books, and from what she could see they were all about music. A few books on songwriting, books on the history of rock, a lot of biographies, but the majority were songbooks, the music and words of the Beatles, the Doors, the Police, the Byrds, Elvis Costello, Neil Young, Creedance Clearwater Revival, Talking Heads, Bob Dylan, Crosby, Stills & Nash, the Clash, Dire Straits, R.E.M., The Cure—everyone. And all well-thumbed and all—here was that housewife thing again—arranged in alphabetical order. David had once told her that he could play anything, and if these books were any indication, he most definitely could. Again, she was impressed.

The top of the bookshelves were covered with knickknacks and a few framed photographs. The largest picture was of his family: David, his mother, his father, his two sisters. They look so normal, Madeline thought as she studied their attractive, well-adjusted smiling faces. But then he had said his family was normal, hadn't he. And speaking of normal, she had to wonder: Was it a little weird to have a picture of his family here, in the bedroom? Oh, stop it Madeline! she told herself. You can't judge other people by yourself. Bella's apartment did not have a single picture of Spam and Polly, and Madeline certainly could not imagine putting a picture of those tight unhappy faces in her bedroom. But obviously David's family did not paralyze him; obviously their benevolent gaze did not interfere with his lovemaking. Still, Madeline would at least have thrown a sweater over them. Well, never mind. Two of the other pictures were of David and Hanson playing music, and in another picture David was shaking—Madeline peered closer—Joe Strummer's hand. Hmm—she'd have to ask him about that one. There were no pictures of women or any other lingering memories from other relationships. In fact she had not seen anything that indicated a woman's presence, or even female visitors. But David would not have lied to her: she had asked him if he was seeing anyone else, he had said no and she believed him. She had no reason not to. Anyway from what David had said it seemed he was somewhat picky—she could not imagine an endless stream of women going in and out of his apartment.

The phone rang. David opened his eyes, shook his head. He simultaneously kissed her and reached a hand over to the bedside table to pick up the receiver.

"Hello?…Hey, Hanson." He drew Madeline into his arms, put his chin on the top of her head. "No, not much…Madeline's here, we're hanging out…I'll ask her." He cupped the receiver with his hand. "Are you hungry?"

She looked up at him and nodded.

"Do you want to meet Hanson and Alison at East LA?"

"Okay."

"She says fine…Okay, at seven…About a quarter of an ounce. You want me to bring it?… I'll roll a few joints…No, that's okay…All right, we'll see you at seven."

He hung up the phone and pulled her so she was laying on top of him, her face just above his.

"How do you feel?" he asked, running his hand through her hair.

"Happy."

"You look it. Listen, after dinner, do you want to come back here?"

"Oh—I don't think I can. The temp agency called me on Friday, I have a two-day assignment at The Big Cigarette Company. I should go home, get a good night's sleep."

"Don't tell me I have to wait until Tuesday night to see you again."

"Well—it looks that way. I can't meet you at ten-thirty the night before work."

"I wish you didn't have to work. I wish you were here all the time, waiting for me."

She laughed. "Well, I have to work. I may not pay rent, but I need money for books, clothes. And savings."

"What are you saving for?"

"Mmm—I don't know. I just save. I spent a lot of my savings when I was living down the shore, so now I want to build it up again."

"You're lucky you don't pay rent."

"How much do you pay?"

"Three hundred fifty."

"That's great. I mean, for a place of your own, without a roommate. Unless you consider Bridget Harrigan your roommate."

He laughed. "Not exactly, no."

"What's she like?"

"Well, let's see—she's in her sixties, she's got flaming red hair and she wears really tight clothes. Lots of cleavage. And she has a boyfriend—Paddy Muldoon, a retired cop. But the best thing about Bridget is, she has no sense of smell."

"What do you mean?"

"She smoked for thirty years, and somewhere along the line she lost her sense of smell. She quit a long time ago, but it never came back. Which means she has no idea when I'm getting high."

"But what about Paddy Muldoon?"

"He's usually here in the evenings when I'm out. But if he's ever noticed anything, he hasn't said a word. He and Bridget are my buddies; they think I'm great."

"So tell me, what's with the elves?"

"Lucky and Leapy?"

"They have names?"

"They're gifts from Paddy; they protect the house."

"This is a pretty wild scene here at 10 Willow Terrace, wouldn't you say?"

"Between me and Bridget and Lucky and Leapy, I suppose so." He kissed her. "Are you getting tired up there hanging over me?"

"No. It's nice being on top."

"We didn't get around to that, did we? Next time."

"Next time," she laughed.

"I didn't hurt you, did I?"

"No. I mean, I'm a little sore, but that's only normal. It's been awhile."

"It's been awhile for me, too."

"How long?"

"A little over three months."

"Three months!" she laughed. "For me it's been more like three years. Well, two and a half, to be exact."

"And that's one of the things I like about you."

"So maybe it's better if we don't see each other until Tuesday. I think I need a little time to recover."

He sighed dramatically. "If you say so. I suppose I can hold out till then."

"I guess you'll just have to."

"But I'll be thinking about you," he said, running a finger along her cheekbone. "Will you be thinking about me?"

"Mmm hmm."

"And we can at least talk on the phone. What time will you get home from work?"

"I'm working from eight-thirty to four-thirty, so I should be back around five-fifteen, five-thirty."

"So I'll call you before I go to rehearsal. Listen, it's almost seven, we should get up and get dressed. And I need to take a quick shower. Are you any good at rolling joints?"

"No."

"Well, we'll be a little late then. We can smoke as I roll. Do you want to take a shower too?"

"I think I should."

"Well then, we'll have to do it together, won't we?"

"Your bathroom is so clean, I'm afraid I'll make a mess."

"Don't worry about it, I'll clean up."

He got out of bed, opened the closet, and took out a thick white bathrobe. As Madeline watched him she suddenly remembered that awful thought: *This man is a stranger.* Well, clearly she had been wrong. It had just been some sort of blind panic, because she certainly did not feel like that now.

The bathrobe over one arm, David came to the bed and held out a hand.

"Come with me," he said.

CHAPTER 10

On Call

Madeline was on call.

Which meant it was seven-thirty on a Monday morning, and she was sitting in the temp office wearing a plaid skirt, white cotton blouse, short black jacket, black stockings, and low black heels. She had signed in on the clipboard at the receptionist's desk (Madeline Boot, Displaywrite 4, 7:25 a.m.), then sat in a molded plastic chair and pulled out the tea she had bought at a nearby deli. Five other people were also on call, but they did not speak to Madeline and Madeline did not speak to them.

After battling the crowds at Port Authority, then battling the crowds as she walked across Forty-first Street, it would have been nice to sit somewhere a little inspiring. The temp office, however, could not have been uglier: the carpet was dull grey, the walls beige, the chairs also grey not to mention plastic and connected, and there was not a single poster on the wall unless you counted the framed notice that said TIME SLIPS MUST BE IN BY 6:00 P.M. THURSDAY OR YOU WILL NOT BE PAID. And yet judging from the client list, this was a rather exclusive agency—surely they could have afforded to spice up the place. But more than the decor, it was the atmosphere that depressed Madeline, because everyone was tense and on edge. Madeline did not know and did not want to know the inner workings of the office, but she had witnessed enough bitchy exchanges to understand that something was wrong. And once when she had a problem with her check she had to call accounting, and while on the phone she heard someone say, "You tell Miss Madeline Boot not to screw up her time slip again." Only her counselor was friendly: her name was

Lynn, she was short and plump with glasses and frizzy brown hair; she always called Madeline "Honey," and once tactfully suggested that Madeline upgrade her wardrobe so she could work with the more senior people at The Big Cigarette Company.

But the worst part of the temp agency was the receptionist. She was a pretty, big-boned girl from Long Island, the kind of person who is sickly sweet to those above her and sneeringly condescending to those below. When Madeline first came to sign up at the agency, the receptionist looked her up and down, then without a word handed her a clipboard with an application. Madeline was at the agency almost two hours filling out forms and being tested on the computer and, finally, talking to Lynn, and all the time the receptionist acted as if Madeline was some street bum blocking her light. And the receptionist could not have been more than nineteen years old.

Madeline was halfway through her tea when the receptionist blew in, an almost bursting deli bag in her hand, her long brown hair flying behind her as she stalked by the temps. "Don't anyone tawlk to me," she commanded, "because I am in a FOUL mood." She went behind her desk, wrestled off her coat, flicked a few switches. She picked up the phone, angrily punched numbers, then with the phone balanced between her shoulder and ear started unpacking her bag of food.

"Angie? Hi. I'm so pissed. You won't baleeve what happened…Naw, we didn't go there. We should have, but we didn't. Lissen, 'cause you're gonna die when I tell you…"

Madeline sighed. And a good mood was no better, because then the receptionist would flirt with the (predominantly gay) male temps, and show off her much vaunted ability to recite every Billy Joel song from memory. And sometimes she even sang, which was excruciating. But this was a bad mood morning, and now everyone's ears were burning with her boyfriend Mark's latest horrible unforgivable "toe-tally immature" misdeed. Madeline looked at a thin quiet black woman sitting across from her; Madeline and the woman often exchanged smiles at such times, and sure enough the woman looked up and sent Madeline a grin. Madeline smiled back—at last, human contact.

Madeline sighed, and tried once again to find a comfortable position in the plastic chair. No luck. She was tired, but she had her tea, and probably had an hour or so until someone from The Big Cigarette Company called in sick. She had a great deal to think about this morning, because this morning David had asked her to move in with him.

Two weeks had passed since the Sunday afternoon at David's apartment, two of the best weeks of Madeline's life. She and David were completely, wildly, passionately in love. They saw each other as often as they could, and it would not be an exaggeration to say they had sex constantly. Before David went to work, when he came home from work, before he went to rehearsal, after rehearsal, before going out with Hanson and Alison, after going out with Hanson and Alison—the minute they were alone they fell at each other, most times not even making it to the bedroom. Madeline was scared and inhibited at first, but no more: she had adjusted quickly to her good fortune, and was greedily drinking in all the love and affection. David was crazy about her; he could not keep his hands off her, not even in public, and under the warmth of his enthusiasm Madeline felt healthy and strong and—even she had to admit it—beautiful. In the mirror of David's spotless bathroom she would look at herself after another night of lots of sex and little sleep, and she was always amazed at her flawless skin and lively, happy eyes.

She had overestimated her abilities this morning, however. For the first time she had consented to stay at David's the night before work—a night of separation seemed impossible, and David swore they would be in bed by eleven. Well, they were in bed by eleven, but they did not get to sleep until two, and when the alarm rang at six-fifteen Madeline was startled out of a deep dream. She shut off the alarm and sat up. Her head was swimming in sleep, and her whole body felt stuffed and numb. Not good.

She stumbled into the shower, then stumbled into the bedroom and quickly dressed in the clothes she had brought the night before. David was laying in bed watching her dress when suddenly he said, "This is crazy, you having to bring clothes here. Why don't you just move in?"

She looked up, her blouse half-buttoned. "Are you serious?"

"Very. That way I'll have you here all the time. It'll be easier."

Madeline sat down on the bed and ran her hand through David's hair. "Living together is a big decision. It's not something to decide at six-thirty in the morning, which is a time of day you don't normally see."

"I've been thinking about this for awhile, not just this morning. Are you saying you don't want to?"

"Are you kidding? I'd love to. It's just—" She sighed. "My sister."

"What about her?"

"She'll freak out. I remember when I went to live down the shore, it was awful for her. She doesn't have any children, and I guess I'm sort of her child."

"But then you were moving far away—with me you'll just be a few streets over."

"That's true... Anyway, I don't think I quite believe you. I'll call later from work when you're more awake to ask if you really mean it."

"I do really mean it, and if you ask me later I'll be insulted." He pulled her towards him, and put his mouth close to her ear. "We're practically living together anyway, don't you think?"

"Yes..."

"And we're in love, right?"

"Right..."

"So talk to your sister tonight, okay? That way you can move in as soon as possible."

"Okay." She put her arms around him, and they kissed deeply.

"You look nice in those clothes," he said, running a hand along her stockinged leg and up under her skirt.

"I look goofy. Listen, I better go."

He laid back on the bed, his hand still caressing her leg. "I wish you didn't have to go. You know I can't keep my hands off you."

"I noticed."

"Do you mind?"

"Not at all. But I really have to go," she said, reluctantly moving her leg from his hand.

"You'll talk to your sister tonight?"

"I promise."

Well, that was a promise rashly made, Madeline thought as she stared into her tea. Because although David did not know it, he was not a favorite at 821 Washington. Not at all. And it was Bella's fault for opening her big mouth. The Sunday night after Madeline and David first made love, Madeline returned home and sat in the kitchen, listening as Bella described her day in Brooklyn with the Dellasandandrio clan. And then Bella said, "Tell me about your day—is David good in bed?"

Madeline looked at the wall, then looked back at Bella. "How do you know?"

"Well, we can start with the fact that you're walking like a cowboy. Not to mention the fact that your skin is glowing like you just had a facial. Don't tell me I don't know the signs."

So Bella knew, and that was fine, but the next night when Michael was over and they were all eating ice cream Madeline dropped her spoon and Robert said, "What is wrong with you tonight? At dinner you dropped your fork, during Scrabble you dropped your letters twice—I've never seen you so clumsy."

"That's what happens when you start getting laid," Bella said.

"Bella!" Madeline said. Robert made a choking sound, and Michael gave Madeline a short, sharp look.

"Well, it's true," Bella said. "You've been spaced out all night."

"I thought, Madeline," Robert said, his voice taut, "that you had better judgment than that."

Here it comes, she thought. "What I do, Robert, is none of your business."

"It is when you're setting yourself up to be hurt."

"You know nothing about it."

"I know that this guy is a bum."

"You've never even met him, so how can you say that? Anyway, for your information, David and I are in love."

"Oh, I see—love. He loves you so much he can't even be bothered to meet your family."

Tears leapt to her eyes. "That's not fair."

"It's not fair, but it's true."

"Robert," Bella said, putting an arm around Madeline. "Maybe David's just shy."

"Obviously not shy enough," Robert said coldly.

Bella gave Robert a warning look, and he did not say another word. And after that night Robert never mentioned David's name: all jokes about David not picking up Madeline ceased, and every evening when she got up to leave Robert stared at her stonily.

It was all so unnecessary, Madeline thought, drinking the last of her tea. Robert was not the most observant person in the world—he certainly wouldn't have noticed that she was walking like a cowboy. But now the truth was out, and the way Robert was acting Madeline felt like she was living in a 19th century Sicilian village. Was it not the 1980s? Was she not a modern woman? She and David were in love, they were using birth control, so what was Robert's problem?

"...coulda told me that, but no, not Mawk. We had to march right into that club and there they were, his dumb ass brother and—Hold on Angie...Classic Temps...One moment...His dumb ass brother and his even dumber ass friend. I ask you, was it necessary they be there? Can we never have an evening alone?"

So Madeline was naive if she thought she could go home and blithely announce that she was moving in with David. Maybe she should ask Michael to help her? But no—although Michael had never said a word for or against David, he definitely emanated an air of disapproval. Michael always helped her when she needed him, but he was too principled to help if he did not approve. Better to keep Michael out of it, she decided. This time she would face Bella and Robert on her own.

One of the counselors came out and called in two of the temps. A moment later the temps came out, put on their coats, and left. It was close to eight-thirty, and Madeline was torn between wanting to earn some money and wanting to go home at eleven-thirty and crawl into bed for a few hours. It could go either way, but Mondays were usually busy. Madeline could imagine some poor secretary with a raging hangover calling in sick, then the secretary's boss calling personnel, and personnel calling Lynn...

"Madeline?"

She looked up. Lynn was in the doorway, a small piece of paper in her hand.

"The Big Cigarette Company. Come on in, honey, I'll give you the info."

Madeline rose, and as she passed by the receptionist's desk the girl looked her up and down disdainfully. One day, Madeline thought, I'm going to publish a book of short stories, and then I'm going to come in here and shove it up her nose, and we'll see if she can recite the words to every Billy Joel song with a wad of paper in her sinuses. The thought cheered Madeline immensely, and she gave the receptionist a winning smile.

*   *   *

On the bus home. Madeline's shift had been from 8:30 to 4:30, so with fast footwork she had managed to cross 41st Street in only fifteen minutes. The Red Apple bus was waiting at the gate; she hopped on, put her dollar in the slot, and took a seat in back. She was lucky to miss the crowd, the five o'clock mass of people that spread through the streets and subways and buses and trains. No one sat next to her, and as the bus pulled away she curled her feet up on the empty seat.

It had been an easy day, she thought as she watched the familiar sights fly by. A good day, even. She had worked for one of the top dogs and, as usual, the higher up the boss the less she had to do. The man had an enormous office, and Madeline had sat in a lushly carpeted area with expensive plants and exquisite artwork. In other parts of the building six secretaries were crammed into similar spaces; you couldn't even have a phone conversation or swear at your computer without being overheard, but today Madeline was in first class. At ten o'clock the man gave her a one paragraph letter to type, and after that he came out with his coat and said, "I'll be at meetings the rest of the day. Put any messages on my desk." Hallelujah, Madeline thought, watching him put on his expensive wool coat and walk out the door. Now I can write. She was an expert at writing in noisy, adverse circumstances—and had in fact been writing for an hour before she typed the lone letter—but she so much preferred silence and peace. She spent the next hours writing, and nothing, not even a phone call, disturbed her private world.

In the Lincoln Tunnel now, the green tiled walls and eerie lights flashing by her window. Madeline twisted in her seat, trying to get comfortable. In the afternoon she had called Devon in Connecticut and Rose at her Wall Street job, and filled them in on the latest development. Devon had suggested caution, but Rose was gung ho: "Listen, you tell your old-fashioned overprotective brother-in-law he has no right to tell you how to run your life. You've got yourself a great man, you don't want to lose him just because you're afraid of what Robert will say." And Madeline called David just to say hello; Hanson was with him, so she spoke to him as well. They both sounded high as kites, and Madeline was shaking her head and smiling as she hung up the phone. But they get their work done, she thought, so I can't really criticize them. Then she printed out fresh copies of two short stories, wrote a few letters, and at 4:27 turned off the computer and slipped some office supplies into her bookbag. All in all, a good day.

The bus was in Hoboken now, rumbling down Washington Street. Just before Ninth Street Madeline pulled the wire above her head and rose out of her seat. She maneuvered her way down the aisle of the moving bus, and when it lumbered to a stop at Ninth and Washington she thanked the driver and got off. She stood a moment in the cold, trying to decide what to do. Although it was a painfully obvious buttering-up gesture, she went into Finness Floral Shop and bought a ten dollar flower arrangement, then went to Vito's Deli and bought fresh mozzarella and sun-dried tomatoes. Thus armed, she went home.

The lights were on when she entered the apartment. It was too early for Bella to be home, but Robert worked odd hours and was often home in the afternoon.

"Hi Robert," she called out.

"Hi," he called from the TV room.

Madeline took off her coat, changed into sweatpants, a T-shirt, and sweater, then went into the kitchen where she put the flowers in a vase and arranged the food on a tray with crackers. She put the vase on the dining room table, then brought the tray into the TV room. Robert was sitting on the couch drinking a beer and reading a book of critical essays on George Eliot, which struck Madeline as even more painful than reading George Eliot herself.

"What's all this?" Robert said, looking up as Madeline put the tray on the coffee table. "Did you break something?"

"No, I didn't break anything. I just felt like doing something nice."

"Hmm," he said suspiciously. He put down his book and started arranging mozzarella on a cracker. "How was work?"

"Good. Easy. I typed a letter, then my boss left for the day."

"I cannot get over how much money you make for so little work. You know, if there's ever any kind of economic crash, you temps will be the first to go."

"Well, I don't know much about economics, but there's always going to be secretaries and they're always going to be calling in sick."

"Did you get your writing done?"

"Of course."

"Good. I know I tease you about not making any money, Madeline, but I see how hard you work and I respect what you're trying to do."

"Well, thank you Robert. So how's George Eliot?" she asked, nodding toward the book.

"Oh." He sighed. "I wanted to read over a few things for class tomorrow. People write such horrible things about her, it's really disturbing."

"Like what? What do they say?"

"Well, one scholar wrote a forty-page essay trying to prove that Lewes influenced her work so heavily he ought to be considered her co-author. I think that the biggest insult for any writer is the implication that they're not responsible for their own work."

"I don't see how he could be considered her co-author—according to the biography I read, she never rewrote anything." And it shows, she thought privately.

"That's this man's point—he says that because Lewes didn't let her hear anyone else's criticism, he was her only critic and therefore shaped her work. And, according to the essay, damaged it. Which is nonsense, because you can't damage perfection."

Madeline fixed a cracker and kept silent. For Robert's sake she had tried to wade through the whole oeuvre: *Scenes from a Clerical Life, Adam Bede, The*

Mill on the Floss, Silas Marner, Felix Holt, Romola, Middlemarch, Daniel Deronda. She had loved *Middlemarch,* and *Silas Marner* was at least short, but when she was about a hundred pages into *The Mill on the Floss* she went to Bella and said, "I hate this book! It's the most dank, dismal, depressing thing I've ever read in my life. You know I finish everything I read, but I can't finish this—I'll get so depressed I'll end up killing myself."

"Isn't that ironic, since that's exactly what the main characters do."

"And I can see why—if I was trapped in this book I'd kill myself too."

"Madeline," Bella said. "You have to finish it. You have to finish it, and you have to find something good to say about it to Robert."

"But I'll be lying."

"What do you think I've been doing all these years? Every marriage has compromises, and since you're an extension of this marriage you have to make some too. Robert will die if he thinks you don't like Ms. Eliot."

So Madeline swallowed her criticism, and Robert was left in the happy delusion that the two women he shared his home with worshipped George Eliot as much as he did. Bella and Madeline could say nothing when Robert put a framed drawing of her in the bathroom, and they could say nothing when, in honor of Eliot's birthday, Robert read them selections of her work. At least then there was cake, and Madeline could amuse herself by trying to make Michael laugh. Now, however, she had to be careful: she had to show interest but not too much, or she would be corralled into reading a forty-page essay.

Thankfully, Bella came home. She came into the TV room wearing her black coat and red beret, her cheeks pink from the cold.

"Well, isn't this a cozy scene," she said cheerfully. "My two favorite people, and mozzarella. From Lisa's?" she asked, picking up a piece and popping it into her mouth.

"From Vito's," Robert said. "Madeline bought it."

"What's wrong?" Bella asked, turning to Madeline. "Did you break something?"

"No," Madeline said. "I'm just being nice."

"Who are you trying to fool? The moment I saw those flowers I knew something was up. What's going on?"

"It's nothing bad. In fact it's something good."

"Hmm. Listen, can we order Chinese? I'm not in the mood to cook."

"I'll cook," Robert said.

"I've been dreaming about Szechwan-style tofu all the way home, Robert, and I don't think that's one of your specialties. I'll call now," she said, leaving the room, her voice and clicking heels trailing down the hall. "And I'll give Michael a call, maybe I can catch him before he eats."

Madeline was tempted to run into the kitchen and tell Bella not to call him, but on second thought maybe it was better if he came. Michael always exerted a calming influence on Robert, and perhaps his presence might convert a hysterical Sicilian explosion into a mild outburst.

Michael came, the food came, they were eating in the dining room when Michael said, "These flowers are beautiful." He reached out and gently touched a snapdragon, his finger running along the delicate lilac curve.

"Madeline bought them," Bella said. "She has to break some bad news, and the flowers are supposed to butter me up. Robert got mozzarella."

"Bad news?" Michael asked, turning to Madeline. "Is something wrong?"

"Nothing is wrong, and I don't have bad news. I just have—news."

"Let's talk about it after dinner," Bella said. "I don't want anyone using chopsticks for weapons."

"Perhaps I should leave…" Michael said.

"Oh, don't be silly, Michael," Bella said. "If this *news* is bad enough for flowers and mozzarella, I think we're going to need you." Bella looked at Madeline. "Are you pregnant?"

"No, I'm not pregnant. And can we please do this after dinner? I can't eat with all of you staring at me."

After dinner Madeline cleaned up the half-empty tins and rice boxes and broken fortune cookies, her mind all the time scrambling for the proper words. But it was no use: by now they were all so suspicious they expected the worst, maybe even suspected the truth. Madeline spent a long time in the kitchen putting away the food and loading the dishwasher, and when the time came to go back into the dining room she found she could not move. She sat on a stool staring at the refrigerator, her stomach a mass of nerves. Maybe if I stay here long enough, she thought, they'll forget I have to tell them something. Or maybe a spaceship will come and take them all away or, better, zap them with a stun gun that makes them bow to my every desire. Or maybe—

"Madeline," Robert called. "We're waiting."

Madeline sighed. She rose, turned off the kitchen light, and started walking down the narrow hall, step by painful step. One would have thought there was a guillotine awaiting her, but actually it was worse: Robert was at the head of the table, his eyebrows drawn, his mouth grim and serious. His hands were stretched before him on the table and his fingers were slowly, steadily tapping. Bella had moved over to Madeline's seat, her arms folded and her expression slightly mocking. Only Michael offered some hope: his large green eyes were soft and worried, and as she sat down he winked at her gently. Like someone offering a last cigarette, Madeline thought. She sat opposite Robert, but dared not look at him; she stared at the place mat, unsure where to start.

"I'm prepared to have my evening ruined," Robert said, "so please, just spit it out and get it over with."

"Well," Madeline said, "I have a little announcement to make. David asked me to move in with him, and I said yes."

Robert slammed both his hands on the table. "No. Absolutely not."

"Madeline…" Bella said.

"I forbid it," Robert said. "I absolutely forbid it."

Madeline saw red. "Excuse me, Robert, but you seem to be misinformed about one very important fact: you are not my father, and you cannot tell me what to do."

"That's right, Madeline, I'm not your father. But aren't I the one who took you in when you were seventeen years old and completely messed up? Aren't I the one who helped protect you from your most self-destructive impulses? And aren't I the one who paid for your food and shelter all these years? I may not be your father, but I'm sure as hell the next best thing considering that your real father is off in Arizona being crazy."

"Robert…" Bella said.

"What the hell is wrong with you, Madeline? Why don't you choose a nice normal guy who treats you well instead of this David who has you running out of here at all hours of the night and who doesn't even have the courage to meet your family?"

"David *does* treat me well," Madeline said hotly. "He loves me, and he wants me to be happy, which is more than I can say for you!"

"Oh—I don't love you? I don't want you to be happy? That's all you have to say after all these years?"

Michael rose. "I should go."

Bella put out a hand. "No, Michael, please stay. We need you."

"No, really, I should go. This is between all of you, it's not my business." He went to the door and Robert followed him. Madeline heard Robert murmur something, then Michael murmured back. She turned to Bella, her eyes wide and pleading. Bella sighed, then moved her chair closer to Madeline and put an arm around her.

"Wonderful," Robert said as he slammed the door. "Now you've chased Michael away." He came back into the dining room. "Oh, this is great—when I see you two like that I know I don't have a chance. Don't cross me on this one, Bella, because I'm not changing my mind."

"Look, Robert, I want you to calm down. You said what you think, now I'm going to say what I think."

"On the contrary," Robert said as he took his seat. "I've only just started."

"Robert, for one minute can you please just shut up?" Bella sighed, and turned to Madeline. "Okay, Maddy, it's like this: we have no objection to you seeing David. It's great that you found someone, and it's great that you're serious about each other. Fine. But we haven't met him. Can you imagine how that makes us feel?"

"You don't have to imagine the worst," Madeline said huffily. "You could try trusting me."

"Well, based on your history with men, you can at least understand why we're so concerned."

"My history with men? What history with men? In all the years I've lived with you two I've never had a real relationship, except that thing with The Virgin, and that doesn't count. The problem is, you two don't want me to grow up; you don't want me to be what I am, which is a woman with a sex life."

"Maddy—try to see it from our point of view. When you first came to live with us you were a *child* with a sex life. You were fucking everyone, and you had no idea what you were doing, you had no idea about love or sex or relationships. It killed me to see you making the same mistakes as me, don't you see? So we were strict with you. You did what you wanted anyway, as I recall, but by the end of college you had your shit together. And as for us stopping you from having a boyfriend, that's nonsense—we never stopped you from dating, we were glad when you dated, but you never really liked anyone you went out with, which was not our fault. And then when you went through that religious thing you didn't date because you didn't want to which, again, was not our fault. Do you see what I mean?"

Madeline was silent.

"And now there's this David and okay, it's great, you're in love and you want to move in with him. And we're concerned. Of course we're concerned. It's because we love you so much. And more than that, Maddy—we cherish you. You're our little Madeline, you mean so much to us. And we want you to be with a man who feels the same way, but we've never even met this guy, so we don't know how he feels."

"He *loves* me!" Madeline said, tears streaming down her face. "I'm telling you, he *loves* me."

Robert sighed. Bella shot him a dirty look.

"And if you're so obsessed with meeting him," Madeline said, "then fine, I'll bring him over. But he rehearses until ten every night, so it's not like he can come over and have dinner."

"Have you ever heard of a little thing called weekends?" Robert said.

"I have the perfect solution," Bella announced. "This Sunday Patty is coming over for brunch so she can meet Michael—why doesn't David come too?"

"No," Robert said.

"And why not?"

"Because I don't want you dragging Michael and Patty into our business."

"Oh, Robert—if the poor guy comes over by himself he'll feel like it's the Spanish Inquisition. This way there'll be other people, it'll be more relaxed—and it'll help take the pressure off Michael and Patty."

"David doesn't rehearse on Sundays," Madeline said, wiping her eyes. "I'm sure he can come."

"I still think it's a bad idea," Robert said.

"And why's that?" Bella flared. "Because you want to see him squirm, is that it?"

"I wouldn't mind. But no, it's what I said—why put Michael and Patty through something that's sure to be a complete and total disaster?"

"It won't be a complete and total disaster if you show some manners. Listen, Robert—if David comes over and you're not polite, I swear to God I'll kill you." She turned to Madeline. "So, what do you think? Will you ask him?"

Madeline nodded. "I'll ask him tonight."

"*Again* you're going out with him?" Robert said.

"Yes, Robert, again. Because when two people are in love they want to be together. Is that so odd?"

Robert shook his head.

"So, are we done?" Bella said.

"I'm going to move in with him," Madeline said. "I'm going to do it whether you like it or not."

"I'm sure we'll like him. Won't we, Robert?"

Robert snorted.

"So, case closed. Well—poor Michael, we really did chase him away. Give him a call, Robert, tell him we're done tearing out each other's throats."

Robert went off to the kitchen, and came back with a long face.

"Michael's in for the night," he said gloomily. "He's working on his sutra, and he's at a point where he can't stop. So no Scrabble."

"We could rent a movie," Madeline suggested.

"I guess so," Robert said. "But you have to go get it, Madeline, that's your punishment." And then he went over to Madeline and awkwardly kissed her cheek. "I yell at you because I love you. You know that, don't you?"

"Mmm hmm."

"So you're not mad at me?"

"I guess not. Give me the card for the video store."

"And money for ice cream," Bella said. "Don't forget money for ice cream."

CHAPTER 11

Brunch from Hell

"Okay, Bella," Madeline said, coming into the kitchen. "I swept the floors, I fluffed the pillows, I took the biggest offending specks from the windows, I cleared off the coffee table, I dusted the piano and the dining room table and all the chairs, I set the table, I vacuumed the TV room, and I put all the Scrabble things out of sight. And I cleaned the bathroom. So what's next?"

"Make yourself a cup of tea, sit here and keep me company."

Which is exactly what Madeline hoped Bella would say. She put on the kettle and sat down on a stool, watching Bella chop carrots and sip wine. The two sisters were both wearing sweatpants and sweaters, although Bella had for some reason already put on fancy earrings, large fake pearls surrounded by large fake diamonds.

Madeline glanced at the clock. It was eleven-thirty, and everyone was supposed to arrive at twelve-thirty. Michael would come earlier, of course—he and Robert always had a private beer before such events, steeling themselves for the torture to come. Robert did well at parties, Michael not so well, but whenever Michael was being fixed up there was always a tension in the atmosphere that called for a slight degree of inebriation. As for Bella, well, Bella always got tipsy at their parties. She was a happy drunk, at least; she just got more and more animated, which was not a bad thing for a hostess. Madeline was stone cold sober as usual, but if there was ever a moment when she needed a drink it was now. Right now.

"How are you doing?" Bella asked, glancing at Madeline. "You feel okay?"

"I'm so nervous I could barf."

"Did Robert say anything to you?"

"No. He's in the TV room reading you-know-who's poetry. He lifted his legs when I vacuumed, but that was it."

"Well, I read him the riot act this morning. Your water's boiling."

"What do you mean?" Madeline said as she hopped off the stool. She took a mug from a cabinet, and a tea bag from the canister on the counter.

"I told him that if I detected even a glimmer of rudeness I'd throw him out the window. And I mean it," Bella said, taking another sip of wine. "I can't promise he'll be friendly, but at least he won't be rude."

"Thanks, Bella," Madeline said, giving her a hug.

"Oh, Maddy." Bella put down her knife and hugged Madeline back. She kissed Madeline's hair, then smoothed it with her hand. "I'm sure it's going to be okay. After all these years Robert is well-trained, so don't worry."

"I'm worried. I feel so much pressure."

"I just wish Michael would feel a little pressure," Bella said, releasing Madeline. "He is as usual completely blasé about this whole thing. I might as well have invited Uncle Harry for all the excitement he's showing."

"Bella, you're the only one who hasn't realized it, but Michael doesn't want to get fixed up. He as much as told you so."

"Well, Michael doesn't know what's good for him."

Madeline fixed her tea and sat at the counter, stirring aimlessly. The night of Madeline's announcement she had met David at Narrow Grave's rehearsal space, and as they walked home arm in arm she told him about the fight, leaving out Robert's harshest words. David was disappointed that she would not be moving in that night, but he had readily agreed to brunch, saying that anyway it was high time he met her family. And he had understood when she told him it was better if she stayed home Saturday night so she could wake up early and help Bella get ready. They had plans to see Jonathan Richman in The City, but David said no problem, Hanson and Alison would keep him company, and he could just scalp Madeline's ticket. They spent all of Saturday together making love and talking; they decided that when brunch was over they would call a taxi and move Madeline's things. So as of tonight, Madeline thought, we'll be living together. Unless, of course, something awful happens at brunch.

Someone knocked. Slowly. Madeline heard Robert jump up and answer the door; Michael came in, and the two men walked into the kitchen.

"Hi Michael," Madeline said, looking up from her tea. Michael was wearing grey khakis and a button-down shirt and he looked, she thought, a little pale.

"Hello Madeline."

"Hi Michael," Bella said, holding her knife at arm's length and giving him a kiss on the cheek. "Don't you look handsome and ready to meet someone."

"Don't start, Bella," Robert said. "And let me at the refrigerator—I never needed a beer so much in my life."

"Now, Robert," Bella said. "Remember our little talk about your attitude."

"I remember," Robert said, opening the refrigerator and taking out two Dos Equus. "And I remember very vividly the image of myself laying on the pavement with my brains spread out all over Washington Street."

"See what you have to look forward to, Michael?" Bella said. She rested her hip against the counter, her glass of wine in her hand. "Nothing like domestic bliss."

"We men will be in the TV room," Robert said. "But don't feel you have to call us when someone comes. We won't mind if you leave us out of this altogether."

"Ha ha," Bella said. And, after they left, "*Men*."

"I'm going to get dressed."

"Mmm, me too. Would you put this platter on the coffee table on your way? Careful, don't drop it."

Madeline took the heavy silver platter with glass wedges and walked slowly down the hall, the glass trembling with each step. Bella had filled the wedges with carrots, celery, and crackers, and in the round dish in the center she had heaped her special eggplant dip. Madeline could not decide if the platter was stately or gaudy; it had been a wedding gift from Robert's mother, who claimed it had been in the family for years. Which doesn't mean anyone used it, Madeline mused as she set the platter on the coffee table. She looked into the dining room—the door to the TV room was firmly shut. Robert wasn't joking, she thought as she went to her room. He and Michael really wouldn't mind if they were left out of the brunch altogether, if by some lucky accident no one ever opened the door and dragged them out. But Robert had been married to Bella long enough to know that such lucky accidents never occurred.

Madeline pulled down the shade and took off her clothes. She dressed with care, putting on a clean bra, new underwear, and new black stockings she had bought in The City; then she put on one of her nicest outfits, a dark maroon dress of heavy cotton with an empire waist and gleaming black buttons down the front. The sleeves were long but not cuffed, the hem reached just below her knees, and the scooped neckline showed off her long neck and the soft skin above her breasts. Most importantly, the dress was comfortable; she could eat as much as she wanted without feeling the tug of a tight waistband. She put on a pair of small but real diamond earrings, a graduation gift from Bella and Robert, and she put on an amethyst ring, and a diamond ring that had been her grandmother's engagement ring. She spritzed Opium behind her ears, on her wrists and in her cleavage, slipped on a pair of low black heels, then went to the bathroom to brush her teeth and hair. She bent over and brushed her hair from the roots to give it more body, then stood and flipped her hair away from her face. She examined herself in the mirror—well, other than her panicked expression, she looked quite nice.

She went into Bella and Robert's room. "Well?" she asked Bella. "How do I look?"

"My, my!" Bella said, looking up as she pulled on her stockings. "Breaking out the stones! You look fabulous. And me?"

Bella gave her stockings a final tug, then twirled around. She was wearing a dress similar in design to Madeline's—not surprising since they had bought them at the same store during the same shopping spree—but Bella's dress had a shorter skirt, and instead of maroon it was black with orange flowers.

"You look great," Madeline said. "As usual."

"Are we not the hottest chicks in Hoboken?"

"Was there ever any doubt?"

"Tell me, is Robert wearing jeans? I can't remember."

"He's wearing jeans."

Bella went to the door and stuck her head in the hall. "Ro-*bert!*" she yelled. "Get in here and change your pants." She turned to Madeline. "You go sit with Michael, I'll stay here and supervise Robert."

Robert appeared in the hall just as Madeline was passing the bathroom. She ducked into the bathroom to let him pass, and as he walked by he gave her a quick look and said, sniffing, "You're wearing too much perfume."

"And you're wearing jeans, so go change."

Michael was sitting on the couch with his legs crossed, a book of George Eliot's poems open and balanced on one knee. He looked up when Madeline walked in.

"You look nice," he said, smiling faintly.

"Robert says I'm wearing too much perfume," she said, falling into the green armchair.

"I don't think so."

"How's George Eliot and her poems?"

Michael smiled. "Excruciating."

"Michael, you have the patience of a saint to be able to sit and talk with Robert about these things."

"I don't mind talking about the poems, I just don't like reading them. Which stays between you and me, of course."

"Hey, you never said a word about me not finishing *The Mill on the Floss*—I never even told Bella that."

The buzz of the doorbell split the air. David? No, he would never be so prompt. Bella's high heels clicked into the hall, then Bella sang into the intercom, "Hel-looo!"

Madeline sighed. "Bella's already well on her way." She looked at Michael closely. "Are you okay? You're kind of pale."

"Mmm—I'm all right. I didn't sleep well last night."

"You were humiliated because you lost at Scrabble. But it's your own fault—the only reason I won is because you gave me 'xeric.'"

Someone tapped rapidly at the door—not David. And sure enough when Bella opened the door there was a burst of mutual female screeching: "Oh, I'm so happy you're *here!*" "Oh, I just love your *dress!*"

Madeline looked at Michael. "Well," she said. "Looks like we have to get out there."

Michael let out a long, tired sigh, then picked up his beer and stood. Madeline opened the door and they walked into the dining room. And there she was by the piano, Bella's friend Patty. Madeline took one look at her, just got the briefest sense of her, and felt one hundred percent sure that nothing would ever happen between this woman and Michael. Not that Patty wasn't pretty, because she was: she was short and curvy with big brown eyes, a perky nose, and a full mouth with big teeth. Her tight black suit showed off her curvaceous body to perfection, and except for her crooked lipstick her makeup was tasteful and flattering. But just watching her stride across the room to shake Madeline then Michael's hand, just watching her big smile and gesturing hands—what was it? Patty just wasn't for Michael, Madeline was sure. Which was a relief. But why? Madeline asked herself as she sat next to Michael on one of the flowered sofas. Well, probably because any girlfriend of Michael's would surely be a factor in her life, and Madeline had never made friends with anyone like Patty. Madeline was generally rather languid, whereas Patty exuded a hyper energy; Patty sat on the other couch, but she did not keep still—she picked up a carrot, crossed her legs, uncrossed them, smiled at Michael, scanned the room restlessly. She seemed impatient, as if she was dying to shove aside the furniture, roll up the rugs, and teach everyone how to mambo. Madeline felt exhausted just looking at her.

"So," Bella said, clapping her hands together. "Tell me, Patty, what do you want to drink? I'm drinking red wine, you can help me polish off the bottle."

"Red wine would be lovely," Patty said, smiling toothily. "Where's Robert?"

"He was wearing jeans, if you can believe it, so I ordered him to change. I'll go get your wine now. Michael, you still okay with that beer? And Madeline, club soda? Okay."

Bella left. Michael was busy studying the crease in his khakis so Madeline said brightly, "Tell me, Patty, is this your first time in Hoboken?"

"As a matter of fact it is. And what a cute little city! I passed some lovely antique stores on the way, they were as good as anything in The City. Bella is always raving about how wonderful it is here, and now I know why. And it's so close to Manhattan, the bus ride was, what, ten minutes? Fifteen? That's nothing."

"And where do you live?"

"Chelsea. I love it there, I just love it. And you, Michael?" Patty said, turning to him, her voice taking on a tinge of coyness. "Do you like living here?"

Michael looked up from his pants. "I do."

"Did you ever live in The City?"

"I used to live in Brooklyn, and later I lived up by Columbia."

"Oh, *Brooklyn*. I *love* Brooklyn. Where did you live?"

"In Park Slope. Before it was gentrified."

"Oh my God, what a pity you left, because it's simply gorgeous now. Too bad you didn't buy a building, it would be worth a fortune now."

"Well, I did buy a building, actually."

"So what on earth are you doing living here?"

"Well—my ex-wife lives there."

"Oh. Right. Bella said you were divorced. Me too," she said, leaning forward confidentially. "Horrible, isn't it?"

Michael smiled quickly, then went back to studying his pants. Fortunately Bella came back, Robert in tow. Apparently Robert had met Patty at *Psychology Now*'s Christmas party; they exchanged greetings, and Robert sat on the couch next to Patty. Bella pulled over the piano bench and sat facing them, her wineglass as always glued to her hand.

"So," Bella said, taking them all in with a happy glance. "As soon as David gets here I'll bring out the appetizers. I made these cool little samosa things, they're stuffed with cheese and peas and onions—you'll love them."

Robert looked at his watch, then at Madeline. "He's late."

Madeline's cheeks reddened. "He is not! What time is it?"

"Twelve-forty."

"Oh, Robert! Everyone is fashionably late for these things. Not that there's anything wrong with being on time," Madeline said hurriedly, looking at Patty, "but I would say that most people, when they're invited for twelve-thirty, come a bit later."

"Not me," Patty said cheerfully. "You tell me twelve-thirty, I'm here on the dot." Madeline wanted to break each and every one of Patty's big teeth, but then Patty winked at her and said, "But that's probably a little neurotic. Remember, Bella, that article in *PN* a few months ago, all about the psychology of being early, being on time, and being late? It was fascinating," she said, looking at Madeline and—again coyly—at Michael. "Just fascinating."

"And what did they say about people who are late?" Robert asked. "That they're selfish and don't respect other people?"

"Robert," Bella said. He looked at her, and she pointed out the window.

"Actually, no," Patty said, picking up a carrot slice and nibbling as she spoke. "It said that people who are always late are angry and controlling. Or, they just have a different sense of time. You know, like people from the Mediterranean countries or from Latin America. Countries where it's hot. Which reminds me of a precious little story a friend of mine told me: she used to be married to a Greek man, and once when she asked him how long it would take them to go somewhere, he said 'Well, it takes twenty minutes to go and twenty minutes to come back, so let's say an hour.'"

Everyone laughed politely, and the conversation continued, Bella and Patty and Robert telling anecdotes about late and early people. Robert did not say another word about David, but he kept checking his watch and sighing. Madeline's stomach twisted into a series of hard knots; and with every minute that passed, every minute without a ringing doorbell, her agony increased. Her hands, ice cold now, grappled each other on her lap; she took a sip of club soda hoping it might calm her down, but it tasted so sharp and sparkly she almost spit it out on her lap.

"Well," Bella said, leaning over and turning Robert's wrist so she could see his watch. "I'm sure you're all quite hungry. I'd like to bring out the hors d'oeuvres, but we really should wait for David. Madeline, you're sure you told him twelve-thirty?"

Madeline nodded, miserable.

"Well, it's five after now. We'll give him five more minutes, then—"

The doorbell rang. Oh, thank God! Madeline flew out of her seat and ran down the hall to the intercom. She pushed the button and said breathlessly, "Hello?"

"It's David." His voice was half-man, half-machine.

She pushed ENTER, then went to the front door and opened it. She leaned against the door, her hands folded over her acrobatic stomach. Steps thudded on the stairs, getting louder and louder until Madeline saw David's head, and then he was in front of her smiling. He was here; now everything would be fine.

"Oh, David," she said, taking his hands. "I'm so glad you're here."

"Of course I'm here," he said, laughing as he leaned over and kissed her. He looked calm and happy, not a care in the world.

"Come in," she said. "Everyone's here."

She pulled him inside and shut the door. She held out her hands for his coat; he undid the buttons, and as he shrugged it off she saw to her absolute unmitigated horror that he was wearing the flashy shirt from The Beat'n Path gig. Oh no! she thought. Not that shirt! It had not looked bad in the dark of The Beat'n Path, but in the cruel light of Sunday brunch it was positively garish. She wished she could do a Bella and send him home to change, but he was already late and, how ridiculous, she couldn't ask him to do something like that. Maybe one of Robert's shirts? she thought wildly. No—there was nothing she could do.

David took her in his arms and kissed her. "I missed you last night," he said, looking into her eyes, one hand stroking her hair.

"And I missed you."

"You look pretty. And you smell good." He buried his face in her neck and lightly bit her skin.

"We better go in," she said, pushing him away gently. "Everyone's here."

"How are they?"

"Mmm—okay, I guess."

"Don't worry, I'll win them over. Come on, let's go."

He took her hand and walked confidently down the narrow hall. Madeline trailed behind him, trying to convince herself that his shirt was not so bad, but it was, it *was*. Then they were in the living room.

"Everyone," Madeline said. "This is David." Please ignore his shirt.

"And I'm Bella," Bella said, rising and extending her hand. "It's so nice to meet you."

"Oh no, the pleasure's mine," David said. "Madeline talks about you so much, it's great to finally meet you."

Robert had risen as well. After an extensive examination of David's shirt he put out his hand. "I'm Robert," he said curtly.

"Nice to meet you," David said, shaking Robert's hand. Then Michael rose, he and David shook; Bella introduced Patty, then said, "So David, what can I get you to drink? The women are drinking red wine and the men beer, but don't feel obligated to follow party lines."

"I'll have a beer."

"Why don't you sit here next to Michael. Maddy, come with me to the kitchen so we can get David's beer."

Madeline shot Bella a look—they couldn't leave David unprotected, not so soon! But Bella had already linked her arm with Madeline's and was dragging her into the hall.

"Why did you do that?" Madeline hissed when they were in the kitchen. "Robert will eat him alive!"

"I wanted to talk to you, silly. Madeline, he is *cu-ute!*"

Madeline smiled. "I told you so."

"And he has a nice body, and he holds himself well. He's a real hotty."

"I told you."

"And that's quite a shirt. Does he always dress like that?"

"Oh God—I wish he hadn't worn it. I'm sure Robert is horrified."

"Don't worry, it'll be okay. David looks like someone who can handle himself." She opened the refrigerator and took out a beer. "You can open this; I have to get my samosas out of the oven."

"Do you need help?"

"Actually, yes—can you get the big silver platter out of the cabinet down there? And cover it with napkins, these things are a little greasy."

Bella and Madeline were arranging samosas when Patty burst in.

"Hey, Patty," Bella said. "How's it going?"

Patty clutched Bella's sleeve, her perfect blood-red nails sinking into the cloth. "Bella," she said in a hushed, dramatic voice. "He is *gor*-geous! Just *gor*-geous!"

It took Madeline a moment to realize that Patty was talking about Michael.

"I told you so," Bella said.

"And he's smart, and he's sexy. Oh my God—do you think he likes me?"

"Well—it's difficult to tell with Michael. He's on the quiet side."

"Well, if anyone can draw him out, it's me." She held down the hem of her jacket and wiggled her hips. "Tell me, how do I look?"

"Terrific. Only your lipstick is a little crooked."

"I'll go fix it. And Bella," she said, her voice again dropping dramatically. "Thank you."

Patty left. Madeline looked at Bella and raised an eyebrow.

"And what's that supposed to mean?" Bella asked.

"She's not his type."

"Madeline, you tell me, what is Michael's type? I've tried intellectuals, career women, athletic women, widowed women, maternal women, neurotic women, there was even that nice woman I met at Lisa's who was into Tai Chi—he didn't want any of them. So now I'm trying a sex hungry woman. And if things don't work out between him and Patty, that's it, I'm through."

"Why do you say she's sex hungry?"

"Oh my God, all she ever talks about is her dildo collection. And whenever one of the editors has a question about female sexuality, they go ask Patty—and she's in advertising."

"Do you think Michael likes her?"

"Do you?"

"Well—he sort of smiled at her once."

"Doesn't mean a thing. He has excellent manners, he would never be mean to someone. Come on, let's go."

Patty was in the midst of explaining her job when Bella and Madeline walked in. Bella put the platter on the coffee table, Madeline handed David his beer then sat between him and Michael. David put an arm around her shoulder and smiled into her eyes. "Hi," he said.

"Hi. You okay?"

"I'm fine."

"So David," Bella said, back on her piano bench with her wineglass in one hand and a samosa in the other. "Tell us all about your band. Patty, David is in a rock band, they're poised on the verge of success."

"Well," David said, his hand curling around Madeline's shoulder. "There's not much to tell. The band's called Narrow Grave, we've been together about ten years, we cut two albums with The Small Record Label and now The Big Record Label is interested in us. But nothing's definite."

"Oh, David," Bella said. "You're much too modest, you left out all the good stuff! What David didn't say, Patty, is that his band was written up in *Rolling*

Stone and they get airplay and they're so much in demand they have to turn *down* gigs. Isn't that right, David?"

"Pretty much. And you, Bella, you work at *Psychology Now*?"

"That's right. I'm one of the assistant editors. I'm the oldest one in my position, but that's because I got a late start in life—I only graduated college six years ago, when I was thirty."

"Oh, now Bella's the one who's being modest," Patty said, reaching for the wine bottle. "She practically runs *PN*. Everyone there loves Bella."

"And you, Robert?" David said, turning to Robert. "Madeline says you teach literature at Columbia?"

"That's right," Robert said tightly.

"My husband Robert," Bella said expansively, "is one of the country's foremost experts on George Eliot."

"Tell me, David," Robert said, leaning over and looking David in the eye. "Do *you* like George Eliot?"

To the uninitiated it was a simple question, but Madeline knew that her entire future rested on David's reply. Madeline looked at Bella; Bella raised her hand and crossed her fingers. Please God, Madeline prayed. Let him at least have read *Silas Marner* in high school. She looked at David and held her breath.

"I don't know," David said, picking up his beer from the table. "I've never read him."

Him? *Him*? Oh no; oh my God, no. Only the greatest reserves of strength prevented Madeline from sinking her face into her hands and weeping. She glanced at Robert—he looked pained, seriously pained. Bella emitted a snort of laughter that involved expulsion of food, Michael's expression was neutral, and only Patty had the presence of mind to say, kindly, "Actually, David, George Eliot is a woman. 'George Eliot' is the pen name for a woman named Mary Ann Evans."

"Oh," David said. "Is that so?"

"Well," Madeline said, laughing shrilly. "George Eliot is a woman, and Evelyn Waugh is a man. So much for English literature."

"Yes," Robert said, sighing sadly. "So much for English literature."

Madeline did not think it was possible for David to further lower himself in Robert's eyes, but then to her complete and utter horror David reached into the front pocket of his offensive shirt and pulled out a pack of rolling papers and a folded plastic bag of pot. Oh fuck! she thought. Fuck, fuck, fuck! And not because Robert was against smoking—during Bella and Robert's evening parties a joint or two usually circulated; Bella and Madeline smoked, and so did Robert and Michael on occasion. No, the problem was that it was Sunday afternoon: in David's world that was as good a time as any to get stoned, but in Robert's world it smacked of indulgence and moral decay. Poor David—Madeline had not wanted to hurt him, and so had not told him the full extent of Robert's disapproval. Probably David thought he was doing a good and generous thing: some people brought flowers, he had brought pot. Madeline had mentioned that the others sometimes got high, and David naturally assumed it would be okay to roll a joint. But it was not; no, it absolutely was not.

As David rolled away, Bella bravely carried the conversation, telling anecdotes about *Psychology Now*—anecdotes that emphasized just how wonderful Patty was. Madeline pretended to listen, and pretended not to notice Robert: he was staring at David with narrowed eyes, his hand steadily tapping the arm of the couch. The arm was upholstered so the tapping made no noise, but each time Robert's fingers made contact Madeline's nerves stretched tighter and tighter. It was never a good sign when Robert tapped.

David lit the joint, took two deep hits, then passed it to Patty.

"Not me," Patty said brightly. "I never smoke."

She passed the joint to Robert; by his expression one would have thought Patty had just handed him a decapitated baby. He passed the joint to Bella, who interrupted her story to take two long hits. Then Bella passed it to Michael, who passed it at once to Madeline. Michael and Madeline's eyes met for a moment, but Madeline could not read his expression. She took a superficial hit off the joint, then passed it to David.

"…because Patty could sell anyone anything. And she has great ideas—remember, Patty, when you went after those Freud freaks? Patty convinced them to advertise a bust of Freud and we were all laughing and laughing, we thought, Who on earth is going to buy this piece of junk?, and then two weeks after the issue hit the stand Patty gets a call from the Freud people and they're *ecstatic*, they say they're getting a stack of mail every day, the orders are just *pouring* in. So now they're one of our most regular advertisers. What did they advertise last month, Patty? It was a scream."

"Bronzed cigars with a little plaque saying, 'Sometimes a cigar is just a cigar,'" Patty supplied.

"That's such a scream. Isn't that a scream? Michael, did you ever hear anything so funny?"

"Very funny," Michael said.

"Pass that wine over here, Patty. And people *buy* these things. You know, David," Bella said, waving the joint, which was once again in her possession. "This pot is really good."

"Keep the rest for yourself," David said, winking at her. "I'll roll another for me and Madeline."

Robert emitted an unidentifiable noise; Bella shot him a look, then said to David, "Why, aren't you a gentleman! I like this guy, Madeline; you have to bring him around more often."

Robert rose. "I'm going to the kitchen to get another much needed beer," he said. "Michael, I think you could use another. David?" he asked coldly.

"I'm fine," David said, meeting Robert's eye and smiling.

"And bring in another bottle of wine, Robert; Patty and I are almost done with this one. And get Madeline another club soda. Maddy, you haven't said a single word! Where is my little sister and her scintillating conversation?"

Madeline smiled weakly, and kept silent.

"So Michael," Patty said, thrusting her curvy black suited body over the table. "Bella tells me that in addition to being a professor you're a translator?"

"That's right," Michael said.

"What do you translate?"

"Well," Michael said, clearing his throat. He had his beer in one hand, his other arm rested on the back of the couch and he looked, Madeline thought, more pale than ever. "I've translated 'The Diamond Sutra' and 'The Platform Sutra' and 'The Flower Ornament Scripture,' and now I'm working on something called 'Verses on the Faith Mind,' which is often referred to as 'The Faith Mind Sutra.'"

"Isn't that interesting? But tell me, what is a sutra, exactly? Is it a religious text?"

"Some people define the word 'sutra' as a teaching by the Buddha, but actually many people have written sutras. And yes, I suppose you could say they're religious texts—they're Buddhist texts, in any event."

Robert came back and passed out the drinks. Patty hung over the table a moment, waiting for Michael to go on, but he was busy tracing the label of his beer with his fingernail.

"Michael is not one to blow his own horn," Bella said, filling Patty's glass then her own, "but I can tell you that his translations were extremely well received."

"Really?" Patty said. "How wonderful."

"We love our Michael," Bella said, reaching over and pinching Michael's cheek. "Isn't he cute? Our very own upstairs bachelor."

Oh my God, Madeline thought. Bella is totally bombed. And stoned; she had polished off the rest of the joint, and was still sucking on the roach.

"So Bella," David said. "Madeline tells me you used to be quite a Deadhead."

Another blunder—because although Robert accepted Bella's past, it was not his favorite topic of conversation. Which David did not know: Madeline had told him that when Bella was young she was wild, and she never exactly defined wild, although among other things it included the fact that Bella had racked up a list of lovers the number of which could only be estimated. Once Madeline tried to pin Bella down, and Bella had said, "Three or four different men every week over a period of five years—you do the math." Whatever the number, most of the list had been racked up during Bella's days following The Dead, and as a result The Dead were sparsely mentioned at 821 Washington. Which was something David did not know, and something Bella forgot, because the two of them launched into a lively laughing conversation about Jerry and Bob and Pig Pen and Phil and Donna and Mickey ("A friend of mine fucked him," Bella said cheerfully). And "Dark Star" and "China Doll" and "Brokedown Palace," and so much intimate Deadhead detail that everyone else was completely left out. And the two of them were talking so loudly it was impossible for anyone else to start an alternative conversation. So Robert tapped, Michael stared at his beer, Patty smiled and drank, and Madeline once again hoped for an alien invasion.

And Madeline had another problem. Whenever David's hands were not occupied by the fresh joint he and Bella were passing, they were wandering all over Madeline. Again, David was just acting as he always acted, the way *they* always acted, so what did it mean, she wondered, that now in front of her family and Michael she wanted him to act differently? It seemed like an important question, but it flew out of her mind before she could pin it down and save it for later contemplation. Anyway she was too busy to think: there was David's hand massaging her upper thigh—she put her hand on his and clamped it tight, but now his other hand was on her shoulder, the fingers reaching down and stroking her exposed skin. She took her other hand and grabbed his fingers together, but no matter what she did she could not stop his mouth: as he listened to Bella, laughed or told his own Deadhead stories, he kissed her constantly, his lips running over the side of her face and nuzzling her ear. She liked that he touched her all the time, but not here, not here! He probably thought he was showing everyone how much he loved her, but Madeline knew that

Robert saw only a strange man pawing his sister-in-law. And once she dared look at Michael; he felt her glance and turned to look at her, and the expression on his face shocked her—he looked disgusted. Michael had never, ever looked at her like that! She panicked; she looked at Michael pleadingly, wanting him to be on her side. He stared at her some moments, then shook his head and looked down at his beer. Well, she thought, at least now I know where he stands.

Bella, meanwhile, had gone into the kitchen to check on the lasagna, and on her way back she went to the bookshelves and pulled out an oversized softcovered book. Oh no—the coffee table Dead book, the one with the picture of Bella doing hair. Bella, book and wineglass in hand, wedged herself next to Patty so she could show David the picture. Patty moved over to give Bella room, and Robert was squeezed into the corner of the couch, which did nothing to improve his disposition. David and Bella, however, were in Deadhead heaven; the book was open and resting on their knees, and they passed a joint while Bella flipped through the pages.

"It's in this section here, I can never remember the page number. Here it is, that's me!"

Indeed it was. Bella was in profile, bending over a sitting woman, a pair of scissors in her hand. Bella's thick black hair was down to her waist, and she was wearing a flower-splattered mini-dress; and because she was bending over, one could see all of her long thighs and the round curve of her buttocks. A wooden sign propped on the ground proclaimed: I DO HAIR. PAYMENT: $2—A JOINT—WHATEVER.

"That 'whatever' must have been pretty interesting," David teased.

"Oh, believe me, it was," Bella said. "But I don't want to shock your young ears."

"Bella," Patty laughed. "You are something else. How could you let anyone take a picture of you with your ass hanging out like that?"

"I have a nice ass, so what do I care?"

"I don't even think you're wearing any underwear."

"Oh well—I probably wasn't." She looked at Patty, and they both gave a screech of laughter, their heads banging together. So Patty is totally looped as well, Madeline thought. When oh when will this brunch ever end?

"Oh, and this guy here," Bella said, pointing to another picture. "He was my old boyfriend. He sold beaded necklaces, I still have a couple. And this guy—oh God, what a story." Bella pointed to a picture of a man in a leather cowboy hat and mirror sunglasses, a sheaf of multi-colored tickets fanned out in front of his mouth. "He was a scalper. And he was the only one with a watch, but let me tell you about this watch. Written on the face in big black letters it said 'TIME TO FUCK.' So, you know, you'd ask him what time it was, and he'd hold out his watch. You know: 'What time is it?' 'Time to fuck.'"

Patty threw back her head and gave a scream of laughter. David laughed too, and turned to Madeline to see her reaction; she smiled weakly and said nothing.

"I knew *you'd* like that story," Bella said, winking at Patty. "And do you know, that became his nickname. You know, like, someone would say 'I need some tickets' and you'd say 'Well, go ask Time to Fuck.' But the funniest thing," Bella said, laughing so hard she held her stomach, "the funniest thing of all is that I *did* fuck him."

"Bella," Robert said, looking at the ceiling.

"I did fuck him, and you know what? He was horrible! I mean, the man was *pathetic*! So why in God's name he was wearing that watch I'll never know."

Bella and Patty screamed with laughter, little Patty so overcome she put her head in Bella's lap and pounded the book with her hands. Bella was weeping, her face smothered in Patty's back. Madeline snuck a glance at Michael; he had his eyes closed and was shaking his head, but he was smiling. As for Robert, he had a huge black thundercloud on his forehead, and was staring accusingly at—of all people—David. Robert blamed David for everything: David had gotten Bella stoned, David had asked her about The Dead, David had encouraged her stories—it was all his fault. Madeline knew Robert, and she knew that Robert hated David. Hated him. And David had no idea. He was, as a matter of fact, in paradise: he was laughing at Bella's story, he was smoking a joint, and he had managed to work a hand in Madeline's dress until his fingers were mere inches from her breast. He couldn't be happier, and he couldn't be more unaware that only fear of jail and Bella were preventing Robert from leaping across the coffee table and snapping his neck in two.

A buzzer rang out. Bella lifted her head. "It's the doorbell," she said. "Is someone else coming?"

"That, Bella," Robert said, biting off each word, "is the timer in the kitchen. That means that the food is ready."

"The food's ready!" Bella sang out. She lifted Patty off her lap and got up, then danced out of the room and down the hall singing, "Food's ready, food's ready!"

David kissed Madeline's cheek. "Your sister is a riot," he said. "She's so much fun."

"She sure is."

The buzzer stopped; hysterical laughter pealed from the kitchen.

"Madeline," Robert said murderously. "Would you please detach yourself from your boyfriend and go help your sister?"

"Okay."

Madeline ran down the hall into the kitchen. She found Bella on the floor next to the open oven, laughing hysterically.

"Bella," Madeline said, kneeling beside her. "What is it?"

"It's these potholders," Bella said. She held up two black and white potholders shaped like cowheads, complete with long eyelashes and red lips. "These are the funniest fucking things I've ever seen."

"Bella," Madeline said, taking her sister's hands and pulling. "*Bella*. Come on, we have to bring out the food."

The food was simple, thank God, just lasagna and salad. With some difficulty Madeline wrestled the potholders away from Bella, then took the glass casserole dish full of bubbling lasagna and put it on top of the stove. The salad was in the refrigerator; Madeline took it out and found six wooden bowls and the wooden salad utensils.

"Bella," she said. "What are we going to do about salad dressing?"

"Oh, I've got *lots* of dressing," Bella said. She stood and began pulling bottles out of the refrigerator. "Thousand Island, Blue Cheese, Roquefort—which looks a little moldy, but oh well..."

"Bella!" Madeline said, almost in tears. "We can't bring out forty different kinds of dressing! Tell me, did you have anything special planned?"

"I did. An olive oil thing. I'll make it now."

"Do you think you can?"

"I can." Bella stood up perfectly straight, and slapped her own cheeks. "I guess I'm a little fucked up, huh? I'm sorry, Maddy, I'll make it up to you. Bring me the olive oil and a few lemons from the fridge."

And with Madeline's assistance Bella was able to make dressing. She was just shaking the glass container to mix the oil and vinegar when Robert walked in, that black thundercloud still lodged on his forehead.

"Are you all right?" Robert asked, staring at Bella.

"Fine and dandy. Madeline and I were just making salad dressing. Go, take out the lasagna, tell everyone to sit down. And make sure Michael sits next to Patty."

Robert took the lasagna; Madeline smiled at him as he left, but he did not even glance at her.

Madeline sighed. "Robert hates David," she said.

"Does he? Well, don't you worry, because I think he's great. Here, take these bowls, I've got the salad. And I promise, from now on I'll be good."

They walked down the hall without incident, then entered the dining room. Robert was at the head of the table close to the door, with Michael and Patty on his left. There was an empty chair on his right for Madeline, and David was sitting next to it. Bella put the salad on the table and sat at the other end of the table, between Patty and David. She winked at Patty, and patted David's hand. "I'm fine now," she said, smiling. "Just a little fit of giggles. Won't happen again."

Robert looked up from cutting the lasagna. "Let's hope not," he said.

"*Well,*" Bella said as Robert passed out the food. "I think I've told enough stories for one day. Now, David, don't be modest, tell us all about The Big Record Label. I've always been so fascinated by the process, you know, how stars are born. And the psychology of it—you know, how when your dream comes true and it's not what you thought? Patty, remember that article we did a few months ago, the one about the lottery winners? David, did you know that most lottery winners are in debt after a year? Not that *you'll* ever be in debt," she said, touching David's arm, "I just mean, is it everything you thought it would be? You know, success?"

And from that moment, David took over. He started off slowly, modestly, talking between bites of lasagna, telling anecdotes about The Big Record Label, including how the VP was so charmed by Madeline he gave her a joint of Thai stick (Madeline did not dare glance at Robert during that story); and then as it became clear he had a captive audience in Bella and Patty he relaxed, grew more confident, and was soon pouring out story after story about life in the underground and above ground music scene. Bella and Patty hung onto his every word, laughing hysterically at his jokes, oohing and aahing, encouraging him to go on, all the while filling their wineglasses from the fresh bottle that was intended for everyone but instead found itself permanently parked between Bella and Patty's plates.

In a way, David was not doing anything wrong: Bella had made an effort to draw him out, and he was simply giving her what she asked for. Nevertheless Madeline could not help feeling that David was acting inappropriately. True, Bella and Patty were practically drooling over him, and they had certainly formed a cozy little trio, but Madeline was part of a much different trio, and she wished David would just take into account that Robert had pushed away his plate and was staring at the ceiling, and Michael—well, Michael had a look on his face that Madeline could not bear. He was sitting slightly away from the table, his hands folded elegantly on his lap, and he was staring at David. His features were composed but his brow was slightly drawn and his eyes were piercing. David did not know Michael and so would never notice, but Madeline knew what was hiding behind that gaze. And she saw, unhappily, that it was true: David was making a fool of himself. Bella and Patty were already drunk and worked up, and all his stories—particularly those that touched on sex—were just whipping them into a further state of hysterical excitement. He was making them laugh, but *anything* would have made them laugh, witness Bella and the potholders. Maybe their laughter made David feel good, but there were other people in the room; he should have turned the floor over to Robert, or Michael, or even herself. She had seen David like this before, and had been charmed, so why was it suddenly so excruciating? Because, she thought, I want them to like him, I *need* them to like him. This was the man she loved, the man she was going to move in with and maybe, just maybe, the man she was going to marry.

How could she stop him? She couldn't, for he was unstoppable. Even when Bella rose unsteadily to clear the dishes and bring out ice cream, David went on, now just talking to Patty, with occasional glances at Madeline. Poor Patty: all through dinner she had sent Michael coy fluttering glances, but Michael had not responded in kind—as if Michael could do anything coy and fluttering. So what was Patty to do? She was here to be fixed up with Michael, Michael was polite but, let's face it, absolutely indifferent, and a woman had to save her pride. So with Bella gone—Madeline could hear her singing "Sugar Magnolia" in the kitchen—Patty had hoisted her elbows on the table and was leaning over staring at David, her big mouth open and laughing, her pert nose crinkling, her curvy black-suited body wiggling with joy. And when Bella came back with a tray of ice cream bowls and—God help us all, Madeline thought—another bottle of wine, David just rolled on full steam. Madeline ate her ice cream without tasting a bite.

Then finally, finally, David stopped. His ice cream bowl was empty and his string of stories seemingly, hopefully, depleted. He pushed himself back from the table, put an arm around Madeline, leaned over and kissed her cheek. He lifted his hand to her face and began tracing her ear, all the while staring at her and smiling.

So David had stopped, but no one else started. Bella and Patty were in a boozy haze, Robert was a tense coil of anger, and Michael was still elegant, still disapproving. The silence started off small but then it grew and welled and swelled. Madeline felt her cheeks turn beet red, as if she were somehow respon-sible. David was so busy being enamored of her that it took him some time to notice, and when he did notice he said, "Well, everyone is certainly quiet! And Madeline," he said, patting her thigh, "would like to know what you're all thinking."

Michael looked at Madeline. "Is Madeline sure she wants to know what we're thinking?" he asked.

Madeline shot him what she hoped was a withering look.

"Do you know," Bella said, her voice slurring, "that people can actually read minds? We did an article on it a few months ago and—"

"Excuse me," Madeline said, rising from her chair. "I'll be back in a moment."

She went into the kitchen, opened the window, and stuck her head out into the cold, overcast day. She was not even stoned, she just had a horrible head-ache. They had eaten dessert, so when would everyone go home? But it was still early, probably not even four, and Bella would surely make coffee and bring out fruit and, what agony, they might be here for another two hours. I can't bear it, Madeline thought. I just can't bear it. Robert's hatred for David was almost palpable, and Michael—what was Michael's problem? Well, he was her friend, and he probably felt just as Robert did, that her moving in with David was wrong. Oh, fuck them both! she thought angrily, slamming the window shut. It's my life, I'll do what I want.

She filled a glass with water and took a plastic aspirin bottle from the cabi-net next to the phone. She was just popping the aspirin into her mouth when she heard footsteps. She turned; Michael was standing in the doorway.

"I'm not surprised you have a headache," he said.

"And what's that supposed to mean?" she said, narrowing her eyes and sip-ping from the glass.

"It means exactly what I said." He took a few steps forward and leaned against the refrigerator. "May I tell you something?"

"Go right ahead."

"Your boyfriend is a pompous ass."

Madeline took a step back. She had always wanted to see Michael lose con-trol, but now that it was actually happening she felt scared.

"Tell me," he said, "Because I want to be sure. *This* is the man you've been raving about? *This* is the man you've fallen so madly in love with? I thought I knew you, Madeline, but now I think I never knew you at all."

He turned, ready to leave the room. Madeline's fear fell away, and rage took its place.

"Don't you walk away from me, Michael," she said. "Don't think you can make your smug little comments and stroll out of here. You gave me your opinion, and now I'm going to give you mine."

"Which is?" he said, turning around.

"You, you— You're so *slow*."

"Oh. Yes, that's right. I'm slow. I really wasn't aware it was such a crime."

"You're slow! And, and, you're like Mr. Causabon from *Middlemarch* with his Key to All Mythologies—you're so slow you'll never finish translating your sutra, never!"

As soon as the words were out Madeline regretted them. Not because she thought she had hurt Michael—she wanted to hurt Michael—but because it simply wasn't true. But she couldn't stop now.

"Yes, you're just like Mr. Causabon, all caught up in your books and completely unable to love!"

"Oh. So I'm unable to love."

"That's right," she said, suddenly nervous.

"That's what you think."

"That's what I think."

Michael took a deep breath, looked her up and down, then turned to walk away. Madeline picked up the plastic bottle of aspirin and hurled it at his head. The bottle flew past his ear and hit Robert—who was just coming into the room—smack in the center of his forehead.

"Ow," Robert said, holding his hand to his face. "Ow."

"Oh, Robert!" Madeline said, rushing past Michael and putting an arm around Robert. "I'm so sorry, are you okay?"

Robert removed his hand and glared at Madeline. "I come in here to get away from the sight of your boyfriend flirting with my wife and what happens, you hit me."

"David is not flirting with Bella!"

"Oh, he's not? What would you call it?"

"Robert!"

"Let me tell you, Madeline, if you move in with him you're making the biggest mistake of your life."

"How can you say such a thing?"

"Oh, how can I say such a thing? Let me count the ways. We can start with the fact that he's wearing the most obnoxious shirt I've ever seen in my life."

"It's not obnoxious, it's, it's flashy."

"Oh please, Madeline. Don't even try. What kind of person wears a shirt like that?"

"And what kind of person is obsessed with George Eliot? *Oh*—the two of you! Just leave me *alone!*"

She ran past them, flew into the bathroom, slammed and locked the door. Then she sat on the toilet and cried. Now both Robert and Michael were mad at her—no, not mad, it was worse: they were disappointed. They just didn't see David the way she did. Not that David had behaved particularly well today, but he was different when they were alone, when they were alone everything was perfect. Robert and Michael hadn't even given him a chance, not really.

She cried her heart out, and when she was done she felt better. She peed, washed her face and hands, then closed the toilet and sat on it. She had no desire to go back into the living room; she crossed her legs and stared absent-mindedly at the drawing of George Eliot. Eliot had not been known for her looks, and in this drawing she was not the least bit attractive: her eyes were dull, her nose droopy, her jaw long and thick, and her partially open mouth actually made her look a bit stupid. Which was not true, of course, for she was brilliant, perhaps the most brilliant of all the Victorians. Madeline had read Gordon Haight's biography of Eliot and, excepting *Middlemarch*, she had enjoyed it more than any of the novels. Most of all she admired Eliot's courage for defying convention in order to live with the very married George Henry Lewes; Eliot had taken love when it was offered, societal mores be damned. "You and me, George," Madeline said. "You and me both." Well, if George moved in with George, then Madeline could move in with David. She simply had to accept that Robert and Michael would not accept him, at least not for a long, long time. She sighed; she would just have to learn to live with that.

The tears had stopped; she had gained courage, and had even forgiven Robert and Michael, not that she was about to give them the satisfaction of knowing that, but Madeline still did not leave the bathroom. She was being childish, she knew that, but it was so cool and peaceful here with the light green tiles and fluffy white towels; and because they had company Bella had cleared away the jumble of cosmetics on top of the toilet and replaced them with a white china bowl full of delicate blown glass balls. Very middle-class, Madeline thought, but Bella was better off middle-class than running around Dead shows with no underwear.

Running feet pounded down the hall; someone twisted the bathroom door-knob.

"Madeline!" It was Bella, her voice oddly strangled. "Let me in, *now!*"

Madeline leapt up and opened the door. Bella ran in with her hand to her mouth; she raised the toilet seat, sank to her knees, and proceeded to throw up.

Oh no. Madeline left the bathroom and closed the door. Robert came down the hall, his expression simultaneously worried and furious.

"Would you please go sit with our guests?" he said. "I'll take care of Bella."

It was a grim little group in the living room. Michael was sitting on the piano bench looking out the window, and David was on the couch, his brow drawn. Even Patty looked wiggled out—she was sitting next to David, holding out her hands and examining her nails.

"Are you okay?" David asked, grabbing Madeline's hand as she sat. "You were gone so long."

"I'm fine," she said. Michael had looked up when she walked in, and she could tell by his expression that he felt bad about what he had said. She shot him a dirty look—let him suffer, she thought.

"How's Bella?" Patty asked. "Did she—"

"She sure did. What happened?"

"Well, I was in the middle of a story, and one moment I looked over at her and her face was just *green*. Next thing I knew she was running out of the room."

"She'll be okay. Robert's helping her."

David squeezed her hand. "While you were gone I was telling Mike how much you always talk about Bella and how much fun she is."

Mike? Oh no—David just couldn't do anything right today. "Well, Bella's my only family; it's just me and her and Robert."

"But your parents are still alive, no?" Patty asked.

"They're alive, but they're not exactly functioning."

"Oh."

Robert walked in. He sat on the empty couch and took his beer from the table. "Well, you'll all be pleased to know that Bella threw up the entire contents of her stomach, then went into the bedroom and passed out." He glared at David. "She's not used to smoking so much pot—not anymore, anyway."

"Robert," Madeline said. "It wasn't just the pot. Bella and Patty drank about four bottles of wine. Not that it's your fault," Madeline smiled at Patty. "Just Bella doesn't have a very strong stomach. Not anymore, anyway."

"I'm sorry, Robert," Patty said. "I didn't mean to be a bad influence."

"I don't blame *you*, Patty," Robert said, still staring at David.

"Well!" Patty clapped her hands together and stood. "I don't know what Emily Post says, but when the hostess passes out I think it's time to leave." Then she politely went around and shook everyone's hand and said it was nice to meet them; and as she shook with Michael she gave one last wiggle and said, "I hope to see you again, Michael—it was a pleasure."

Robert walked Patty to the hall to get her coat. The minute the front door shut, Michael stood.

"I have to go as well. Good-bye, David; good-bye, Madeline."

David stood and extended his hand. "Nice to meet you, Mike. I'm sure I'll be seeing you again."

Michael shook David's hand, but said nothing. He looked at Madeline; she pursed her lips and glowered. Michael sighed, and left the room.

As Robert and Michael murmured in the hall David leaned over and kissed Madeline. "So why don't you pack up your things and we'll go."

"I don't think we're going to get off so easy."

"What do you mean?"

"I mean Robert."

"He can't stop us."

"But he can try."

David made a face. "He wouldn't do that."

"David, you don't know Robert."

The front door shut. Slow, angry footsteps marched down the hall. Madeline closed her eyes and thought, Here it comes.

Robert came into the living room and sat on the couch. He leaned back against the arm and, staring at David, rested one hand on the top of the couch and started a rapid, furious tapping.

"Well," David said. "I guess we'll be off too. We're going to call a taxi and move Madeline's things over to my place."

"Excuse me," Robert said coldly. "Not so fast."

"I beg your pardon?"

"I want to have a little talk with you."

"Robert..." Madeline said.

Robert pointed a finger at her. "Madeline, for the next half hour you are forbidden to speak. I mean it—not a word."

Madeline sat back on the couch and folded her arms. She was angry, but she knew when she was outmatched.

Robert—skin taut and white, eyes burning—turned his full attention to David. "I would like to have a little talk with you, David. My wife was also supposed to be part of this conversation but, as you know, she is no longer conscious. So I'll have to do this myself. I assume, David, that Madeline has told you that her parents are—well, for lack of a better word I'll say crazy; and because of that Bella and I are responsible for her. Madeline told us about your plan to move in together, and we agreed that you would come here and meet us and then we could all talk. Well—there's no point trying to sweeten things, so I'll just come out and say how I feel, which is that I don't want Madeline moving in with you. And the reasons are, I don't think you've known each other long enough, I don't like the way you've behaved with her, and I haven't been particularly impressed with your behavior today."

David, who had been sitting perfectly straight and listening with great concentration, jumped right in. "Well, Robert, I appreciate your honesty, and I'll try to address your doubts as best I can. I'll start by saying that yes, it's true I haven't known Madeline very long, but it's been long enough to know that I love her. And since Madeline told me that you fell in love with your wife as soon as you saw her, I think you can understand me. And as far as how I've behaved with her—well, I'll have to ask you to clarify that, because I don't know what you mean."

"Why don't you ever come here to pick up Madeline?"

"Well, my band rehearses until ten, ten-thirty, and I thought that was too late to come over. I know you and Bella both go to bed early, I didn't want to bother you."

"What about weekends?"

"Well—" David spread out his hands and looked at the floor. "I don't know, it just never worked out that way. But it was certainly nothing intentional, I wasn't avoiding all of you. And Madeline talks about you and Bella so much I felt like I already knew you."

Robert raised an eyebrow. "It's not the same thing."

"Is there anything else?"

"I don't like the hours you keep."

"Well, it's true I have an unconventional lifestyle, but I think for a musician my life is pretty organized. I mean, I work and practice at the same time each day, it's not like I'm unreliable. And since I work in the day and so do two other members of my band, we can only practice at night. And I can assure you, Robert, that I've never taken Madeline anywhere dangerous, or left her unprotected."

"Do you always smoke so much pot? And do you always flirt with your girlfriends' sisters?"

David inhaled deeply, but kept his cool. "It's true I smoke pot, I won't deny that, but I don't think I smoke too much. And I hardly drink at all; if you noticed I only drank one beer all day. And as for flirting with Bella, you'll have to forgive me, but that's ludicrous. We were just talking. And I think we got along very well, but it certainly wasn't anything you could call flirting. Madeline," he said, turning to her. "Do you think I was flirting with your sister?"

"No," Madeline said, looking at Robert. She was so proud of David she could have hugged him.

Robert closed his eyes and released a long, pained sigh. "Well," he said. "I'm going to be blunt with you. I am one hundred percent against this. I can't give you my blessing because I don't approve of this, not one bit. But I know Madeline, and I know how stubborn she is, so I won't try to force her to stay here. But I swear to God, if you harm one hair on her head—"

"Robert, I value Madeline as much as you do, and I wouldn't be taking this step if I wasn't serious about her." David stood. "Can we at least shake hands and leave on good terms?"

Robert stood and, with an expression of greatest reluctance, shook David's hand.

Madeline jumped up at once. "Well, that's settled. David, give me five minutes and I'll be ready."

She ran to the storage room, pulled out a suitcase, and flew to her room. Quickly, she thought, quickly, before Robert changes his mind! She opened the suitcase and threw in two skirts for work, three good blouses, her black short jacket, two pairs of jeans, three sweaters, four T-shirts, two pairs of sweatpants, underwear, bras, stockings, hair ties, her small wicker basket full of jewelry. She filled her bookbag with all the drafts of the short story she was working on, plus pens, paper, typing paper, envelopes, her submission notebook, her copy of *The Literary Marketplace*, a few novels, and her dictionary. She looked around—what else? Her eyes landed on the framed picture of Flannery O'Connor; she couldn't leave without Flannery.

"Flannery," she said as she removed the picture from the wall. "We're moving in with David."

She clicked the cover on her typewriter and put her lapdesk on top of it, and just as she was zipping up her suitcase someone knocked.

"Madeline? It's Robert."

Her eyes filled with tears. Oh no! He was going to ruin everything, she just knew it. She opened the door and steeled herself.

Robert walked in, his hands in his pockets, his brown eyes sad. He looked around the little room, then turned to Madeline. "You have everything?" he asked.

"Yep."

"Well—in case you need it…" He reached into the pocket of his pants and pulled out a wad of bills.

"Robert! I don't need money."

"Just take it. And Madeline? I want you to know, this will always be your room. We'll keep it this way for you."

"Oh, Robert." She hugged him. "Thank you. And please, don't worry."

"I'm worried."

"Well—" She looked around. "I guess that's it. Robert, don't look so sad! I'll be over tomorrow night for dinner and Scrabble."

His face lit up. "You will?"

"Of course I will. I'm still going to come every day. What did you think?"

"I thought—I don't know."

"Oh, don't be a dumbbell. Come on, help me bring all this stuff into the hall."

Robert called a taxi, and a few minutes later they heard BEEP BEEP from the street. Madeline kissed Robert, then ran to Bella's bedroom. She opened the door quietly; Bella was asleep on the bed, dead to the world.

David grabbed her suitcase and typewriter, Madeline took her bookbag and lapdesk, and they walked downstairs and out to the waiting taxi. Free at last, Madeline thought. Free at last.

CHAPTER 12

Living Together

Living together was wonderful. Being with a man she loved in a nice, clean apartment was heavenly, and Madeline thrived as never before, which made her think that all those men who saw her as a cozy domestic partner had not been totally off-base. Not that she had become particularly domestic in terms of housework or—God forbid—cooking; David took care of all those things, and did a much better job than she could have. No, it was more that living in a sane, loving environment was exactly what she needed. She had such a life at Bella's, but there Bella was mistress of the house, and Madeline more like a child. But now Madeline felt that she was living as a mature woman, and it felt wonderful: she was strong, happy, sure of herself.

The first time she was alone in the apartment was the Wednesday after she moved in. She had worked on Monday and Tuesday, had spent both evenings at 821 Washington, then met David at his rehearsal space. Wednesday morning she and David spent in bed, then at eleven o'clock he went to Maxwell's. Madeline had planned to write while he was gone, but instead she decided to explore the apartment. It was not a big place, but there were drawers and cupboards and closets, so much to look at and get familiar with. She started with the kitchen, opening each drawer and cupboard, learning where David kept the potato peeler and scissors, balls of twine and extra light bulbs. She touched the matching mugs, the plates with the triangle design around the edge, discovered a set of pots and pans, saw two vases tucked behind a pressure cooker. She left the kitchen and moved on to the hall closet, and as she was opening a box in the corner she asked herself, Am I snooping? But no—how could she be snooping if she lived here? Anyway, all the box had was a scarf, two wool hats, and a pair of mittens. No harm done, Madeline thought as she carefully replaced the lid.

As she worked her way through the hall closet, the bathroom linen closet, and the big bedroom closet, as she saw how tidy and organized everything was, she decided that David was very mature. Despite the pot smoking and late hours and whatever associations of flakiness she might have about rock musicians, she realized that David was far more self-sufficient than she was. She asked him once how he kept everything so clean, and he said it was simple: every day when he got home from work he put on some music, smoked a joint, then just did whatever had to be done. Discipline, she thought; he's got discipline. She was disciplined about her writing but, in truth, not much else. She was the type of person who waited until she was wearing her last pair of underwear before she did laundry, and even then she might borrow a pair of Bella's, or just wash a few pairs by hand. And Bella and Robert had a washer and dryer in the apartment, so there was no excuse at all. David, on the other hand, had a hamper and a bright blue laundry bag and, he told her, every Monday before work he took his clothes to the corner Chinese laundry where they washed and ironed and folded everything to perfection. That had impressed Madeline mightily, and then when she opened the bedroom closet she saw—and she actually did gasp—*an ironing board*. The Chinese laundry ironed his clothes, and he still had his own iron. Amazing, just amazing.

Next to the bed was a small chest of drawers. On top was a phone, a clock radio, and a box of tissues. Madeline already knew about the first of the three drawers because that was her diaphragm's new home, a home it shared with gaily colored condoms, a small jar of Vaseline, and extra shoelaces. The other two drawers were unexplored territory, and were just begging for Madeline to open them. So she did. The second drawer had only a well-used notebook and a few pens, and the third drawer was full of similarly well-used notebooks, all with the year of use carefully written in the corner.

Madeline looked at the clock—a little after twelve. David wouldn't be home until two. Is this a moral dilemma? she wondered. Hmm. The notebooks were diaries, definitely diaries. She would take a peek, just the tiniest little peek, and that would be all. Who wouldn't do the same in her place?

She shut the third drawer, opened the second, and carefully took out the notebook. She opened it: the first page had several lines of music, then a gap, then the phrase "An undistinguished birthmark." She twisted her lips—she had heard that phrase before. Of course: it was a line from one of Narrow

Grave's songs. So, she thought, a little disappointed, these aren't diaries, they're David's working notebooks. And he had so many! Well, Madeline, she asked herself, what did you expect? David is a serious artist. She had similar notebooks for her ideas, and as she paged through the notebook she felt a silent bond between her and David. And then on the last page with writing she saw a complicated musical notation and under it the words "Madeline's hair." She felt a shock of pleasure: so he was planning a song about her or, at least, her hair. Because that was the kind of song David wrote: Hanson's songs were about love and death and deep dark emotions like panic, greed, and jealousy, but David's songs were funny and whimsical—he wrote about his first dog and eating beans in Boston and what it was like to be a principal's son. He told her he was in the midst of writing a song about Lucky and Leapy, and searching through the notebook she found bits of description—Lucky's blue jacket and pink nose and cheeks, Leapy's plastic pipe and red hat. She saw no other references to her or her hair but you never knew, maybe the song needed to percolate in his subconscious awhile. David was obsessed with her hair—he was always touching it, smelling it, marveling how it changed color with the light; and he was always thrilled with Bella's hairdos, he was practically ecstatic when Madeline wore Defying Gravity, and once had insisted on undoing it so he could see how it worked. So she really shouldn't be surprised that he wanted to write about her hair. Well, she thought as she put the notebook away. I won't say a word. But the fact that he was even thinking of writing about her touched her deeply.

Gradually her feelings of newness and strangeness—the feeling that she was using David's mugs, playing David's stereo, calling on David's phone—faded away. Getting mail helped: a few days after she moved in David wrote out a new sign for the mailbox (GUGGENHEIM/BOOT) and Madeline went to the post office and filled out a change of address form. Two days later she got her first piece of mail, a letter from Oriana, and she considered it a good sign: if she was getting mail, well, then 10 Willow Terrace was really home. This feeling was sealed by Bella's first visit. Three Sundays after moving in Madeline invited Bella and Robert for coffee and cake. Robert declined, so Bella came alone; she breezed in, kissed Madeline, kissed David, tossed her red beret on the sofa and said, "Nice place. Love the elves." Bella stayed all afternoon drinking coffee and smoking joints and entertaining them with stories from her Grateful Dead days, even showing them the weird loopy dance she used to do in the aisles during concerts. Madeline was happy to see Bella and David getting along so well, and she was proud to have her own place where she could entertain her sister properly. The stable in Swan's Cove had a sad, pitiful air, but David's apartment—*their* apartment—was clean and warm and lovely. When Bella left she hugged Madeline and said, "This living together thing is really agreeing with you, Maddy. You look so beautiful, you're really blooming."

"I'm happy," Madeline said.

"I can tell. See what happens when you get regular sex?"

"Bella!"

"Well, it's true. David is really good for you." She sighed. "I just wish Robert would come around."

"Do you think he ever will?"

"No. Never."

On the way out Madeline knocked on Bridget's door and introduced her to Bella. Bridget was, as usual, dressed to kill in a frilly, low-cut blouse and tight lavender pants. "Oh, your sis-tah! She's gaw-geous, just gaw-geous! You two could be twins, excepting for your hair." Bridget put an arm around Madeline. "You're so lucky to have a sis-tah like Madeline. God didn't put a sweeter creature on this green earth." She pinched Madeline's cheek. "I just love huh."

Which was true. Madeline and Bridget had hit it off immediately, and about once a week Madeline was downstairs in Bridget's apartment sitting on the plastic-covered sofa drinking tea, always careful to put her teacup a respectful distance from the plastic statue of Jesus that graced the coffee table. Madeline decided that she wanted to be like Bridget when she was sixty-eight: Bridget was trim and busty and always well-dressed, as well-dressed as one could be in polyester and nylon; and she was up at seven each morning to take a walk and have coffee at Shirley's on Washington Street, and then it was on to her volunteer job at St. Mary's gift shop. At 12:30 she was home and ensconced in front of the TV for the latest installment of *The Young and the Restless*. "I hear that song and I just cry. It *moves* me, you know what I'm sayin?'" After that a nap, and in the evenings Paddy O'Malley came over for dinner and canasta and, twice a week, bingo at St. Ann's.

"So David," Madeline once asked. "Do you think Bridget and Paddy have sex?"

"Are you kidding me?" he said. "Just look at her—of course they do."

And it did happen on occasion that Madeline heard an odd squeak or moan from the apartment below, but as Bridget never said anything about Madeline and David's occasionally noisy sex life, Madeline never said anything about Bridget and Paddy's.

So Madeline was okay with Bridget, and she was also okay with David's mother. Mrs. Guggenheim called every Sunday at noon; Madeline was always at David's on Sundays, and had listened in on many such calls, but the first Sunday after she moved in she and David were laying in bed talking when the phone rang. David talked to his mother for awhile, then handed the receiver to Madeline. "My mother wants to say hi."

"She knows I'm here?"

"Of course she does. Say hi."

Madeline pulled the sheets up to her neck then took the phone. She was nervous at first, but they had a pleasant conversation: Mrs. Guggenheim said how happy she was that David had met someone nice, wasn't it was wonderful that they decided to live together, she couldn't wait to meet Madeline but it would have to wait until Christmastime since Mr. Guggenheim was at school until then, Madeline and David were of course welcome for Thanksgiving but since David had a date to play music in New York the Friday after Thanksgiving it was too much to ask them to come up to Boston then travel back down again… Then she put Mr. Guggenheim on the phone; he said a brief, friendly hello, then asked to speak to David. And every Sunday after that Madeline spoke to Mrs. Guggenheim, and sometimes during the week as well when Mrs. Guggenheim called to say she was sending David a sweater she had ordered from Lands' End, or letting him know there was a PBS special on Buddy Holly. She was a nice, cheery woman who was utterly infatuated with her son but not, Madeline assured herself, in an unhealthy, sticky way. No wonder David is so sure of himself, Madeline thought; from the moment he was born he had this amazing, stable love. She envied him.

So Madeline was folded into David's life, and he was folded into hers: one Saturday they went into The City and hung out with Rose, another time Devon came down from Connecticut and Madeline took her to lunch at Maxwell's where David waited on them, then when David got off work they all went back to the apartment and got stoned. And once David took a day off and they went to The City to have lunch with Bella; afterwards they got stoned in Central Park, then Bella took them to *Psychology Now*'s offices where they had a great time hanging out with Bella and—sexy and curvy in a fire engine red suit—Patty. Everyone in Madeline's life loved David, everyone except Robert and Michael. Madeline went to 821 Washington every evening and most weekends, but as long as Robert was in the room David's name was not mentioned. If Robert absolutely unavoidably had to refer to David, he used the pronoun "he"; as for Michael, he formulated his words and thoughts so that even "he" was unnecessary. Madeline did her best not to let it bother her, and anyway what did it matter—Bella liked David, and her opinion was the one that counted.

And one of the best things about living with David was his respect for her writing. Whenever she was writing or typing he practically walked on tiptoes, and whenever she got a rejection letter he cheered her up. "Don't give up," he told her again and again. "If they knock you down ten times, you get up eleven. We never gave up, and look where we are now."

Yes—look where David was now. Because only after living with David some weeks did Madeline fully comprehend the extent of Narrow Grave's success. They weren't yet on the cover of *Musician* or *Rolling Stone*, but in the underground music scene they were acknowledged as one of the top bands. And this meant many things: endless phone calls from newspapers and minor magazines and fanzines, calls from managers hoping to sign them, free tapes and CDs, passes to clubs, recognition in the streets, buses, PATH station; and there was even a phone call from—Madeline could hardly believe it—a Mr. Michael Stipe, who left a message on the machine saying he had just gotten around to listening to Narrow Grave's last album and he wanted to call them personally and say it was one of the best things he'd heard all year. Alison and Hanson came over to hear the message, and Alison was so overjoyed she actually taped it. And these were just the calls David was getting—Hanson and Alison got just as many and maybe more. Plus the VP and others from The Big Record Label kept calling; there was no date yet on the informal meeting, but they wanted to keep in touch. "They want to see if we're getting other offers," David told Madeline. Which they were: a few other record companies were calling and sending A&R men to gigs, but it had always been David and Hanson's dream to be on The Big Record Label, so they were biding their time.

All of this was very exciting, and Madeline had to work hard to keep her vow not to let David's work overwhelm her own. One evening she walked in the door carrying two rejection letters, and on the answering machine she heard three messages for David: an A&R man from Another Big Record Label wanted to know about their next gig, The Small Record Label needed him to come in and choose publicity pictures, and *The Hoboken Reporter* wanted to interview him and Hanson for an article entitled "Now that The Bongos have broken up, Narrow Grave is Hoboken's best band." Never mind, Madeline told herself; never mind. The secret was to use David's success to give herself confidence. David had told her stories about Narrow Grave's early gigs when they were lucky to have an audience of four people—and how it felt when one of those four people walked out saying loudly, "This band sucks." And how Hanson's father ridiculed them, telling them Narrow Grave would never make it so why didn't they both do something practical like go to law school? And about being a waiter at Pizzeria Uno in Boston, his clothes so smelly and greasy after work he had to hang them on the fire escape. David used all these things to fire his ambition, and she could do the same, she *would* do the same. She was so proud of David; he had simply refused to quit, and now look what he had achieved. She had been shy at The Beat'n Path gig, but now when they were out in public she enjoyed the attention—she was David Guggenheim's girlfriend, and proud of it.

So everything was perfect, just perfect.

Well—not exactly. There were a few tiny things, a few problems and fears that floated into her mind at odd times—at work watching a document print out, or standing on line for the Red Apple Bus, or waiting for Michael to put down a word during Scrabble. First and foremost, David smoked too much pot. Madeline liked to smoke pot, but David was a potsmoker, and there was a huge difference. David never once left the house without first getting high; it would never occur to him to just do something, instead it was always, "Let's get high and go to a club" or "Let's get high and go buy batteries." Madeline didn't know if David liked to get high before he went out or if he needed to—again, there was a huge difference, and she was afraid to find out the answer. And sometimes it seemed to her David couldn't even be in the house without being high: in the morning when they woke they often made love, and he wasn't high then, but after taking a shower and making coffee David would sit down at the living room table—in his bathrobe, hair still wet—and roll a joint. And sometimes Madeline woke up and found herself alone; when she went out to the living room David was on the couch quietly playing bass, his notebook open on the table in front of him, a lit joint in the ashtray. Then he had to have a joint before he went to work, and another when he came home from work, another before rehearsal, and of course he smoked during rehearsal and then again after. So except for the morning he was always stoned. And looking back on their courtship Madeline realized that of course he was stoned during their first date at Leo's, and of course he had been stoned for every single date after that. And surely he had been stoned when he showed up at Bella's brunch. Such thoughts made Madeline uneasy, and she started to wonder: Who is David? Where is David? What would he be like if he wasn't always stoned? Then her mind would work furiously to defend him: okay, he was always stoned, but where did it show? He worked hard at his career, he never missed a day at work, his apartment was immaculate. Hell, his eyes weren't even red, so if you didn't know, you could never tell. And David never pressured her to smoke; if she wanted to smoke, fine, but if she didn't that was okay too. One morning when she was sitting on the couch listening to him play, he lit a joint and passed it to her.

"Oh no," she said, waving a hand. "I have to write."

"Maybe you'll write better if you're high."

"Or maybe I'll just go to sleep," she laughed. "Or be compelled to go to the store and buy a pint of ice cream."

He laughed, and that was the end of it. But so many times she wanted to ask him: Why? Just sit him down, take his hands, look him in the eye and ask, "David, why do you smoke so much pot?" But she was afraid to hear his answer, so she never asked.

Another little cloud on their horizon was UTIs, better known as Urinary Tract Infections. The first one came a few days after Madeline moved in. She and David had spent the morning in bed, and when she went to the bathroom to pee it felt as if her urine was full of broken glass. Very painful. She crept back to bed, wincing as she laid down.

"Bad news," she said.

He leaned over, kissed her and stroked her hair. "What, you got your period?"

"I consider getting my period good news. No, I have a urinary tract infection."

"Which means?"

"Which means every time I pee I feel like I'm going to die. And I have to drink about three gallons of cranberry juice every day. And we can't have sex for awhile."

"What's 'awhile?'"

"A week."

He moved on top of her. "Does no sex mean no sex at all or no sex with—how should I say—penetration?"

She smiled up at him. "No sex with—how should you say—penetration."

"Oh, then we'll be okay."

The infection cleared up, but it came back a few days later, and then again after that. They experimented a bit and found that she didn't get them so frequently if they just had sex—with penetration—no more than twice a day. But she still got them. Madeline knew the truth, which was that she got UTIs because of the way they had sex. Or, really, the way David had sex. He was a bit rough, and he never changed his style, not once. Poor Madeline: although she had many sexual experiences, she was not sexually experienced. She had been drunk for all her high school and college sex; the encounters had been brief and unloving, and she never even had orgasms. And except for The Virgin—who hardly counted, she could barely remember his face—she had never had an extended relationship, had never been able to leisurely explore what it meant to make love. Her hunger for physical contact was so great that it was a relief just to be touched, but she never asked herself if she liked the way she was being touched, just as a starving person will eat what they can get without quibbling over vegetables being fresh or canned. Madeline accepted David as he was, and took on his style. Mostly she thought they had an amazingly good sex life, but other times a vague worry nagged her, and she was unable—and unwilling—to understand what it meant.

Another problem was that David never read her work. He had read one of her short stories, and part of another; he had praised them to the skies, telling her how great she was. Whenever they went out he was always proud to introduce her as a writer, and whenever friends came to the apartment he always showed off the magazines with her stories. But whereas she knew every one of Narrow Grave's songs, whereas she was making a real effort to learn about music and songwriting and what it meant to have a band, David was not putting any effort into learning about her work. He encouraged her, he was proud of her, but he was not involved. Maybe he didn't know how to be, or maybe he was just too busy. Or maybe, another voice said, he's lazy. Or, worse, indifferent. She did not know and, again, was afraid to ask.

So these were the small things. And then there was the one fight they had, but she couldn't really call that a problem since the whole fight consisted of her straightening David out—and fast. He had made an assumption, and she had shown him that his assumption was wrong.

It was afternoon. David had come back from work, changed his clothes, smoked a joint, and was getting ready to meet Hanson for their voice lesson.

"So what are you up to?" he asked her as he sat on the couch tying his shoes.

She was reclining on the couch reading *Some Tame Gazelle* by Barbara Pym, a book Michael had lent her. She put the book facedown on her lap and said, "I'm going to finish this book, then at six I'm going to Bella's."

"Listen, would you mind doing me a favor? I have a few shirts in the closet that need ironing. They're not dirty, but they could use a quick pressing."

"I beg your pardon?"

"You'll know which ones they are—they're all hanging together, I put them that way so you'd know."

She laughed. "David, you must be joking."

"Why?"

"David—I'm not going to iron your shirts. I don't know if I've ever ironed anything in my life."

"Oh, come on. Everyone knows how to iron."

"Well, of course I know how, but I never do it. They're your shirts, you do it."

"Well, I always do, but I just thought—I mean, you seem to have more free time than I do, so it just seemed logical."

"No, David, I do not have more free time than you do. I also work, and I write, and as a writer I need to read. I do a lot of things; I don't iron."

"Madeline, what's the problem? I just asked you a simple favor."

Oh no, oh no: anger. And David had never seen her get angry, at least not in a full-blown way. The red rawness rose up her throat; she felt it overwhelming her, how she hated to lose control, she was just like her father and here it came, and now she was standing with her hands on her hips and yelling.

"The problem is, David, that I am not your personal slave, and I'm not going to iron your stupid fucking shirts. You take care of your clothes, and I'll take care of mine."

She sat down, trembling. David was stunned. "Madeline...Madeline, look, I'm sorry. Of course you don't have to do it, I just thought..."

She put her head in her hands and started crying. David came closer and put his arms around her. "Shh, shh," he said, stroking her hair. "I'm sorry, I'm so sorry. It was a stupid idea, I won't ask you again. I thought you liked, I don't know, domestic things. You're always saying how happy you are that this place is so clean."

"I'm happy if a place is clean," she sniffed, "but not if I have to do it."

"Okay," he said, putting her head on his shoulder. "It's okay, I understand."

"I'm no good at housekeeping and stuff like that. My mother wasn't either; our house was always a mess. Disgusting, even." She looked up at him. "I bet *your* house was perfect. I bet your mother is a great housekeeper."

"Well—yes. But she made us work as well. She had a list of chores on the refrigerator, and if you did a chore you got a gold star, two if it was a big chore. And as soon as you had ten gold stars you got five dollars."

"Oh my God, that's so cute."

"Well, my Mom's pretty cute."

"Listen, you better go, you'll be late."

"I don't mind. I just want to be sure you're okay."

"I'm okay. It was just—an outburst."

"I'll say." He laughed and kissed her nose. "My Madeline has quite a temper, doesn't she."

"Just sometimes."

He left, and that was it: he kept his word, and never asked her to iron again. So that wasn't a problem, and the other problems weren't exactly problems either—it wasn't as if they were fighting all the time, or had found they were incompatible. The fact was, they were very happy living together; and one night before they went to sleep Madeline was laying in David's arms and he said, "I love you, Madeline. And you know, living together like this, I feel like we're married. Don't you?" He kissed the crown of her head, and she buried her smiling face in his chest, her joy inexpressible.

❧   ❧   ❧

The Saturday before Thanksgiving Madeline was alone in the apartment; David and Hanson had a gig in Baltimore, and would not be back until the next day. She was sitting on the couch with her knees bent, her lapdesk pressed against her thighs. She was reading over—for what had to be the fiftieth time—her new short story. It was twenty-two pages long, typed and printed courtesy of The Big Cigarette Company. She had printed out a final version on Tuesday, and every day while David was at work she read it over and made corrections. She was happy with the story, though there were certain fine points she could not decide on. The second page, for example, had a long sentence that she could not decide how to punctuate. She had tried dividing the sentence with a comma—no, not right. A semi-colon? Also not right. A colon was too abrupt, three dots too wimpy, and dashes were too—well, too spacious. Should it be two separate sentences? No, because then it read too choppy. If only there was another form of punctuation, something half-dash and half-comma. She sighed; no matter what she did, the sentence did not read right, and at this point she had written and crossed out so many times it was getting difficult to read the sentence at all. Oh well—maybe Michael would have a suggestion. It was as her writing teacher had said: some sentences you get right the first time, some in the second or third draft, and some you can never figure out. But Madeline didn't mind; putting on the final touches was the fun part of writing. The blank free-fall of the first draft was over, as were the major revisions of the second and third drafts. By now the plot and characters were set in stone, and it was just a matter of choosing the right words and the right punctuation, just a matter of taking out whatever interrupted the smooth rhythm of storytelling.

Perfect or not, the story was about to embark on its maiden voyage. In exactly two hours Madeline would go to 821 Washington and read the story to Bella, Robert, and Michael. She had always read her stories to Bella and Robert, and then when Michael moved in he was just naturally included. The readings were not at all helpful, because no matter what she read the reactions were always the same: Bella would jump up and exclaim that it was the best most fabulous story she had ever heard—that is, she would say all that if she wasn't crying too much, for from the moment Madeline had started writing she wrote about her family, and it wasn't always pretty. "Wonderful," Bella would say as she laid on the couch sobbing. "Really, Maddy, it couldn't be better." As for Robert, he was so blinded by his love for George Eliot it was difficult for him to believe that literature could concern itself with anything other than the Poor Law, the Reform Bill, and English clergymen in all their wearying incarnations. By way of comment Robert usually said something like, "Don't you think you need more description?", whereupon Madeline would reply, "Robert, this isn't *Middlemarch*, it's a twenty-page story, which means I'm not going to spend four paragraphs describing the tablecloth." Then Robert would sigh, and Madeline would roll her eyes.

As for Michael, he would make a noncommittal comment like, "Very interesting," or "I liked it." But he at least took the story and read it again on his own, and a week or two after each reading he would sit down with Madeline and point out everything from errors in punctuation to misused words to character anomalies. He would say things like, "I don't think he would wear a red shirt, do you?"—which delighted Madeline, because this was exactly the sort of comment her teacher used to make. Madeline did not incorporate all of Michael's suggestions, but the majority of them improved her stories in small but telling ways. At the readings, however, Michael could not be induced to comment; he always claimed he needed to read the story on his own. "What he means," Madeline told Bella, "is that he needs to read it *slowly*."

So the readings were more traditional than useful. But Madeline enjoyed reading out loud, and anyway she wanted the others to know what she was doing. Also it gave her a deadline, because otherwise she was likely to hang onto a story for months, alternating between commas and semi-colons.

She was in the middle of puzzling over a paragraph break when the phone rang. Absentmindedly she reached behind her to the little table with the phone and answering machine.

"Hello?"

"Madeline, it's Alison. I need your help."

"What's up?"

"Well, you know the guys are playing in Philadelphia in three weeks, and I really have to get these cassettes off to the radio stations, plus send notices to a bunch of other people, and I have to do it all first thing Monday morning in hope they'll get there this week, if not Wednesday then Friday or maybe Saturday. The point is, I'm swamped, and I could use some help."

"What about tomorrow?"

"Tomorrow I'm going into The City to get a dress for the VP's dinner. I haven't had a free moment to shop and I won't have another free moment all week. Did you find a dress yet?"

"My sister and I went shopping yesterday." Because, finally, the informal meeting had been arranged: David, Hanson, and their respective girlfriends had been invited to dinner at the VP's home in suburban New Jersey. Narrow Grave had a gig at The Bottom Line—again opening for The Replacements—on the Friday after Thanksgiving, and the dinner was arranged for Saturday. David told Madeline she had to look better than beautiful, and he even gave her a hundred dollars and told her to buy a dress. "Something amazing," he said. "Sexy, but not slutty." Who was she to argue? She and Bella went to a boutique in Chelsea that Patty recommended, and they came away with a sleeveless dress made of strange shimmering copper material that perfectly set off Madeline's skin and hair. The dress was on sale for only $55, and since Madeline could borrow shoes and earrings from Bella they decided to use the rest of the money for sushi. "Is this morally wrong?" Madeline asked Bella as they broke apart their wooden chopsticks. "Of course not," Bella replied. "Don't even think twice."

"Did you find something?" Alison asked.

"I did. Stop by this week and I'll show it to you."

"Maybe tomorrow night—otherwise I don't have a moment, as I said. So can you come over? Now?"

"Well—" Madeline glanced at her story. She had to let it go sometime. "Okay. But only for an hour or so; my sister's expecting me at five. I'm going to read my new story, then we're going out to dinner."

"An hour's better than nothing. I'll be expecting you—ciao."

Madeline put her story in its folder, then put the folder in her bookbag along with some books she had borrowed from Michael, and a hair band she had borrowed from Bella. She combed her hair, turned out the lights, and left the apartment.

It was a classic November day, complete with cold air, grey skies, and an all-pervading feeling of late autumn bleakness, but since Madeline felt happy the bleakness seemed romantic. She walked over to Alison's building, and as she ascended the stairs she noticed that the stick of butter was gone, and in its place there was an old man in slippers, counting change on the floor.

"I think you have a homeless person in your hallway," Madeline said as Alison took her coat.

"That's not a homeless person, that's my upstairs neighbor. Have a seat—want some tea?"

"Sure."

Madeline sat at the kitchen table. As always, the table was a mess; today's mess consisted of piles of cassettes, a stack of fuchsia postcards announcing the Philadelphia gig, three rolls of stamps, a mangy sponge in a dish of water, sheets of printed labels, a heap of small padded envelopes. Madeline snuck a look at Alison; she was relieved to see Alison reach up and take a fresh tea bag out of the glass jar. Madeline had long ago graduated to fresh tea bags, but she always checked to be sure.

"Wanna get high?" Alison asked. "I rolled a joint, it's in the ashtray."

"No thanks. I'm going to my sister's to read one of my short stories, I have to have my wits about me."

Alison set down Madeline's tea. "Well, if you change your mind..." She took the joint out of the ashtray and lit it. "So it's great you're here. Why don't you start putting stamps on the postcards? I'll stick on the address labels—I'd let you put the labels on but I sometimes write a note if I know the person, so it's easier if I do it."

"No problem," Madeline said. She took the stack of cards and a roll of stamps, and got started. The apartment did not feel so claustrophobic today—it was peaceful, even, with the weak grey light coming through the window and *Marquee Moon* playing in the background.

"So," Alison said after snuffing out the joint. "You miss David?"

"Sure," Madeline said, smiling. "But he'll be back tomorrow."

"I miss Hanson," Alison said. "It's no fun being a rock widow."

Madeline laughed. "Is that what we are?"

"You're lucky you caught them at a good time; since you've been going out with David they've hardly toured at all. There used to be weeks when I hardly saw Hanson."

"How on earth did David swing that at work?"

"Are you kidding? They love David, he's their flesh and blood rock star. He could go away for months and they still wouldn't fire him; he gives them cachet."

"I guess I never thought of it that way."

"You and David doing okay?"

"Me and David? We're fine."

"I'm glad," Alison said, darting a look at Madeline. "David needed a nice girlfriend. Hanson and I liked you from the start, you know, and we were really happy when David asked you to move in. David's had a lot of girlfriends, but he's never had anyone move in."

"Well, we're happy. It's nice living together."

"Hanson and I started living together after our first night together. I went with him to his apartment after a Clash concert, and I just never left."

Madeline smiled, but said nothing. David had told her quite a few things about Alison and Hanson's relationship, many which she preferred not to know. Like the fact that they had sexual problems: when Alison got too bossy and neurotic Hanson never said a word, but then he would be unable to have an erection for a week or more. And Hanson didn't like Alison using a diaphragm because he said he could feel it, but he didn't want her on the Pill because it made her fat, and he didn't like rubbers because they lessened the feeling. Alison had tried an IUD, but she got an infection and had to get it removed, so now every time before they had sex they had an argument about birth control. Oh well, Madeline thought as she pasted on a stamp. Alison and Hanson probably knew all about her UTIs, not to mention whatever other sexual details David had chosen to disclose. But Madeline had long since understood that going out with David meant, in a sense, going out with Hanson and Alison.

"So Thanksgiving should be fun," Alison said.

"I'm surprised Plug invited us," Madeline said. "I mean, he doesn't seem the type who does traditional American things."

"Plug's wild, but he's also extremely domestic. He's got this huge Polish girlfriend who he obeys like a dog."

"I've never even met her."

"She hates rock 'n' roll, and she hates Hoboken. Anyway, Thanksgiving in Brooklyn—it'll be fun."

"My sister and brother-in-law are also going to Brooklyn. Not that we'll be traveling with them," Madeline said, sighing.

"Your brother-in-law, hmm?"

"Robert's a nice guy. I mean, he's a great guy. He just—"

"—doesn't like David."

"No. Not at all."

"It's really odd; usually everyone loves David."

"Not Robert. But Bella loves David, they get along great."

"I'd love to meet her. David says she's a riot."

"Well, she says she'll come hear the guys next time they play in town. But I'm sure you'll meet her before that."

They fell silent. The album finished; Alison got up and put on another. Madeline cocked her head and listened to the first few notes—it was The Pretenders' first album, side one.

"So," Madeline said, wetting a stamp on the mangy sponge. "Have you gotten a chance to finish your painting?"

Alison sighed. "No. Like I said, I haven't had a minute to myself."

"You know," Madeline said carefully. "Once Narrow Grave signs with The Big Record Label things'll be easier for you. I mean, The Big Record Label will have their own people to do this sort of thing, right? You know, the publicity department and all."

"Sure, things will be easier in terms of me not having to do mailings, but there'll be a ton of other work. And if they get really big and make lots of money, you better believe I'm quitting my job and going on the road with them. Hanson needs me," she said, hitting a label with her fist to make it lay flat. "And besides, I don't trust groupies."

"But your own work?"

"My own work? It'll keep; I'll get back to it soon."

"Tell me, how did you learn to paint? Did you go to school, or did you just teach yourself?"

"I've always painted. Just—always. And from the minute I could work I started saving money so I could go live in Boston when I was eighteen. I grew up in this awful white bread town in Vermont—we were the only Jews, but even worse than that we never skied, and in Vermont that's like being from Mars. Anyway, so I went to Boston and got a job as a secretary, and at night I took classes at the Museum of Fine Arts. I even won a prize in one of their competitions."

"That's great."

"Yeah, I was pretty happy. Then I stopped taking classes and just worked on my own; I even had a few exhibitions here and there. Then I met Hanson, and a few months later he and David decided to move to Hoboken. I thought I could get some things going here, but it hasn't really worked out."

"Is Hanson supportive of your work?"

"Hanson, as you've observed by now, is a bundle of nerves. He can hardly be supportive of himself, much less me."

Madeline nodded, and said nothing. She felt sorry for Alison, but she was also angry at her and, oddly, a bit jealous. Madeline felt sorry for Alison because she was a talented person—a talented woman—who had gotten offtrack and was not doing her work. And Madeline was angry because Alison should know better: she should pull herself together, set some rules with Hanson, then shut herself in her studio and work. But Alison didn't seem to want to work; by latching herself onto Narrow Grave and making herself indispensable, she was avoiding the hard work of following her own path, her own muse. And this was exactly why Madeline felt jealous: it would be so relaxing to take that shortcut, to fall into David's success and reap the benefits, but she just couldn't do it. Madeline had an inner integrity and an inner drive that refused to let her stop working, and as a result she paid a price: it was painful getting rejection letters, painful watching others get published and wondering if her day would ever come. And here was Alison, a painter, all hot and bothered about sticking labels on postcards; Alison was not getting any work done, yes, but she was also avoiding a great deal of pain.

Madeline's arrogance reared its unsympathetic head: she couldn't help but feel superior to Alison. It wasn't nice, but that's how she felt.

❧   ❧   ❧

When Madeline arrived at 821 Washington, Bella and Robert were sitting on the kitchen floor, peering into a cabinet.

"Hi," Madeline said. "What're you guys doing?"

"Looking for roaches," Robert said. "Bella swears she saw one."

"I took out a pot and there it was," Bella said. "It was living in my saucepan."

"And I say that's impossible; we haven't had a roach in years."

"Robert, I know a roach when I see one. I used to live with about a thousand of them in my place on 113th Street." Bella put an arm around him. "In fact I think that's why you asked me to marry you; you felt sorry for me living in that dump of a room."

Madeline laughed. "I thought Robert asked you to marry him because it was the only way he could get you to sleep with him."

"Well, that too."

Robert sighed. "Actually, I asked her to marry me because I wanted to spend the rest of my life being tortured by you two. I don't think there's another man in the world who could put up with the Boot sisters."

"Where's Michael?" Madeline asked.

"Upstairs. He said we should call him when you came."

"I have to return some books so why don't I just go up and get him."

"Go," Robert said. "We're in no rush."

Madeline took the books out of her bag and went upstairs. She knocked on the door, then waited. And waited. Finally she heard footsteps, and the door opened.

"Madeline," Michael said, smiling down at her. "It's nice to see you."

"Hi, Michael. I came to return these books," she said, holding them out to him. "And to get more, if that's okay."

"Of course it's okay. Come in."

Michael's apartment was, as Bella would say, a trip. It was quiet as a cloister, and had the hushed, solemn air of a library. Which is what it was, really, because no one had as many books as Michael, no one. Bookshelves were everywhere: in the narrow hallway, in the living room, the dining room, the study, the guest room, even the kitchen and bathroom. Another notable feature of the apartment was the rugs. The floors were covered with beautiful oriental rugs that Michael had bought on his travels, rugs in shades of fawn, gold, ivory, and dusky rose. They were all finely woven and soft to the touch; Madeline was always tempted to fall on the floor and roll on them, and in fact once she and Bella did just that. The books were so weighty and everywhere, but the rugs gave the apartment an ethereal floating feeling. The furniture was made of dark wood and rather plain; once Madeline said to Bella, "Michael's furniture is so boring; he should get a beanbag chair or something," and Bella had replied, "You, my dear, know nothing about antiques. That boring furniture is worth a fortune." The apartment's other unique feature was that it always smelt slightly of roses. Madeline had never seen roses in the apartment, and as she couldn't imagine Michael dousing his rooms with air freshener she was always puzzled by the smell. Then one time in the bathroom she decided to take a little stroll through Michael's cabinets, and below the sink she discovered rose-scented furniture oil imported from England. Ah ha, she thought, mystery solved. The smell was mildly sweet, and quite soothing; walking around the apartment she felt as if she were in a private garden, some beautiful walled hideaway in the heart of England.

She trailed behind Michael into the dining room. He carefully replaced the books she had given him, then turned to her and asked, "More fiction?"

"Of course. I told you, no more Thomas Merton."

"All right. Well—my father sent me some novels by a Canadian author named Carol Shields. She's American, actually, but she's lived in Canada for many years. They're all rather short, and they're companion novels."

"Which means?"

"They go together. One novel is about a woman, and the other about her sister. And one novel is about a couple, the first book about the husband and the second about the wife. They're quite good; she has a nice sense of humor."

"Sounds great."

"And they are—where? In the living room."

She followed him through the open archway into the living room. The same grey light was coming through the windows, but the white silk curtains transformed the light into a fragile paleness that laid gently on the dusky pink rug. No wonder Michael's so calm, Madeline thought. There's not one disturbing color in this whole place.

He handed her the books. "And do you want something else?" he asked.

"Well, maybe something to balance out all of this Canadian-ness. Know what I mean?"

"Well, let's see." He walked slowly in front of the bookshelves, hands on hips, his eyes moving across the rows and rows of books. "Have you ever read *Native Son*?"

"No. But I should."

"Here." He withdrew the book and placed it on top of the others. "There's not one Canadian in the whole thing."

"Great. So—you want to go down now?"

"I just have to put some papers away in my study. You can come with me, it'll just take a minute."

Michael's study was above Bella and Robert's TV room. The rooms were identical in size and shape, and Michael even had a couch—dark wood with dark blue cushions—in the same place; but instead of a television and armchair he had a plain, sturdy wooden desk and a wooden file cabinet. And bookshelves, of course. Madeline sat on the couch and put her books next to her; she looked around at all the bookshelves, craning her head to look at the shelves poised above the couch.

"Aren't you afraid these are going to crash down on you?" she said.

Michael looked up from his desk. Several manila folders were open before him, and he was moving papers from one to the other. "No," he said.

"You're the only person I know who has books in every room of his house."

"I don't have books in every room."

"Yes, you do! You even have books in your bathroom."

He closed a folder and looked at her. "But I have no books in my bedroom."

"Oh." She blushed. Then she stood, and peered over his shoulder. "Is that your sutra?" she asked, pointing to a neat stack of typewritten papers.

"Yes."

"Can I glance at it?"

"Of course."

She carefully lifted the title page and put it facedown on the desk. She leaned over and read:

> The Great Way is not difficult
> for those who have no preferences.
> When hate and love are both absent
> everything becomes clear and undisguised.
> Make the smallest distinction however
> and heaven and earth are set infinitely apart.
> If you wish to see the truth
> then hold no opinions for or against anything.
> To set up what you like against what you dislike
> is the disease of the mind.
> When the deep meaning of things is not understood
> the mind's essential peace is disturbed to no avail.

"'When hate and love are both absent,'" Madeline quoted. "How can that be? Who wants to live in a world without love?"

"It's not saying that. It's saying that if you get attached to something by either loving or hating it, you can no longer see it clearly."

"But love *is* attachment."

"You can love something without attaching yourself to it—in other words, without making your identity depend on it."

"Hmm."

Madeline sat down on the couch again, fluffed a few pillows and got comfortable. How naive she had been to believe Michael when he said that he would just take a minute. She watched as he picked up a piece of paper, held it over an open folder, then hesitated; after several long moments he put the paper back on the desk, then picked up another paper from another folder. It was agonizing watching him work, just agonizing; she longed to shove him away from the desk and sort everything out in two minutes flat. A comment floated into her mind, something to the effect of, "Don't worry, Michael, I don't mind waiting until the year 2000 to read my story," but she stopped herself: she and Michael had made up after their fight, but things were still delicate between them. Poor Michael—the Monday evening after the brunch he had come over with no less than four pints of ice cream, and the moment he stepped into the living room he said, "I'll put these in the kitchen. Madeline, will you come with me?"

She exhaled an elongated sigh of annoyance, slammed her book facedown on the coffee table, then followed him down the hall. In the kitchen she stood with her arms crossed, watching as Michael (slowly) put the ice cream in the freezer. Then he turned around and looked at her; his expression was so contrite, his green eyes so big and sad, that she immediately forgave him. Not that she was about to let him off the hook so easily.

"Madeline, I'm so sorry I said all those things to you."

"You've never spoken to me like that before," she said icily.

"I know, and I feel awful. I wanted to call you this morning but I didn't know your new number and anyway you were at work. Will you accept my apology?"

She couldn't stay mad at him. "Oh, Michael—of course I accept your apology. And I guess I should apologize too—I'm sorry I called you slow. I mean, you *are* slow, but you're nothing like Mr. Causabon. I know you'll finish your sutra and, and, I know you're not some withered up old man."

Michael looked out the window and said, "As far as literary insults go, I think being called Mr. Causabon is the worst."

Now she really felt bad. "I know, it was horrible of me. I honestly didn't mean it, I just had to think of something mean to say and that's what popped out. So can we just be friends again? I mean, okay, you don't like David, but neither does Robert. I can deal with it, I guess—I just don't want to lose either of you."

She reddened; she had never said such a thing to Michael before.

He turned from the window and looked at her. "You won't lose me," he said quietly.

"Okay then. So—Scrabble?"

He smiled. "Let's go."

And since then Madeline had gone out of her way to be polite to him. She noticed that Michael looked different these days: he had a strange sad wound-edness around his eyes, and sometimes she was afraid that her Mr. Causabon comment had caused it. Michael was not a Mr. Causabon but he was, no getting around it, a scholarly bachelor; and though he never said a word about how he felt, it occurred to Madeline that maybe Michael was lonely. So she held her tongue as he organized his papers, and when he at last put the manila folders in his file cabinet she said lightly, "Done?"

"Done. Don't forget your books."

When they walked into the apartment they saw that Bella and Robert were not in the living room; Madeline motioned Michael to the kitchen where they found Bella and Robert sitting on the floor, kissing passionately.

Madeline rolled her eyes at Michael, then sang out, "Ex-cuse me! You have guests."

"Oh," Bella said, breaking away from Robert. "Sorry—we didn't hear you."

"So I noticed. When Robert stops blushing can we go to the living room so I can read my story?"

Madeline took her bookbag to the living room and put her story on the piano bench. She glanced again at page two: a comma was best. No—a semi-colon. She still couldn't make up her mind. Robert and Michael came in each carrying a beer, and Bella followed with a box of tissues. Bella used to set out food for the readings, but once she put out pistachio nuts and Robert's loud crunching had distracted Madeline to the point where she had to stop reading and forcibly remove the bowl from Robert's grasp.

"Okay," Bella said, putting the tissues on the table and going over to Madeline. She put an arm around Madeline and said, "This evening we're honored to present the future amazing writer—"

"How can she be a future writer when she's writing now?" Robert interrupted. "That's not logical."

"Shut up, Robert. Anyway, as I was saying, the current amazing writer, Ms. Madeline Boot, reading her story—" Bella peered at the page—"'Never Ever Disobey Me.'"

The story was written in the first person, and began with the narrator as a seven-year-old laying on the floor of the living room on a stack of pillows, listening to her sixteen-year-old sister play piano. The living room was spacious with good furniture, but everything was dusty and faded, clearly in a state of neglect. The narrator was in a dreamy world, reading a book, stopping now and then to watch her sister. No one else had such a beautiful sister, a sister with long black hair held back by a tortoiseshell barrette, a sister immaculately elegant in her sky blue Fairisle sweater, grey wool skirt, and string of pearls. And no one else's sister was a piano prodigy; no one else's sister made such beautiful music with, seemingly, so little effort.

Then their father walked into the room. He was a tall blond man with big hands and a ruddy face, his expression locked into a permanent scowl. The father's voice cut into the swirl of music, asking his daughter to stop playing because he had a headache.

The music stopped. "But Dad," his daughter said. "You know I have that recital next week. If I don't practice now I'll never get this right."

The father looked at her; he said nothing, then turned and left the room. The two girls exchanged a glance; the narrator's sister shrugged, then resumed playing. The narrator fell back into her dreamy world, and the father's interruption was forgotten, smoothed away by time and music. Then footsteps; the narrator looked up, and saw the father walking across the room. In his hands he held an axe.

The music stopped. "Dad—?" the older sister said. "Dad?"

The father strode over to the piano, and in a swift, sure motion, brought the axe down on the lid. There was a painful crack followed by a dark crash of music as the axe hit the wires. Then a scream; then more cracking wood, more crashing notes, flying shards of wood and then more screams, but now they were the narrator's screams coming from the corner where she was cowering, her fear so tremendous she had lost control of her bladder.

Then silence. The father stood panting; the older sister was weeping, her body stretched over the ruined piano. The father hiked the axe onto his shoulder and said, "Never, ever disobey me." He turned on his heel and left the room. The narrator ran from her corner and threw herself on her sister's heaving sobbing body, hoping to comfort her; and what an odd sensation as her body undulated up and down each time her sister sobbed, like being on a strange human roller coaster.

Then years later. The narrator is in a drugstore in her hometown, buying contraceptive pills. A woman she doesn't recognize asks her if she is X's daughter, and the narrator says yes. The woman tells the narrator how wonderful the narrator's father is, how he was such a great softball coach, was so funny and kind, so good with the kids; and what a shame he hadn't been principal of *their* high school, life would have been easier if only the narrator's father had been in charge.

"And what could I do but stand there smiling and saying, 'Really? Is that so? Oh, thank you.' Finally the woman walked away, and as she strode down the aisle I watched her, amazed at the version of my father that lived in her head. Would it have done any good to take out my version, and smother her friendly stories with a few choice tales of my own? It would not have done any good, so I did not do it. But how I envied her—God, how I envied her."

"The end," Madeline announced.

She looked up. Bella was staring at the floor, tears running down her cheeks. Robert had his arm around her, and was gently stroking her hair. "Oh, Bella!" Madeline said, rushing over and kneeling on the floor in front of her sister. "I'm sorry. I'm so sorry. But I had to write it."

"Don't be sorry," Bella said, wiping her tears on Robert's sleeve. "You have to write what you have to write. It's just—" She closed her eyes. "I hate that man so much. The both of them, I hate them so much."

"I know," Madeline said as she hugged Bella's knees. "I know." And Madeline also knew that when Bella moved in with Robert, the first thing he did was buy her a piano.

"Anyway," Bella said. "The story is wonderful. The way you describe the living room, the noises the axe made—it was just like that. I think it's the best thing you've ever written."

Madeline looked at Robert. "Well?" she asked.

He shifted uncomfortably. "It's good, I suppose, but I think it would work better as a chapter in a long novel. That way you could add more description."

"Whatever. Michael?" she asked, turning to face him.

He was sitting on the couch with his legs crossed, his beer poised on his knee. "It's quite good."

"But you need to read it," she supplied.

"That's right."

Madeline sighed, and rested her head on Bella's knees. Well, she hadn't expected anything different. And anyway she hardly cared about her story anymore, she was more concerned about Bella.

"Well," Bella said, "I have to say I don't really feel like going out for dinner. I hope you guys don't mind."

"Why don't we get Chinese food," Michael suggested. "And rent a video. Something funny."

"That's a good idea," Robert said. "Madeline, why don't you and Michael go to the video store? And pick up some Chinese food."

Robert gave Madeline forty dollars as well as the card for Take One Video. They went out into the cold November evening, and as they were walking down Washington Street Madeline suddenly stopped. She turned to Michael, tears in her eyes. "I didn't write it to hurt Bella," she said. "I wrote it so I could forget about it. Do you know what I mean?"

"Of course I do," Michael said gently, his green eyes kind and sympathetic. Which made Madeline feel a twang of guilt—Mr. Causabon! How could she ever have called him Mr. Causabon!

"I didn't mean to hurt Bella," she said, her eyes pleading. "But I did. Seems like I'm always hurting people without meaning to."

"Bella will be fine. Come on," he said softly, taking her by the elbow. "If you walk you'll feel better."

Later they were in the Chinese takeout restaurant, sitting on folding chairs and waiting for their food. The air was warm and steamy, and smelt of hot grease and soy sauce. Madeline glanced at Michael; he had a bag with two videos on his lap, and he was staring at a Chinese calendar, his lips moving slightly as he read the Chinese. Madeline folded her arms and sighed contentedly—she felt better. She had enjoyed dawdling in the video store with Michael, listening as he described movies, arguing with his choices but, since she was making an effort to be nice to him, eventually giving in. Michael's my buddy, she thought. It would be nice if he could be David's friend too, but—oh well.

"Madeline," Michael said suddenly. "Do you know what Tuesday is?"

"What?"

"Tuesday is George Eliot's birthday."

"Oh no. And I don't even have a decent excuse to back out."

"No decent excuses allowed, I'm afraid."

"If he reads from *Felix Holt* I don't think I'll make it."

"*Adam Bede*'s the one I hate." They paused, visions of a dank, dismal evening before them. "And don't try to make me laugh," Michael warned. "It's not fair."

"But Michael, that'll be my only enjoyment all evening! You can't take that away from me."

"There'll be cake."

"Oh God, remember that cake Bella made two years ago, when she tried to draw a picture of George Eliot with icing but it ended up looking more like a horse and Robert got upset?"

"But not so upset that he didn't read."

"What a pity."

"Your food ready," the woman behind the counter called out as she hoisted two paper bags onto the counter.

Michael took one bag, Madeline the other, and they left.

CHAPTER 13

Super Cool

Saturday evening after Thanksgiving, and Madeline was at 821 Washington, sitting on the couch in the TV room and getting a manicure from Bella. The sisters had not seen each other since Wednesday night, and Bella was telling Madeline about Thanksgiving in Brooklyn with the Dellasandandrio clan.

"...a vegetarian's nightmare. Only Italians would serve sausage at Thanksgiving. And there was this one sausage—I didn't touch it, of course, but Robert had a piece and I swear to God I saw white chunks as big as my fingernails. And you just have to wonder, what *is* that stuff? And everyone kept oohing and aahing over how great it was and meanwhile I was about to *puke.* The only things I could eat were the mashed potatoes and string beans and cranberry sauce, but the cranberry sauce was that nasty stuff out of the can, you could still taste the aluminum..."

"Since when does Robert eat meat?"

"Robert, I've decided, is what's known as a reluctant vegetarian. He's a vegetarian by default because he lives with me. I bet he eats meat all the time up at Columbia. Isn't that right, Robert?" Bella called out to the living room, where Robert was reading volume six of George Eliot's letters.

"Whatever you say, Bella," Robert called back absentmindedly.

"See? And his Aunt Maria was there—you know, the one with the hot young thang for a boyfriend? And he was cute, let me tell you..."

Eventually it was Madeline's turn, and while Bella stroked blood-red polish on Madeline's nails Madeline described Thanksgiving in Brooklyn with Plug and his Polish girlfriend. It was the most bizarre Thanksgiving Madeline had ever experienced: the main course was not turkey, but pot. Never in her life had she seen so many joints and so much smoking over such an extended period of time. After two hours of smoking she had crawled into a not very clean bed and fallen into a deep sleep. When she awoke the others were just finishing eating.

"And thank God I don't eat meat because I'm telling you, Bella, that turkey was *pink*. The undercooked flesh of a poor dead animal—but they were all so stoned they didn't even notice."

"So what did you eat?"

"Well, thank God we had brought those pumpkin pies from Carlo's Bakery. Plus Alison brought an ice cream cake. But everyone had such munchies David and I had to go out and find an open store and buy more ice cream. And potato chips, and chocolate bars. And sardines."

"Sounds ghastly."

"Actually it was fun." It hadn't been the safest neighborhood, but the streets were empty and she had held onto David's arm as they giggled their way through the store. And walking back through the icy winds in the cold streets, Madeline had been struck by how beautiful Brooklyn was, and how happy she was to be there with David.

"And thank God I slept," Madeline went on, "because we didn't leave there until one in the morning. We got back to Hoboken around two-thirty, slept all day, then went into The City at seven for The Bottom Line gig."

"I wish I could have gone with you, but we'd already accepted that dinner invitation from my boss. How was it?"

"Good. Great. But it was another late night, we weren't in bed until four."

"And now tonight is the big big night. Is David excited?"

"David is—confident. He feels good."

"Please tell me he's not going to wear that awful shirt," Bella said, blowing on Madeline's nails. "Because one gander at that psychedelic swirl and the deal is off."

"David, thank you very much, bought a new shirt. It's this cool chocolate brown color."

"And the fabric?"

Madeline hesitated. "Well—silk."

"My, my! Silk! You're in real rock star territory now, Madeline."

"Is silk effeminate for a man?"

"Are you doubting David's masculinity?" Bella laughed.

"No, it's just—it seems a little Las Vegas."

"Madeline, David is in show business. Which is why you're wearing red nail polish and four-inch heels. How do those shoes feel now, anyway?"

Madeline grimaced, and looked down at the black leather instruments of torture on her feet. She had tried them on a week ago and nearly fallen over, so every time she had a chance—during Scrabble and George Eliot's birthday party and now during her manicure—she practiced wearing the shoes. But being squeezed and arced out of shape insulted her feet, and even after all her efforts the shoes still caused waves of pain.

"Never mind," Bella said. "You can slip them off when you're sitting. Now, put your hands out to the side to let your nails dry, and I'll brush your hair. Bend over so I can get to the roots."

After lengthy consideration Bella had decided to leave Madeline's hair free—no braids, no crinkles, just clean straight hair. "Your hair has to echo the dress," Bella said, "not distract from it." So after a super duper olive oil conditioning treatment and blow drying, Madeline's hair was soft and full. She bent over, feeling the satisfying tug on her roots as Bella ran the wire-bristled brush through her hair.

"So where's Michael?" Madeline asked. "Shouldn't he be here by now?"

"Oh my God, I forgot to tell you! Big news flash."

"What?"

"Michael, my dearest Madeline, is on a date."

Madeline's head snapped up. "He's *what*?"

"He's on a date. With Patty."

"*Michael* asked *Patty* on a date?"

"Don't scream. And bend over, I'm not done. Actually, Patty asked Michael on a date."

"And Michael said *yes*?"

"Apparently so."

"Do you think they're going to have—a relationship?"

"Honey, I hope they get married. They'd make a cute couple."

"I don't think so. She's not his type."

"Well, he's her type. After the brunch she kept hoping and praying he'd call her, and when he didn't she just took the bull by the horns. So to speak."

"I can't believe it. Do you think they're going to have sex?"

"Probably. I don't know. What's it to you?"

"Nothing. Just—I don't think she's his type. And he didn't seem to like her very much."

"Well, we can only cross our fingers and hope she gets through that shyness of his."

"Michael isn't shy. He's soft-spoken, and he's quiet, but he's not shy."

"Not with us he isn't, but with everyone else he is. Honestly, Madeline, you don't notice anything. Lift your head."

Madeline's hair was a wild mess around her head. "You know, Bella, the day of the brunch I said something terrible to Michael."

"What?"

Madeline looked up at Bella. "I told him he was like Mr. Causabon."

"*Madeline*. You didn't."

"I did. I apologized, but I still feel awful. And I bet that's why he's going out with Patty—you know, so he won't end up like Mr. Causabon."

Bella stood with her hands on her hips and stared at Madeline. "I cannot believe you said something like that to Michael. He is our dearest friend in the world, and for you to call him Mr. Causabon—! I'm not even going to tell Robert."

"Please don't. I'm just telling you because I still feel so guilty."

"Well, never mind. If it spurred him to go out with Patty, then it wasn't a bad thing at all. Michael needs a woman to love him; he shouldn't be alone all his life. Anyway, I'll get all the dish from Patty on Monday. I can try to interrogate Michael tomorrow, but I'm sure he won't tell me a thing."

Bella tamed Madeline's hair, then they went into Bella's bedroom where Madeline put on a fresh bra and underwear, plain stockings and then, the moment of truth, the shimmery copper dress. The style was simple: sleeveless, a scoop neck, molded waist, skirt two inches above the knee. But the material was unique, shiny and mercurial, and the copper color was rich and sensuous, perfect with Madeline's skin and hair color. Bella recombed Madeline's hair, then made Madeline keep still as she carefully applied eyeliner, mascara, and red lipstick. Then Madeline put on Bella's thick gold hoop earrings and, the last step, slipped into the tortuous black heels.

"Madeline," Bella said, stepping back to admire her handiwork. "You look sensational."

"You think so?" Madeline peered into the mirror; to her own eyes she looked hard, doll-like. "You don't think I look like a hardened coke fiend who hangs out at the Limelight?"

"But Madeline, that's exactly the look we're going for! Trust me, you look great. Come on, let's show Robert."

"I don't think Robert will be interested."

"Oh, come on."

Madeline walked unsteadily behind Bella, following her down the hall to the living room. "Robert," Bella commanded. "Look at Madeline. Isn't she a babe?"

Robert glanced up, then looked down again. "You're wearing too much makeup," he said, turning a page. "It doesn't suit you. And your neckline is much too low."

"Robert!" Bella cried. "You are such a—oh! Never mind, Madeline."

"I hope," Robert said, still not looking at them, "that this boyfriend of yours doesn't expect you to dress like this all the time. Because if he does he's destroying all of your natural beauty. Not that he cares."

"Enough, Robert. Ignore him, Madeline—he's living in the nineteenth century, what does he know about fashion? So what time is it now? Oh, almost six-thirty! I'll call a taxi right now."

"Wait, I'll come with you," Madeline said, tottering after Bella.

The VP was sending a car for them at seven. David had gone to Hanson and Alison's at five for a last-minute strategy discussion and—Madeline was sure—some heavy-duty pot smoking. Madeline was to meet them as soon as Bella was done with her, and since walking to Jefferson Street in the cold in heels was deemed impossible, Madeline had decided to take a taxi.

Bella walked Madeline downstairs and waited with her in the front vestibule. "Oooh, it's cold!" she said, hugging her arms around her chest. "I should have brought my jacket. So you'll come over tomorrow night and tell me everything?"

"Tomorrow, or Monday. I'm not sure if we have plans for tomorrow night."

"Well, call me if you can't make it. So—are you nervous?"

"I'm excited but—look, this isn't for me. It's not like I'm going to an editor's house to discuss my stories. My job is just to look good and not embarrass David."

"Wouldn't it be awful if you did something really tacky, like get sick all over the dining room table, or make some kind of awful faux pas?"

Madeline laughed. "Oh, thanks a lot, Bella! I see you have a lot of confidence in me!"

"I'm not saying you will do something like that, I'm just saying wouldn't it be awful if you did. Oh, there's your taxi. Okay," she said, kissing Madeline on the cheek. "Have a great, great time. You're only young once."

"Thanks, Mom."

Madeline ran down the stoop and climbed into the backseat of the taxi. She leaned forward and said, "Third and Jefferson, please."

There was nothing the least bit glamorous about the taxi; it was a typical worn-out Hoboken taxi—the nauseatingly sweet smell of air freshener, the vinyl seats patched with black masking tape—and yet Madeline, her stockinged legs pressing against the vinyl, the unaccustomed taste of lipstick in her mouth, felt as if she was in a Rolls Royce going to Princess Diana's wedding. She had kept her excitement from Bella because it was somehow too private to share. She was just so curious about how the evening would play out, curious to see the VP's house, meet his wife, see what food they served; and curious, of course, to learn what The Big Record Label had planned for David and Hanson. It might be big money, really big money; and David had promised her that if the money was good enough she could stop temping and just focus on her writing. "And on me," he had said, grabbing her by the waist.

In a way Madeline was relieved that she was not expected to say or do much at the dinner, because this way she could watch the others and see how they interacted. She particularly wanted to observe Alison, because as of last night at The Bottom Line Alison had worked herself into a frenzy, unable to talk of anything but the dinner and Narrow Grave's impending entrance into the world of Big Time Rock 'n' Roll. While the club filled up Madeline and Alison had sat together behind the stage smoking a joint, Madeline patiently listening to Alison's speculations and calculations. Alison spoke rapidly, her hands flying, her cheeks rosy, and for the first time Madeline thought Alison was pretty. Well, it would be interesting to see how Alison handled herself; Madeline just hoped Alison had calmed down a little, because at the rate she was going she was about to spontaneously combust.

The taxi pulled up in front of Hanson and Alison's building. Madeline peered up through the taxi window, and saw a faint light in Hanson and Alison's bedroom. She paid the driver, and with her heart racing she dashed up the stairs and into the foyer. She was so happy she didn't notice the pinch of her high heels, nor that her legs had goose bumps. She pressed the buzzer on the mailbox; a buzz replied, and Madeline pushed in the front door.

As she passed the first landing there were no sticks of butter or upstairs neighbors, but there was a much stepped upon slip. Oh well. And as she mounted the stairs towards Hanson and Alison's apartment she was surprised to hear shouting. She stopped a moment; it was Alison, but Madeline could not hear what she was saying. Probably yelling at Hanson to change his clothes, or arguing about how much pot to bring.

It had never occurred to Madeline that anything could go wrong on tonight of all nights, so she was utterly unprepared when she opened the door and saw the scene in the kitchen. There was so much to take in, but she saw the essential image: Hanson sitting at the table with his head back, blood gushing from his nose. Madeline had never seen so much blood: blood on Hanson's face, his hands, his shirt; blood on the table, blood on dozens of wadded-up tissues, blood everywhere. David was sitting across from Hanson, a hand covering his mouth, his skin very pale. He turned to look at Madeline, and she saw that he was crying. Alison was standing in front of Hanson, wearing a short black mini-dress that hugged her stomach unflatteringly; her clenched hands were resting on her hips, and when she turned towards the door Madeline was shocked to see Alison's face twisted with white hot hate.

"Oh my God," Madeline said, going over to Hanson. She knelt on the floor next to him and gently touched his leg with her hand. "We've got to get him to a hospital. Call a taxi, we'll go to St. Mary's."

"He doesn't need a doctor," Alison said harshly. "What he needs is a psychiatrist. Get away from him, Madeline, you'll get covered in blood."

Poor Hanson! Blood was flowing from both his nostrils, and he was crying so hard he was practically hyperventilating. Crying with one's head thrown back, however, was never easy; Hanson's sobs were more like gasps, and his Adam's apple convulsed painfully.

"Get away from him, Madeline," Alison repeated. "He doesn't deserve our sympathy."

Madeline turned and looked at Alison steadily. She felt the anger rise from her stomach to her throat, and she was just about to make a retort when she understood that she was beaten—the hateful twist of Alison's features spoke of a fury Madeline could never match. Madeline stood and, in a hopefully dignified manner, went around the table and sat next to David. She took his hand, then reached over and wiped away some of his tears.

"What happened?" she asked softly.

David took his hand away from his mouth, grabbed a clean tissue from the almost empty box and wiped his face. "Everything was fine, we were sitting here smoking a joint and laughing, and then his nose started bleeding." David looked at her, his eyes pleading. "What are we supposed to do now? The car will be here in twenty minutes."

"Well—we'll ask the car to wait. Or call the VP and cancel; he'll understand."

"Oh, he will?" Alison said sarcastically. "He will? 'No problem, boys; and now that I see you don't even have your shit together enough to make it to a simple dinner, we'll just sign up another one of the five million bands that're dying to be on our label.' You're wrong, Madeline—we can't cancel. But we can't go. So what the fuck are we supposed to do?" She leaned over and shouted in Hanson's face, "See what you've done? See what you've destroyed? We've only been waiting for this for years and now you fuck it all up with one of your fucking nosebleeds!"

"Alison!" Madeline said, putting her arm around David. "It's not his fault."

"It's not? It's not his fault that he's weak and pitiful?"

And that's exactly what you like about him, Madeline thought. "Look," Madeline said. "Why don't David and I go? We'll explain about Hanson's nosebleed, and we'll say you guys will come over later once the bleeding has stopped."

"We could do that," David said. "Because we can't cancel; that's impossible."

Alison thought a moment. "It's better if you say I have a nosebleed," she said. "I don't want them to think Hanson gets nosebleeds all the time."

"But Alison," David said. "Hanson *does* get nosebleeds all the time. And that's not exactly a secret in the music industry. This is who we are; we're not perfect. Which doesn't mean they won't sign us."

"I don't agree."

"Alison," David said tightly. "I've made up my mind: Madeline and I will go, and you and Hanson will follow just as soon as you can."

"Fine," Alison said, tears welling up in her eyes. "Fine. For the first time we're about to hang out with real people, with people who are actually in power and do things instead of all this fleabag shit we've been putting up with— For the first time we're about to do something real, and now I can't go. Because of Hanson."

"Alison," David sighed. "They'll be other dinners. This is just the beginning, and you know it."

Alison sat down and took a deep breath. She looked up at the ceiling, weeping steadily now. "You know, Hanson," she said. "I have put up with so much because of you. I left Boston, which I never wanted to do, and I took this stupid shitty job as an office manager, which is another thing I never wanted to do. Every day I haul myself out of bed and get on the PATH and get on a subway, and every day you sleep until noon and then what do you do all day, you hang out playing guitar and listening to records. You have a nice life, Hanson, and I'm the reason why. I hate my life here, I hate every minute of it, and the only thing that's kept me even the least bit sane was the hope that someday your music would take off and I could tell all those fucking people at my office to just go fuck off." She looked at him. "I don't know why I bother with you. You're not that handsome, and you're certainly not a good lover. And you know, most of the time I find you boring. That's the truth, you know; you bore me."

Without even knowing what she was doing, Madeline stood and walked through the apartment until she came to the rehearsal room. She shut the door behind her and, still in her coat, laid down on the carpeted floor and closed her eyes. There is so much hate in the world, she thought. There is just so much hate. She wished she could walk out the door and go to 821 Washington and fall into Bella's arms, far away from these people.

A bar of light fell across her face; she opened her eyes and saw David come into the room.

"Madeline," he said, sitting next to her. He pulled her up and into his arms. "Don't you flake out on me, too. Are you okay?"

"Is she done?"

"For now."

"David," Madeline said, putting her head on his shoulder. "They're really sick. They have one of the sickest relationships I've ever seen."

"Well, this isn't the first time I've had to sit through something like this, so I guess I'm used to it. But it's new for you, hmm?"

"Actually, it's not new at all. It reminds me of my parents."

"Did they—was that a beep?"

The sound repeated: beep beep!

"It must be the car," he said. "Are you going to be okay?"

"I'll be fine. Just get me out of here."

They left the rehearsal room and went back into the kitchen. Now Alison was sitting down, her head resting on Hanson's lap. Madeline did not even say good-bye; she just went out into the hall and waited for David.

"Okay," he said, shutting the door behind him. "We'll call them when we get there."

"What will we do, send the car back for them? That's expensive."

"It doesn't matter; The Big Record Label is paying for it. Come on, let's go."

They walked hand in hand down the stairs, and when they opened the front door Madeline laughed.

"Oh no," she said. "This isn't happening."

Because it was not just a car, some stately dark blue sedan or new model Ford; it was a white limousine, complete with tinted glass and uniformed driver.

"They're joking," Madeline said. "I mean, they're joking, sending a car like this."

"It's not a joke. Come on."

David spoke to the driver, then they opened the door and entered a luxurious womb complete with purple velvet seats, a TV, small bar, and phone.

"This is so bizarre," Madeline said. "I feel like I'm living out someone else's fantasy."

"Look," David said, taking a small box off the coffee table. "Remote control." He pressed a button, and a piece of tinted glass slowly rose and sealed them off from the driver. He looked at Madeline and smiled. "So?" he asked.

"So this is how we're going to travel from now on? No more PATH, no more Red Apple bus?"

"Well, I wouldn't turn in your bus pass just yet. But this is pretty cool, isn't it?"

"Hmm. I feel weird."

"You know, you never took off your coat so I never saw how you look."

Madeline shrugged off her coat and moved back on the seat. "Ta da," she said, spreading out her arms.

David looked her up and down, nodding his approval. "You look perfect, just perfect." Madeline put her coat back on, and snuggled herself into his arms. He stroked her hair and sighed. "That was some scene back there, hmm?"

"Let's forget about it. We can't help them now."

"You're right. Let's just smoke a joint and relax."

"David! We can't smoke in here."

"Madeline, we can do whatever we want." He reached into his coat and took out a joint and lighter from his shirt pocket. "In fact, one is supposed to do drugs in limousines, didn't you know that? And," he said, lighting the joint and taking a deep hit, "one is also supposed to have oral sex."

"Oh, is one?

"Mmm hmm," he said, smiling and handing her the joint.

"Excuse me, but I don't think so."

"Why not? There's plenty of room."

"David! Didn't you ever read *The World According to Garp*? A woman accidentally bit off a man's penis doing that."

"That's only a book."

"Sorry, David—fantasy's over. I'm not going to do that; what if we get into an accident?"

"We won't get into an accident."

She put her hands on his chest and pushed away from him. "You're not kidding, are you? You really want me to do that."

"Why not?"

"It's so tacky."

"Never mind. But you'll kiss me, won't you? I hope no one's ever gotten their lips bitten off in any of the books you've read."

"Of course not," she said. "Kissing's fine."

Forty-five minutes later the limousine pulled into the driveway of what appeared to be a modest two-story house in a typical suburban neighborhood. There was not much space between the houses, and Madeline was surprised that the VP did not have more property. Yet when she came out of the limousine and stood in the driveway, she peered around the side of the garage and saw that in fact the house was very big, and that the fence running along the driveway and garage continued past the house and went up into a stand of woods where it disappeared out of sight. Odd, Madeline thought; houses for rich people who want to appear modest.

The front door was typical except for a brass doorknocker in the shape of a guitar. Cor-ny, Madeline wanted to say to David, but she stopped herself: maybe it wasn't so corny to him. David pushed the doorbell, and moments later a maid in a black dress and white apron opened the door. She was quite young, and looked Hispanic.

"Good evening," she said in accentless English. "Do come in."

My goodness, Madeline thought as they walked into the marble foyer, letting the maid take their coats. We are in the land of the rich. She tried to be inconspicuous as she greedily drank in the room, wanting to remember each detail so she could tell Bella. The floor was deep green marble, and the walls half-covered with white marble; above the marble the walls were white and decorated with a few very abstract and very expensive paintings. A DeKooning, a small Pollack, and a Barnett Newman. If these were the paintings they put in their foyer—! She had a wild urge to go over to the DeKooning and lay her cheek on it; she loved DeKooning, and some form of worship seemed in order, but then the maid beckoned them to follow her. They walked a few steps down a wide hall, then the maid turned right.

"Your guests are here," she announced.

"Thank you, Lucinda," Madeline heard the VP's deep voice. "Show them in."

The maid stepped aside and indicated that they should go in. Oh my God, Madeline thought as they entered the large room. Is that a goldfish pond? Yes, it was; a goldfish pond, smack in the middle of the living room.

"Good to see you, David," the VP said, stepping up to them and pumping David's hand. "And you look lovely, Madeline. And Hanson? Alison?"

David stood very straight and looked the VP in the eye. "Just before we were about to leave, Hanson got a nosebleed. He'll come later when the bleeding stops."

"Well, that's a shame. Still, I'm glad you two are here. Come, sit down; my wife will join us in a minute, she's just putting the baby down."

He indicated a grouping of small couches just past the goldfish pond. If Madeline had been completely at ease she would have stopped, put her hands on her hips and said, "Why the hell do you have a goldfish pond in your living room?" Instead she took a discreet look into the sunken marble pool; she saw multi-colored fish lazing through waving seaweed.

"You like the koi?" the VP asked, stopping and smiling at Madeline. "They're my pride and joy."

"They're called koi?" she asked.

"They're Japanese goldfish. Aren't they gorgeous?" He kneeled at the side of the pool, supporting himself on his long bony arms as he leaned over to stare at the fish. "Come down here, I'll show you my newest one."

Madeline glanced at David; he smiled, and indicated she should kneel. But between these awful heels and her tight short dress, how was she supposed to get all the way down there? She slipped out of her heels and half-knelt, half-fell at the VP's side.

"See?" he pointed. "The gold one."

"She's beautiful," Madeline said. "And she really is gold."

"She's not swimming much at the moment; she's still recovering from the drugs."

"Drugs?"

"I had her flown in specially from Japan, they had to give her a mild narcotic for the flight. She just arrived this morning. Oh well." He stood, and reached out a hand to help Madeline. "I don't want my wife to catch us looking at them. She says I spend more time with them than the baby."

"How old is your baby?" David asked.

"Six months. He's my other pride and joy. Now, let's see—we need drinks. Come, let's go sit." He led them over to two small couches, then picked up a phone on the coffee table and punched two numbers. "Lucinda? We're ready for drinks now." He looked at David and Madeline. "What would you like?"

"A beer for me," David said. "And Madeline would like—"

"Mineral water," she said.

"You like Guinness Stout?" the VP asked David. "That's what I'm drinking."

"Sure."

"Two Guinness Stouts and a Perrier. Lemon or lime?" he asked Madeline.

"Lime."

"How does that work?" David asked when the VP put the phone down. "Is that a special phone for the house?"

"Oh, this is one of my favorite toys. It's an ordinary phone, but it has a special program so I can call anywhere in the house. Watch this." He punched two numbers and put the phone to his ear. Madeline watched him carefully. His skin was pale, his eyes large and blue, his teeth big and white, and his blond hair cut short and ever so slightly punk. He looks like a bunny rabbit, she thought. A big, tall bunny rabbit.

"Now I'm calling my wife. Hi honey…Yes, they're here. I'm just showing them how the phone works…Okay." He pushed a button and put the phone down on the table. "See?"

"That's really cool," David said.

"It's Japanese. Nowadays everything cool is Japanese. David, right behind you on that table is a red lacquered box—pass it over to me, I'll roll a joint."

As the VP deftly rolled, he told Madeline and David about a book he had just bought which described all the latest Japanese inventions. David was in his sincerely listening pose—he had his elbows on his knees, hands clasped, mouth serious, and eyes fixed on the VP's face. Madeline half-listened, preferring instead to drink in the room. First there was the couch: it was black and made of an unknown luxurious fabric, something between suede and velvet. As she ran her fingers over it she thought she had never felt anything so soft and sensuous; she couldn't tell if it was an animal skin or some new Japanese design, but whatever it was she wanted to line all her clothes with it. She thought about a Richard Pryor monologue where he described going to a Playboy centerfold's apartment, and how the couch was so luxurious he thought, "Never mind if she doesn't fuck me, I'll just fuck the couch." Madeline laughed out loud, but thank God David laughed a split second later—apparently the VP had said something funny.

And the room—more paintings. One wall was filled with one of Susan Rothberg's horse paintings, a beautiful sepia-colored horse with a large sepia X behind it. And there was a Milton Avery seaside landscape, the colors touchingly fragile. And a Rothko on another wall, the painting so big only a few inches of wall appeared on either side. It was, for a Rothko, remarkably cheery, with green, yellow, and black stripes. Again she had that urge to make bodily contact with the paintings, but she held back: she thought about Bella saying it would be awful if she did something tacky, and certainly rubbing herself on the Rothko would qualify.

Otherwise the room was rather empty; there was the pond, another grouping of couches and chairs by the bay window, a few tables here and there—all black and lacquered, very sleek and probably very costly—and on top of the tables were boxes, dozens of boxes of all colors. Good place to hide your drugs, Madeline thought as she accepted the joint from the VP. All in all the room was beautiful; the art was able to breathe, and except for the boxes there was nothing cluttered or extraneous about the decor. This is what heaven would be like, Madeline thought as she passed the joint to David. And if there were books, the room would be perfect.

She looked over at David. He was pulling on the joint, nodding as he listened to the VP talk about liens and property taxes. Madeline knew David didn't give a damn about things like that, but what else could he do? Madeline was proud of David—he had handled the whole Hanson problem so directly and honestly. If he had hemmed and hawed about Hanson's absence the whole evening would have started on a false note, but as it was Madeline felt relaxed and, honestly, thankful that Alison wasn't here to destroy things with her nerves and ambition. David was also nervous, also ambitious, but you would never know by his behavior.

"I'll give Hanson a call now," David said as he passed the joint to the VP.

"We'll just send the car right back," the VP said. "It's hired for the evening, so it's no problem."

David punched Hanson's number in the phone and waited. Madeline questioned the wisdom of David calling in front of the VP, but if he left the room it would look as if he had something to hide.

"Alison? It's David." Madeline faintly heard Alison's hysterical voice. "We're all here right now," David interrupted her. "Okay…Okay. Wait a moment." David looked at the VP. "It doesn't look like Hanson can go anywhere tonight."

"Let me speak to him a moment," the VP said.

"Alison? Alison—listen, put Hanson on…Hi…Yeah, it's okay…Wait, here he is."

The VP handed the joint to Madeline, then took the phone. David put his arm around Madeline; she reached up to her shoulder and took his hand.

"Hey Hanson. Listen, sorry about the nosebleed…I'm sure, I'm sure. Look, I just want to say, it's no problem. I have a few things I need to tell you guys, so I'll just tell David and you guys can discuss it…No, because anyway I didn't expect answers from you guys tonight, I knew you'd need time to think things over. I'll just discuss it all with Dave here, and then we can set up a meeting at my office. Sound good? …No, please don't worry…Sure. Bye."

The VP put down the phone. "He feels really awful that he can't come, but as I said, I can just as easily tell you everything. There's no need to hold things up; we want to get you guys on vinyl as soon as possible. But," he said, clapping his hands, "we can talk business after dinner."

"Sorry, sorry, sorry!" a high female voice called out. "The baby just wouldn't go down."

A short woman in a tan and black muumuu rushed into the room, her little hands flapping in agitation. Madeline and David stood to shake her hand, but instead of shaking she planted wet kisses on their cheeks. She had a red afro, a space between her teeth, wide flaring nostrils and over-large brown eyes. And she was heavy; when she sat and leaned back Madeline saw her huge braless breasts flop to the sides.

"I hate formality," she said, patting the VP's knee. "I feel like I know both of you already. You're David, of course, and you're Madeline. And Hanson?"

The VP explained about Hanson's nosebleed.

"Oh God," she said. "Oh, lord. Tell me, does he eat a lot of dairy?"

"I beg your pardon?" David said.

"You know, milk, ice cream, butter? Because dairy reeks havoc with your sinuses, that's probably why he gets nosebleeds."

"Honey," the VP said with an edge in his voice. "Nosebleeds have to do with veins, not sinuses."

"Well, excuse me! It's all packed up in there somewhere, isn't it? Roll another joint, honey, that one's just a roach. Well, thank God the baby's down! I'll have two hours of peace at least. I'm breast-feeding," she said to Madeline. "You know how it is."

"Actually, no," Madeline laughed. "Not personally. But a friend of mine has a baby."

"Oh, really? How old?"

Madeline didn't think the VP's wife really wanted to hear about Devon and her child, but she asked question after question about Devon's pregnancy, her delivery, the consistency of her breast milk, Devon's diet while pregnant and while breast-feeding—the works. "And you?" she asked Madeline. "Do you want children?"

"Yes," Madeline said. "I definitely do. But not until I'm older. When I'm thirty, maybe."

"Good for you," the VP's wife said. "I waited too. And this way David's band will have time to get off the ground, and you can enjoy his success before getting tied down."

"Oh," Madeline said, blushing. She looked over at David; he was talking to the VP about California marijuana harvests. "We're not even engaged."

"Not yet," the VP's wife said, winking. "Don't worry, your day will come."

Her husband passed her the joint and she took three long, deep hits. Should she be getting high while breast-feeding? Madeline thought not.

"Your turn," the VP's wife said, handing Madeline the joint. "So tell me about you: David told my husband you're vegetarian. What's your diet like?"

So David continued talking with the VP, and Madeline continued with the wife. Or rather the wife continued, her wide nostrils flaring, her big eyes moist and eager as she told Madeline all the excruciating details about her diet. Madeline wished she and David could communicate telepathically so she could say, "Please help me; please fold me into your discussion so I can be free of this woman." But the situation was delicate, and a good impression essential; Madeline did not dare slip David a meaningful look while passing him the joint, or even discreetly step on his toes. No, this had to be suffered through; Madeline pasted a brittle smile on her face, her head swimming in stonedness as the VP's wife talked on.

"…became macrobiotic two years ago. It changed my whole life, everything. I remember when I went on my first brown rice fast—that's ten days eating only brown rice, it's terribly cleansing. Anyway, on day five my urine was *brown*. I mean, dark brown, like coffee. I called my nutritionist—he's a fabulous guy, I can give you his number—and he said it was a good sign. I said, 'Good sign! My urine looks like espresso and you say that's good?' But he insisted, and I swear to God, after the fast was over I never felt so good in my life."

"Really," Madeline said.

"Then of course when I got pregnant my husband freaked out, he said I had to start drinking milk and eating dairy and we had so many fights. He tells me I'm macro-neurotic. Macro-neurotic—isn't that funny?"

"Very."

"So I gave in to him, I gained fifty pounds while pregnant and I'm still trying to get rid of it. My big concern now is mucus; I feel like I'm full of it. Do you know what I mean?"

"I know exactly what you mean."

The phone buzzed twice, and the VP's wife picked it up. "Ready? Lovely." She put down the phone and clapped her hands. "Dinner's ready; just follow me."

The dining room had more art—Frank Stella, Jasper Johns, and on the wall behind David was a canvas that could only have been a Munch. Madeline almost whimpered in delight. The table and chairs were of grainy white wood that Madeline thought rather ugly, but just by virtue of the fact that it was here she had to assume it was très chic and très expensive. She wished she had a camera so she could show Bella; but who knew, maybe such dinners were to become commonplace in her life, and maybe she could bring Bella along some time.

Lucinda brought out Cornish game hen, wild rice, peas, and stuffing. Madeline knew David had said she was vegetarian, but obviously they had forgotten, or maybe they thought she ate chicken. Then Lucinda brought out two more plates of food and put them in front of the VP's wife and Madeline.

"We can keep each other company while the men eat animal flesh," the VP's wife said, winking at Madeline.

Madeline looked down at her plate. There were a few spoonfuls of brown rice, a small pile of seaweed, three slices of pickled beets, and a quivering slab of tofu. Help, Madeline thought. She didn't mind macrobiotic food; once after a lecture Michael took her to a macrobiotic restaurant in the Village and she had really enjoyed it. But this food was completely without sauces, and the quantities were so small it broke her heart. She had hardly eaten all day because she was sure there would be mouthwatering appetizers and course after course of savory dishes. She had counted on plenty, and here she was with tofu. How she longed to look across the table at David and roll her eyes! But she couldn't.

During the meal David took over. It was practically a repeat of his brunch performance, but this time David could do no wrong; the VP and his wife laughed at everything David said, and seemed utterly charmed by his stories of rock 'n' roll life. David was unstoppable, his color rising, his enthusiasm growing with every laugh and encouraging word. And suddenly Madeline had a painful thought: Were they really charmed, or were they just being nice because David was, as the VP had said, about to make them a lot of money? She was too stoned to judge accurately. She thought about herself, agreeing with the VP's wife about mucus. Robert would have said, "I have no problem with mucus," and that would have been that; Bella would have said, "With all the problems in the world I don't have time to think about mucus"; and Michael would have blinked and said, "Mucus?" in a way that closed the subject once and for all. And what had she done, grinned and nodded like an idiot. She picked through her mound of seaweed, suddenly feeling lonely and out of place. And cold; why on earth did she wear a sleeveless dress at the end of November? As the others talked and laughed she kept a smile pasted on her face, but she hardly heard a word of their conversation.

When the dinner dishes were cleared no one mentioned dessert; a little ice cream would have lifted Madeline's spirits considerably, but instead the VP stood and announced, "And now I'm going to steal David. Madeline, you and my wife can hang out together in the den."

"Okay," she said. She gave David a smile of encouragement; he smiled back, looking completely unconcerned.

The den was a small room off the kitchen. Madeline kept hoping the VP's wife would bring out cookies or something, and when she picked up the phone and punched in two numbers Madeline's hopes rose wildly, but instead the VP's wife said, "Lucinda, bring Dilby in. It's time for his feeding."

"Dilby?" Madeline asked. "That's an unusual name."

"It's my maiden name. It's actually his middle name, but we call him that anyway—his full name's William Dilby Peterson. Have you heard of Dilby Appliances?"

"Of course."

"Well, that's me."

Money, Madeline thought. Big money. "Tell me," she asked. "Are you the art collector? Because you have some beautiful pieces here."

"It's all mine. Most are from my father—he has so much he's run out of wall space—but a few I picked up myself."

"I love the DeKooning."

"That's one I bought. It's nice to have someone appreciate it, because it's all lost on my husband—he cares more about his goddamn goldfish. Here he is! Here's my little Dilber! Come to Mommy!"

Lucinda passed over a chubby blond baby. "He's so cute," Madeline said, reaching out and stroking his soft blond hair. She loved babies, especially the way they smelt; Bella always said that the two best smells in the world were fresh baked bread and just washed babies.

"Cute, and hungry." The VP's wife unzipped her muumuu part way and hauled out an enormous breast. The nipple, Madeline was surprised to see, was dark brown, and she wondered if that was because of breast-feeding or if it always looked that way.

"Do me a favor, Madeline? On the table next to you is a black box with a dragon on it? There's a pipe and some pot in there, why don't you fill it up and we'll smoke a little. Breast-feeding is so boring, I need something to do."

"Okay," Madeline said, praying she wasn't contributing to the rearrangement of Dilby's brain cells. Seemed to her the THC would cancel out all the seaweed, but again, she didn't feel she could say how she really felt.

They smoked, and soon Madeline was so stoned she was dizzy. She wanted to kick off her shoes and lay down, she wanted to take the expensive looking green pastel blanket off the rocking chair and draw it over her, but she couldn't; this wasn't Thanksgiving at Plug's, she couldn't just pass out.

"Where's the bathroom?" Madeline asked, standing unsteadily.

"Back in the hall, just past the dining room."

Madeline followed instructions, but once out in the hall she heard murmuring voices. She had assumed that David and the VP had returned to the living room, but the voices were coming from a little alcove across from the dining room. She cautiously stepped over to the alcove; the door was slightly open, she saw a massive desk and paneled walls covered with gold records, but she could not see David or the VP. She heard them, she saw smoke in the air, but they were invisible. It reminded her of something: yes, the movie *Rosemary's Baby*, the scene where Rosemary's husband, unbeknownst to Rosemary, makes a deal with the devil.

Oh, Madeline, she told herself. You really are stoned. In the bathroom she splashed her face with cold water, but it didn't help; once back in the den the VP's wife said, "You must be cold—here, cover yourself with this blanket." Madeline agreed at once—she slipped off her shoes, tucked her feet under her, took the soft green blanket and covered herself to the chin. Her eyes grew heavy as the VP's wife talked about coffee enemas and electrolytes; softly, imperceptibly, Madeline slipped into a delicious black sleep.

❦   ❦   ❦

"Madeline? Madeline?"

David. In front of her. Shaking her gently.

"Madeline, it's time to go."

She sat up like a shot. "Oh God, I'm sorry—I fell asleep, I couldn't help it."

"Well, it's two in the morning, no wonder you're tired."

"Two in the morning! You mean you've been talking all this time?"

"Yep. Come on, they're in the living room, we'll say good night and then we'll go."

Madeline searched sleepily for her heels. Two o'clock! Dinner had ended around ten, which meant they had been talking for almost four hours. Was there really that much to say? She followed David into the living room; she said good-bye to the VP and his wife, apologizing for falling asleep.

"Don't worry," the VP's wife said. "Happens all the time. Next time we won't keep you up so late."

The VP walked them out to the car, and they stood a moment before opening the doors. "So talk to Hanson," he told David. "And call me on Monday. You can take your time thinking it over, but not too much time, if you know what I mean."

"Okay," David said. "Monday. Thank you for everything."

"Oh no," the VP laughed. "Thank *you*. I'm just glad we got to you before anyone else did."

David opened the door and they were once again enclosed in the humming velvet luxury.

"So?" Madeline asked, taking David's arm. "How was it?"

"You know, Madeline," he said. "If you don't mind, I'd like to have a few minutes to think. I feel pretty confused."

"Okay." Surprised, she leaned her head on his shoulder. She was still sleepy, but it was impossible to sleep now; she was far too curious to learn what had happened. She glanced up at David; he was looking out the window, biting his thumbnail.

"David," she said softly. "What's wrong? Because something's wrong, I can tell. Don't they want to sign you?"

"Oh, they want to sign me. Me and Hanson."

"So that's great."

He looked at her and shook his head. "No, it's not. Because they don't want the rest of the band."

"But that's impossible!" she laughed. "What band has only a guitarist and bassist?"

"You don't understand. They want to replace Jessie and Plug."

"But why?"

"The VP says they're not good enough musicians. Which is bullshit, because Plug is a great drummer, he's really something else. And Jessie—he plays guitar almost as well as Hanson, and he's been with us from the beginning. And I told the VP all that, and he finally admitted they were concerned about our image."

"Your image?"

"It seems Jessie is too old. So he's forty-two, so what? And Plug isn't very photogenic. Or so the VP thinks."

"I don't see what difference any of that makes."

"The way the VP sees it, since we can get comparable musicians who have a more interesting look, then that's what we should do. And that, in fact, is their bottom line. If we agree to that they can get us studio space in a month and we can begin cutting a record."

"Don't do it, David!" Madeline said. "Find another label. You're the one who always said you can sign anywhere. I mean, you can just keep cutting records with The Small Record Label—they don't have any problem with Jessie and Plug."

"We're tired of being on a small label. And the VP says any other label will tell us the same thing."

"You don't know unless you try."

"If we start shopping around, he'll get wind of it. It won't look good. And if we wait too long *we'll* be forty-two, and then no one will want us either."

Madeline's eyes filled with tears. "This is terrible," she said. "And we all just had Thanksgiving together."

"Well, he gave me a little time to think it over. But I pretty much know what I have to do. Goddammit!" he said, hitting the seat with a fist. "I went through this with Raller, and now I have to go through it again."

And for the second time that night, David cried. Madeline held his head to her shoulder, wiping away his tears, kissing his hair. And she remembered what the VP had said at The Beat'n Path: no business is as hard as rock 'n' roll.

CHAPTER 14

Surprise

Madeline was sitting directly behind the bus driver, so instead of pulling the wire she leaned forward and said, "Next stop, please."

The driver pulled over to the corner of Fourth and Washington. He cranked open the door, and a blast of cold air swept into the bus and onto Madeline's stockinged legs.

"It's a cold one," the driver said.

"It certainly is," Madeline laughed. "Good night."

"Good night."

It was about quarter after five and already it was dark; Washington Street was lit with neon and bright windows and, a recent addition, strings of white lights hung above the streets, the middle lights wrapped around wire in the shape of a bell, star, or crooked Christmas tree.

Madeline hesitated; if she hurried home she could catch David before he left for rehearsal, but she also needed to stop at the grocery store and pick up soy milk, orange juice, and flowers. She wanted to see David, but necessity won out. Maybe she would surprise him and show up at the studio before ten so she could walk him home, maybe they could go out and get something to eat.

Two weeks had passed since their dinner with the VP, and what a two weeks it had been. The morning after the dinner David woke up with agonizing stomach pains. "I can't do it," he told Madeline. "I just can't do it." He called Hanson, and Hanson and Alison came over for an emergency conference. Despite Madeline's resolve to stay out of Narrow Grave's business, she had her opinion and was ready to fight the others. But to her surprise, they agreed;

even Alison felt that The Big Record Company was asking too much. "You'll lose your sound," she insisted. "Jessie and Plug are both very distinctive players." And during their powwow both Jessie and Plug called to find out any news; David put them off by saying nothing was definite, and each time he hung up the phone his face was twisted in pain.

The next morning David called the VP to set up a meeting; the VP fit them in that afternoon and David and Hanson went to the plush corporate offices and said they could not agree with The Big Record Label's terms. At which point, David told Madeline, the VP said, "Okay. Let's split the difference." He told them they could keep Jessie on the condition that he dyed his hair and allowed the public relations department to say he was thirty; Plug, however, had to go. "And that's really our final offer," the VP said. "Think it over." Which totally blew David's mind; as he told Madeline, the VP had agreed so instantly it was almost as if the whole thing had been a test, some sort of weird initiation rite. "And yet," David said, "he and I argued about it for hours on Saturday night. I feel like they're playing with us."

That night after rehearsal they broke the news. Plug took it pretty well; he said he had been expecting something like that, and since he'd only been with the band two years he knew he couldn't ask them to lose a lucrative contract just for his sake. Everyone had expected Plug to go crazy and destroy things, but instead he behaved with great dignity, even saying he'd be happy to break in his replacement. Jessie, on the other hand, was furious. He refused to dye his hair, refused to lie about his age, refused to be packaged into some MTV-acceptable product. At which point Hanson's nerves broke, and he got a nosebleed, which left David to convince Jessie that, really, he had no other choice. Jessie insisted they did have a choice: another label. "Then you set it up," David told him. "You go out and you negotiate with more of these assholes, because I don't have the stomach for it." Jessie walked out in a huff; he didn't show up at rehearsal the rest of the week, then on Friday night he left a message on David and Madeline's machine: "Okay," he said. "You win. But I'm not going to a beauty salon." So they called Bella into action; the next day Jessie came to 10 Willow Terrace, and Bella dyed his hair jet black and cut it into a punkish style. Hanson and Alison were also there, and everyone agreed that Jessie looked thirty, maybe even twenty-nine. Jessie liked the new look, and in fact he felt so good he asked Bella on a date. Bella laughed. "Didn't you notice how I sometimes refer to a person named Robert? That person is my husband, and if he knew you asked me out he would kill you. Sicilian style." Jessie backed down, but Madeline could tell that Bella was pleased.

So all was well. David called the VP, the VP invited David, Hanson, and Jessie to a meeting; a lawyer was hired, and now the contract—eighty pages at last count, the lawyer had told David just the night before—was being banged out. Narrow Grave was on its way.

But David had not bounced back. The stress and strain and back and forth had been too much for him, and he had moments where he sat on the couch absolutely listless, saying nothing and smoking joint after joint. He even fell behind on the housework, so it was Madeline who brought their clothes to the Chinese laundry, Madeline who vacuumed and did the dishes. She was worried about David; all the responsibility had fallen on him and he had managed beautifully, but he was paying a price the others did not see. And she really knew he wasn't well when he didn't ask her to have sex—she had contracted another UTI after the VP's dinner, and when she told David they should take a break from sex so it could really clear up he said, "Sure, no problem." Which is what he always said, but usually after four or five days he began hinting, asking if she didn't feel better, and since the worst of the pain was gone by then she always gave in. But this time he had said nothing, which is when Madeline knew David was not himself.

She was doing her best to cheer him up, which was why she spent five dollars on fresh daisies and bought a six-pack of Dos Equus beer. But I hope he perks up soon, she mused as she walked home hurriedly in the cold. He needs to clean the house before his parents come. Because at long last, on December 26 to be exact, the parents Guggenheim were coming to stay with David and Madeline for five days, and Madeline knew that no matter how hard she tried, her housekeeping wouldn't be earning any gold stars from Mrs. Guggenheim. She was curious about the visit for a number of reasons, one of which was seeing David straight—because how could he get high if his parents were here? She asked him about it and was disappointed by his reply: "Anytime they visit I'm always running out to the store for them, so it's no big deal to stop in the park and smoke a joint. I don't let them cramp my style." Oh well, she thought, opening the gate, mentally saying hello to Lucky and Leapy. You can't have everything.

She opened the door to the apartment. The lights were on, and David was sitting on the couch smoking a joint.

"Oh, you're still here!" she said. "I thought I'd missed you."

"Rehearsal's starting later today."

"Oh?" she said, putting the packages on the counter, unpeeling her hat, scarf, gloves, and coat.

"Come sit down," he said, patting the couch. "I want to talk to you."

"Sure. Just give me a moment to put these in water." She unwrapped the daisies and took a large cut glass vase from the cupboard; she filled it halfway with water and shoved the flowers inside. "You'll have to arrange them," she said, carrying the vase over to the table. "You know I'm no good at it. So!" she said, sitting next to him, leaning over and kissing his cheek. "What's up?"

"Well, I wanted to talk." He stubbed out the joint. "About us."

"Okay."

"Well, what I want to say is—it's not working."

"What?"

"Us."

"What do you mean?" she laughed. "Everything's fine."

"Well—it isn't for me."

"What's wrong? Did I do something? Tell me, we'll talk about it."

"No, it's not anything you did. The truth is, I'm bored."

Bored. Bored? Madeline's head snapped back as if he had slapped her. *Bored*: what a horrible indictment.

"But I'm not bored," she said, her voice small. "I'm not bored at all."

"I know, and that's what makes this so hard." He sighed, and stared at the coffee table. "Madeline, I think it would be best if you went back to live with your sister."

Something started roaring in her head. "You—you want me to move out?"

"I think it would be best. I mean, there's no use prolonging things."

"Prolonging things?! David—we're in love! We're living together! You don't just say, Move out. We've got to talk it out, we've got to work on things."

"Madeline, for the past two weeks I've been miserable. And I've tried working on things. And I know it won't work."

"But—David! The past two weeks have been the craziest weeks of your life! I don't even see how you had a moment to think about us. This is just some kind of reaction to all the stress."

"No, it's not," he said quietly. "Look—the VP and I talked about a lot of things that night. He tried to prepare me for how my life is going to change. My life is going to change a lot, Madeline. And I think it's best if I'm just totally free for whatever those changes might be."

"I don't understand."

"What I'm saying is, anything could happen. We could go on tour for six months—and not just in America, but in Europe. And I just want to do all that without looking over my shoulder, worrying about you." He sighed, and looked at her. "I guess this wasn't a good time for me to get involved with someone. I'm so sorry, Madeline. I never meant to hurt you."

"But—but you told me when we met how you wanted someone to share all this with."

"I know I said that, and at the time I meant it. But now I feel differently."

And suddenly she felt tremendous relief: he wasn't breaking up with her, he just didn't want to live together anymore. Okay—her pride was hurt, it was a blow, but at least they'd still be together.

"David!" she said, putting a hand on his arm. "I'm sorry, I misunderstood you. You don't want to break up; you just don't want us to live together. I can handle that."

He shook his head. "No, Madeline. What I mean is, I want us to break up."

That horrible roaring started again, like the sound when you put a seashell to your ear, but magnified a thousand times and coming from somewhere behind her eyes. Her lips went completely dry, and her hands started shaking.

"Are you—are you saying you don't love me anymore?"

"Not like I used to, no. Oh, Madeline," he said, reaching out a hand and touching her cheek. "I'm so sorry. You can't imagine how sorry I am. You're one of the most wonderful girls I've ever met, but I just can't do this anymore."

Her eyes felt strange; they were as dry and chapped as her lips. "But it's almost Christmas," she said. "I have a present for you. And your parents are coming. They want to meet me."

"I know. That's why I wanted to do this now, before they came."

It was so strange. She heard his words, but she didn't believe him.

"But David—you're the one who suggested I move in. It was your idea. And remember all those things you said to Robert? You really fought him on this."

"I know. And now I see I was a little hasty. It seemed like a good idea at the time; we were so in love, and we always wanted to be together—"

"And now?" she said, her voice strangled. "And now you don't want us to be together?"

"No, I don't. Now I think you should move out."

She licked her lips. She felt some kind of scratching inside, as if a wild animal were caught in her chest. She blinked several times, hoping to stop the stinging in her eyes. The apartment looked strange, suddenly; everything was very bright and vivid.

"But you, you told me you weren't going to hurt me. And I slept with you. I hadn't slept with anyone in so long, I was scared even to let a man touch me and I, I opened up to you. I trusted you."

"Madeline, I swear to God I never meant to hurt you. I guess this is just how I do things. I mean, you meet someone, you sleep together, you get to know each other, and if you break up after a few months, well, no one's traumatized."

"That's not the only way to do things," she said quietly. "You can get to know someone by talking and by doing things together, and if you find you're compatible then you sleep together."

"Well, that's another style."

That was her style. And instead of sticking to it she had given into his style, and now she was going to pay.

Oh my God. He was not sitting next to her telling her these things. She put her head in her hands. "Don't do this to me, David," she said. "Please, please, don't do this to me."

"I'll help you move, of course. We can call a taxi. In fact I'll call now."

"But all my stuff—I have so many things here."

"I did all that for you. Everything's in the bedroom."

She stared at him, then rose and went into the bedroom. Sure enough, on the bed was her suitcase, her typewriter, her lapdesk, two large and one small plastic shopping bag.

"I was nervous while I was waiting for you," David said, coming up behind her. "I needed something to do."

She moved to the bed and touched her typewriter. Then she went to the bedside table and opened the top drawer: her diaphragm was gone.

"It's in your bag," he said.

"I see." She sat on the edge of the bed and looked up at him. "You're very thorough. There's no trace of me anywhere." She took a long shaky breath. "And the bathroom? Did you take all my stuff out of there?"

"It's all in that small plastic bag. Well—I'll go call a taxi now."

Madeline looked around the room. This is not your room anymore, she told herself. This is not your room. She suddenly remembered David's Christmas present; she had hidden it behind the plastic box where he kept unmatched socks and stray buttons. She went to the closet, stood on tiptoe, and felt behind the box. She felt a shock run through her as her fingers touched empty shelf. She went to the bed, opened her suitcase, and there it was, tucked into a corner, a small wrapped box. It was a ring, a beautiful gold ring embedded with a piece of jade. David had admired it in the window of a store in the Village, and Madeline spent $300 of her savings to buy it for him. She hid it behind the box over a week ago, and somehow he knew. She picked the present out of the rest of the clothes; he hadn't touched the wrapping, hadn't even been curious what it was. And somehow that hurt worst of all. She had no idea David could be so ruthless.

Numbly she put the box back in and closed the suitcase. She took a slow look around and saw, yes, he had forgotten something: her framed picture of Flannery O'Connor. The picture was propped just behind David and Joe Strummer; Madeline rose and plucked it from the shelf, then sat down on the bed and bent her head so her forehead touched the cool glass.

"Madeline?"

She looked up. David was in the doorway.

"They'll be here in five minutes. I'm going to start taking all this stuff down."

"David." Her fingers grabbed the picture; she had to keep her voice steady. "I don't want to do this. I don't want to leave."

"Madeline, you have to leave."

"But I don't want to."

He sighed. He came over to the bed and sat down next to her; he took her in his arms, and for a moment joy flooded back. It was going to be okay, he wasn't going to make her go. But then he took his arms away; he held her by the shoulders and said, "I'm going to take your stuff downstairs now."

He grabbed the suitcase and the small plastic bag, and he left the room. She sat in a dull daze as he returned to take the two large plastic bags, then returned again for the typewriter and lapdesk. Then he came back for her.

"Come on, Madeline. The taxi'll be here any moment. You need to put on your coat."

She sat and stared at the picture in her lap. Peacocks—what was it like to live with peacocks? Actually Flannery had written a whole essay on just that subject, but Madeline couldn't remember a word of it now. And why hadn't anyone ever told Flannery to lose those cat glasses and get a more flattering hairstyle? Obviously Flannery didn't have an older sister.

"Madeline. Come on, let's go."

She looked up at him. "I still love you."

"Madeline." His voice was pleading now. "Madeline, you have to get up. Come on."

He grabbed her hand and pulled her off the bed. Still holding her hand he led her to the kitchen counter where she had dropped her coat. He took the picture out of her hand, put her arms into the coat and buttoned it. Then he wrapped her scarf around her neck, put her wool hat on her head, moved her fingers into her gloves. He replaced the picture in her hand and then led her downstairs.

They stood in the small foyer, waiting. All her things were on the sidewalk next to the curb, standing in a pool of street light. Which wasn't very smart; someone could have stolen something. But it was a cold night; everyone was too busy going home to worry about a pile of things on the sidewalk.

Madeline looked at David; his arms were folded and he was staring into the street. His eyes looked sad, but his jaw was tight and determined. And suddenly she remembered their first date at Leo's, remembered him leaning over the table and staring at her, hanging on her every word.

Beep beep! "Here it is," David said, pushing open the door.

The taxi driver had stopped on Willow Street. With his breath coming in frozen puffs, he helped David bring Madeline's things to the taxi, then opened the trunk and hastily put everything inside.

"Cold!" he said cheerily to Madeline as David led her inside the taxi.

"Cold," she agreed.

In the taxi David explained to the driver that they were going to 821 Washington where they would leave the young lady and her things, then he needed to go over to Second and Grand.

"You're going to rehearsal?" she asked him.

"Of course."

She looked out the window.

The ride was short: only four blocks up to Washington, then two blocks up to 821. The driver offered to bring Madeline's things inside but David said they could manage. The driver opened the trunk and put everything on the sidewalk; David handed the plastic bags and lapdesk to Madeline, then took the typewriter and suitcase himself. They walked up the stoop and David said, "Madeline—the keys?"

She put down the bags and reached into her pockets for her key ring.

"And while you're at it," he said, "I guess you might as well give me your keys back."

She looked at him, then down at her key ring. All the keys looked the same to her. David sighed impatiently, then he put down the suitcase and typewriter and deftly flipped through the keys. He maneuvered two of them off the ring and put them in his pocket.

"Now which one is for this door?" he asked.

"I'm not sure," she said faintly.

"Okay," he said. "I'll just try all of them." But he guessed right on the first try; he propped the door open with his foot, then handed her the keys.

They made their way up the stairs. It was a beautiful staircase: when Bella and Robert first moved in they spent many weekends sanding and stripping the wood, then shellacking it so it gleamed rich dark brown. The stairs were carpeted in dark blue, and there were even little brass bars holding the carpet in place at each step. And the two landings they passed had healthy ferns in brass pots. Bella and Robert had really done a nice job.

Then they were in front of the apartment. David put down the suitcase and typewriter and cracked his knuckles. "Well," he said. "I'll call you in a few days, see how you're doing. I'm really sorry about all this, Madeline, but it's for the best. You'll meet someone else, you'll see."

He leaned over, kissed her cheek, then turned and walked down the stairs.

His foot had just touched the third floor hallway when Madeline threw down the plastic bags and lapdesk and ran down the stairs, running so fast she almost tripped over her feet. David, who was halfway down the hall, looked back in surprise. Madeline fell down on her knees and wrapped her arms around his waist. She squeezed her face into his legs and said, "Don't leave me, David. Please, please, don't leave me." She looked up at him, love and fear pouring out of her grey-green eyes. "Please don't leave me. Please, please don't."

David's eyes were also full of tears. He closed his eyes, put his hand on her wool hat. Then he unwrapped her arms from his waist and held her hands in his own.

"Madeline," he said, looking at her both tenderly and fiercely. "I have to do this. Don't make it any harder than it already is."

He reached down, kissed her gloved hands, then left, this time taking the stairs two at a time. The front door slammed.

He was gone.

She knelt there for some time. She could follow him to his rehearsal space, go there and talk to him, try to make him change his mind—but no. No. She swallowed. Everything was so bright, so odd.

She walked up the steps. She went to the door and knocked. Nothing happened; she must have knocked too softly. Anyway everyone was home; she could see a bar of light from under the door, could smell garlic bread. She knocked again.

She heard Bella's rapid eager footsteps. Then the door opened; good smells and a pool of light fell into the hall, and there was Bella, standing in front of Madeline.

"Maddy! I was worried about you, you're late. Why didn't you use your key? We ate already, and Michael just came—but what's all this? Why do you have all your things?"

CHAPTER 15

Shock

Madeline laid in bed under her flowered bedcover, on her side in the fetal position. Her eyes were open, and she was staring at her bookshelves.

She had been up for hours. She had not moved, she just laid in bed watching as the rectangle of light thrown by her shaded window changed from dark grey to light grey, listening as the noise on Washington Street changed from occasional rumbles to full-blown morning traffic. And then one moment a bar of white light appeared alongside her open door: Robert had woken up, and turned on the hall light. Some minutes later she heard voices and footsteps, then the smell of coffee drifted into her room. The sounds grew and faded, grew and faded, then heels clicked determinedly down the hall, and the white bar widened.

She looked up. Bella was in the doorway.

"Maddy? Are you awake?"

"Mmm hmm," Madeline said, looking again at the bookshelves.

Bella came into the room and sat on the bed close to Madeline. She wore a green silk suit, white collarless shirt, a thick gold necklace, gold hoops, and a jangle of gold bracelets. Her perfume was strong and sweet, and as she bent forward to feel Madeline's forehead the scent pricked Madeline's nose.

"Did you sleep?"

"A little. Not much."

Bella sighed. "I would give you more sleeping pills but I don't think it's a good idea. It was okay for the first night, but we shouldn't make a habit of it." She bent down and picked up an empty box of tissues. "I'll bring you more.

And I'll throw all these away," she said, waving her hand to indicate the crumpled balls of tissue that littered the carpet next to Madeline's bed.

Madeline said nothing.

"I have to go now, I have an early meeting. But as soon as I'm out I'll give you a call. Get up and answer the phone, okay, or I'll worry. Robert'll call you too. Okay?"

"Okay."

"And try to eat something. There's still stuffed shells from last night, they're in the fridge."

The bar of white widened farther. Robert.

"Hi, Madeline," he said. He stood awkwardly by the bookshelves, his hands in his pockets. He was in what Bella called his professor-wear, brown trousers and a thick brown corduroy jacket. "Did you sleep?"

"No," Bella said. "Not really. I told her we'd call her. You can call after your nine o'clock class, okay?"

"Okay. And I'll try to get home early, but I have a few student conferences that I can't miss."

"Well, it's almost finals, it's not easy for you to get away. But I should be able to leave at five. Okay, Maddy, I'm going now. Robert," Bella said as she stooped and gathered the tissues, "bring another box of tissues from the bathroom, okay?"

Robert left the room and Bella, hands full of used tissues, leaned over and lay her cheek on Madeline's. Neither sister said anything, and they stayed that way until Robert came back and put the tissues on top of the closed typewriter, which was back in its old spot on the desk next to the bed.

"Okay," Bella said. "I'll call you. You're going to answer the phone, right?"

"I will," Madeline said.

Bella kissed Madeline's cheek, Robert patted her hair, then they left. Murmurs, clicking heels, doors shutting, Bella's laugh, then the bar of white disappeared and the front door slammed shut.

Madeline sighed, and closed her eyes. She inhaled deeply, her breath shaky and weak. Except to go to the bathroom and answer the phone, she hadn't left her bed since—when was it? Two nights ago; Bella had led Madeline into Bella and Robert's bedroom, and then when it was time to go to bed Bella took Madeline into her own room. Robert had brought in the suitcase, typewriter, and plastic bags, but Madeline had touched nothing; the suitcase was still on the floor next to her closet, the plastic bags resting on top.

Except for the first night when Bella gave her two sleeping pills, Madeline had hardly slept, and all she had eaten were two crackers—it was all she had been able to force down. The only thing she wanted to do was lay in bed and think about David. The entire day before all she did was go over their relationship, running through all their conversations, all their dates, all the times they made love, and the only conclusion she could come to was that they had been happy. Even the past two weeks, they had been happy. She just couldn't believe she was the cause of David's depression; he had been so involved with The Big Record Label, they hardly had time to be alone. He must still love her. He must.

And then she would remember Tuesday night. She would close her eyes and steel herself against the biting wave of pain. She had replayed the conversation so many times she knew it by heart, but she just couldn't match that conversation with the rest of her memories. Was there something David wasn't telling her? Had someone said something about her, had he met someone else? How could his feelings change so quickly? She didn't really understand why he had broken up with her: first he said he was bored, then he said he wanted to be free because of the new record contract. So which was it? Last night she and Bella had talked it over, and Bella couldn't understand either. Madeline asked Bella to think back on the day she had spent at their apartment dying Jessie's hair: Had David acted strange? Had he seemed bored, worried, unhappy? Bella knit her brow and thought a long time; finally she said that other than the fact that David hardly touched Madeline, everything had seemed normal.

Which gave Madeline hope. Maybe this was a passing whim, a temporary panic; maybe David—coming home to an empty apartment, sleeping alone—would see his mistake. In fact she felt sure that he would, and just this thought made joy flicker inside her. But then Tuesday night would flood back: his definitiveness, his ruthlessness, his determination to get her and every trace of her out of the apartment. And—the worst memory of all—her down on her knees, begging him not to leave, and him taking away her hands and running down the stairs, running away from her.

But every time the phone rang, she was sure it was him. She laid sluggishly in bed, but at the first ring of the phone she was always up and running down the long thin hallway. But it was never David. Or anyway, not yet.

Men always come back. That was Devon's theory, anyway; Madeline remembered Devon telling her that all of her old boyfriends, with only one or two exceptions, had tried to return to her. Devon said that men needed longer to understand how they felt: after a breakup a woman cries nonstop for a month, then slowly gets back on her feet. Men pretend nothing is wrong, but after about six months the truth sinks in and then, like clockwork, they show up at your door, hoping to win you back.

But six months! Madeline could not wait that long; she needed David now. She missed him so much—less than two days, and already she was almost out of her mind missing him, missing his touch, the way he smelled, the way he laughed, the concentrated look on his face when he played bass, the softness in his eyes when he played with her hair—everything. She missed everything. They had been so happy together! She played over their courtship again and again, the dates at the beginning when all they did was talk, how it was later once they started sleeping together, and how happy they were when she moved in. It was a happy, magical time, and she saw no reason why it had to end.

He would come back. He had to. Because if he didn't, how was she supposed to live?

The morning passed in a lethargic haze. The phone rang twice, but it was just Bella and Robert. And then a little before eleven Madeline raised her shade and watched Washington Street, hoping David might pass by on his way to work. But he must have walked down Bloomfield, because she didn't see him. How odd, she thought, laying back in bed. He was at work now, at Maxwell's, corner of Eleventh and Washington Street, a mere three blocks from where she laid missing him. She imagined herself walking into the restaurant and him rushing over to her, glad to see her, eager to tell her he had made a mistake and wanted her to come back...

She sat bolt upright in bed. She would go! Yes, she would go and see him. Why not? If he was feeling badly, if he was regretting what he had done—and she was sure he was—why prolong their agony? Maybe he was ashamed to call her after what had happened; maybe he was afraid of Robert, afraid of confronting him on the phone. She would take the first step, she would make things easier for him.

It was a great idea. But she wouldn't go while he was working; she would wait outside, and when he came out they could go back to the apartment and talk. And maybe—yes, just maybe—they would make love, patch things up, start fresh.

Energy surged through her: yes, she would go.

She took a shower, washed and blow-dried her hair. Her face was puffy from crying and sleepless nights, but she borrowed some of Bella's makeup and made herself presentable. It was important not to be pitiful. His last memory of her—on her knees, begging—had to be erased. Because anyway that wasn't who she was. Madeline never begged anyone for anything; it was important that David know that.

She was ready by one o'clock. His shift was over at two, but he sometimes left earlier if there were no customers. The idea of missing him made her almost hysterical, so she decided to go at once. She could peek in the window and see if there were many customers, then station herself across the street next to Helmers'. Luckily the windows at Maxwell's were covered with Venetian blinds; he wouldn't see her, or at least she hoped not.

She put on her coat, hat, scarf and mittens, then went out into the day. Stepping outside, the world looked woozy and grey, cloudy and damp and Decembery. If it rained, or snowed, then how would she wait for him? She couldn't miss him, she just couldn't.

She walked up Washington Street, her heart pounding crazily, cold fear alternating with joy. The closer she got to Maxwell's the more her anguish grew; she was dizzy from nerves and lack of food, but as she approached the corner of Eleventh and Washington she steeled herself. She peeked into the front window of Maxwell's, stooping slightly to see through the blinds—she saw three full tables, another waiter and then—oh! there he was, carrying a tray of drinks. He was wearing jeans and a red corduroy shirt, and as he set down the drinks he said something that made the customers laugh. Seeing him gave her hope: he was just David, after all. Her David.

Well. What to do now? She watched a little; the table of drinkers appeared to be his only customers, she would wait across the street until they left and then she would come back and wait for him by the door. That wasn't desperate, was it? She wasn't making a scene, wasn't interfering with his work. She didn't look all wild and freaked out—a little swollen around the eyes, perhaps, but it was cold outside, anyone would think it was from the cold. She wasn't here to beg, she was here to be reasonable, to give him a chance to ask her back. She was just making things easier for him—nothing wrong with that.

She dashed across the street and stood in the doorway of Helmers'. She was hungry, very hungry, but her stomach was a tight stretched nerve and anyway she didn't dare leave her post and risk missing David. The entrance to Maxwell's was on Eleventh Street; she kept her eyes glued to the sidewalk in front of the entrance. After a few minutes a couple came out, then maybe fifteen minutes later three women—secretaries from Stevens, probably—stumbled laughing onto the sidewalk and walked unsteadily over to Hudson Street. David's party consisted of two couples and—yes, finally, here they were, coming onto the sidewalk, hesitating a moment then walking to Washington Street and heading downtown.

Here goes, she thought. Chips of ice fluttered through her chest as she crossed the street and walked to the entrance. But she shouldn't stand directly in front of the door—too desperate. No, over by the side, closer to Hudson Street, and when he came out she would step forward, lightly call his name; he would turn and see her and then—well, then they would see.

She waited. She was cold; she moved from foot to foot, sometimes lowering her head to stop the dizziness. She looked up at the sky: grey and full, so heavy it appeared it might fall. One moment she wanted to run back home, the next moment she was sure she was doing the right thing; through it all her heart skipped wildly, with occasional strange cold flashes bursting in her head.

She was terrified.

A noise; the door opening, laughter, voices. Two waiters bundled up in coats and behind them in his black wool coat—David.

"David," Madeline said, stepping forward.

He turned, and when he saw her his carefree expression closed slightly. "Oh—Madeline. Hi."

Everyone stopped. The other waiters said hello; they of course knew Madeline through David. Madeline could tell at once they knew that she and David had broken up—there was an odd distance in their voices, as if they were unsure how to treat her.

"See you guys tomorrow," David said. The others waved good-bye and hurried towards Washington Street. "Well, Madeline," David said. "What can I do for you?"

"Well, I was hoping we could go somewhere to talk? I mean, if you're not busy or anything."

She wanted him to suggest the apartment or the Malibu or even—lowest of lows—The Castle Point Diner, but instead he said, "Why don't we walk over to the park?"

Elysian Park was at Hudson and 10th Street. It was a curious park; the ground was mostly covered in concrete, and the playground had black plastic underneath the rides. There was a grassy area behind this, and a lovely view of Manhattan, but the initial impression was a bit sterile. "The park without a park," Bella always called it.

"Okay," Madeline agreed. "Let's go there."

David walked quickly. He was beside her, but there was at least two feet between them; he said nothing, just strode quickly, his eyes trained straight ahead. None of this boded well, and an agitated anxiety ran from Madeline's chest to her stomach and back again to her chest. She wanted to open her mouth and say something, anything—a casual inquiry about work, or the band—but words were impossible. All the easiness between them was gone; the swirl of dark purple had been replaced by concrete.

The park without a park was empty except for two high school boys smoking cigarettes, and an old woman feeding pigeons out of a battered brown paper bag. David sat down on one of the benches and Madeline sat next to him, careful not to sit too close.

She wanted him to start. She had gone to him, yes, but if he wanted to ask her back this was his opportunity. There was no fear of confronting Robert on the phone, there was no one else around. If he was going to say he was wrong, this was the moment.

He glanced at her, smiled briefly. "I don't know if you know this," he said, "but your brother-in-law called me."

"Oh my God—Robert?"

David nodded. "He told me off. I mean, he *really* told me off. Then a few minutes later your sister called to apologize, and then when she was done apologizing *she* told me off."

Madeline closed her eyes, mortified. "David, you have to believe me, I knew nothing about it."

"I didn't think you did."

"I'm going to kill them."

"Don't be angry at them. They did it because they love you, that much was clear." He paused. "And some of the things they said were true. But they were both wrong when they said I never loved you. I really did love you; I wouldn't lie about something like that."

"And now?" Madeline asked, not caring about the desperation in her voice. "Now you don't love me? Now you feel bored?"

He nodded.

"But David—" It was all she could do to stop herself from reaching out and shaking his arm. "Look, all couples go through rough spots. This boredom you feel—maybe it'll pass. If we just stick things out—"

"It won't pass. I know it won't."

"Well—then I really don't understand. Is the problem that you're bored, or that you want to be free because of the record contract?"

"It's both."

"But when did you start to feel this way? Because I thought we were happy. I mean, this is really coming out of the blue for me." Her voice shook, and her eyes once again started that dry stinging.

"Well, I guess it all started after we went to the VP's house."

"But that's only two weeks! Two weeks of unhappiness doesn't cancel out two and a half months of happiness! Don't you see that?"

"Madeline, all I know is that I felt like I was drowning. All of your love, having you at home every day—I felt like you were strangling me."

She was so astonished she gasped. "But David—you asked me to move in with you! You wanted me to love you!"

"I did, but then it turned out to be too much for me." He sighed. "I'm sorry."

"So," she said, the word stretching and trembling. "Are you saying that there's no chance of our getting back together again?"

He at least had the decency to look her in the eye. "No, Madeline. There's no chance."

"None? None at all?"

"None."

"But how—" She stopped, closed her eyes. Don't cry, she told herself. Don't cry. "How can two people love each other so much, and then suddenly there's nothing?"

"I don't know. Sometimes it's like that."

"I love you," she said, her eyes wide and pleading. "You stopped loving me, but I never stopped loving you. I love you with all my heart."

He looked at the ground and said nothing. Then he raised his head and looked over at the playground. "I'm sorry, Madeline. I'm sorry I'm hurting you so much. I really did love you, but then—I don't know, it just went away. I still like you, though; I mean, you're a wonderful person." He looked at her. "I'd say we could still be friends, but that's probably not enough for you."

"No," she said. "It's not."

"Well—" He shifted his legs, put his hands in his coat pockets. "Listen, I better go. I have a couple things to do before rehearsal."

She nodded. "Okay."

"You'll be all right?"

"I'll be fine."

"I'll call you sometime, see how you are. Okay?"

"Sure."

"Well—bye." He lay his hand on her wool hat, then left. She watched him walk to the corner of 10th and Hudson; he turned the corner, then disappeared.

A hard gasp escaped her. She couldn't ignore the truth any longer, and the truth was that David had moved on. He was done with her.

That sense of gasping didn't leave; it was as if her body was stuck in a position of exhalation. And when she tried to breath in she could only take in a little air. She thought it would pass but with each inhalation it became worse; she could hardly breathe in at all. To compensate she started breathing very fast, inhaling rapidly and shallowly. She put a hand on her stomach, another on her throat. She recognized that she was in the middle of some kind of panic attack; she wanted to call out to the old woman and the high school students, but she couldn't make a sound. The rapid, shallow breathing had a life of its own, she couldn't stop it if she wanted to. For one wild moment she thought she would die right there on the bench in the park without a park, but then she remembered her legs—she could walk, of course she could walk. She was close to home, she just had to get to Tenth Street, then go over to Washington and walk down a block. It wasn't far; she could make it.

Normally such a walk would take less than five minutes, but Madeline could hardly breathe, and she was scared her throat might close up completely. She inched her way home, taking steps forward whenever she inhaled her little bit of air. She passed no one on Hudson or Tenth, but when she finally turned the corner at Washington an older woman was just ahead of her. Madeline wanted to fall into the woman's arms, but no, she couldn't ask a complete stranger to take her home. She passed a few more buildings, and then her breath became so shallow and painful she had to sit on the stoop of a building. But resting didn't help; her throat just got tighter and tighter, and all she wanted was to be home. Please God, she prayed as she rose off the stoop. Please just let me make it home. I don't care if I die, but don't let me die on the sidewalk like a stray dog. Please, just let me get home.

Step by painful step, breath by constricted breath, Madeline walked down Washington Street. At the corner the light was green, she crossed the street and then, yes, there it was, the stoop to 821. She carefully made her way to the building and with great effort walked up the stoop. She had problems with her keys—at first she couldn't find them, then she dropped them, but finally she opened the door and nearly fell into the building. The gleaming banister, the blue carpet, the brass rods—she was home.

She walked up the stairs with great difficulty, and at last, at last, she was in front of the apartment. And suddenly she remembered: she had left her keys in the front door.

It was too much for her. She started to cry, and with every sob that little bit of air was more difficult to take in. She could at least take puffs of air before, but now her throat had constricted to the size of a spaghetti stick. She laid down in front of the door, curled into the fetal position, and closed her eyes.

Time passed—how much she was not sure—but one moment she heard someone say, "Madeline?"

She lifted her head. Michael was standing above her.

"Madeline, what's going on? I found your keys in the door." He dropped his briefcase and knelt at her side. "Madeline, what's wrong? Look at me."

She felt gentle hands on either side of her face; her head was turned, and she found herself looking at Michael. She saw his large green eyes and his drawn brow.

"You're hyperventilating," he said. "Let's get you inside."

She was aware of the door opening in front of her and then, it felt like a miracle, she was suddenly off the ground, weightless, her arms around Michael's neck and her head on his shoulder. And then she was sinking into softness. Thank God: her bed, her books, her little room. But still she could not breathe; she closed her eyes and continued fighting for air.

"Madeline. Madeline—open your eyes and look at me." She opened her eyes. Michael was sitting on the side of the bed, bending over her. "I know you're scared, but I want you to do as I say. There's a very simple way for you to breathe normally again. Here."

He cupped his hands together and held them in front of her face, totally covering her mouth and nose. She panicked—what was he doing, cutting off her air altogether? Her eyes went wild; she grabbed his hands and tried to pull them off her face.

"Madeline," he said sternly. "You have to trust me."

She continued to struggle; he sighed and then, his expression half-angry and half-sad, leaned over her, and with the weight of his body pressed her back against the bed, his hands clamped tightly over her nose and mouth.

"Just breathe," he said quietly. "Trust me—all you have to do is breathe."

She scratched at his hands; he tightened his lips but did not budge. Her eyes were large and terrified, his soft and sad.

"Trust me," he said. "You have to trust me."

He was bigger than she was, and he was not about to budge, so she did as he said. Her eyes threw knives at him, but gradually, slowly, the stick of spaghetti widened, and Madeline no longer felt she was going to die. She dug her nails out of Michael's knuckles and let her hands rest on his. No, she wasn't going to die, but she still had to contend with the fact that David was gone. At the thought of him her throat suddenly contracted again.

"Keep your mind empty," Michael said. "When you're better you can tell me what happened. Okay?"

She nodded.

About ten minutes later he slowly lifted his hands off her mouth. "You should be okay now. Do you think you'll be all right if I leave you alone a moment? I want to make you some tea—you need something hot in your throat. You'll be all right?"

She nodded.

He rose from the bed and left the room, his footsteps slowly fading down the hall. A few noises from the kitchen drifted into her room, and Madeline held onto them: he'll be back, she told herself. He's just making you tea, then he'll be back. And he was, for Michael, surprisingly quick; one moment there were footsteps, the footsteps grew and grew, then he was back in the room with a teacup in his hand.

"I put in sugar, but no milk. It's rather hot, but that's what you need. Can you sit up?"

She shook her head no. Michael put the teacup on top of her typewriter, then put his hands under her armpits and gently lifted her into a seated position. He tucked a pillow behind her, then took the teacup from the typewriter and filled the spoon with tea.

"Open," he said.

She opened her mouth, and he poured the tea down the back of her throat.

"Hot," she said.

"I know. I'll try not to hit your tongue. This should open your throat for good. Open again."

Sitting with her mouth open and head tipped back, Madeline felt like a baby bird being fed by its mother. Teaspoon by teaspoon, the tea eased the constriction in her throat. Then the teaspoon clicked against china, and Michael put the empty cup on the typewriter.

"Better?" he asked.

"Better."

He took her hands. He had nice hands, warm, strong, and soothing, but the sight of the red scratch marks made Madeline turn her head in shame.

"Do you want to tell me what happened?" he asked softly.

"Well," she said, her voice weak. "You, you know that David broke up with me."

"Robert told me. And I was here the night you moved back, although you didn't see me."

"Well, I thought it must be a mistake, I thought he regretted what he'd done, so I went to see him at Maxwell's. I waited till he got off, and we walked to the p-park without a park."

"And what happened?"

She squeezed her eyes shut and shook her head.

"Oh, Madeline." He clasped his hands around hers. "I'm sorry you're in so much pain."

"He doesn't want me anymore. He says, he says that my love strangles him. And he says that he's bored."

Michael smiled sadly. "I don't see how anyone could be bored with you."

"That's what I thought. But apparently not. How can this happen, Michael? How can someone love you, and then just not love you at all?"

Michael looked down at their hands, and said nothing.

"Oh, Michael, spit it out. I know you want to s-say something."

He knit his brow. "Well, I would say, I suppose, that only a person who doesn't know themselves very well would do such a thing."

"I think David knows himself well."

"I don't."

"You were expecting something like this, weren't you? You and Robert both." Again Michael looked at their hands. "Come on, Michael. Tell me."

"You're upset, Madeline. We shouldn't talk about this."

"Michael—please. Please tell me. Because I feel, I feel like I'm going crazy. I thought he and I were happy. I had no idea— Tell me, what was it you saw? What did you and Robert see that Bella and I didn't?"

Michael was silent.

"Michael."

"Madeline, I don't think—"

"*Michael.*"

He sighed. "Well. I don't know. I can't speak for Robert, of course, but you're right, I didn't feel your relationship would last. At least at first that's what I thought, but as time went on and you stayed together I thought perhaps I was mistaken."

"But why? Why didn't you think it would work out?"

"Well, when I met him at the brunch, and when I observed his behavior, he struck me as being—well, superficial. And I wasn't at all happy with the way he spoke to you."

"What do you mean?"

"Well, he didn't speak to you. He just—how can I say this? He just ate you up with his eyes. I didn't get the feeling that he really understood you, nor that he was particularly interested in trying."

"Oh God." She turned her head to the side.

"I'm sorry, Madeline. We shouldn't talk about this now."

"Oh, Michael—I know this sounds dramatic, but I feel like I'm dying. I can't bear all this pain."

"Your happiness doesn't depend on him. I know you think it does, but it doesn't."

"It does depend on him, Michael. It does."

She started crying again, her face turned into the pillow. Michael brought his hand to her face and moved a lock of hair off her cheek. She looked up at him—he was watching her intently, his expression deeply concerned. She closed her eyes again; her crying escalated and rose into hysteria. She was breaking down completely, all her control slipping away. Every so often Michael held a tissue to her nose and instructed her to blow, then once again took her hands.

When she was too exhausted to cry anymore she opened her eyes and stared dully at her bookshelves.

"Madeline? Do you want more tea?"

She shook her head no.

"Isn't there anything I can do for you?"

She tried to smile. "You'd be a great nurse, Michael; you shouldn't have become a professor."

"The two professions are not as different as they seem."

"Am I, am I keeping you from something? I mean, it's almost finals, don't you have papers to grade?"

"Even if you were keeping me from something I still wouldn't leave. And my students aren't handing in their papers until tomorrow, so don't worry."

"Thanks, Michael. You saved my life. No, I mean it—when I left the park without a park and was walking home, I was ready to die. I really didn't think I was going to make it."

"Well, you're fine now. You just have a broken heart, and that's not fatal."

"It feels fatal."

"Well, it's not."

The apartment door opened. "Madeline?" Bella's voice rang out. "I'm home." The door shut. "Is Michael with you?" she called. High heels clicked down the hall, and Bella came into Madeline's room still in her coat and beret, Michael's briefcase in her hand. "What's going on?"

"I found Madeline in the hall when I came in," Michael said, dropping Madeline's hands and rising off the bed. "She was hyperventilating."

"What happened, honey?" Bella asked, sitting on the bed and stroking Madeline's forehead. "Where did you go?"

"I went to see David."

"I'll go into the other room," Michael said.

"No, Michael, stay," Madeline said. "I don't mind." And in between sobs and gasps she explained how she had waited for David and how they went to the park without a park and how he said there was no chance they would get back together.

"And he said, he said that he felt like he was drowning. Because of having me in his house, and because of me loving him."

"That fucking bastard," Bella said as she tenderly stroked Madeline's hair. "I'd like to rip his eyes out."

"And," Madeline said, looking at Bella accusingly, "he said he got a couple of phone calls?"

"Oh. I was hoping you wouldn't find out about that."

"Phone calls?" Michael asked.

"Well." Bella took off her beret and smoothed her cap of black hair. "Yesterday morning at work Robert called me and said he had just called David and—well, apparently they had a little conversation. So, wanting to fix things, I called David myself. Because I agreed with you, Maddy, I thought you two would get back together again. Men get the jitters sometimes; I was sure David would come crawling back, and I wanted to be sure that Robert hadn't fucked things up for you. So I called him."

"And?"

"Well, I did apologize for Robert. But the truth is, Maddy, David was just so—he wasn't cold, exactly, but he had obviously made up his mind. And I thought of you laying in bed crying and I couldn't help it, I lost my temper."

"What did you say?"

"Well, the words 'scum of the earth' may have slipped from my lips. And body parts were threatened. But believe me, compared to what Robert said to him I was kind. Anyway, Maddy, it doesn't matter—if he really wanted you back Robert and I wouldn't be enough to stop him."

"So that was your impression, that he doesn't want me back?"

"That was my impression."

Madeline looked at the ceiling. "This is too much for me, Bella," she said. "I can't handle this."

"Yes you can," Bella said stoutly. "You most certainly can. Michael," Bella said, looking up at him. "Thank you. You really are the best friend we have."

And I called him Mr. Causabon, Madeline thought. She put her head into the pillow and started to cry. Bella sighed; she put a hand on Madeline's back and started rubbing.

"Will you stay for dinner?" Bella asked Michael. "It's the least we can do for you."

"Of course I'll stay. Anyway I'm worried about Madeline."

"Madeline," Bella said. "I have to start dinner, but Michael will sit here with you. Okay?"

Face still in the pillow, Madeline nodded.

"Tell me what you want to eat. I'll make anything you like."

"I'm not hungry."

"You haven't eaten a thing in two days. You have to eat."

"I said I'm not hungry."

"Okay, okay. Well," she said, rising off the bed. "I'll leave you in charge, Michael. And your briefcase is here—I found it out in the hall."

"Thank you."

Madeline wept. She wept so much she began to scare herself, but she could not stop. Michael said nothing, but he kept a hand on her shoulder and helped her blow her nose. And often he held a folded-up tissue to her face and gently wiped away her tears. Mostly she forgot he was there, but sometimes she looked up and saw him watching her. Once it made her angry: how could she let him see her like this? It was not so much how she looked, although she was certainly no prize with her swollen eyes and matted hair; it was more the raw weakness she was displaying, the pitifulness of her situation. She wanted to scream at him, to shove him and tell him to go away, but as she lifted her head to speak she saw him folding a tissue; he did it so gently, so *slowly*—she couldn't be mad at him.

And then she heard Robert's voice. She opened her eyes and saw the two men standing and looking down at her. Then one moment she noticed that the weight on the bed was lighter; she looked up and saw Robert sitting in Michael's place.

"I told Michael to go upstairs and change," Robert said. "He's been here all afternoon?"

Madeline nodded.

"Here, take a tissue." He handed her a tissue, then put his hands together and twisted them awkwardly. He looked at Madeline, then looked at the bookshelves. "You know," he said. "I'll always remember the first time I saw your sister. She walked into my Victorian Literature class, she sat in the front row and she had a look on her face like she'd kill anyone who tried to talk to her. She looked so tough and mean but, I don't know, I just had this feeling she was scared to death, and I fell so in love with her. She had long hair then, remember? As long as yours but with bangs. Anyway—I was crazy about her. Just completely crazy. I went to the Registrar's office and read over her records and application, I walked by her apartment building, I bought new clothes so I'd look better in class, I even scheduled mandatory conferences so I could have a chance to be alone with her. Finally I asked her out, I had to practically beg her to go out with me, and even when I managed to get her to see me regularly she never dropped that mask, not once.

"And then she changed. It took months and months but finally she started to open up and when she did she used to cry all the time, she cried just like you're crying now. I used to pick her up to go out and instead of going anywhere I'd just hold her and let her cry. She told me everything then, about your parents, about her dreams of being a pianist and how everything went wrong, about all the men she slept with and how none of them cared about her…and she also told me about you, she spoke about you all the time, she said she was afraid you'd end up like her and she wanted to help you. She made me promise we'd take care of you, and I swore to her I would.

"And do you remember when you came to live with us? You had a weird punk hairdo and you wore all that black eyeliner—I felt like I'd brought a wild animal into my house. And the first night you were with us you drank every beer in the house and passed out on the couch. But then things got better, remember? You and I became friends, I helped you with your homework, I read your stories, I taught you all my Scrabble tricks. And slowly you changed into such a beautiful young woman. Bella and I are so proud of you, Madeline. And now all this—I feel like I've failed you."

"Oh Robert," Madeline said. "It's not your fault. You warned me, and I didn't listen."

"But I should have done something. I should have stopped you from moving in with him."

"You couldn't have stopped me, Robert. Please don't blame yourself."

"But I *knew*," Robert said. "I just knew he was no good. That day he came over for brunch, I took one look at him and I knew he would break your heart."

"You just didn't like his shirt."

"It wasn't the shirt, Madeline. It was the way he was with you, how he looked at you, the way he pawed you—I knew he didn't love you."

"But he did love me."

"As much as someone like him can love anyone. The person he loves the most is and always will be himself. Believe me, I know the type."

"He says—he says I bore him. He's bored with me."

"That's ridiculous," Robert snorted. "He's just the type of man who never gets serious about women. That was obvious to me from the start."

"But he fought you, remember? When he wanted me to move in? If he really didn't want me he could have just caved in."

"Maybe you were a challenge. Or maybe he just likes to get his own way."

She squeezed her eyes shut. "You and Michael saw the truth all along, and Bella and I wouldn't listen to you."

"What did Michael say?"

"I had to drag it out of him, but he basically said the same thing as you. And he said that D-David is a person who doesn't know himself very well."

"That's a typically measured Michael comment. But I have to agree."

"But Robert," she said weakly, staring up at him. "I still love David. I love him so much, and he just doesn't want me."

"You'll get over him, Maddy. He doesn't deserve someone like you."

She said nothing. She drew one of the pillows to her stomach and crunched it against her body. Some time later—fifteen minutes? twenty?—Bella was kneeling before her, a glass of water and a pill in her hands.

"Maddy, honey, I want you to take this."

"What is it?"

"It's a tranquilizer. I still have a bottle from my last miscarriage. It won't knock you out but it'll relax you. You're a little bit hysterical; I think you need something."

"Okay." Obediently she lifted herself onto her elbows, took the pill out of Bella's hand and swallowed it.

"Now some water—good. I'm going to turn out the light and let you rest. Do you think you can rest a little?"

"I'll try. But don't close the door—I don't want to be alone."

"Okay."

The pill worked. The edges of the pain softened; Madeline's thoughts broke and gently drifted away. She heard the clink of knives and forks, and then she must have slept because when she woke the others were in the living room talking. She heard her name and, still wrapped in her covers, moved to the foot of the bed so she could eavesdrop.

"…used her," she heard Bella say. "He was attracted to her, he fucked her, and then when he got tired of fucking her he kicked her out. That asshole—if he was in front of me right now I swear I would strangle him."

"I think we all would," Michael said. "But that doesn't help Madeline."

"Poor thing. She's been crying her eyes out for days now. Thank God she's finally getting some sleep."

"I blame myself," Robert said. "I didn't like him from the start, even before I met him. I should have stopped her—and I should have stopped you, Bella; you kept encouraging her."

"You were right, Robert," Bella admitted. "He was in fact a slimy musician. I can't believe someone would do this to our little Madeline."

Madeline moved back to the head of the bed; she had heard enough. Our little Madeline! Please… She put her head in her hands. And now that the tranquilizer had worn off, now what? Nothing. Nothing was next, except pain. All the time she had been sleeping pain had been waiting for her, hunched at the end of the bed like a vulture.

She laid in the dark room with her eyes opened. She was frightened.

CHAPTER 16

Pain and Knowledge

The next day Madeline had Bella call the temp agency and tell the obnoxious receptionist that Madeline had mononucleosis and would be out of work indefinitely. That taken care of, Madeline was free to stay in bed.

There were a few details to be dispensed with, of course; in between Christmas shopping and holiday parties Bella stopped by the post office and changed Madeline's address, and she also managed—with a great deal of charm and fast talking—to get a complete cash refund for the ring Madeline had bought for David. And a few days after the breakup Bella came into Madeline's room with a full brown shopping bag; the bag had been left in the foyer with a note in David's neat handwriting: MADELINE BOOT. Madeline tore the bag open—it was the clothes she had left at the Chinese laundry, but there was no note or other sign of life from David.

So that was it. But inside Madeline the terrible process of weaning had begun. A thousand threads connected her to David, and it quickly became clear that changing her address and returning his ring were the least of it. The most vivid pain was physical. After years of not being touched suddenly there was David, and she had grown used to the touch of his hands on her body, the feel of sleeping against him, the pleasure of having someone to throw her arms around and hug. Now that these things were gone, her body was screaming. She talked to Bella about it, and Bella said she had felt the same way when Robert went to England for a George Eliot conference.

"He'd gone to other conferences before, but only for two or three days whereas this was for two weeks and let me tell you, I was dying. Don't you remember what a bitch I was? It was because I missed him, I missed touching him."

"But at least you knew he was coming back," Madeline said. She was sitting in bed, still in her nightgown, her chin resting on her knees. It was four days after the breakup, a Saturday afternoon. "David's never coming back."

"You'll find someone else, Maddy. And in the meantime you can't expect to feel better when you're laying around in your nightgown all day."

"I can't go outside. I feel like if I go outside Christmas is going to eat me alive."

"Well, it is pretty hairy out there. But still, a walk wouldn't hurt."

Madeline shook her head. She just couldn't imagine going outside, never mind taking a shower and getting dressed.

Bella sighed. "You can't stay holed up forever, Maddy."

"It's only been a few days."

"Maybe it's my fault. I shouldn't have given you my tranquilizers."

"Without them I'd be crying all day. Now I just cry half the day."

Bella reached out a hand and smoothed Madeline's hair. "Well, I guess it's okay for now. Listen, I lined up a babysitter for you tonight: Michael's going to come down and keep you company. I wouldn't mind missing this party but it's Robert's department head, we have to go."

"Michael doesn't mind?"

"Not at all. He says anyway he has to stay home and grade papers."

"That must take him forever."

"I shudder to think of it."

"So he's not going out with Patty?"

"Honey, that relationship is dead as a doornail. Yesterday Patty told me she called him and asked him out for Sunday, and he said he was flattered by the offer but he didn't think they should go out anymore." Bella sighed. "At least I tried. But do you know, they went out three times and Michael didn't even try to kiss her? She said she practically threw herself at him, and he turned her down."

"I told you she wasn't his type."

"Well, I guess you were right."

So that evening Madeline laid on the couch, listening as Bella—in a black mini-dress, dangling red earrings, and the infamous four-inch black heels—instructed Michael on his duties. Michael sat in the green armchair, leaning his head against his hand and listening to Bella.

"I left money by the phone, you can order in Chinese or whatever you want. Not that Madeline will eat anyway, but it's worth a try. And I bought more Earl Grey tea, I know it's your favorite; I left it out next to the kettle. And our phone number is next to the phone."

"Bella," Madeline protested. "You act like you have to be on suicide watch with me."

"Madeline, you know as well as I do you can't bear to be alone." She turned to Michael. "This morning Robert and I went out for breakfast, and when we came back Madeline was crying because she missed us."

"Everything will be fine," Michael said. "Don't worry."

So for the next hours Madeline laid on the couch dully watching as Michael worked his way through a pile of student papers. She knew she was in trouble when she didn't even get agonized by the sight of him slowly bringing his pen to paper, lifting the pen without making a mark, then staring thoughtfully in the air. She closed her eyes and sighed. She couldn't stop thinking about David. It was Saturday night—where was he? Over at Hanson and Alison's getting high? At a club in the city? Somewhere in Hoboken? They hadn't had any plans as far as she remembered. She knew his schedule by heart, and she had a good idea what he was doing almost every hour of the day. It was a form of exquisite torture, but she couldn't help herself; it was impossible for her to just cut off the way he had. And everything reminded her of him, everything: she couldn't watch *Cheers* because it took place in Boston, and David was from Boston; she couldn't watch *The Young and the Restless* because Bridget watched it, and thinking of Bridget was one step away from thinking of David; she couldn't eat Bella's lasagna because it reminded her of the lasagna at the infamous brunch; and she couldn't bear to comb her hair because David used to like to do that. It was silly, illogical, masochistic, but she couldn't help herself: he just popped up everywhere.

Michael raised his head. "I'm going to order food now. Is there anything particular you want?"

"No."

"You have to eat something, Madeline."

"There's ice cream in the freezer. That's all I want."

He sighed and shook his head. "All right. I'll bring you a bowl."

"You can dispense with the formalities and just bring me the carton and a spoon."

And so while Michael slowly ate egg drop soup and moo shu shrimp, Madeline dug into a pint of Ben and Jerry's Coffee Heath Bar Crunch. Thank God for ice cream, and thank God for Bella's tranquilizers, because without them Madeline would have been a screaming mess. But ice cream and pills couldn't take away her pain entirely; she still felt bruised inside and out. That morning she had looked in the mirror: her face was drawn and sad, her skin ashy, and her eyes swollen and red. All her glow, all the new beauty that came with David's love was already gone. He wouldn't find me attractive now, she thought. And so what? He wasn't coming back, so it didn't matter how she looked.

She finished the ice cream and put the empty carton on the floor. She closed her eyes, and when she woke Michael was sitting on the couch, staring at her.

"What's wrong?" she asked him.

"You were crying in your sleep."

"Really?" She pulled the cover up to her chin. "Great—it's not enough that I cry when I'm awake, now I can't even get any peace when I sleep."

"You know what you should do?"

"I think you're going to tell me."

"Stop the ice cream and stop the pills, and just let yourself feel pain."

"Michael, if I do that I'll die. I swear I'll die. And anyway it's almost Christmas," she said, her eyes filling with tears. "Do you know what that means? Do you know how terrible that makes everything? I just want to get through the holidays without falling apart. Can you understand that?"

"I understand. It's just—"

"Just what?"

"Well, you're not learning anything this way. All this pain can teach you something, if you let it."

"Michael, if you knew how I felt right now you would never say such a thing. Believe me, my way is the best way."

❧   ❧   ❧

The closer the holidays came, the more Madeline buried into herself. She spoke on the phone to Rose, Devon, Spencer, and Oriana, but otherwise she did not attend Spencer's annual party, did not buy gifts, did not even send Christmas cards. And she did not shower, did not wash her hair, and rarely changed her clothes. She refused to leave the apartment, and since Bella kept her supplied in ice cream, there was no need to.

Christmas Eve she was laying on the couch watching *Hawaii Five-O* when Robert came into the room. Columbia was closed for a month; Robert had nothing to do except read George Eliot and take care of Madeline.

"Here," he said, handing her two packages. "Early Christmas presents."

"For me?" She rose a little, and carefully unwrapped the paper. One present was a box of Godiva chocolates, and the other a copy of Charles Dickens' novel *Our Mutual Friend*.

"Thank you, Robert."

"I thought it might take your mind off things. And a book is infinitely better than—" He motioned to the television set.

"I know, but I can't read right now."

"Frankly, Madeline— Look, can you shut off the TV? I can't think with it on."

"Okay." She pointed the remote control and clicked.

"Frankly, Madeline, I'm worried about you. It's been a week and a half now, and you're not any better. I have vacation now, you and I can do things if you want. And Bella's going to take a few days off—we're going to do our annual ice skating trip to Rockefeller Center, plus there's a lot of other things we plan to do. You should come with us."

"I can't, Robert. I just can't. I think of going outside and it's too much. Everyone's rushing around and they're all so happy and Christmasy. I just feel like I'm dead inside."

"Don't say that, Madeline."

"Robert, how would you feel if Bella left you?"

"Well—I'd die."

"You see?"

"Madeline, you can hardly compare Bella and me with you and David."

"I loved him. And we lived together. What more do you want?"

"Okay, okay." He paused. "So—what if I ran a hot bath? Would you get in it?"

"No."

"It's those pills. I'm going to flush them down the toilet."

"You do and I'll go down after them."

He stared at her. "You are so much like your sister it scares me. Oh—that was Michael on the phone. He's going to stop by on his way out."

Michael was going up to Cambridge to spend Christmas with his father. Madeline had met Michael's father several times; he was exactly like Michael, same looks, same height, same calm manner, except he was twenty-five years older and had an English accent, and his hair was grey instead of sandy.

"So he won't be around to sit with you. We do have to go out sometimes, so you're going to have to be alone."

"How long is Michael going away for?"

"Ten days."

"Oh." Bella always said Michael must be getting laid somewhere, and she was sure he had an old flame tucked away in Cambridge.

"So you have to prepare yourself to be lonely."

"Rose is going to come and see me one day. Devon too."

"Well, that's good. And you know, a new year can be a new start. You think you might celebrate 1988 by taking a shower?"

"I can't think that far ahead."

Slowly, excruciatingly, the holidays passed. Madeline, fortified with tranquilizers and ice cream, lived out each day in a haze. On Christmas Day she curled up on one of the couches and absentmindedly opened her gifts: books from Robert (*Mary Barton*, *The Voyage of the H.M.S. Beagle*, *The Moonstone*, volume one of Dickens' Christmas stories) and from Bella earrings, a silk scarf and—what on earth had Bella been thinking?—a red lace nightgown; and from both of them, $200 in cash and a beautiful leather binder for her short stories.

"It's a dead animal product," Bella said as Madeline looked at the binder. "I had a moral dilemma, but in the end I couldn't resist."

Madeline nodded. She was so touched she began to cry.

"Don't cry, Maddy," Bella said, curling next to Madeline on the couch and taking her in her arms. "Please don't cry."

"I feel so stupid," Madeline said. "I didn't get anything for either of you. I couldn't go shopping, I just couldn't."

"That's okay, honey. You're having a hard time now; we understand."

So Christmas passed. But the next day Madeline felt worse, because she knew today was the day Mr. and Mrs. Guggenheim were arriving in Hoboken. This was the day she was supposed to meet them. The discrepancy between the way things were supposed to be (her and David sitting in their apartment, drinking coffee with his parents) and the way things were (her laying on Bella and Robert's couch in her bathrobe, an empty carton of ice cream on the floor) hurt so much she felt almost mad with grief. She felt tight and cramped and pained, like someone had clasped hands around her chest and was squeezing as hard as they could. And in order to escape the pain, she did something which she knew was dangerous: she let herself fantasize about getting back together with David. Madeline had always been a first-rate fantasizer, and she immersed herself completely in all the rich details: a phone call, an invitation to come over, David apologizing, she and David making love, then his parents coming in from a day of shopping in The City and David explaining who she was and how they were back together again. The images in her head were so vivid she could hear David's laugh, smell his mother's perfume. And for the duration of the fantasy she was happy—or, at least, pain-free. It was a wonderful feeling, and then it all came crashing down when, for instance, Robert walked into the room looking for his copy of *Felix Holt.* The moment she opened her eyes, the fantasy collapsed. Nothing had changed: it was still just her in her bathrobe on the couch, still with that squeezing pain in her chest.

Nevertheless, she continued fantasizing. Anytime the pain became unbearable, she slipped into an alternative, preferable world. It got to the point where she would spend hours in this world, and it didn't even matter if Bella or Robert were in the room, or if the television was on. She knew it was unhealthy, but she promised herself she would stop once the holidays were over; she just needed something to get herself through, and all Bella and Robert's suggestions—let's go to the movies, let's go to Coliseum Books, let's go to Dojo's—wouldn't, couldn't help her. Devon and Rose both called frequently, and both offered to visit, but Madeline asked them not to: "I'm no fun now. Wait until after the holidays." Rose came anyway; she just showed up one day and spent the whole afternoon holding Madeline's hand and listening. Which helped, but not much, because Rose was not David. And what Madeline needed was David. If he had called her, all her joy would have come back. Her energy, too: she would have leapt off the couch, jumped into the shower, dashed over to 10 Willow Terrace and thrown herself in his arms. But he never called.

Curiously enough, Alison called. Once after Madeline woke from a nap she went into the kitchen and saw the red light blinking on the answering machine. She pushed the Play button and heard, "Hello, this is Alison, I'm looking for Madeline? Madeline, I just want to say I'm really sorry about what happened, I think it's a shame. I would have called sooner but, you know, what with the holidays everything's kind of crazy. So please give me a call and we can go out for a cup of coffee." The sound of Alison's voice reminded Madeline of her old life, and for a moment she felt a surge of joy—maybe everything wasn't lost. Because it wasn't just David she missed, it was also the lifestyle and the music and all the people she had met through him—Hanson, Alison, Jessie, Plug,

Bridget—she had been folded into a whole other world, and she had felt comfortable there. True, the late hours and pot smoking were a bit much for her, but otherwise she had really enjoyed hanging out with musicians and being part of the scene. Her life had expanded in ways she had never dreamed, and now all that was gone. In the long run, they were all David's friends; it was David's world, not hers. She couldn't imagine going to one of Narrow Grave's gigs, hoping for a crumb of David's attention—no, she was too proud for that. Nor could she imagine returning Alison's call. Madeline had really hated Alison the night of the VP's dinner, but the next day when Alison and Hanson came over to discuss the VP's ultimatum Alison had been calmer, and she had been so strong about not breaking up the band. And one moment she pulled Madeline aside and apologized profusely for her behavior the night before: she said she was completely edged out, and there was no excuse for what she did. Madeline was never good at holding grudges; she hugged Alison and said it was okay. But now, to go out and meet Alison—impossible. Just seeing Alison would make her cry, and how long before one of them mentioned David's name? Twenty seconds, thirty tops, and then Madeline would really break down. No: she would not let any of them know how the breakup had affected her. She might be in her bathrobe all day, she might have greasy hair and dark circles under her eyes, but she still had her pride.

New Year's Eve arrived. Bella and Robert never went out on New Year's Eve; they always had a romantic evening at home, so in order not to spoil their good time Madeline took three tranquilizers and was fast asleep by nine o'clock. When she woke it was three a.m., and the apartment was dark. It's a new year, she thought, then crept down the hall to the bathroom where she swallowed two more pills.

On the Monday after New Year's Eve Madeline was home by herself. Bella and Robert had gone into The City to ice skate at Rockefeller Center. The trip was an annual tradition, and as Madeline was a good skater she always enjoyed herself. Robert also skated well, but Bella was useless, and to see Bella on ice was guaranteed to cheer anyone up. Bella and Robert begged her to go; Bella was almost crying, saying they were going to Tavern on the Green afterward and wouldn't Madeline like to go there, but Madeline shook her head no. "I can't," she said, crying. "I just can't." So they left her on the couch. The moment the door shut Madeline almost rose to stop them—but no, she was right. She couldn't go.

She was laying dully on the couch watching *Cagney and Lacey* when someone knocked. Slowly. Madeline turned off the TV and shuffled to the hall. She opened the door: Michael. "Hi," she said. "Come on in."

She shuffled back to the TV room and climbed into her nest of blankets. Michael followed her, and sat in the green armchair. He was wearing khakis and a dark green sweater that was certainly a Christmas gift, and he looked, as always, calm and handsome.

"How was Cambridge?" she asked, rousing herself to be social. "Did you have a good time?"

"Madeline. In all the time I've been gone, have you ever left this apartment?"

She shook her head no.

Michael looked at her steadily, then stood and left the room. "Michael—?" she called weakly. She heard him walk down the hall to her room; a few moments later she heard him walk towards the kitchen, and heard the closet door open and shut. Then he came back into the TV room. He had a pair of jeans, a T-shirt, and a thick sweater draped on one arm, and her coat, scarf, and hat on the other. In one hand he held mittens and a pair of socks, in the other her sneakers.

"I'm going upstairs for my coat and my wallet, and when I come back down I want to find you ready."

"No, Michael," she said, shaking her head. "I can't."

"I'll be down in five minutes."

"But my hair—"

"I don't care. Five minutes." He left the room and went out the front door.

Madeline was stunned. Fuck him! She didn't have to do what he said. And since when was Michael so forceful? Nobody told her what to do; she would lock the door and when he came down she wouldn't let him in. She didn't want to go out, and she wouldn't.

But there had been something in Michael's voice, something that would not take no for an answer. It reminded her of Michael in the kitchen on the day of the brunch, and she did not care to have a repeat of that scene. So, cursing him aloud, she rose off the couch to change her clothes. He had forgotten underwear, naturally, so she went to Bella's room and took a clean pair from Bella's drawers. After she was dressed she went into the bathroom to brush her teeth. She looked at herself in the mirror: she looked dreadful. Her skin was dead white and pasty, her eyes dull, and the area under her eyes swollen and dark. Her hair was plastered to her head; she put it back in a barrette, which helped a little. Then she went back into the TV room, put on her coat, scarf, hat, and mittens, and sat on the couch. Five minutes came and went. Only Michael, she fumed, would need more than five minutes to dash upstairs, grab his wallet, and throw on his coat. If slowness was a crime, he would have been executed years ago.

Someone knocked. Slowly.

Madeline went to the door and threw it open. "Okay," she snapped. "You got your way, I hope you're happy. Where are we going?"

"We're going to take a walk, and then we're going to eat sushi."

Sushi...her weak spot.

"Come on," Michael said gently. "Let's go."

"I don't have my keys."

"So go get them."

Madeline walked down the stairs, banging her feet on every step, sighing loudly at regular intervals. Michael walked behind her, probably to make sure she didn't escape. When she arrived at the ground floor foyer, she was surprised by a sudden feeling of panic. She was dizzy, and had to lean against the wall.

"Are you okay?" Michael asked, taking her elbow.

She looked up at him, tears in her eyes. "I'm afraid."

"Afraid of what?"

"Afraid of running into David."

"We won't run into him," Michael said firmly. "Come on."

He opened the door and they walked outside. Madeline stood on the steps and blinked; she felt as if she had just left her spaceship and had landed on another planet. It was just Hoboken, just Washington Street, but the colors were so vivid, the sounds so fresh. She looked up at the sky; it was thick and white and wintry.

"It's going to snow," she said, turning to Michael.

"Not for a few hours. We have time."

"Where do you want to walk?"

"How about up to Stevens?"

"Okay."

They turned down Ninth Street and walked over to Hudson. If they went left they would reach the park without a park and could walk up from there, but Michael must have remembered; he turned right, and they walked down Hudson to Eighth Street. Madeline stopped; she looked up the steep hill that led to the Stevens' campus.

"No way I can walk up that hill," she said.

"Let's go down to Fifth, we can walk up from there. Okay?" he said, looking down at her and smiling.

"Okay."

At Fifth and Hudson there was Stevens Park, a real park with grass; they walked along the edge of it, then turned left. They walked through a parking lot and arrived at the campus gate and the faux castle guard tower. They walked through the gate and into the campus, walking on an asphalt pedestrian path past the gym, past dorms, past classrooms and the library, then they arrived at the main administration building. Just behind it was the Hudson River, and across the river, silent and dignified, Manhattan. There was a circular lookout with benches; Madeline and Michael walked over to a bench and sat.

"It's rather cold," he said. "We don't have to stay long."

"It's nice," she said. The cold stung her face, and she liked it. She looked at Michael; he and everything else seemed far away, as if a curtain stood between her and the world. Sadness welled up inside her; she looked down at her feet and began to cry.

"Here," Michael said, handing her a handkerchief.

"I think," she said, wiping her eyes, "that you're the only man in the world who still carries handkerchiefs."

"No, I'm not. There's my father."

"Well, you and your father are practically twins, so I guess I'm not surprised." She folded the handkerchief and handed it back to him. "How is your father, anyway?"

"Good. Very good, actually. He has a girlfriend."

"Your father?"

Michael nodded. "A widow. She works at one of the Harvard libraries."

"Late blooming love, hmm? Did you meet her?"

"I did. She's a nice woman. They're cute together. And best of all, she seems completely and utterly sane. Which is something my father needs."

"You mean, after having been with your mother so many years."

"Yes. So," he said, turning to look at her. "Are you hungry?"

"Very."

"We'll probably be a little early, but if we walk slowly…"

"Michael, I'm sure we'll walk slowly."

They walked around campus, behind the administration building, past the President's house, past the graduate student dormitory, past a few rambling fraternity houses, and then were once again on Hudson Street. They walked down to Kobe, a Japanese restaurant on Washington Street between second and third. A Japanese woman in a blue kimono and white obi was just turning the sign in the door from CLOSED to OPEN. The restaurant was peaceful; water burbled from a tiny waterfall in a small garden, the sushi chef was quietly slicing, and two waitresses in kimonos were standing silently in back. The hostess led Madeline and Michael to one of the booths; a dark blue cloth with white symbols hung in the opening, shielding them from the rest of the restaurant. One of the waitresses came over with hot towels, and Michael asked for green tea and menus. The waitress poured tea from a white clay pot with a wicker handle into cups decorated with shallow indentations and flying cranes. Madeline pulled her cup closer and blew on the tea to cool it.

"So," Michael said, handing her a menu, "have whatever you want."

"Anything?"

"Anything."

She cocked her head. "Even the uni, which is so expensive?"

"Even the uni."

"You should stop me, Michael. I'm capable of running up a very high bill."

"I'm putting it on my credit card, so don't worry."

"Well…if you're sure."

"I'm sure. I want to see you eat something that doesn't come out of a Ben and Jerry's carton."

The waitress returned, and Madeline reeled off her order: miso soup, shrimp and vegetable tempura appetizer, two pieces of uni, a yellow tail roll inside out, and the sushi deluxe. Then Michael ordered, and when he was done the waitress laughed and said, "Good for you, you pronounce everything right."

"Well," Michael said, then released a string of sing song.

The waitress clapped her hands in delight, and answered him in the same strange music. She called over the other waitress, and soon the three were talking in earnest, the women making tiny bows, their faces lit with joy. Madeline felt like she was listening to birdsong; it was very beautiful, but she had no idea what it meant.

"Well," Madeline said when the two women finally went away. "You certainly made a good impression."

"One of them was born in Kyoto, and that's where I used to spend summers with my father. It appears I used to walk by her grandparents' house almost every day."

He explained that his father first brought him to Japan when he was six; mornings when his father did research in the Kyoto University Library, Michael had language lessons from an old Japanese man.

"Isn't Japanese rather difficult for a six-year-old?" Madeline asked.

"Oh no, I loved it, I loved drawing the characters. And my tutor was a wonderful man; he was a retired professor from Kyoto University, he was very learned. In the mornings we studied Japanese, and in the afternoons he took me to temples and explained their histories and all the symbolism."

"In English?"

"In Japanese. I didn't have much trouble learning it; children pick up languages quickly. And when I was ten he started me in Chinese—it wasn't so bad because I already knew many of the pictograms from Japanese. I used to love sitting in his garden, it was tiny but perfect; he had placed every rock himself, and he had a name for each one of them."

"He's not still alive, is he?"

"No. He died when I was twenty. But last summer I stayed with his daughter and husband for a few days. Apparently the other waitress knows of them."

The waitress brought the appetizers they had ordered as well as five small dishes of cooked seaweed, dumplings, and other delicacies.

"What's all this?" Madeline asked.

"It's on the house."

"Michael, I have to come here with you more often! I never get treated like this."

She asked him more about living in Japan as a child, and she listened intently as he described his father's translation work, how his mother couldn't come because she was "resting," but that was okay since Michael and his father both needed a break from her, how they rented the same house each summer and how the man down the street was a transvestite, and how Michael studied the tea ceremony and flower arranging. Madeline was enjoying the conversation and the food and then suddenly she remembered: David was gone, and he wasn't coming back. She kept her eyes focused on Michael's face but she couldn't help herself; it was as if there was a button in her chest labeled CRY and when a thought or sound or smell pushed it, there was no use, the tears flowed out.

"Madeline—?"

The waitress parted the blue cloth and placed their sushi on the table. She looked at Madeline, then singsonged at Michael. He singsonged back; she rushed off and returned with two hot towels. She put one around her fingers and softly dabbed Madeline's cheeks.

"Is it the food?" she asked. "You don' like the food?"

Madeline laughed. "No, the food is fine. Please don't worry."

The waitress left, and the blue cloth once again sealed them off.

"Did I say something that hurt you?" Michael asked. "I didn't mean to."

"No, Michael, you didn't say anything. The truth is," she spread her hands, "I'm a mess. I'm just one big fucked-up mess and I don't know what to do with myself."

"Madeline." He reached across the table and took her hand. "Tell me what's been going on."

So she told him, haltingly, about taking tranquilizers and living in a fantasy world, how she was supposed to meet David's parents, how lonely and dazed she felt, and how she knew she was a burden on everyone but she just felt so helpless, so helpless and tired and lost.

"I can't live without David. I can't. There's no love in my life anymore, there's no love and there's no joy. But if I don't do something soon I'm going to dissolve in a puddle on the couch."

"Well, tell me what you think you should do."

"I think I should stop taking tranquilizers, and I should stop fantasizing about something that's never going to happen. Because David's not coming back, Michael; he's not."

"Okay. What else?"

She sighed. "Well—I need to take a shower, that's for sure. And wash my hair. And I should probably get back to work, although I can't think of anything more depressing. I wish I could write, but that just seems impossible."

"Your writing will come back, don't worry. And although you don't believe it, you're going to feel better. That day will come; you just have to hold on until it does." He released her hand and picked up his chopsticks. "And I should know—I speak from personal experience."

"You do?" She moved her sushi in front of her and looked at him curiously.

"Well, you know I'm divorced, but what you don't know is that my wife left me. For another man." He twisted his mouth. "And not just another man, but one of my friends."

"Oh, Michael. That's terrible."

"So it was a double loss. It was like—well, like if Bella left Robert for me. You can just imagine how Robert would feel."

"Robert would die. I mean it; he would just curl up and die."

"Well, I pretty much did that. And I not only lost them, but I lost my house. And the cat."

"Oh no—you had to leave your cat! I had to leave my cat Spike when I moved in with Bella and Robert since Robert's allergic. It was awful."

Michael nodded. "So you understand. She was beautiful—her name was Dorje, she was a grey tabby; she used to sit on my desk when I worked. Anyway. It was difficult. I guess my wife and I had been drifting apart for awhile, but I still had no idea. Apparently she'd been having affairs for years."

"Michael, I had no idea you'd been through something like that! You're always so—I don't know, so cool, calm, and collected."

"Well, I don't talk about it much. Robert knows."

"But Bella doesn't, or she would have told me."

"Robert doesn't tell Bella everything."

"*She* sure thinks he does."

"Well, he doesn't."

"So your ex-wife—was she pretty?"

"Yes."

"Do you—do you still love her?"

"No."

"Do you ever talk to her?"

"No."

Poor Michael, out on the street with no wife, no friend, no house, and no cat. As they ate Madeline probed delicately, and Michael told her how he managed to get an apartment through Columbia and about the day he moved all his books and how it was snowing and how his ex-wife screamed at him that he had always ignored her and was lost in a world of his own and she wanted a real life with a real man who didn't have his head in books all day. When he asked her if it was absolutely necessary that this real man be his best friend, she slapped him. And by the time Madeline and Michael had stopped eating, Madeline saw that as bad as her situation was, she at least was able to fall into the arms of people who loved her. If she had to leave David and go find a new apartment, some cold, empty place—she didn't even like to think of it.

After extensive and elaborate good-byes between Michael and the entire staff of the restaurant, Madeline and Michael went up front to pay the bill. She tried to peek at the total but he covered it with his hand. "Never mind," he said.

"I'm just curious."

"It's none of your business."

"If you say so." She looked out the window. "Michael, look, it's snowing! Hurry, or we'll get caught in it."

But Michael was not able to hurry, and when they went outside snow was falling rapidly.

"I don't have the right shoes for this," Madeline said. "I told you we'd get caught."

"Hold onto my arm; I won't let you slip."

She tucked her hands around his arm, and they inched their way up Washington Street. The snow fell heavier; Michael took a pair of earmuffs from his pocket and put them on his head.

"You're not only the only person who carries handkerchiefs," she yelled up at him through the snow, "but you're also the only one who wears earmuffs."

"My father wears earmuffs."

"I should have guessed."

Bella was waiting in the open doorway as they came up the stairs.

"Oh, Michael, thank God you've got her! When we came home and Maddy wasn't here I was ready to call the police, but then Robert said you'd be coming home today so I hoped—come in, come in and get dry. And you," she said, tweaking Madeline's nose, "you could have left me a note."

"I'm sorry, Bella, but it all happened kind of suddenly. I was *forced* outside."

"Well, it did you good, you have some color in your cheeks. Leave your wet things here and go sit with Robert in the living room. I'll bring you some tea."

Robert and Bella were on one couch, Madeline and Michael on the other, and four mugs of tea and a platter of canolis were positioned around the coffee-table books.

"So how was ice skating?" Madeline asked as she reached for a canoli.

Robert patted Bella's knee. "Aside from your sister nearly decapitating a child, it was just fine."

Bella snorted. "Listen, Robert, it wasn't my fault that kid fell down in front of me. Anyway I skated over the scarf, not the child."

"One of the mothers started passing around a petition to ban Bella from the rink."

"Oh, shut up! I would be a better skater if you took the time to teach me instead of skating off by yourself so you can show off."

"Bella, I've spent hours trying to teach you how to skate. The problem is, you have weak ankles. It's a genetic flaw; you can't help it."

"But Madeline skates well."

"Well, looks like Madeline got the blonde hair and the strong ankles."

"Thank you, Professor Dellasandandrio, for your enlightening explanation. Now what I want to know is, how did Michael get Madeline off the couch."

"He went into my room and got my clothes and he said he'd buy me sushi."

"Sushi—why didn't I think of that?"

"You two should know," Michael said, "that Madeline has made some decisions."

Madeline looked at him. "I have?"

"Over dinner Madeline told me that she is not only going to stop taking tranquilizers, but she's going to wash her hair and go back to work."

Madeline gave Michael a dirty look; she had not said she *would* do those things, she had said she *should* do those things.

A look of relief passed between Bella and Robert. "So Maddy," Bella said. "How about taking that shower now? And when you're done I'll blow-dry your hair and braid it for you. I'll even do Defying Gravity."

Madeline sighed. She didn't want to. But they were looking at her so hopefully, and after everything they had done for her she couldn't disappoint them.

"Okay," she gave in. "That sounds fine."

✻   ✻   ✻

So Madeline was better. But what was better? She was out of her bathrobe and off the couch, her hair was clean, she was going to work, answering her mail, playing Scrabble—and yet she still felt miserable. She woke, dressed, took the bus into the city, went to work, took the bus home, and all the time she felt wretched. If Michael had just left her on the couch she could have continued crying, but since she had given in and rejoined the world she couldn't cry all the time, she had to stuff down her feelings. Michael and Bella both said that wasn't the point; the idea was that being out in the world would take her out of herself, but it wasn't working that way—the world went on around her, and she was still just Madeline, Madeline without David.

She never saw him. Her worst fear and her greatest hope was that she would run into him, but she never did. Once on Washington Street she saw Raller, but she ducked into the Hoboken Farmboy and avoided him. And Alison left a few messages, but Madeline was still not strong enough to talk to her. As for David—well, he lived his life in Hoboken, she lived hers, and their paths did not cross. She saw posters for Narrow Grave gigs on lampposts, so she had a general idea what he was doing, and of course she still knew his daily schedule by heart, but there were 40,000 people in Hoboken, and of the ones she passed in the street, sat with on the bus, waited behind in stores, none of them was David. She still hoped that he might call her, but as the days and weeks passed without a word, she saw that he meant what he said: there was no hope of getting back together.

Worst of all, she couldn't write. She tried a few times, but she had no inspiration; after writing a paragraph or two she always stopped in frustration. She felt as if something was blocked up inside her, and if she could take that something away the writing would once again flow. But only David could take that something away: one word from him, and she knew her energy would be released. But he didn't call, so she stayed stuck. She was tempted to reclaim her place on the couch, but Bella said that if she did she'd have to start paying rent. Not knowing what else to do, Madeline worked: she told Lynn that she would take any work anytime, and Lynn set her up on longer assignments—two weeks at The Big Cigarette Company, a week at The Large Japanese Securities Firm, ten days at The Enormous Brokerage House, another two week gig at The Big Cigarette Company. Because the assignments were longer she actually had to work, but she didn't mind; it was either typing or *Cagney and Lacey* reruns, and at least with typing she made money. Her bank account grew, and sometimes she thought about taking a trip to Europe, where she'd never been; or maybe to Nepal—Michael had recently told her about his trips there, and it sounded like a wonderful place. But no—if she couldn't forget David in Hoboken, it was naive to think that spending money and going halfway around the world could make her forget him either.

Evenings she spent at home playing Scrabble with Robert and Michael while Bella played piano. This was the best part of her day; for some reason she felt less awful while playing. She still felt dull and sad, but in her home, surrounded by family, the pain softened.

But how long, how long would it last?

Weeks passed; February passed, and still Madeline was not well. Sometimes she cried, but sometimes she was so sad she couldn't feel anything. She knew the others were worried about her. She often caught Bella staring at her, and Robert was forever bringing her books: *Martin Chuzzlewit, North and South, The Woman in White, Vanity Fair*, as if Victorian literature could cure a broken heart. Michael was especially kind, and made a real effort to get her out of the house. Robert would leave their Scrabble game to answer the phone, and Michael would turn to Madeline and quietly ask if she had plans that weekend, and if she didn't perhaps she'd like to go see a movie at Film Forum, or watch a tea ceremony demonstration at The Japan Society, or hear a lecture at The

Open Center. She rarely had plans, so she always said yes. Sometimes she forgot herself and managed to have a good time, but most times the lecture or demonstration would end without her having heard a word. Michael never got angry when she admitted that she had been too spaced out to pay attention, and he always took her out to eat afterwards. Except for ice cream most food still tasted like ashes, but once in awhile she got excited by a new restaurant or dish, and she would have some moments of happiness before remembering that she couldn't be happy, because David no longer loved her.

One Scrabble night in early March, Madeline, Robert, and Michael were in the living room waiting for Bella to bring in ice cream. As Robert and Michael discussed the etymology of the word "gemeinschaft," Bella came in with four bowls on a tray; she put three bowls on the table then handed one to Madeline. The bowl had no ice cream, just a piece of folded paper. Madeline looked at Bella; Bella raised her eyebrows and said nothing. Madeline unfolded the paper and read:

Dearest Madeline:

I don't think you should eat any ice cream tonight. You're getting kinda fat.

Signed, A Concerned Friend

Madeline threw the note on the table. "Fuck you, Bella."

Robert picked up the note and read it; he shook his head, and passed the note to Michael. "Bella," Robert said. "You have absolutely no tact."

"Well, it's true," Bella said. "She is getting fat. Worse, she's getting lumpy. Michael, you're objective—isn't Madeline getting fat?"

"I think Madeline looks fine."

"Thank you, Michael," Madeline said. "'A Concerned Friend'—Bella, you are really too much."

"Oh, come on, Maddy. I didn't know how else to tell you. And you have such a lovely figure, I don't want to see you turn into a blob."

Madeline stood. "Well, if all my *concerned friends* don't mind, I'm going into the kitchen to get some ice cream."

But the next day she did not have a temp job, and when she woke up she went into Bella and Robert's room and stripped. She looked at herself in the mirror: it was true. Her stomach protruded, her hips bulged, and her thighs were—there was no other word for it—lumpy. All that ice cream had to go somewhere, and it had decided to distribute itself between her waist and knees. Not a pretty sight.

Madeline put on her clothes and rushed to the kitchen. She dialed Bella's number at work.

"Hello, this is Bella Dellasandandrio."

"You're right."

"Hi, Maddy. I'm right about what?"

"I'm lumpy. What should I do? I can't stop eating ice cream, it's my only pleasure in life."

"Well, if you can't change your eating habits you can at least take an exercise class."

"You mean aerobics?"

"Why not? Face it, Maddy, you've got to do something. If you don't shed those pounds now you may never lose them. Patty takes aerobics three times a week; she swears by it."

"You don't exercise."

"Yes, I do. Instead of taking the subway I walk twenty blocks to and from work each day. All you do is walk to the store to buy ice cream, and last time I checked that wasn't exercise."

Bella was right. So Madeline had a new project: find an exercise class. She went to the YMCA on 13th and Washington to get their schedule, but the woman at the front desk told her that aerobics classes were already in session and it was too late to join. Madeline was relieved; she had taken a few aerobics classes here and there, and they hadn't suited her personality—she had never been fond of jumping up and down. She walked to the Hoboken Farmboy to buy some non-fattening food, and while waiting on line with her powdered miso soup, soy milk, granola, and tofu, she spied a yellow poster on the large and crowded bulletin board: YOGA FOR WOMEN. Yoga, she thought as she handed her items to the checkout clerk. I could do yoga. She *had* done yoga, had taken classes in college to fulfill her physical education requirement. She paid for her food, took her grocery bag, and stood in front of the poster. The studio was at Eleventh and Willow, there were several classes each day, and each class was only $6, less if you bought a monthly card. The bottom of the poster had strips of paper with a phone number; Madeline ripped off a strip and carefully put it in her pocket. I will be lumpy no more, she thought as she left the store and walked onto Washington Street.

So a few minutes before six there was Madeline in a large room with hardwood floors, wall-to-wall mirrors, and blue exercise mats. Five other women were in the room; each had taken a mat from a pile in the corner and was laying on top of it. One woman was sitting with her legs out and her upper body stretched on top of her legs, two other women were talking softly, another was sitting in the lotus position, and another was laying flat on her back. Madeline sat on her mat, glancing around and feeling shy; it was always hard doing something new with strangers, like being a five-year-old on the first day of kindergarten. At least the teacher had been nice; the studio had a changing room and a small office, and when Madeline walked in she went to the office and told the woman that she was the one who called earlier that day.

"Oh, you're here," the woman said in a flutey English accent. "Brilliant! You don't know how many ring up and never show. You can pay me now, then hop into the other room and change. You don't need to change? Then leave your coat on a hook—if you have any valuables leave them with me. I'm not worried about the other women, but we do get the occasional nutcase roaming in. And I'm Beverly," the woman said, extending a hand.

"Nice to meet you," Madeline said as they shook. Beverly appeared to be in her late thirties; she had a mop of curly grey-brown hair, piercing blue eyes, big cheekbones, and a good-sized nose. You could never call Beverly pretty, but she radiated energy and self-confidence. Madeline liked her immediately, and decided that Bella would like her too.

"Will you be teaching the class?" Madeline asked.

"With my assistant Genna," Beverly said. "I'm training her to take over some of the classes."

And as Madeline sat on her mat, Beverly came into the room with a young woman who had to be Genna: she had a cute, perky face, sunstreaked brown hair cut into bangs and pulled into a slick ponytail; she was lithe and vibrant and healthy, and had the nerve to fit into a nifty navy blue bodysuit and even niftier navy blue leggings with white polka dots. I hate you, Madeline thought as she watched Genna limber up. You're fit and together whereas I'm lumpy and fucked-up. Madeline was wearing maroon sweatpants and one of Robert's Columbia sweatshirts, and just the quickest glance in the wall-to-wall mirrors was adequate proof that she was many pounds from fitting into a nifty bodysuit. Genna's waist was the same size as one of Madeline's thighs, and as Beverly stood and asked them to sit cross-legged and close their eyes, Madeline felt a frustrated despair—was she about to have a humiliating experience? Well, she had already paid her money; she might as well stick it out.

The first two postures were easy, and hardly even postures: sitting cross-legged, then just standing. The next posture was called the triangle, and involved standing with spread legs, bending sideways and looking at the ceiling. Not too bad, although Madeline's left side was much stiffer than her right. Then another standing posture, and now Madeline's breath was coming faster, and her leg muscles were burning. Then Beverly announced the warrior pose: it was a deceptively simple pose, just bending one knee to the side and standing with arms outstretched, but after a few moments Madeline's thigh was burning unbearably. Beverly appeared to really like this pose; as Genna held the pose in front of the class, Beverly strode around the room, lifting one woman's arm, pushing another's bent knee, all the while calling out, "This is the pose of the warrior! Imagine yourself on a beautiful white horse, charging into battle! Think of all the battles you've fought in your life, breathe deeply, and CHARGE!" Oh, shut up, Madeline thought as she stood in agony, her entire thigh on fire. Beverly came up to her then; she lifted Madeline's arms a little, which made everything hurt more, then she said, "You're not breathing, love. Take deeper breaths."

Madeline breathed into her chest, but Beverly wasn't satisfied. She put a hand on Madeline's stomach and said, "Breathe from here. Breathe so that my hand rises."

Madeline breathed in deeply, and to her horror the breath hit the Cry Button, and at once tears rolled out of her eyes and onto her cheeks.

"Oh dear," Beverly said. She made a motion for Genna to take over the class, then led Madeline out of the studio and into the office. Beverly brought two chairs side by side and sat with her arm around Madeline.

"I'm sorry," Madeline said, taking a tissue from Beverly. "I didn't come here to cry. Just I breathed and—" She looked up helplessly.

"It's okay, love. Everyone cries at least once."

"I'm just, I'm just feeling kind of fragile these days. Someone recently broke up with me—actually, someone recently kicked me out—and since then..." She shook her head and looked down at her hands. "The truth is, I'm a mess. I have no energy, I eat too much ice cream, and my body feels like a carcass I'm dragging around."

"Don't worry, love, we'll fix you up."

"But I have no energy. I don't even know if I can do this class."

"Listen," Beverly said, taking Madeline's hand and looking her in the eye. "I can't say you'll never be sad again, and I can't say you'll never get kicked out again, but if you stick with me I can show you an energy source that will never leave you."

"What's that?"

"Your own body. You have everything you need right now; you just need a little guidance."

"But I'm fat. I mean, I look at G-Genna and I know I'll never be able to do the things that she does."

Beverly snorted. "Genna! When Genna came here two years ago she was twenty pounds overweight and smoking a pack a day. You're in much better shape than she ever was. So come on, let's go back in."

Embarrassed, Madeline trailed Beverly into the studio. No one said anything; Beverly just bounded to the front and started shouting. The woman next to Madeline shot her a sympathetic glance, but otherwise it was as if nothing had happened.

The rest of the class was not bad. What Madeline found interesting was how some postures—particularly those that involved balancing—were as easy as crossing her legs, whereas others were sheer torture. She was shocked to find that she couldn't do something as simple as sit on the floor with legs in front and back straight; Beverly gave her a small pillow to sit on, but Madeline still could not touch her toes without bending her legs. Beverly said not to worry, many women had problems with that posture, and in fact two other women were also using pillows. Madeline also didn't like the Hero pose; they had to sit on their haunches, link their hands and raise them above their heads. The muscles around her knees screamed in agony, and Beverly didn't help as she stalked about the room yelling "You are a hero! Take the posture of the hero, and don't be afraid of your breasts! Small, big, firm, droopy—let your breasts be your heroes!" But Madeline loved the wheel: she laid on the floor with knees bent and hands flat on the floor by her head, then in one movement she lifted herself up into the air, her whole body bent into an arc. She used to do the pose as a child, walking around the house that way to make Bella laugh. And the shoulderstand was easy, as was the plow, the posture after the shoulderstand where you dropped your legs to the floor and bent your knees by your head. Then at the end they went into the corpse position: Beverly turned down the lights and everyone laid on the floor with their eyes shut, breathing deeply. Beverly asked them to visualize themselves in a canoe in a long lovely river, sitting with straight backs, paddling along with swift, sure strokes. Madeline hated canoes and any sort of water sport, so she imagined that her river was very shallow, and that Bella was in the canoe with her and they had a big picnic basket full of their favorite foods. Madeline drifted into a light sleep, then Beverly turned the lights back on. As the women stretched and started leaving, Beverly stood in front and cried, "Warriors! Don't forget that you're warriors!"

As she walked home, Madeline wondered if the other warriors were in as much agony as she was. But it was just the first class, after all. She decided to go again the next night, and if it worked out she would go five or six times a week. She did feel a little better, a little lighter, but whether that was from deep breathing or crying she didn't know.

At the apartment Robert and Michael were sitting at the dining room table, the Scrabble board set up and waiting.

"How was it?" Bella called out above the piano music.

"Not bad."

"Is that my sweatshirt?" Robert asked.

"I didn't think you'd mind," Madeline said as she took her seat next to Michael. "You have so many."

Robert looked at Michael and sighed. "I can't win. Between the two of them they've completely overpowered me and taken over my life. Even my clothes aren't mine."

"Oh, Robert. Tell me, are we clockwise or counterclockwise tonight?"

"Clockwise," Michael said, passing her the bag of letters.

Good, she thought as she selected T D O R Q A L. Now I just have to hope that Robert gets a phone call so Michael can help me.

They were a half hour into the game, Robert had just put the word HARD-WARE on a triple word score square and was feeling very pleased with himself, and then the phone rang.

"That's 39 points, Michael," Robert said as he rose from the table. "And don't forget my fifty bonus points for using all my letters."

"I won't," Michael said.

As soon as Robert disappeared into the hall Madeline put her letters in front of Michael. "Well?" she asked.

Michael looked at her and smiled. "I'll do my best," he said. He was still staring at the letters when Robert's footsteps came back into the hall. Madeline quickly took her letters back and looked up innocently when Robert came in.

"It's for you, Madeline."

"Who is it?"

"A guy. Not David."

Strange, Madeline thought as she hurried down the hall. I wonder who it could be. She grabbed a stool and brought it over to the phone. "Hello?" she said.

"Hi, Madeline? This is Jessie. You know, from Narrow Grave."

"Oh. Hi Jessie."

"Hi. Well, I just wanted to give you a call. I've been thinking about you, wondering how you're getting along."

"I'm fine," she said defiantly. "Just fine."

"I'm glad to hear it. Listen, I was wondering—would you like to go out to dinner sometime? Like this weekend, maybe?"

"What?"

"Dinner. You know—a date."

"Jessie, I don't think—"

"Look, if you're worried that things'll be weird with David, don't. I already checked this out with him, he said it was no problem for him if we went out."

She felt as if someone slammed a hammer into her chest. "Listen, Jessie," she managed to say. "I'm flattered, but I can't go out with you."

"But why not? We always got along so well. Are you seeing someone else?"

"Good-bye, Jessie." She hung up the phone. She grabbed her elbows and hugged herself, squeezing her eyes shut. The pain was cold and strong and it came in waves, as if someone was throwing buckets of ice water on her head. Slowly she rose from the stool, walked down the hall, and went into her room. She shut the door and laid on her bed; she saw nothing, heard nothing.

Someone knocked. Slowly. Then the doorknob turned and Michael walked into the room. He sat on the edge of the bed and looked down at her. "I've been elected to find out what's wrong," he said. "Will you tell me?"

Madeline turned her head and looked at him. "That was one of David's bandmates. One of the guitarists."

"And what did he say?"

"He asked me out on a date. He told me he asked David if it would be okay, and David said it would be no problem. No problem. And do you know, Michael, if I dated someone in David's band that would mean I'd be seeing David all the time. And him saying no problem means it wouldn't bother him—it wouldn't bother him to see me with another man, it wouldn't bother him to know I was sleeping with someone else. I mean, here I am—I can hardly get through each day, I can't even take a yoga class without crying, and here David is so completely over me that I could date someone in his band and he wouldn't care the least. I don't think I've ever been so humiliated in my life."

"So you said no?"

"*Of course* I said no. I'm not a masochist. Tell me, Michael—am I overreacting? I feel like—I don't know, I feel like David just slapped me."

"You're not overreacting."

"I hate him," she said quietly. "I just hate him. How could he be so insensitive? How could he think I was over him?"

No more Scrabble that night. And when Madeline woke the next morning her jaw was sore from clenching it in her sleep. She was furious. And the more she thought about Jessie's phone call, the more furious she became. She had no temp job and nothing to write, so she spent all morning in bed thinking. The dull numbness was gone, and in its place was an anger so strong she felt she could kill someone. David, in particular. And she felt scared, because this must be how her father felt. At such moments she realized that no matter how hard she and Bella tried to distance themselves from their parents, there were still areas where they would always be Polly and Spam's children, and Madeline's temper was one of them. This was Spam's anger, the kind of anger that could destroy a piano, strangle a hamster, throw a child through a glass window, or any of the other memorable ways Spam had chosen to express himself over the years. The pounding heat of the emotion frightened Madeline, but at least—thank God—part of her was rational. There was a little corner of sanity that told her not to jump out of bed and run to David's house and slam his head against the wall. Because she could have done that; she felt capable of anything.

She called Bella, but Bella was out to lunch with one of the writers. Not knowing what else to do, Madeline stalked up and down the long narrow hall, her arms wrapped around herself, her thoughts and emotions black. I hate him, she thought. I really hate him. She started crying from frustration, from not knowing what to do with all this pollution inside of her. She wanted to punish David. Maybe she should go out with Jessie, go out with him and be in David's face all the time. But what good would that do? David wouldn't be jealous, and Madeline would just end up hurting herself. She could go to Maxwell's and chew him out in front of everyone. No—she would look like a ranting raving crazy woman. But she felt so hurt; she had to do something, even if it was just leaving a nasty message on his answering machine. Oh, how she hated him for going on with his life as if she never existed! And for kicking her out the way he had! He could have at least tried; she knew unmarried couples who went to counseling, and she would have done that. Or at least she could have moved out on a trial basis, and they could have still dated. But no—David didn't want to try. It was as Bella had said: he was attracted to her, he fucked her, and when he was tired of fucking her he kicked her out. In the beginning when she was unavailable he was all charm and flattery, and then when she slept with him she was still new and fascinating, but after that? Time to move on. And I was so stupid, she thought. I was actually flattered that he was so attracted to me. She was lonely and frightened after her experience at Swan's Cove, and so she was vulnerable to his charm—because any other time she would have seen through someone like David, she was sure of it. From the first it was all about the way she looked, and all about getting her into bed. He was willing to sleep with her on the first date when he hardly knew her! He didn't want her, he just wanted her blonde hair and breasts and vagina.

Oh God, she thought, sinking into the couch, head in hands. Oh God, how could I have been such a fool. If all she had wanted was sex, fine, but she didn't want just sex, she wanted to be in love, and she assumed that David felt the same way. But he didn't; it was all about getting into her pants. Oh, he liked her well enough, and maybe he even thought he loved her, but Madeline saw now that David had never really loved *her*—he had loved her blonde femaleness. Things he said came back to her, how the first time he saw her he thought, "I've got to have her." He called that love at first sight, but it was just wanting to fuck at first sight. And a cold horror swept over her as she suddenly understood that *nothing she said had ever mattered to him*. That first night at Leo's, if instead of talking about her writing she had told him that she was on the FBI's most wanted list, David would still have smiled and been just as attentive, because it was never her words that he was interested in. And she saw—bingo—that this was why he had such a long string of problematic relationships. He didn't go out on a date to listen and learn about the woman he was with; he went out on a date so he could have sex. And then a few months later, after the conquest had been made and the sex was not so fresh, he decided it was time to break up. And that's what he did with her. Only she wasn't problematic, so he invented the excuse about the record contract—but the real truth was what he first said, that he was bored. Only he hadn't taken it far enough; if he had been honest, he would have said, "I'm bored with fucking you." And that's why it truly would not have bothered him if she went out with Jessie; it was okay for Jessie to sleep with Madeline, because David had already covered that particular piece of ground.

Oh God. And she had fallen so in love with him.

Madeline wept angrily. So now she saw what Robert and Michael had seen all along; they tried to warn her, but she hadn't listened. She hadn't wanted to. And Bella? Well, Bella had never been a good judge of men; the only reason she was with Robert was because Robert had refused to give up on her. And anyway Bella always had a weak spot for musicians, witness her years in the Grateful Dead traveling circus. But most of all Bella wanted Madeline to be happy, and since David made Madeline happy that was good enough for Bella.

But he asked me to move in with him, Madeline thought. I talked to his mother on the phone. She hadn't imagined all that, and she hadn't been wrong to think it meant something. She thought it over, and decided that David had really wanted her to move in—but what had he said? "I want you here all the time. It'll be easier." Easier to sleep with you. And sure, she talked on the phone with his mother, but when the time grew near for them to meet, David broke up with her. And for the first time she saw that David was not an emotionally stable person. Not that he was crazy, but he simply was not mature. He was mature enough to dedicate himself to his music, mature enough to organize all facets of Narrow Grave, mature enough to have a job and clean clothes and matching mugs in his kitchen cabinet, but he wasn't mature enough to have a deep relationship with a woman. He didn't know how to have a woman in his life. Or maybe he didn't really want a woman in his life; maybe he wanted the sex, but not the woman.

Madeline sat in the living room, thinking and crying, thinking and crying. And the more she saw the truth, the more her anger grew. She got up to call Bella; she was in the hall walking towards the kitchen when someone knocked. Slowly.

Madeline threw open the door. Michael. In khakis, a white oxford shirt, and dark blue sweater.

"I came home from work a little while ago," he said. "I wanted to stop by and see how you are."

Madeline motioned him inside and instructed him to sit on one of the couches. Then, pacing up and down the small room, she explained everything she had been thinking. Michael listened carefully, his eyes following her as she stalked from wall to wall. And when she was done, when she had said for the fiftieth time that she was so angry she could kill someone, when she fell on the couch exhausted, Michael looked at her and smiled.

"Good," he said.

"*Good?* Michael, I don't think you understand. I don't think you have any idea the kind of anger I feel."

"I wouldn't say that. I used to have terrible revenge fantasies about my ex-wife."

"Such as?"

"Well, let's see." He looked at the ceiling a moment. "She was a photographer, so I used to have a lot of fantasies about destroying her work. You know, exposing all her unprocessed film, or bursting in on her darkroom while she was working. And I also used to fantasize about taking bad pictures and sending them to her agent and saying they were hers. You know, stealing some of her stationery, forging her signature, doing all that and basically destroying her career."

For the first time that day, Madeline laughed. "Why, Michael!" she said. "You are vicious! I hope you never get mad at me."

"I could never get mad at you, Madeline."

"Let's hope not. I can just imagine you writing some awful trite short story and sending it out in my name."

"But the point is, I never did any of those things. All the fantasies were just a means of discharging anger. You have to let yourself feel it, or it'll destroy you."

She thought a moment. "I want to kill him, Michael. I'm that angry."

"So imagine killing him."

"Oh—I don't really want to kill him. But I want to hurt him; I want him to suffer."

"So imagine hurting him."

"But I don't really want to hurt him."

"Exactly. But you want to get rid of the anger. I can't say what will work for you, but I know what worked for me: I used to have very elaborate revenge fantasies, and I also wrote dozens of letters that I never sent. I called her every name I could think of, and described all the horrible things I wanted to do to her."

Again Madeline laughed. "Where is our nice calm Michael?"

"But don't you see? The reason I'm calm is because I don't carry all that around with me. Whatever I feel, I let myself feel it."

"But aren't you afraid you might go berserk?"

"No. I trust myself."

"It's different for me, Michael. I come from a family of berserk people, we have a history of violent behavior."

"As did my mother. But I still trust myself. Look, why don't you and I make a pact that if you really get to the point where you think you'll do something violent, you'll come see me and we'll talk about it. Okay? That way you have a safety net."

"But what if it's eleven in the morning and I'm seized by an uncontrollable desire to burst in on David's work? I almost did that today."

"Then get on the bus and come find me at Columbia. You can do that."

"I guess so...Okay. Let's make a pact."

"Good."

He stayed with her until she left for yoga; when she returned it was the usual evening of piano music and Scrabble, but after Michael left and Bella and Robert went to sleep, Madeline sat in bed with a pen and a pad of paper on her lapdesk. "Dear David," she wrote. "I hate your guts." She held the pad up and read it over; it seemed like a good start. And then before she knew it, she was writing at a white heat, covering page after page, pouring all her anger and disgust and pain onto paper. She may not have been able to write short stories, but she was certainly able to write a nasty letter to David. When she was done she was trembling with exhaustion, but she also felt clearer than she had in months. While massaging her cramped fingers she sat back and read. She was shocked at the vileness that had come out of her; she had actually written things like "You stupid fucking asshole, I hope you burn in hell"; but she had also written things like "I didn't deserve to be treated that way," and also funny things like "I hope your bass has a power surge and you electrocute yourself on stage." Michael was right; it was really good therapy.

Over the next weeks the sad numbness made an occasional appearance, but mostly what Madeline felt was anger. She wrote nasty unsent letters religiously, and she began to feel somewhat lighter. And yoga helped. Madeline took classes with Beverly every day but Sunday, and while her lumpiness had not gone away she definitely felt stronger and more limber. And she found that instead of getting annoyed at Beverly's cheerleading—because wasn't yoga supposed to be a quiet, meditative experience?—she started to appreciate Beverly's imagery. One day during the warrior pose Madeline imagined herself on a white horse, holding a bayonet and wearing a suit of armor with an elaborate helmet with huge red and blue feathers; she was charging along at top speed and then—bam! There goes the bayonet into David! After that the pose seemed easy, and became one of her favorites. Other postures were still torture, but with most of them she had just needed to get a little limber before she could enjoy the nice stretch they gave. She concentrated and worked hard, and one day as she was putting away her mat Genna came up and said, "You know, you're doing really well. You've made a lot of progress." Madeline thanked her, and in a moment of generosity complimented Genna on her nifty navy blue bodysuit. And as Genna walked away Madeline decided that she didn't hate her anymore; after all, Genna's only crimes were being pretty and in shape.

And in general it was good therapy to be in a room with a group of women who, like her, were trying to find some kind of peace and inner power. There was quite a bit of crying; Beverly often had to lead someone out of the room, but they usually came back and finished the class. Madeline wondered what the other women were going through, and she often wondered what Beverly had been through until one day Beverly casually let slip that her ex-husband used to beat her. And one evening as Madeline laid in the corpse position she remembered Roberta, her rebirther down the shore, another woman who had been through a great deal and was now helping others.

And after awhile all Beverly's talk about warriors and heroes and courage really began to make sense to Madeline. She was still so hurt by the fact that David had seen her just as something to have sex with, and so it was nice to work with Beverly, who never discussed physical appearance. Beverly's definition of being a woman started from the inside out, and with Beverly's guidance Madeline began to experience herself differently. She felt less embarrassed about being pretty, and at the same time felt that, despite what everyone said, being pretty didn't matter very much. Look at Beverly: she was not conventionally good-looking, but she carried herself like a queen. Bella was like that too: she had squandered her youthful good looks with drugs and wild living, and as a result her face was deeply lined, and she looked much older than thirty-six. But Bella didn't give a damn; as she once said to Madeline, "This is what I look like. And if someone doesn't like it, they can go fuck themselves." Madeline had always felt ambivalent about her good looks; they seemed important, but the whole thing was so ephemeral and intangible. Being pretty had made David want her, but it didn't make him stay, did it? So never mind all that; much better to be a warrior than a doll.

Madeline talked about Beverly so much that one Saturday Bella decided to come along with her. Madeline was surprised at how well Bella did, and even Beverly commented on Bella's suppleness. Madeline was afraid Bella would make some comment about the benefits of regular sex, but for once Bella held her tongue. They arrived home laughing and talking, and found Robert and Michael in the living room.

"What are you two discussing?" Madeline asked as she flopped on the couch next to Michael.

"Thomas Carlyle's essay on heroes," Robert said.

Madeline grabbed her breasts and proclaimed, "My breasts are my heroes."

Bella and Michael laughed; Robert looked pained and said, "Bella, make her stop."

"Oh, Robert," Madeline said. "That's one of the things the yoga teacher says."

"I don't know about her; she sounds a little weird."

"She is not," Bella said, cuffing Robert's head. "She's just a nice feminist Englishwoman. Say!" Bella's eyes lit up. "Maybe she'd like to meet Michael. She's English, he's half-English—why not?"

"Oh no," Madeline said hurriedly. "Beverly has a boyfriend. He came by one night, I saw him."

"How do you know it was her boyfriend? Maybe it was her brother."

"I don't think her brother would stick his hand down the back of her pants."

"Oh. Guess not."

So Madeline was better. Still angry, but better.

❦   ❦   ❦

Then the most important revelation came. Important, unexpected, and at the same time completely familiar.

It was Wednesday morning, a few days after she and Bella had gone to yoga together. It was early April, and outside the rain poured down. Madeline was sitting on her bed, her lapdesk and pen and paper in front of her. She still couldn't write, but she liked to wake up early and read—Michael had lent her a number of books by Aldous Huxley, and now she was reading Huxley's biography and finding it hard to put down. Then one moment her mind drifted off, and she started thinking about David. She tried to push him away and return to the book, but he inserted himself between the words and she could no longer concentrate. So she sighed, put her book on top of the typewriter, and got ready to write another angry letter. She had not written many in the past days; as Michael had predicted, she was tapering off. But now it seemed like a good idea to let out an explosion of feeling so she could go on with her day.

She had covered half a page and was writing in earnest when she stopped. Something was wrong. She tried to go on but couldn't; she reread what she had written, and two sentences stood out as if in neon: "How could you do such a thing to me? I would never do something like that to someone."

But I did do something like that to someone, she thought. That's what I did to The Virgin.

The Virgin. It wasn't that Madeline had ever forgotten him, but she also never thought about him. And now the relationship ran through her mind: her temping at a law firm the summer after she graduated from Barnard, him just out of law school, awkward and nervous, not knowing how to give orders. He was quite good looking; tall with wide shoulders, dark blue eyes and thick brown hair. She worked for him for a week while his secretary was on vacation, and Friday at five o'clock as she stood by his desk watching him sign her time card, he suddenly looked up and asked if she wanted to have dinner with him.

"I can't date clients," she said.

He handed her the time card. "I'm no longer your client."

Well, she thought, why not? They went out to dinner and she had a nice time, but she knew at once that they would never work as a couple. His politics were conservative, for one thing, and while she wanted to live as a bohemian artist it was clear he was cut out to be a straitlaced lawyer. But he was cute, and clearly enamored of her. He had grown up in West Virginia and gone to Duke as an undergraduate and for law school, and he had a bumbly innocence that she found attractive. He took her out to dinner almost every night for two weeks, and never once tried to kiss her. She wanted him to kiss her, and as the dates passed and he took no initiative, she decided it was time to take action. So one night she put her diaphragm in her purse, and while they were standing outside a restaurant and he was hailing a cab to take her to Port Authority, she threw her arms around him and kissed him. He was surprised, but he kissed her back.

"Let's go to your apartment," she whispered in his ear.

"You're sure?" he asked.

"I'm sure."

They took a taxi to a lonely half-furnished apartment in the East Nineties. The Virgin had only been in town a few months, and the law firm kept him so busy he hadn't had time to buy furniture or decorate. So in a bedroom with no posters on the wall and no furniture other than a mattress on the floor, Madeline threw off her clothes, laid down on the mattress, and pulled him on top of her.

"You want to—?" he asked.

"What do you think?"

So they did. Madeline knew she didn't love him, knew it couldn't last, but it was nice to have someone to sleep with, and she decided to just enjoy it while it lasted. Bella and Robert couldn't believe she was dating a lawyer, and in order to see for themselves they told Madeline to invite him to brunch. The night before Madeline slept at his apartment, then they took the bus to Hoboken. They were going through the Lincoln Tunnel and Madeline was telling him how Hoboken was much nicer than New York; he listened, nodded, then said, "Well, when we get married we can live in Hoboken. I'm not very fond of New York myself."

Madeline wanted to hit her ear to make sure she had heard correctly. Married? With him? He was joking, he had to be. But the comments escalated; soon anytime they were together he said something about marriage or children, and she started feeling uneasy. The decisive moment, however, was when they were talking about birth control; she told him about the time in high school when she took The Pill but had to go off it because it made her fat. As she spoke he had a strange look on his face, and when she was done he said, "So I guess you weren't a virgin with me."

She laughed. "Of course not! And what a ridiculous double standard—you certainly weren't a virgin with me."

He looked at her with great seriousness. "I never said that."

Her heart sank—he had been a virgin! When she went home the next morning she told Bella, and Bella said, "Madeline, you're in way over your head. This guy wants to marry you, so if you're not serious about him you should end it now before he really gets hurt."

The next time Madeline saw him she was too scared to tell him; she hated breakup scenes. But the time after that he asked her if she wanted to go to West Virginia and meet his parents, and Madeline knew Bella was right. She waited until a Saturday night; she went to his apartment and found him pouring over a newspaper looking for a movie for them to see. Madeline sat next to him and told him in a halting voice that she was sorry, but they had to break up.

He cried. And the sight of him, a big tall strong man with his head in his hands weeping—it was horrible. She explained how he was more serious than she wanted to be, they had different lifestyles, she was only twenty-two and not ready to meet parents, get married, have children. He tried to talk her out of it, but she was firm; and as she was walking out the door he said, pitifully, "Call me if you change your mind." She shut the apartment door with a feeling of great relief: thank God that was over.

But it wasn't. He called her repeatedly, begging her to give him one more chance; and when she refused to take his calls anymore, he started writing her letters. The letters became a family joke; Bella would come in with the mail, toss a letter to Madeline and sing out, "Another letter from The Virgin!" Madeline read all the letters out loud, and showed Bella and Robert how he corrected his mistakes with Wite-Out. Robert just shook his head and asked Madeline what she had done to the poor guy. Finally Madeline received a letter from The Virgin saying he could no longer bear all the memories in New York, and was transferring to a law firm in Seattle; Madeline had danced around the apartment with joy. He still wrote her from Seattle, but gradually the letters trickled out, and the last one she received had to be two, three years ago.

And now, sitting in bed, the rain hitting against the window, Madeline felt a hot, humiliating shame. I broke his heart, she thought. I completely broke his heart. And he felt as badly as I've been feeling these past months, maybe even worse. And she saw—oh God, the shame was so strong, like a knife ripping across her chest—she saw that she had actually behaved worse than David. At least David had loved her; maybe he hadn't loved her as fully as she would have liked, but David was not a liar, and would never have said he loved her if he didn't. But Madeline had not loved The Virgin; she could remember laying in his arms after they had sex, how he would run his fingers through her hair and tell her how lonely he was in New York and how happy he was to find someone to love. She had kept quiet; she felt sure he didn't really love her, and was just saying so. Talk about warping reality to fit your own needs! Of course The Virgin had loved her; but because she didn't want him to, she just assumed he didn't. Oh God! she thought, pushing her lapdesk on the floor, raising her hands to cover her reddening cheeks. Oh God—I *used* him! I used him for sex! At least David had loved her, at least they had a life together, but except for that one brunch Madeline never introduced The Virgin to her friends or incorporated him into her life. Even the brunch had been something of a joke, at least from her side; she had mostly wanted to see Bella and Robert's expressions when they saw her walk in with a corporate lawyer. She had used him; he took her to nice restaurants and gave her orgasms, but she had never really cared about him. But he had cared about her. He hadn't been able to forget her. And all those letters, those pleading letters—she had laughed at them. And the Wite-Out—oh, the Wite-Out. He had taken such care with each word, as if that would somehow bring her back. And all she had done was laugh.

Madeline buried her head in her hands and moaned. And she remembered something—yes, from a book she had just read, which one? In the last weeks she had gone through so many: *Chrome Yellow, Point Counterpoint, Brave New World*, now the Huxley bio—but no, it wasn't from Huxley. Before that—yes, she had read *Giovanni's Room* by James Baldwin. It was Bella's book, and she had returned it to the bookcase in their bedroom. She ran down the hall to Bella and Robert's bedroom, found the book, and sat on the floor ruffling through it. The scene where the men were in the bar talking, a line had jumped out at her and—yes, here it was:

"There are so many ways of being despicable it quite makes
one's head spin. But the way to be really despicable
is to be contemptuous of other people's pain."

She shut the book. She lay her head against Bella and Robert's bed. David
had not been contemptuous of her pain, not when they broke up and, she was
sure, not now. But she had laughed at The Virgin. Even that, calling him The
Virgin—he had a name. Bill. William. William Baker.

She put her face between her knees and covered her head with her arms.
Shame, shame and pain—and it was worse than the pain she had felt when
David broke up with her, because this was the pain of seeing herself clearly. She
had done all those things to Bill, had forgotten about him for years; she had
lived in complete ignorance of what she had done, blithely going about her
days, considering herself a kind, considerate person, and now with David she
felt so victimized—and all along there was Bill, and what she had done to him.
Life was so odd; years pass, and you are suddenly able to see your past more
clearly than when you were living it. But this seeing clearly—it was agonizing.
And it stopped her mind: where did this behavior—this careless, selfish behavior—fit in with her idea of herself?

"But I didn't know!" she said aloud. "I was young and stupid then, and I
just didn't know." If she had to do it over again she would never, ever do such a
thing—and she had actually learned from the relationship, because after Bill
she had never gone out with anyone for more than three or four dates—she
always ended things the moment she knew they had no future. So she had
learned, she had grown—but still, what she had done to Bill was wrong. He
had loved her so much—maybe even loved her still—and she had been so
careless of that love, careless and even scornful.

"But I didn't know," she repeated. "I didn't know."

She tried to comfort herself. She had only been twenty-two, was still recovering from a fucked-up childhood and a nightmare adolescence; then Bella
and Robert saved her, and college was a good experience, but as far as men and
love and sex went, she didn't know anything then. She had acted the way she
did out of pain and ignorance. If she had known then what it was like to lose
someone you love, she never, ever would have toyed with Bill. Never.

Oh God, Madeline thought. Look what we do to each other. Look how
much we hurt each other. We need to be more careful; we need to take better
care of each other. And she started crying, different tears than any she had ever
cried before. She cried for herself, she cried for Bill, and she even cried for

David because the truth was, David hadn't known either. He met her, he was attracted to her, he thought he fell in love with her—he hadn't known he would hurt her. And he surely had no idea the pain she was feeling now. She did not forgive what David had done, but she could understand why he did it. He hadn't known; like everyone else he was just barreling through his life. And even if he had known, if he was a fucked-up person who deliberately hurt people—again, she couldn't forgive his acts, but she could have compassion for a person who was so ignorant and in so much pain. Because only a person who was ignorant and in pain would deliberately hurt someone else.

"I'm sorry, Bill," she said aloud. "Wherever you are, I'm sorry."

She crawled up onto the bed and laid with a pillow pressed against her chest and stomach. She cried, and as she cried she had the strangest feeling in her chest, as if something was being pulled out by the roots. She cried a very long time, and when she was done she laid quietly. The room was deeply shadowed; the sky outside was dark and heavy, and a light rain was falling. Madeline felt tender and bruised, and there was still that odd sensation in her chest. She felt—it was odd to say, but she felt as if there was less of her. Something was gone. Less of her, yes, and at the same time amidst the tender bruised feeling, there was some kind of peace. Wait a moment! she said. I know this feeling.

It was Merger.

No—how could it be? She hadn't felt Merger in months; besides, she had done nothing to bring it on. She had just been living her life and now, boom, here it was. It was the same peace, the same feeling, as if she had melted around the edges and was no longer separate.

Wow.

The phone rang. Madeline ran into the kitchen and picked up the receiver. "Hello?" she said, sitting on a stool.

"Hi Maddy. What's up?"

"Hi Bella. I'm okay. I was just sitting in your room."

"You sound funny—have you been crying?"

"Yep."

Bella sighed. "Because of David?"

"Actually, I was crying because of Bill."

"Bill? Who's that, David's evil twin?"

"Bill. Bill Baker. You know—The Virgin."

"Oh God—don't tell me you got another letter from him."

"No. But I realized that I really hurt him."

"You're just realizing that now?"

"You mean you knew?"

"Of course I knew! I felt so sorry for the guy, and I felt sorry for you. That's why I used to go along with you when you laughed at his letters, I thought it was just your way of dealing with your pain."

"I wasn't in pain then, but I am now. I really hurt him, Bella. Worse than David hurt me."

"I know."

"It's no good to be careless of other people's feelings."

"I agree. It's better to be extra careful. Which is why I always say you shouldn't sleep with someone right away. Sometimes it works out, but usually someone gets hurt."

"Well, now I've been on both sides of it."

"That's good—it means you're ready for a Robert in your life. Too bad I can't clone him."

"Don't make me your next fix-up project, Bella. I still feel pretty shaky."

"But you're better."

"I'm better. And I don't hate David anymore. I don't love him either, but I know I don't hate him."

"So you're over him."

"Let's say I'm 75% over him. Or maybe 65%."

"That's good enough for me. Oh, Patty just walked in, I have to go. See you tonight."

"Tell Patty I said hi. Bye."

Madeline hung up the phone. Still sitting on the stool, she leaned over and put her forehead against the cool windowpane. She closed her eyes, and breathed deeply.

CHAPTER 17

No Ram Dass

Seven o'clock on a Saturday night, and Madeline was standing with Michael outside a brick building on 78th Street between Third Avenue and Lexington, waiting on line to hear Ram Dass. It was quite cold for early April, and Madeline was bundled up in her black wool coat and green scarf. She was hungry, too; Michael always took her out to eat when they went to lectures, but he generally took her out afterwards, and she had been so wrapped up in thought all day that she had only eaten an apple and two chocolate chip cookies. Well, once they got their tickets maybe she could run over to a deli and buy some almonds.

The line was long but it moved rapidly, and soon Madeline and Michael were in a crowded foyer, standing before a card table with two women and a cash box. A sign on the card table and another on an easel said SOLD OUT; behind the card table a crowd of people were talking and laughing, creating a hum of noise and excitement.

Michael gave his name to a blonde woman with a Dutch boy haircut and glasses with multi-colored frames. The woman scanned a typed list, then looked up. "I don't see you here," she said. "It's Eliot with one l?"

"That's right."

"Well, maybe they put you with two l's. Hmm—no. I don't see you." The woman turned a little red. "I'm sorry."

"Sorry?"

"I can't let you in. We're sold out."

Michael knit his brow. "But I can assure you that I called and left my name. I spoke to a young man, and he said he would put my name on the list."

The woman sighed. "He must have forgotten. It happens sometimes."

"Perhaps the other list—?"

"It's a photocopy of this one."

Madeline tugged Michael's sleeve; he turned and looked at her. "Do you want me to make a scene?" she whispered. "I can, you know."

"I'm sure you can. But no, it's not worth it." He turned back to the blonde woman. "Should we wait? Perhaps there'll be free seats if people don't show."

The woman gestured at the line behind them. "I really doubt that. Look, I'm terribly sorry; I believe you, but my hands are tied."

"Oh well." Michael turned to Madeline. "Why don't we get something to eat?"

"That's fine. I'm pretty hungry anyway."

When they were out on the street and away from the line Michael said, "I'm sorry, Madeline."

"Michael, it's not your fault. I know you're super-reliable, I know you called and left your name. We can see him another time."

"He's a very good speaker," Michael said wistfully.

"Don't be sad, Michael. Anyway, I'm so hungry my stomach would have been rumbling through the whole thing and you wouldn't have heard a word."

He smiled. "Oh, you think so."

"I know so. So tell me, do you know any good restaurants up here?"

"This isn't really my part of town. We can just walk until we find something."

"At the rate you walk I'll die of hunger. Look, across the street—it's an upscaley diner. Let's go there."

The diner had all the traditional features—a counter, revolving dessert case, red vinyl seats—but the menu featured unexpected dishes like bean burritos and homemade pizza, and the prices were a bit steep. Madeline leaned her open menu against her mouth and looked at Michael.

He looked up from his menu. "What?" he asked.

"It's expensive."

"Do you think so?"

"We can go someplace else."

"Don't be silly. I can afford it."

"You always pay, and I never do."

"But I'm the one who asked you."

"Still, I should pay half."

"You can pay for the bus ride home."

"Oh, two dollars!"

"Madeline," he said, smiling. "I said never mind. Professors make quite good money, and other than books and you I don't have any expenses. It's my pleasure to pay."

"Well, if you insist…"

Madeline ordered a Caesar salad and bean burritos, and Michael—after a long, excruciating examination of the menu—ordered the same, and a Heineken.

"So," he said as the waitress walked away. "You were quiet on the bus ride in. Are you feeling all right?"

"Actually," she said, folding her hands in front of her. "I feel very good. Something sort of amazing happened to me this week. Painful, but amazing."

"I noticed you've been preoccupied. I thought you were upset about—"

"David?" She shook her head. "David's the least of it. Do you want to hear? It's kind of a long story."

"Tell me."

So she explained about Bill Baker and her realization that she had hurt him, and how this led her to a feeling of compassion and pity, and how these feelings, oddly enough, led to the calm peace of Merger.

"The weird thing is, I went down the shore and tried to break all my sensual attachments so I could have an experience of Merger. I thought if I divorced myself from the sensual world I'd have the feeling of Merger all the time and nothing would bother me. I chased Merger for five months and by the end I was so exhausted and freaked out I gave it all up. And then I came back to Hoboken and threw myself into a relationship with David, I got my heart totally broken and was, as you recall, dying, and then in the midst of that pain, boom—Merger. Isn't that weird?"

"No," Michael said. "Not at all. Go on."

"And the really weird thing is, it's not like that pain has gone away. I'm only about 70% over David, so I still feel sad and angry, and yet I feel a kind of peace. I didn't know the two could co-exist, I thought you were either blissed out or in hell, but I'm sort of doing both at once. And then, something else really weird—you know how I've been reading that Aldous Huxley biography? Well, I read this one line that seemed to really confirm what I've been thinking. I memorized it:

"'And then there is the sense that *in spite of Everything*—I suppose this is the Ultimate Mystical conviction—in spite of Pain, in spite of Death, in spite of Horror, the universe is in some way All Right, capital A, capital R.'" Eyes shining, Madeline leaned across the table. "I read that and I just got so excited. If only it were true, Michael! If only things *were* All Right, really All Right. Sometimes I think they just might be. And I think that's what my feeling of Merger is—it's a sense of All Rightness. A sense of being in exactly the right place at exactly the right time. But it doesn't ever seem to last. I mean, I have these revelations, I feel good, and then I forget. Only when I think and read a lot does the feeling stay. And yet now I know—or I think I know—that even when I'm feeling pain the feeling of Merger, of All Rightness, is never far away. Which is probably what you were getting at when you told me that my pain could teach me something. Isn't that right?"

"I didn't know it would teach you all this, but yes, that's what I meant. Pain isn't a punishment, and it isn't something to throw away. It's part of life and has its own richness."

"Tell me, Michael, this All Rightness—do *you* feel that way?"

"Mmm—yes."

"All the time?"

"Well—yes. Mostly."

"Describe it to me. Tell me what it's like to be you."

"Well. Let's see." He took a sip of beer. "It's primarily a physical sensation. Relaxation. As if every cell is completely relaxed. And sort of what you said, about being in exactly the right place at exactly the right time. And it's also, as you said, not about not getting angry or excited or sad, it's more like—well, like a child in a room padded with pillows. The child can bounce and scream as much as it likes but it's protected on all sides. And it's not being afraid of death."

"Are you afraid of death?"

"No."

"I am. I'm so terrified I can't even think about it."

"I used to be as well. It's something I worked on for years through my reading and meditation and translations—well, it's a long story, I can explain it to you another time. But for now I can really say that I'm not afraid."

"Why? Because you don't believe your body is the whole story?"

"Exactly. I think we all have something—we all *are* something—that can never be taken away from us. Not even through death. So there's nothing to lose, and therefore nothing to hold on to. And yes, I would agree with Aldous Huxley: in spite of everything, the universe is All Right."

"So what's the point of being alive? If everything is All Right, why bother?"

"Well, there's many answers to that question, but I can give you my opinion. We're here to relieve suffering, and we do that by giving love. If we understand the All Rightness, if we manifest it and show it to others, we help the world heal itself. And when I say suffering, I mean our own as well as others'. After awhile the distinction between self and other blurs, and you're simply relieving suffering. And giving love. That's why we're here, I think."

Madeline thought a moment. "That's a beautiful philosophy, Michael. That's such a nice way to see life."

"Well, it's certainly not something I came up with on my own—it's been around for millennia. But I agree with it."

"But one thing bothers me. And it's been bothering me for several days now."

"What's that?"

"Hitler."

"Hitler?" The waitress set down their salads; Michael picked up his knife and fork and poised them over his bowl. "What does Hitler have to do with this? Did you break his heart as well?"

"Michael. Of course not. And I'm perfectly serious: Hitler throws a wrench into this whole thing because, tell me, how can concentration camps be All Right? How can the suffering of all those people—and not just the victims, but the people who survived—how can that be All Right?"

"Hitler isn't separate from the universe. You can't accept everything and reject him."

"But I do reject him! He was a monster."

Michael wrinkled his nose. "That's a little too simple. Hitler was a human being—he was of his family, and he was of his time. I'm not condoning what he did; in fact, like most everyone else, I abhor what he did. But it's as you said about David—you can't forgive the acts, but you can have compassion for the person."

"I have no compassion for Hitler. And that's exactly my point. Look—the last few days have been, I don't know, it's like the whole world's turned upside down. For me to see that I did exactly what David did, for me to feel such compassion for myself and for him—it was amazing. And I can apply it to everyone, and I've been doing that. Let me give you an example: our waitress. She has got the nastiest, frizziest red hair, and when I looked at her I just thought,

Yuck. And then I thought, 'Madeline—what are you doing? Haven't you had days when your hair was a wreck? Why are you so hard on people?' And I know why I'm like that—it's the way Polly was always so critical of my appearance, and I'm just doing it to someone else. So I have compassion for myself, and for the waitress, and maybe even a little for Polly. Do you see what I'm saying? It's like I see *through* myself, and I see through others. But I can't see through Hitler."

"Then you should read about his childhood. Alice Miller writes about him in *For Your Own Good*—Bella has the book, and so do I. Hitler had a horrible childhood—beatings, humiliations, poverty—and Alice Miller's theory is that when you look at how he was treated in childhood, you can see that he treated the Jews in the same way. Most people take their frustration out on their families, but unfortunately Hitler had a wider arena in which to act out. Just as you said—your mother criticized you, so you criticize the waitress. It was the same for Hitler but far, far more tragic, for both himself and others. He was a person, Madeline—a person with a psychology, and even a heart. You had a bad childhood, you had abusive parents—can't you feel sorry for others who had the same problems?"

"I do. But look, Michael, there's a difference between criticizing the waitress and organizing concentration camps."

"On one level, yes. Obviously. But on another level, both you and Hitler were acting out of pain. Remember what you told me before? How even if David deliberately hurt you, you couldn't forgive him, but you could have compassion for a person who was ignorant and in pain—because only a person who was ignorant and in pain would do such a thing. Remember?"

"Yes."

"So?"

"So—I have to think about this." She speared an anchovy and piece of lettuce on her fork, then burst out, "I can't believe that you, you of all people, you who won't even swat a mosquito, is sitting here defending Hitler."

"I'm not defending him, I'm trying to understand him. And you can't stop someone like Hitler until you understand him. Look—you read *Native Son*, and you told me you felt sorry for Bigger. Bigger, who killed a young woman and stuffed her in a furnace. Why did you feel sorry for him?" Madeline chewed, and said nothing. "I'll tell you why—it's because Richard Wright was able to show why Bigger murdered. He showed the world through Bigger's eyes. Murder is wrong, yes; but it's not enough to glance at a picture of a murderer in the paper and think, 'He's a monster.' You have to go deeper, you have to see the world through their eyes and understand their childhood and their pain. Remember when you told me you wanted to kill David?"

"Oh, come on. I didn't mean it."

"No, Madeline. The impulse was the same, except you were brought up to believe murder is wrong. But you know, people do kill others just because they broke up with them; in fact most people are murdered by someone they know. There's stories in the paper every day about jealous lovers and vengeful wives. You just have more control, and more love in your life. For instance, I know you would never do anything like that because you couldn't bear to hurt Bella."

"That's true."

"But not everyone has a Bella in their life. And not everyone is as intelligent as you, or as well-educated, and not everyone has a talent for writing to fall back on. And again, that's not to say that murder or incest or concentration camps are acceptable. People harm each other—we have to see that, we have to be intelligent. All I'm saying is that alongside that acknowledgement of harm, we can try to understand one another. It's hard work, and it's heartbreaking. It's like you said—look at what we do to each other. But the important thing is to look. If you refuse even to look, then nothing will ever change. And our everyday life is not always murder and concentration camps, but if we stay awake we can have all sorts of small victories. Like you, realizing what you did to your old boyfriend—that's a moral victory, that's spiritual evolution. It makes you grow up and take responsibility and vow never to do the same thing again." He paused. "Did he really use Wite-Out?"

Madeline nodded. "Yep."

"Poor guy."

"I know, you don't have to tell me."

"Would you ever—would you ever consider getting back together with him?"

"Michael! Are you crazy? I feel bad for him, but I'm not going to sacrifice myself in order to make amends." She sighed. "I thought about writing him a letter, but he might misconstrue my meaning. It's weird, but I'm asking him for forgiveness on my own, silently. I feel like it helps. I only hope that one day he might understand me, and forgive me. And if he doesn't, well, at least I understand myself. It's so painful," she said, pushing away her empty salad bowl. "I mean, I think of all the fucked-up things I did in my life—all the times I hurt people, all the times I made a fool of myself, and all I want, all I really really want, is that when other people remember those things they don't think

'That Madeline Boot was a complete fuck-up' but rather 'Poor Madeline—she must have been in a lot of pain to do what she did.'"

"You can't control what others think," Michael said. "But if you do that for others, if you try to understand their pain—well, it's as I said, you're helping the world heal itself."

She smiled. "I suppose I am, aren't I? It's not easy. And I'm going to have to think about this Hitler thing very carefully. I'll read that book and then we can discuss it. Okay?"

"Okay."

The waitress set down their burritos; Madeline asked for a bowl of guacamole, and after the waitress brought it Madeline said timidly, "There's something else I realized."

"What's that?"

"I realized how precious it is when someone loves you. I mean, even if you can't return their love, you should respect it. That's why what I did to Bill was so bad—I was scornful of his love. And that's why what David did was bad—he said my love smothered him, and that made me feel like I was wrong to love him. But it wasn't my fault that I loved him—it was something beautiful, it was, it was a gift."

"You say you're 70% over him?"

"That's pretty good, isn't it? I mean, after four months. How long did it take you to get over your wife?"

"A long time. But now I'm, let's see—I'm 150% over her."

"Oh," Madeline laughed. "That much? I need a little more time for that."

"I think 90% is good enough."

"Good enough for what?"

"Good enough for starting something new. With someone else."

"I suppose so. Good burritos, huh?"

"Very good."

As they ate they spoke again about Madeline's recent experience of Merger, and Michael said that when he was in Nepal he also realized that he didn't have to retreat in order to have a spiritual life. Madeline knew that Michael had been to Nepal many times, and had actually lived there for a year and a half after college, but now for the first time he told her that after college he had gone to Nepal and had no intention of coming back; he had already honed his ideas about relieving suffering, and had decided that the best way to do this was by meditating constantly.

"Constantly?" she asked. "How constantly?"

"Well—constantly. As in all the time."

"Didn't you eat?"

"When I remembered. I got very thin, and my hair grew long. And I wasn't particularly clean, either."

"But Michael, you would look cool with long hair. You shouldn't have cut it."

"Well, cutting my hair was a symbol of my willingness to re-enter life. Or at least the Harvard Ph.D. program."

"What did your dad think of all this?"

"He was patient. And I'd already been accepted to graduate school, and since he was on the faculty he convinced them to hold a place for me. After a year he got a bit frustrated and he actually came to see me. We had a fight, a really big one. I told him he was trying to turn me into himself."

"Isn't that exactly what happened? I mean, you and your dad are like bookends."

Michael laughed. "That is exactly what happened. Oh well. But my translation work is different from his—he doesn't translate sutras. Anyway, in the long run I felt as you do, that I needed to be in the world. By teaching and translating I can help others. And myself."

"And me," she laughed. "You help me so much, Michael. But what I want to know is, who helps you?"

"My father. And a friend in Nepal—I write him letters. And Robert."

"Robert! Robert doesn't have a religious bone in his body."

"But he has a very good heart, and he's very logical. And he's a good listener. My background is Eastern language and philosophy, so it's good for me to hear another point of view."

"But is it good to hear about George Eliot?"

"Robert's love for George Eliot is one of the most admirable things about him. As is his love for your sister. Robert is one of the most loyal people I've ever met. And he's very loyal to you, you know; he loves you very much, you're like a daughter to him."

"I know. When I was at Barnard he used to help me with my homework. Can you imagine? My own father never did that."

"Can I tell you something?"

"Go ahead."

"All your experiences in the past months have really changed you. You're more mature. Even your face—you look older."

"Michael! You never tell a woman she looks older! You must be the only man on earth who doesn't know that."

"But I mean it as a compliment." She rolled her eyes. "Really. Your eyes, your mouth—it becomes you."

"Well—thanks. I guess it's like when you're really sick, you look different after."

"Something like that. Anyway—do you want dessert?"

"Of course I want dessert. Let's get the menus back."

"I think I saw coconut cake."

"That would make me so happy."

Yes, the waitress with the frizzy hair said, there was coconut cake. Michael ordered two pieces as well as tea, which he gracefully prepared for them. Madeline felt happy: the worst of the pain seemed to be over, and her revelation had not gone away when she talked about it. She still had a great deal to think about, that was for sure, but she was not afraid. No, she was not afraid at all.

CHAPTER 18

Alison Again

Madeline was in the TV room reading Aldous Huxley's novel *Antic Hay*. She had her feet up on the couch, her brow drawn, a finger pressed to her lower lip. Outside it was a fresh April day; she was still not able to write, so she spent the morning rereading Flannery O'Connor's essays *Mystery and Manners*, then she had gone on a walk to clear her head and think about what she read. Now she was back home, deeply engrossed in the novel.

The phone rang. She rose, still reading, then reluctantly put the book face-down on the couch and ran down the hall to the kitchen.

"Hello?" she said breathlessly.

"Madeline? It's Alison."

Madeline's stomach sank, and at the same time a thrill of excitement ran through her. The old world, David's world. "Hi Alison."

"I called you so many times, but you never called me back."

"Well…"

"You don't have to explain, I understand. But I'd really like to see you; I'd like to talk. Are you free this evening?"

No. She had yoga, then Scrabble. But she wanted to see Alison; it was something she had to do, some kind of postmortem of her relationship. And out of nowhere a wild hope arose: maybe Alison had a message from David! Maybe he felt sorry, maybe he wanted to get back together and was sending Alison to test the waters. A few days ago Madeline had told Michael that she was 70% over David, but in that wild moment of hope she was as much in love with him as ever.

"I'm free until about seven-thirty, then I have plans here."

"So why don't I meet you on my way home from work? Say, six o'clock?"

"Okay."

"Where should we meet?"

"How about Ben & Jerry's?"

Alison laughed. "So you remember my sweet tooth. Okay; see you then."

Madeline hung up the phone and drifted back into the TV room. She resumed her position on the couch and picked up her book, but instead of reading she lay the book across her chest, then covered her eyes with her palms. This is masochistic, she told herself. You shouldn't go see Alison. But she was curious about David and the band and how everyone was doing; it was so odd to know they were going on without her, still getting high at Hanson and Alison's apartment, still going to the Malibu Diner, still hanging out at clubs. She never saw any of them, and except for Jessie's phone call and almost running into Raller, there had been no contact at all. And she wanted a little contact, even though she knew it would hurt—because despite the moment of hope, Madeline knew in her heart that David wasn't coming back. He wouldn't send Alison to talk to her, it just wasn't his style. She sighed, and lifted the book from her chest. Well, I'm in for it now, she thought, her eyes refocusing on the page. I am most definitely in for it now.

At five minutes to six she was in the brightly lit store, sitting on a white chair in front of a small white table, digging her spoon into a hot fudge brownie sundae: a brownie, two scoops of Coffee Heath Bar Crunch, thick hot fudge, fresh whip cream, and wet walnuts. Never let it be said that Madeline did not know how to comfort herself; and as she took the first bite she felt armed and ready. When she first walked into the bright store she thought it was a bad place for a meeting: better a dim corner in some smoky bar where she could cry without making a scene. But as she ate she looked around at the cheerful colorful posters—cows, rainforests, Ben and Jerry's bearded smiling faces—and she felt protected, as if she were in a kindergarten. And there was a bathroom, so she had a place to run if she did start crying.

The door opened at quarter past six. Madeline looked up and there was Alison in a trench coat and sneakers, carrying a huge black leather purse. Her hair was in disarray, and her glasses looked foggy.

"Hi," Alison said, dumping her bag on a chair and wrestling off her trench coat. "I'm so sorry I'm late. Let me get something and I'll be right with you."

Alison strode over to the counter, and as she quizzed the counter girl about whether the low-fat ice cream was really low-fat, and which had less calories, the yogurt or the low-fat ice cream, Madeline examined Alison's clothes. Alison was wearing a suit, a real suit, cranberry colored with a skirt to the knees, a jacket, and a crisp white shirt. Just like an adult, Madeline marveled. So professional. But Alison was still Alison; as she set a huge banana split on the table she said to Madeline, "We should have smoked a joint, then this ice cream would really taste good."

"Oh, no," Madeline laughed, "because then I wouldn't have been able to stop."

"What did you have?" Alison asked, raising her eyebrows at Madeline's empty bowl.

"A hot fudge brownie sundae."

"I couldn't decide between that and a banana split, but as you see I got the banana split."

"With low-fat ice cream?"

"Oh, I finally said fuck all that. What good is ice cream if it has no fat? You want some?"

"No thanks, I'm full."

Alison piled a piece of banana, ice cream, and whip cream onto her spoon, then transferred the whole load into her mouth. As she chewed she studied Madeline. "You look different," she said finally. "Did you lose weight?"

"Actually I gained weight then lost it, so the answer's yes and no."

"It's something," Alison said, cocking her head. "Did you dye your hair?"

"No," she laughed. "Actually, a friend of mine told me I look older."

"Oooh, that hurts."

"It was meant as a compliment. Oh well, what can you do. Anyway—you look good. I never saw you in a suit before."

"Please. If anyone told me ten years ago I'd be wearing something like this I would have shot myself. It's from Burlington Coat Factory, only $35. You ever go over there? You should; everything's dirt cheap."

"I've passed it a million times on the bus but no, I've never stopped in. I'll have to go sometime."

Silence. Alison ate, and Madeline played with her empty sundae dish.

"So," Alison said. "I hear Jessie gave you a call."

"He sure did."

"He's still interested in seeing you. He told me just last week that if I ever saw you I should pass that on. So consider it passed on." Alison dug her spoon deep into her banana split and did not look at Madeline. "Would you ever consider going out with him? It would be fun having you around again; we miss you."

"Well," Madeline said lightly, "I make it a policy never to go out with anyone who's already asked out my sister."

"That's right, he did ask your sister out, didn't he?" Alison looked at her. "But I know that's not the real reason you won't go out with him."

"No," Madeline said. "I guess it's not."

"Madeline? I'm sorry. I'm really sorry for how David treated you."

Tears sprung into Madeline's eyes; she took a napkin from the black dispenser and dabbed her eyes. "I guess," she said, her voice shaking, "I guess I still don't really understand what happened."

"How could you? You didn't know David that well."

"And what should I have known?"

"Well, for starters, the fact that David is the master of the three-month relationship."

"What do you mean?"

"Madeline, I've known David for eight years, and in all that time he's never ever gone out with a woman longer than three months."

"You're kidding."

"Nope. We even time him, and I can tell you, it's never a day over three months."

"But—I wish you had told me. I wish *someone* had told me."

Alison smiled sadly. "And if I had? What would you have thought? 'Oh, there goes Hanson's bitchy girlfriend, interfering in our relationship'? It wasn't my place to tell you. Usually we don't let ourselves get attached to David's girlfriends, but with you it was different, we really liked you. And maybe it would have worked out differently—he did ask you to move in, after all."

"I wish he hadn't," Madeline said bitterly. "If we had just broken up, okay, but to get all excited about moving in and then having to move out again." She sighed. "But I can't blame him entirely; I could have said no."

"Well, David is extremely persuasive when he wants something. He would have hounded you until you did what he wanted."

"Still—I should have known better."

"Don't be so hard on yourself. David is very charismatic; it's no accident he's in the business he's in."

"How is the band, anyway?"

"Great. They're up in Bearsville, New York recording their new album. They should be back in a week or so."

"Oh." Madeline frowned and looked at her hands.

"Don't be sad, Madeline. Look—what can I tell you? David is probably the most ambitious person you'll ever meet. He doesn't have the emotional resources to have a real relationship—all his energy goes into his music."

"But he needs to have sex, right? So he gets involved for a little bit, then gets out before things get serious. Am I right?"

"Well." Alison lifted her hands. "He does like women. Especially blondes."

"I thought so." Madeline closed her eyes. "Why didn't I see it? Everyone else did, but not me."

"He did love you, Madeline. In his way. In fact, I would say he loved you more than any of his girlfriends. Certainly more than this new one."

This new one? Alison might as well have dumped a bucket of ice onto Madeline's head. "He's seeing someone?" she managed to say.

"Yes. But God, don't be jealous, not for a moment. She's a total lush; in fact the first time she came to our place she got drunk and threw up in the bathroom. It won't last."

"How long—how long have they been going out?"

"About a month."

"You say this woman drinks—but you know, David doesn't like it when people drink a lot."

"Oh, I know. And that's exactly why it won't last; the whole relationship is programmed to destruct. David always picks women like that. Except for you; you were different. Which is why we thought it might work out. And you know, we bug him about you now and then, but he doesn't seem interested in getting back together. Sorry to say."

"He's never even called me. Not even once, just to say hello. We were living together, we were totally in love—or so I thought—and then, boom. Nothing."

"Well, that's David—he gets really cold and abrupt, and he just drops people. He gets scared, I think, but that's still no excuse."

"But I remember with The Big Record Label—when we were coming home from the VP's house David was crying in my arms because he didn't want to hurt Plug and Jessie."

"Madeline, that was about the band. Band is family, and everyone else is just in the way. How do you think they've managed to come so far?"

"But you know, you can be good at what you do and still be human, you can still have relationships. Like my brother-in-law—he's very successful in his field, but he also loves my sister. And me." And Michael was another example, but Alison didn't know him so Madeline did not mention him.

"I agree. But we're talking about David and Hanson, and that's just how they are. Look, you're ambitious about your writing, I know that, but your ambition can't even begin to touch theirs. And there's two of them, so they just feed off each other."

"I just understood something," Madeline said slowly. "I just understood that I never had a chance with David. He's married to Hanson, isn't he?"

Alison nodded. "I managed to squeeze in there alongside them but yes, you're right—the real relationship is between the two of them. There's nothing sexual going on, mind you, it's just that they do something for each other. I don't know—they stimulate each other creatively, and I suppose that's the biggest turn on there is." She shrugged. "Women come second. And there's lots of us around."

Madeline tapped a finger against her lip. There was something she desperately wanted to ask Alison, but she didn't know if it was her place. Oh well, she thought. What the hell.

"Tell me, Alison—what do *you* get out of all this? I mean, your relationship with Hanson, with someone who will always put his work before you and will always want you to put your work second? If that's not too personal a question to ask."

"Not at all—I ask myself that all the time. But I know the answer: it's that from the time I was a small child I swore I would never, ever get stuck in some godforsaken suburb. I've always wanted something—I don't know, for lack of a better word I'll say glamorous. A certain kind of life, with a certain kind of people. Being with Hanson will get me there." She shrugged. "It sounds cold, but it's the truth; I can't dress it up for you."

"No, I appreciate your honesty… But tell me, what kind of life? What kind of people? I mean, people like those snobby A&R men? Or the VP? I mean, he was nice, and he's rich, but other than his house I didn't really envy him."

"It's a beautiful house, isn't it?" Alison said wistfully.

"So you've been?"

"A couple times. But at least I got fed better than you did."

Madeline laughed. "All that money and they feed me seaweed. But seriously, Alison—you've got so much talent, and I'd hate to see it go to waste. You've got to fight for your work, you've got to fight for the time to do it. Look—I'm not an expert on art, but I really liked your pictures; I've never seen anything quite like them. It would be a pity if no one ever saw them."

"I understand what you're saying, Madeline, and I appreciate it. And my work *is* important to me. But I want a certain kind of lifestyle, and Hanson's music will get me there faster than my painting." She sighed. "In my way I guess I'm every bit as ambitious as Hanson and David. Which is why we all get along. Don't get me wrong—I love Hanson. But I probably wouldn't have stuck it out with him if we didn't have the same goal. And that goal is Narrow Grave's success."

"But your work!"

"I know. I know. And one day I'll get back to it. Believe me, when Hanson does finally make it big and we have a house like the VP's I'm not going to sit around having babies and eating tofu. Then I'll get back to my painting. Until then—" she smiled resignedly—"we have to keep fighting to get there."

Madeline nodded. She felt the familiar feeling of scorn arising, but this time she caught it, and she asked herself: Why? Why do you despise women who sacrifice themselves for their men? While reading Aldous Huxley's biography she wanted to scream every time she read about his wife Maria's perpetual sacrifices—Maria had actually found lovers for Huxley, and even selected presents for them! And when the Huxleys lived in California Maria often listed her occupation as "Driver" because that's what she did all day, she chauffeured the Great Man. So Madeline, she asked herself as Alison took her banana split to the counter and asked for more whip cream, have you no compassion for these women? Have you no compassion for their lack of confidence, their lack of boundaries? And can't you remember how David's success was so seductive, and how much you enjoyed walking into a room and having everyone stare at you? Looking at David, mostly, but also looking at you? If you didn't have Bella and Robert encouraging you, if you hadn't had your teacher, where would *you* be today? Hmm, she thought. Hmm.

Alison put her freshly whip-creamed banana split on the table. "I had to pay a quarter, can you imagine? Help me out with this, I can't finish it alone."

"Well, if you insist."

As they ate Alison asked Madeline what she had been doing the past months. Madeline didn't tell Alison about the hours she had logged on the couch; she simply said it had been a bit hard getting back on her feet again, but with the support of family and friends she had managed. She also told Alison about Yoga for Women, and Alison was enthusiastic; she said maybe she would come someday. And then Alison asked about Madeline's writing. "Are you working on something?" she asked.

Madeline shook her head. "No. Actually, writing's been a bit difficult since David and I broke up."

"Now it's my turn to lecture you: don't let what happened with David interfere with your work. It would be a shame if you let it get you down so much."

"I guess it really shook my confidence, getting dumped like that."

"You need a new boyfriend. Are you seeing anyone?"

"No."

"What about Jessie? He really likes you, Madeline. I mean, I know he's a
flirt, but he'd like to settle down. He told me he really envied David, having a
nice woman like you to come home to. Just give him a chance and you'll see; in
time you won't even notice David, he'll just be another person in the band."

"Oh, Alison, it's really sweet of you, but I can't. It would be too—I don't
know, too pathetic."

"I disagree. It's not pathetic to take a chance with a man who likes you. You
need to get back into action. And it would be fun hanging out again; I'm all
alone with these men all the time, I need a woman around."

"There's David's new girlfriend."

"That drunk? Please. Anyway, she's only good for two more months. So will
you think it over?"

"There's nothing to think over. I can't imagine dating Jessie. Sorry."

They talked a little longer, then Alison said she had to get home and call
Hanson—a reporter had called, and Hanson and David needed to know about
it. Outside Ben and Jerry's Madeline and Alison hugged each other, and as Alison walked away—her step determined, her large purse swinging out at pass-
ers-by—Madeline wondered if she would ever see her again. Probably not; and
suddenly she felt sad. But otherwise, she thought, turning and heading towards
home, I'm fine. I'm just fine. In fact, I can't believe how fine I am. Here Alison
tells me all this bad stuff about David and here I am, walking down Washington Street, feeling just fine. It's strange that I'm so fine, she thought, tears welling up in her eyes. It's really so strange. And by the time she was at Seventh and
Washington she was crying in earnest. Oh fuck! she thought. Not again; no
more crying.

She ducked down Seventh Street and turned onto Bloomfield; she plunked
herself down on the nearest brownstone stoop, put her head on her knees, and
cried in earnest. She couldn't help it: the idea of David with someone else, even
if she was a drunk, made her half-crazy with jealousy. Surely the woman went
to his apartment, surely they had sex in the same bed where she and David had
had sex so many times. David was 150% over Madeline, that was for sure. And
learning about David's inability to have a relationship longer than three
months—if only she had known! If only Spencer or someone had told her! But

I probably wouldn't have believed them anyway, she thought. I wanted a boy-friend, and I wanted to be in love; after a certain point I wanted that boyfriend to be David, and then there was no turning back. But she should have known. She should have gone slower, should have asked more questions, should have understood that a person who is always stoned has problems. But he was so handsome, so charming, and he had a way of looking at her that made her feel special and beautiful and sexy—and then when he stopped looking at her, all those feelings went away. But remember Beverly, she told herself. Remember being a hero, a warrior. You don't need him if you want to feel special; you don't need his eyes in order to see yourself. What was it that Michael had said? "You think your happiness depends on him, but it doesn't." And it really doesn't, she told herself. It really, truly doesn't.

But she still felt horrible.

Suddenly a well-dressed young woman with a briefcase stood in front of Madeline; obviously she wanted to get into her building. "I'm sorry," Madeline said, rising hastily.

"Are you okay?"

"I'm fine," she said, shoving her hands into her jacket pockets. "I just needed to—you know."

The woman looked at Madeline sympathetically. "Honey, believe me, I know."

Madeline smiled and hurried down Bloomfield. Then her step slowed; God, she felt awful. Her chest felt as if someone had pummeled it, and her eyes had that familiar stretched swollen feeling. By the time she arrived at the apartment she was crying again. She didn't want to burden the others, so when she came in she walked past the laughing voices in the living room, went into her room, and shut the door. She threw herself on the bed and, tucked into the fetal posi-tion, had a good cry.

Then someone knocked. Slowly. She raised her head, and watched as the door opened and Michael came into the room.

"Hi," she said weakly.

"Hello, Madeline." He handed her a box of tissues, then sat on the edge of the bed. "Obviously something has happened?"

She nodded. And, haltingly, she told him about her meeting with Alison, and what Alison had told her about David. "And I know, I know I said I was 70% over him, and that might even have risen to 72%, but this still kind of caught me off guard."

"It's only normal you'd be upset," he said sympathetically. "It's like a slap in the face, isn't it."

"It's like a hundred slaps in the face. I feel so jealous I could kill both of them."

"Well, why don't you come out and play Scrabble instead? It'll do you good."

"I can't," she sniffed. "I'm too busy being miserable."

"Well," he said gently. "I'd really love to see you and Robert fight. I had a hard day myself; I could use a little cheering up."

"You?! You never have hard days."

"Of course I do."

"What happened?"

"Mmm—one of the professors in my department said some rather harsh things about my new sutra. It was all from jealousy, but still, it was hard to hear."

"Wow. I'm sorry, Michael. It's still going to get published, isn't it?"

"Oh, of course. In fact just today one of the editors at Columbia University Press told me they'd like to see it in a few weeks—they're quite excited about it. But in our department it's customary to let people see what you're doing and this one man—I still can't believe what he said."

"Let's go to his house and let all the air out of his tires."

Michael smiled. "He lives in an apartment, and he takes the subway. But the point is, I need you to cheer me up, so why don't you come out and join us?"

"I may start crying again."

"I'll take that chance."

But she didn't cry; and while in the middle of a fierce argument with Robert about whether he had given her only four minutes on the timer, she suddenly remembered David, and her heart sank. But Robert was sitting across from her, tapping his fingers, demanding she apologize for questioning his ethics, so she had to put David aside and go on with the life taking place before her.

CHAPTER 19

Another Surprise

One good thing came out of Madeline's conversation with Alison: she started writing again.

The morning after the meeting at Ben and Jerry's Madeline was laying in bed crying when suddenly she sat up and shouted "Enough!" The empty apartment rang with her cry; she wouldn't have been surprised if someone on the street had heard her. Then she said it more quietly: "Enough." She was tired of mourning David—she had to get on with her life. She jumped out of bed, took a shower, put on her favorite jeans and a long-sleeved red T-shirt of Robert's that she had long coveted, then marched back into her room, made her bed, propped up her pillows, sat down cross-legged and placed her lapdesk on her knees. She grabbed the pen and pad of paper laying on top of her typewriter.

"Okay, Madeline," she said. "Write."

So she wrote. Not about anything in particular; in fact all she did was write a detailed description of her room, and then spent nearly an hour trying to describe her writing teacher's face. But when she was done she felt different; she felt, for the first time in oh so long, emotionally balanced.

The next day was the same, except she described Bella and Robert's faces, then wrote about the women in her yoga class. On the third day she had a breakthrough: it was a Saturday, Bella and Robert were in the living room drinking coffee and reading, Madeline was in her room writing about the waiting room at her temp agency when suddenly she heard the words, "I want a man." She stopped writing, and frowned; where had she heard that? She thought a moment, then—yes, that's what she said to Devon the night she met Billy Ray Bonner. That would be a good first line for a story, she thought. She wrote it down, and then she was off; her pen raced over the pages, and soon she was ripping completed sheets off the pad and putting them facedown on her typewriter. At one point Bella knocked on the door and said that she and Robert were going out for lunch, did Madeline want to come? "I'm writing," Madeline called out, not removing her eyes from the page; then before she knew it the apartment door opened, Bella and Robert's voices filled the air, and the spell snapped. She put down the pen, and as she massaged her fingers she read through the twenty or so pages she had written. The beginning was shaky, there were many awkward sentences, but the story held together; and more, the story was funny, the first funny story she had ever written.

She spent the next two weeks rewriting. Usually she took longer for revisions, but the story was surprisingly well-structured despite the fact that she had not written an outline or any notes beforehand. And she had another reason for finishing quickly: she was anxious to read it to the others, and once finals started Robert and Michael would not have a free afternoon to sit and listen. She wanted to send the story out to magazines as soon as possible, and she also wanted to begin a story about Bill Baker, a.k.a. The Virgin. In fact that was the title she had selected for the story: "The Virgin." And after that? She had so much material! College, Hoboken, all her word processing jobs, her time at Swan's Cove, her relationship with David—it would take years to work though all that, by which time she would have even more experiences. She was excited, and it showed: she flew around the house, flew to her temp jobs, flew to Yoga for Women. A new well of creativity had opened up, and she remembered something that the Greek writer Costas Taxtsis had written. She had read Taxtsis' short story collection "The Change" at least ten times because she was so in awe of his perfect, painfully honest short stories about a childhood surrounded by unstable adults; and yet in one of his essays he wrote that he was unable to write much about his adult years because it was easier to write about the time when he had not been responsible for what happened to him. And so it was with Madeline: she had never been able to break away from her childhood. She had documented so many sad painful memories—hers and Bella's—and if she wanted she could do so still. But now she had leapt into her adult years, and had honestly described what *she* had done, not just what Polly and Spam had done to her; and maybe, just maybe, this was the first step towards freeing herself from Polly and Spam. She never spoke to them, and rarely thought of them except when she was writing, but that was external distance. Now for the first time the distance was internal; now for the first time she had a hint of true freedom.

The reading was scheduled for the last Sunday in April. The weather was perfect—blue skies, fluffy white clouds, fresh breezes flowing through half-open windows. It was four o'clock, and Bella, Robert, and Michael were sitting in the living room, waiting.

"This story is different," Madeline said by way of introduction. "Which means Bella won't have to cry."

"But I'm ready to cry," Bella said.

"But you won't."

Madeline read. She knew that Robert would be scandalized by the story, and sure enough she noticed his ears turning red as the plot unfolded. George Eliot had never picked up a man in the Columbia Pub, after all. But Bella and Michael laughed frequently, and when Madeline finished she put the last page facedown on the piano and, eyes bright, cheeks flushed, said "Well?"

"Madeline," Bella said, rising up and hugging her. "That was the best thing you've ever written. And it was so funny! You should always write funny things; forget about Polly and Spam."

"I'm trying to. Robert?"

Robert sighed. His earlobes were quite pink, and his features were twisted in pain. "It was really—descriptive, wasn't it?"

"You always say I should be more descriptive."

"Yes, but not about—"

"Sex?" she supplied.

"It's rather—indelicate, don't you think?"

"Robert, how can you have that attitude and at the same time be married to Bella, who has the foulest mouth in the universe?"

Bella laughed. "Are you kidding me? Robert loves my foul mouth."

Robert shot her a warning look.

"Don't let his red ears fool you," Bella went on. "Repressed people are always the ones who are wildest about sex. I mean, look at the Victorians, they had the best pornography of anyone."

"Bella," Robert said. "Would you please, please stop? Please?"

Bella rolled her eyes. "Oh Robert—you're such a prude. So tell us, Michael, wasn't Maddy's story great?"

Michael was sitting with his legs crossed, one arm resting along the back of the couch. He smiled at the two sisters. "It was wonderful. Really wonderful."

Madeline grinned happily; Bella put her arm around her and said, "See? It's unanimous. Well, almost unanimous. Robert?" she said threateningly.

"Okay," Robert relented. "It was good. So what are we going to do about dinner?"

"Oooh, I don't feel like cooking! Let's order a pizza. With eggplant and garlic."

"And I can go buy ice cream," Michael said. "Madeline? Would you like to come with me to Ben and Jerry's?"

"Sure." She collected her story and put it in its folder. "Let me just put this away and get my sunglasses."

As they were walking out of Ben and Jerry's, each carrying freezer bags with two pints of ice cream, Michael said, "Why don't we walk home through Stevens' campus?"

"But won't the ice cream melt?"

"Mmm—these bags are pretty secure, I think we can make it."

"Well, okay. If you want." They crossed the street and walked on Fourth Street over to Stevens Park. The park was full of children and parents and colorful clothes and screams of laughter, and as Madeline and Michael walked through the park she felt a fluttering lightness in her chest. She was happy not to be depressed, and she was happy to be writing again.

"You know, Michael," she said as they walked through the empty parking lot on the edge of the Stevens' campus, "my story was based on a real incident."

"That's what I assumed."

"Does that shock you?"

"Shock me?" He laughed. "No. You and Bella have always been very forthcoming about—well, about—"

"Being reformed sluts?"

He looked at her and smiled. "Yes, about that. And anyway, we all do things we're not proud of."

"Not you."

"Yes, me. Of course I've done stupid things in my life."

"But not recently."

"No, not recently. But I'm forty years old; I've had a great deal of time to straighten out."

"I can't believe you were ever crooked to begin with."

"No, I suppose I wasn't very."

They walked up the steep pedestrian path, and when they were by the administration building Michael suggested they sit on one of the benches overlooking the Hudson River.

"Are you sure?" Madeline said. "I'm a little worried about this ice cream."

"The ice cream is fine."

But all the benches were filled with families, Stevens students, and kids from Hoboken High. Madeline and Michael walked on the small lawn behind the administration building, and there on the lawn was a small path leading to a white marble bench. They sat, and Madeline took a worried peek into her bag. She reached in and felt the sides of the ice cream containers; frozen, but a little soft in places. She sighed; Michael was so slow there was no telling how long he would need to sit here.

They sat in silence for what seemed a very long time. Madeline was just about to suggest they leave when Michael suddenly asked her if she was still in love with David.

"In love with David?" she repeated. She stuck out her lower lip. "No. Yes. A little, maybe. I don't know—why?"

"I was just wondering," he said.

"It's pretty obvious he doesn't want to see me. I mean, he never even called me, not once."

Michael looked at her, and said nothing.

"To David I was like a lemon," she said, shoving her sunglasses on top of her head. "He squeezed out the juice, and when he was done he threw me away." She wrapped her arms around her stomach and sighed.

"I'm sorry," Michael said. "I didn't mean to upset you."

"Actually," she said decisively, "I don't love David anymore. I could never love someone who treated me like that. I mean, I did love someone who treated me like that, but I don't anymore. Love him, that is." She looked at Michael. "And what about you and Patty?" she asked shyly. "It didn't work out?"

"I knew it wouldn't."

"But why? What was the problem?"

"It was the same problem I had with all the women your sister set me up with."

"And what was that?"

He turned and looked her straight in the eye. "The problem was, they weren't you."

Madeline stared at him. She drew her eyebrows together and moved her head back a little. Had Michael just said what she thought he said? No—it was impossible. She cocked her head and looked at him; his expression was composed and serious, and he was still looking directly into her eyes. Which meant— Madeline felt all the blood drain from her face. She opened her mouth to speak, then shut it. For the first time in her life, Madeline was absolutely speechless.

They sat like that some time, Michael continuing to look at Madeline, and Madeline opening and closing her mouth like a guppy.

"Well," Michael said finally. "Shall we go? I think the ice cream is starting to melt."

They walked through campus and down Ninth Street, and all the time Madeline kept sneaking glances at Michael. Had he really said—? Did he really mean—? Michael never said something if he didn't mean it. Never. So that meant— But no, she told herself. It can't be. It just can't.

She waited for him to resume talking, to give details, but he just walked slowly, lightly gripping the bag of ice cream. As usual he was in khakis and a white button-down shirt, as usual his sandy hair was smooth, and his handsome features calm. He was just Michael, just plain old ordinary upstairs neighbor Michael, but she felt scared, as if he had just said "I'm Ted Bundy, and you're my next victim." She began to sweat profusely; Michael noticed, and offered her a handkerchief which she stoutly refused. Then when they arrived at 821 she dropped her keys twice while trying to open the door. The third time Michael picked up the keys and opened the door himself. He handed her the keys and she muttered, "Thanks." Once inside the building she raced up the stairs, but she caught herself at the second landing; there was no need to be rude. She waited, listening in despair as Michael's quiet, measured steps came up the stairwell; and then there he was, walking towards her. She looked at her bag of ice cream furiously, and when he was beside her she resumed walking, slower this time, but still not looking at him.

At the apartment door she didn't bother with her keys; she pounded on the door until she heard Bella's voice. "All right, all right! Why don't you use your keys, that's what they're—Madeline!" Bella said when she opened the door. "You are white as a sheet! Did something happen?"

"I was thinking about Ted Bundy," she said weakly.

Bella shot her a look. "You are so fucking weird. Give me that ice cream; the pizza'll be here in a minute. Honestly, Maddy, are you okay? Did you run into David or something? Michael, you tell me."

"We didn't see anybody," Michael said simply.

"Not even Ted Bundy? Oh, Madeline—you have such an active imagination. Ted Bundy's in jail, anyhow. Isn't that right, Robert?" she called out. "Ted Bundy hasn't been executed yet, has he?"

The pizza came a few minutes later, and in between the bustle of setting the table and cutting the pizza and accusing Robert of stealing cheese off her slice, Madeline calmed down. And as she sat and chewed, listening to Robert and Michael discuss the war between the locals and yuppies in Hoboken, Madeline decided that she had misheard Michael. He hadn't said, "The problem was, they weren't *you*"; he had said "They weren't *true*" or maybe some word like "mu" or "kru" or "gu." Michael had a large vocabulary, after all; he had just used some word she didn't know, some word like "chateaux" that had a lot of letters but was short when you pronounced it. Michael was not the type to slip in foreign words to sound impressive, but maybe just this once he had succumbed to temptation and said something in Japanese or Chinese—or, hey, maybe even Sanskrit—and she, like a big dumbbell, had misunderstood. Yes, that must be what happened; there was no other explanation.

So she relaxed, and she even laughed at a story Michael told about a letter he read in *The Hoboken Reporter*, and she didn't even mind when he looked at her and smiled. He probably thought she was so silly, not saying a word the entire walk home! She was embarrassed, and to atone for her sins she cheerfully agreed when Michael suggested they play Scrabble. They cleared off the table; Bella went to the piano to play Mozart, and Madeline, Robert, and Michael sat down to play. They played without interruption for almost a half hour, and then the phone rang. Robert had just put down a word, and as he rose to get the phone he said, "Your turn, Madeline; be sure to set the timer."

The minute Robert was in the hall Madeline slid her letters in front of Michael. He stared at them for, as usual, a long time, but the sound of Italian pouring from the kitchen meant Robert was talking to his mother or father and so would be on the phone a long time.

"Here," Michael said, slowly rearranging her letters. "You can put them in front of the 'n' over there."

"'Lepton?'" she said. "What does that mean?"

She looked up at him, and he looked at her. It was the same way he always looked at her, the way he had been looking at her for years—there was a soft light in his green eyes, and in the midst of this softness a directness, an intensity, even. She stared back at him, and in that moment she saw the truth, and try as she might she could not misinterpret it.

Michael was in love with her.

"It means," he said, "a class of subatomic particles. They interact weakly."

"Oh. Well—thanks." Hands shaking, she put the letters on the board. She took new letters, then folded her hands and studied them furiously. She snuck a glance at Michael; he was looking at his own letters. *Slow*, she thought. There he goes, being slow again. He must have felt her looking because he turned his head, but she whipped her head back and stared at her letters.

Michael still had not put down a word by the time Robert came back.

"I was on the phone at least ten minutes!" Robert said. "Which means it should be my turn. Didn't you set the timer?"

"It just ran out," Madeline said.

"Oh—I really believe you, Madeline. What word did you put down?"

"Over there. 'Lepton.'"

"'Lepton?'" Robert raised an eyebrow.

"It's a class of subatomic particles. You don't believe it's a real word?"

"Oh, I'm sure it's a real word. I'm just wondering how you happen to know it."

"Why, Robert! As a writer my knowledge is vast and wide."

"Hmpf."

"Which means?"

"Which means, Madeline, I wonder if you've been cheating."

"Excuse me—did I hear my name and the word 'cheating' in the same sentence? I must say, Robert, I am gravely offended."

"I wouldn't put it past you to crack open the dictionary when I'm out of the room."

"That is a vicious accusation."

And so on. Madeline managed to finish the game without once looking at Michael, but when they had finished and were waiting in the living room for Bella to bring out the ice cream, her glance happened to intersect his and there they were again, those green eyes full of love.

"Madeline!" Bella said as she set down the bowls. "I want you to go to the bathroom and take a look at yourself! I have never seen you so pale. Robert, Michael, look at her lips—they're *grey*. Something is wrong with you, Madeline."

"I'm fine," she said weakly.

"You don't look fine. Maybe you should lay down."

"Well—maybe I should. I'll just finish my ice cream and go."

"Go now and eat it in bed. I'm afraid if you sit up you'll pass out."

So Madeline rose and, clutching her bowl of ice cream, hurriedly left the room. As she was closing her door to a small crack she heard Bella say to Michael, "Are you *sure* you guys didn't run into David? Maybe she saw him and you didn't..."

Madeline decided to shut the door completely, claustrophobia or not. She needed to be alone, and safe. She put the bowl of ice cream on top of her typewriter, and laid on her bed to think.

Michael was in love with her.

How could he be in love with her, and how could she not know it? She thought back to the first time she saw him, when she was sitting on the couch admiring his good looks and thinking he would be nice to have as an upstairs neighbor; he had turned to look at her and—she hadn't liked him. Something in his look put her off. And she remembered how Bella had called her into the dining room to meet him ("This is my little sister Madeline, she lives with us"), and how Bella made coffee and brought out cookies, and then Robert, Bella, and Michael discussed the apartment. Afterwards the conversation turned general, and one moment Michael turned to her and asked what she did. "I write," she said snottily. He continued to ask her questions; she had not been particularly friendly, either then or in weeks to come, but then one day Michael asked if he could see some of her stories. She thought a moment, then agreed—but her motives were less than pure, she knew he was published and she thought maybe he would have some contacts. She gave him a few stories, then two weeks later he came by when Robert and Bella were out, and they talked about her work for hours. His comments were so incisive, his criticism so delicately phrased, that gradually he won her over; she dropped her snotty attitude, and in no time was clutching her hands together and, eyes shining, telling him how she started writing in grammar school, how she loved writing more than anything, and how she felt when her first short story was published. Michael listened carefully; he encouraged her in her dreams, and said that whenever she wanted she could show him her work. Then he suggested a few books, and that led to her going with him to his apartment, the first time she went there with him alone. She saw so many books she wanted to read, and at one point as she was sitting on a beautiful rug, a pile of books in her lap, she suddenly thought: But I'm in Michael's apartment, and I don't like him. She looked up at him; he was standing with a book in his hands, looking at the shelves. He was so mild and harmless, just a typical distracted professor—she decided he wasn't so bad after all, and might be nice as a friend. And he had been awfully nice about her writing. So that must have been the moment their friendship really started.

And after that? Well, they had gone to see Krishnamurti together, and then went regularly to talks at Columbia and other places in The City. Plus he was at their apartment almost every day to play Scrabble or see Robert. And in all that time she had never imagined that he was in love with her. He was always kind and respectful and polite; it never occurred to her that those things meant love. And he never touched her, or tried to touch her, or talked about touching her; other than accidental brushings of their hands while playing Scrabble or sitting on the bus—the kind of thing that could happen with anyone—he never touched her. When she was sad about David he took her hand, and when she was sad about Bella he took her elbow, and then there was that time walking home from the Japanese restaurant when she took his arm—but did any of that mean love? And in the months since her breakup with David, nothing had really changed: she still saw him every night for Scrabble, and they still did things in The City. And then today, out of the blue, he said what he said at Stevens, and then tonight when she saw the way he looked at her—and it was the way he always looked at her—she understood that he loved her. She was very puzzled; it was a new, crucial piece of information that was not new at all. It had always been there. So how had she missed it? How had Bella and Robert missed it? And now that she knew, she couldn't unknow it; Michael was in love with her.

She took one of her pillows and put it over her head. She couldn't *bear* it if Michael loved her; she just couldn't bear it. He was so— It would be so— She couldn't put it into words, but she just couldn't bear it. Flickers of joy started to spread through her, but then she pushed them away. She couldn't accept Michael's love; it was too much love, somehow. And if she loved him back it would mean—why, it would mean growing up. It would mean creating a family, and for her family meant Polly and Spam and all that was suffocating and painful and wrong. But Madeline, a sensible voice inside her said. You also have your family with Bella and Robert. It was an entirely different kind of family, a family loving, stable, and warm. And for the past years Michael had been part of all that; he was always so steady and kind, and he was always so supportive—so *enamored*—of everything she did. So what more do you want? the sensible voice asked. What more could you possibly want?

Madeline rolled onto her side. Michael was a good man, there was no use denying it. She thought about the hundreds of evenings—and there were literally hundreds—that he sat by her side while they played Scrabble. And then it struck her: Scrabble. Scrabble! Oh, Madeline, she thought. You are such a dummy. Do you really think Michael came to the apartment night after night just to play Scrabble? The man had a Ph.D. from Harvard, was fluent in Japanese, Chinese, Sanskrit, and Nepali—playing Scrabble was the only thing he could think to do every evening? Oh God, she thought, putting the pillow over her head again. He came because he wanted to see *me*. And why, for that matter, had she played so much Scrabble? Before Michael came she and Robert had played once, maybe twice a week, but otherwise she had a number of things she could have been doing. It dawned on her that she played Scrabble because she liked being with Michael. It was nice being around someone who loved her, although she had never thought of it that way until now. Only Robert was truly interested in the game, but for her and Michael it was some kind of elaborate courtship ritual, a safe way to spend time together.

But it's not like I *love* him, she thought. He was her friend, obviously, a very good friend, but—love? A relationship? Sex? Sex with *Michael*? Oh no—it was unthinkable. She couldn't even begin to imagine it. And anyway she had been in love with David. But Madeline, the sensible voice said. Even during the three months you were with David you still saw Michael almost every day. In rain, cold, and snow you trudged over from Willow Terrace to 821 Washington. You did all that just for Scrabble? But I loved David! she told the voice. I know I loved David. You did, the voice said. But you never lost Michael. If you had lost him—if he had moved, or gotten serious with Patty—you most definitely would have noticed.

Patty. *Patty*. Madeline had hated the fact that Michael went out with Patty. And when Bella said they were no longer dating, Madeline felt so relieved. And when had Michael stopped seeing Patty? Why, when David and Madeline broke up.

It was like a big puzzle; in the beginning all the pieces were in chaos, but now every piece she grabbed fit in with the others, the pattern was emerging, and there were less and less loose ends. The more she thought about it, the more she saw that although Michael had never said he loved her, he had nevertheless told her so with everything he did.

Suddenly she sat bolt upright: the letter! The letter Michael had written her from Japan!

She threw her pillow to the floor, ran to her closest and—where was it?—there, in the back corner, the old shoeboxes where she kept letters. The one on top had the most recent letters; she grabbed it and brought it to her bed. She emptied the box onto the bed and flicked through the letters. There: a heavy cream envelope. She sat back on the bed and took out the thick letter. The first pages were about meditation and her problems—she skimmed over them and then, yes, the last part:

"Most important of all, Madeline, you must not be so hard on yourself. You are such a lovely person; you are sweet and talented and intelligent and funny and, your best quality of all, you have an inner purity, a radiant goodness. I think it is this last quality that you are really trying to bring to blossom through all of your meditation and spiritual searching, but I must tell you that this goodness of yours is obvious for those who are sensitive to such things. You have a pure, natural spirituality, a clear preference for what is good and true and beautiful, and this quality is so attractive and wonderful. You needn't spend your time trying to eliminate the parts of yourself that you don't like; instead you should focus on loving yourself exactly as you are. I think if you do this you will find that you are extremely lovable."

After that he told her the date of his return, and promised to call her as soon as he came home. Which he did. And then, as if for the first time although it wasn't the first time, she noticed how he signed the letter: "With greatest affection." And what was the greatest affection? Love. The greatest affection was love.

She held the letter next to her chest, and with her free hand put the pillow back over her head. And how had she reacted when she received this letter? When the Federal Express man handed it to her and she saw it was from Michael? She had been *disappointed*. Dark red shame spread from her belly up into her chest; the heat spread to her head, and she felt her cheeks burn. Michael had, in as discreet a manner as possible, poured out his heart to her, and although she had liked the letter, although it had helped her, she still wished it was from an editor. Well, that would be her secret; she would never tell Michael or anyone how she had felt. It wasn't quite as bad as what she did to Bill Baker, but it was in the same spirit: she was incapable of recognizing when someone loved her, and as a result she hurt people. It was as if she didn't want to know when someone loved her, or as if she couldn't believe it. Yes, that was it: she couldn't believe it, and she didn't know how to accept it. Anyone who had taken a psychology class could tell her this was because of Polly and Spam's emotional battering, but okay, it was time to pass that, time to grow up and not be scared. And that's how she felt: scared. Terrified. Unable to accept the beautiful gift being offered. With that first look Michael had offered her love. It was as if he held out a precious jewel, a sparkling emerald large and perfectly cut, held it out to her and said, "Here, this is for you." It blinded her;

she had covered her eyes and turned away. And in response he stood exactly where he was, patiently holding the jewel, waiting for her to take it. In time she had opened her fingers a little; she could stand the light if she shielded herself against it. Over the years she had stepped closer, opened her eyes a little more, and eventually she had taken down her hands altogether. And now after three years, it was time to take the jewel.

But she couldn't. She was scared.

But why be scared? Why, when Michael loved her in such a gentle, sweet way?

Because— Because— The only answer she could come up with was, Because it felt weird. No one had ever loved her this way before. Bella loved her in a motherly smothering way, Robert loved her in a gruff-unable-to-express-himself way, but Michael loved her gently and sweetly. He really is a wonderful man, she thought, taking the pillow off her head. He was a good man; and whereas David was probably the most calculating person Madeline had ever met, Michael was completely at harmony with himself and the world. So what the fuck was my problem all these years? she asked herself. And she remembered: the problem was, Michael was slow. She had held back realizing all of his good qualities by her perpetual indictment: Michael was slow. But rejecting Michael for being slow was like rejecting a beautiful spread of sushi because the pile of ginger was slightly askew. It was illogical. Stupid, even. Or, the sensible voice said, just the kind of thing someone would do if they were afraid. And you, Madeline, are afraid. So he takes ten minutes to drop a dollar's worth of coins into the busfare machine, so he needs a half hour to finish a bowl of ice cream that any normal person would polish off in five minutes—that's no reason to reject his love.

The wall of fear rose up. I can't, she told herself. I just can't. And I can't because—I'm not sexually attracted to him. There! That was a legitimate reason. But under inspection even that fell apart. Michael was a very attractive man; she had thought so the first time she saw him. But she never let herself *feel* that attraction; she had always cut those feelings off anytime they threatened to arise. She tried to imagine kissing him, his face drawing closer to hers, his eyes shutting—no. She couldn't do it. He was too— The whole thing was so—

Laughter in the hall. Madeline lifted her head; Michael must be leaving. She crept to her door and opened it a crack. Michael was leaning on the hall door with his hand on the knob, and Bella and Robert were standing in front of him, their arms around each other. She looked at Michael as he smiled, watched his sun wrinkles deepen.

She shut the door quickly and threw herself on the bed. Michael was in love with her—now what was she supposed to do?

CHAPTER 20

Happy End

The next night at dinner Madeline was picking at stuffed shells, listening to Robert describe a student who had come into his office that day claiming she was having a nervous breakdown and so needed an extension on her final paper.

"So I gave her the extension," Robert said, cutting stuffed shells with his fork. "I felt sorry for her. And a few hours later who do I see arm in arm with some guy, laughing and going into The Marlin? So now I feel like an idiot."

"But it still might be true, Robert," Bella said. She had finished eating, and was sitting cross-legged on her chair. "Just because you're in the middle of a nervous breakdown doesn't mean you can't laugh and go have a drink at The Marlin. Maybe you giving her an extension made her feel better."

"Or maybe I'm a complete fool. But she was so distraught! Her eyes were swollen, she was clutching a tissue…"

"Don't worry about it, honey. Worse comes to worse, you just made a bad call. And even if she's not having a nervous breakdown, she would still have to be having some kind of problem if she went to all that trouble to go to your office and lie. Know what I mean?"

"I suppose."

"And where is Michael?" Bella asked, looking at her watch. "It's past seven-thirty."

"We won't be seeing much of Michael this week," Robert said, dabbing his mouth and beard with his napkin. "His sutra is due at Columbia University Press on Friday, so he's going to be tied up every night."

"He can at least come down and have ice cream."

"That's what I told him, but he said he really has to concentrate."

Madeline's cheeks burned, but she said nothing. At her temp assignment, then at Yoga for Women, and now at dinner, her stomach had been doing flip-flops at the thought of seeing Michael. She didn't ever want to see him again, and at the same time she had been waiting impatiently for his slow knock. And now he wasn't coming, not for the entire week! She was disappointed, but also relieved; she still didn't know how to answer those big green eyes. Oh well, she thought. I'm sure I'll run into him at some point.

But she didn't. One morning when she was in her room making her bed she heard him come in and pick up Robert so they could travel to Columbia together; she had stood by the door, listening to Michael's low careful tones, but she didn't dare go out into the hall. When he left she felt sorry that she hadn't seen him. Don't be silly, she told herself, giving her pillow an extra hard fluffing. You have nothing to say to Michael, nothing.

And yet all day Friday she was in a state of nervous excitement. Surely he would come by tonight to tell her all about his encounter with his editor, and all the last-minute changes he had to make. She loved hearing about these sort of things, and Michael always went into great detail for her. At seven o'clock she flew out of Yoga for Women, and practically ran home. He wasn't at the apartment when she arrived, but it couldn't be long now; she took a quick shower, changed her clothes, and joined Bella and Robert in the dining room. They were almost done eating, and in her place was a bowl of ravioli covered by a plate. She ate quickly, not tasting anything, then helped Bella clear the table and fill the dishwasher. She looked at the clock: almost eight, and still no Michael. Maybe he had plans with other friends? Maybe his editor was taking him out to dinner? Robert would know. Madeline and Bella finished the dishes; Bella was wiping the counter with a sponge when Madeline asked, her voice painfully casual, "Any special plans tonight?"

"Nope. You?"

"None. Just Scrabble, I guess. That is, if Michael comes over."

"Well, if he doesn't we could watch a video."

"Should I go ask Robert if Michael's coming? You know, so if he says he's coming I won't go out to the video store and miss him. Miss Scrabble, I mean."

"Let's go together," Bella said, turning out the light.

Robert was in the living room reading a book on Victorian architecture. Bella plucked the book out of his hands and put it on the coffee table. "So, professor," she said, putting her hands on the arms of the chair, leaning forward and kissing him on the cheek. "What's up for tonight? Is Michael coming for Scrabble?"

Robert ran a hand through Bella's hair. "Michael, my dear wife, is in Cambridge."

"Cambridge!" Madeline cried. "Why on earth did he go there?"

Robert looked at her curiously. "Maybe it has something to do with the fact that his father lives there. Why do you look so upset?"

"I'm not upset, I'm just surprised. Michael hardly goes anywhere for the weekend."

"I think he wanted to give his father a copy of his sutra."

"So Robert, Madeline is willing to go out and get a video."

"I changed my mind," Madeline said. "I think I'll just go to my room and read."

She curled up in bed and held a pillow to her stomach. What was going on? Michael was avoiding her, that much was clear. He had gone away for the weekend, and he hadn't even bothered to stop by and tell her so, or at least say hello. Five whole days had gone by, and not a word from him, not even a glimpse of him. Did he have a change of heart? Or was he hurt by her silence and so had retreated to Cambridge? Or—and the thought nearly stopped her heart—maybe Bella was right, maybe Michael did have an old flame up there, and maybe he was nursing his broken heart with a quick roll in the hay. Not that I care, she told herself stoutly. Not that I care at all. Still… Maybe Robert knew more, maybe if she pumped him for information he could tell her. She left her room and went into the hall; the living room and TV room were dark, and Bella and Robert's bedroom door was closed. She sighed; she wouldn't be seeing them the rest of the evening. She went back into her room to read *Those Barren Leaves*. Another exciting Friday night, she thought as she curled up on her bed.

The next day Madeline wrote, went to yoga, stopped by Spencer's but got no answer when she yelled up at his window. A mutual acquaintance happened to pass by, and he told her that Spencer had left for Amsterdam two days before. Oh well. She thought about going for sushi, but nowadays she always went with Michael, and if she showed up at Kobe without him the waitresses would ask about him and what would she say? "Michael's up in Cambridge having sex because I broke his heart." Not that I care, Madeline reminded herself again. What he does is his business. Yet all through eating an egg salad sandwich at Shirley's, all through buying shampoo at Crabtree and Evelyn's and glancing at books at The Literary Shop, the thought of Michael nagged her. What was he doing, who was he with, why had he stayed away so long? Would he ever come to the apartment again or was he finished with her? He had opened his heart, and she had done nothing but open and close her mouth like a guppy. So now that was it, he was done with her? But that wouldn't be fair, she brooded as she trudged home. He didn't even give me a chance to decide. Not that there's any doubt what I'll decide, not really, but at least he could have given me a little time. All this is new for me; I need time to get used to the idea that he loves me and maybe later—her thoughts would go no further, but all she knew was he shouldn't have given up on her so soon. He should have known to give her time.

Back in the apartment she put her packages in her room, then peeked into the living room. Robert was reading about Victorian architecture again—should she interrupt and cross-examine him? Better try Bella first. She went down the hall and into Bella and Robert's room. Bella was sitting on the bed in her bathrobe, her hair in a bright blue towel, pieces of cotton stuffed between her toes. The radio on the bedside table was on, and Bella was singing softly as she shook a bottle of red nail polish. Madeline flopped on the bed on her stomach, and put her chin in her hands.

"Hi."

"Hi. How was yoga?"

"Okay."

"Did you eat?"

"I had a sandwich at Shirley's, then I did some shopping. Now I'm bored."

"Take off your shoes and grab some cotton, I'll give you a pedicure."

"Okay." Madeline kicked off her sneakers, pulled her socks off with her toes, then rolled on her back and sat up. "Funny," she said as she grabbed a handful of cotton puffs from the bag. "I guess I usually do something with Michael on weekends, and now that he's in Cambridge I don't have anything to do."

"So call someone."

"Rose has a hot date, Devon has relatives visiting, and Spencer is in Amsterdam."

"So hang out with us. We're going into The City to see a double feature of *Frenzy* and *Psycho*, then we're going out to eat."

"You sure I won't be a third wheel?"

Bella laughed. "Madeline, you've been our third wheel for ten years! By this time we're a tricycle. Know what I mean?"

"I guess. Okay, I'll come with you." She sat in silence watching as Bella carefully stroked blood red polish on her toenails. Bella had beautiful feet, white and arched with slender toes that lined up in a graceful curve. "Bella?"

"Hmm?"

"You know how you always say you think Michael has an ex-girlfriend he sees in Cambridge? Why do you say that?"

"Because Michael is a very sexual man who has, as far as I know, no sex life."

"Why do you say he's very sexual?"

"Only because it oozes from every pore of his body. Haven't you ever noticed the way he touches things? I remember one time I was watching him wipe a glass, and all I could think was, I wish I was that glass."

"Bella!"

"Oh, Madeline. You know what I mean. I'm madly in love with Robert, but that doesn't mean I'm blind to other men. Michael is really sexy. He's one of those shy, soft-spoken types—you know, still waters that run deep and all that. Men like that are great in bed."

"Whatever. But tell me, Bella, did Michael ever *say* anything that made you think he has someone in Cambridge?"

"No. Call it women's intuition. Robert says I'm completely off-base, but what does Robert know."

"Michael doesn't go to Cambridge all that often, so he couldn't have a girlfriend there, could he?"

"No, he definitely doesn't have a girlfriend. I'm just saying he probably has an old flame who he calls up and screws. You know, some nice Harvard professor who was in his Ph.D. program. It's just my little theory. Okay, your turn. You want red or pink?"

"Pink."

And all during the walk to the PATH station, all during the ride to 9th Street, all during the two movies at the Eighth Street Playhouse, Madeline was tortured by the thought of Michael rolling around in bed with some fabulous sexy woman. By the time Janet Leigh was in her car and on her way to the Bates Motel, Madeline knew a great deal about this woman: she had cascades of red hair, pure white skin, perfect features, long legs, lots of curves and big breasts, bigger even than Madeline's. And she was totally brilliant; she was fluent in as many or more languages than Michael—they were probably laying in bed right this moment, holding hands and telling jokes in Chinese. And she lived in a beautiful Cambridge apartment decorated with plain dark wood furniture—because this woman would know about antiques—and charming exquisite artwork she had picked up from all her travels—because unlike Madeline who had never even been to Europe, this woman was as well-traveled as Michael. And she was older, more mature; and she was published, and well-respected in her field. She was, in short, everything that Madeline was not—and at the moment when Norman Bates pulled aside the shower curtain and Bella sunk her nails into Madeline's arm and screamed, Madeline was ready to tear out her hair with jealousy. Michael is in love with me! she told the woman. Get your hands off my Michael.

My Michael.

Oh no. That was the sort of thing Bella said about Robert. "My sweet little Robert," Bella would coo when Robert walked into the room. "Isn't he just the cutest thing in the world?" Or she would jump on his lap and pat his head: "My Robert. My sweet darling Robert." Madeline tried to imagine herself leaping onto Michael's lap, and for the first time she could actually envision physical contact with him, even if it was just sitting on his lap and tweaking his nose. Michael was awfully cute and sweet, there was no doubt about that. More cute and sweet than Robert, she thought, stealing a glance at Robert's thin face with its concentrated expression. Well, Robert wasn't too bad, but Michael was more her type. He was tall, for one thing; she liked when they were walking and she had to crane her neck to look up at him. And he had all those wrinkles by his eyes—she liked them. And he had a nice mouth, nice even teeth, and a nice laugh. And he never bragged, or caused a scene, or got hysterical. And he was smart, very very smart...

"Madeline?" Bella whispered.

"What?"

"You look a million miles away. What are you thinking about?"

"Nothing. I'm not thinking about anything." Snap out of it, Madeline, she told herself. Pull yourself together. Forget about Michael, forget about redheads. There's nothing you can do now; he'll be back tomorrow, and you'll see him then.

❧   ❧   ❧

But she didn't.

Five o'clock. Six o'clock. Seven o'clock. Eight o'clock. Where was he? Had he even arrived home? She had been in her room reading, too far away to hear any noise from the staircase. Robert and Bella said nothing about Michael during dinner, but then they weren't the ones who had broken his heart.

By nine o'clock she was wild with panic. Maybe his plane had crashed? Maybe he had taken a job at Harvard? Maybe he had asked the redhead to move in with him? Or, maybe worst of all, maybe he had come home and had no plans to come by and see her. She had to know if he was home—should she call and hang up if he answered? That was so childish; and what if at the exact moment he picked up the phone Bella came into the room and asked, "Maddy, who are you calling?" No—no good. But she had to know; if the plane crashed, or if he was in an accident, they would notify his father, not Robert and Bella. She decided to go outside, cross the street, and see if there was a light in his apartment. Yes, that was the solution. She grabbed her keys and was halfway out the door when Bella stepped into the hall.

"Where on earth are you going at this hour?"

"I—uh—have to mail a letter."

"Can't it wait till tomorrow?"

"No, it can't." She closed the door and ran down the steps. Was it worse if he was there or if he wasn't there? But even if she didn't see a light he might still be home, might just be sleeping—but no, she decided that if there was no light she would go home and call Newark Airport and ask if there had been any crashes, and she wouldn't even care if Bella and Robert heard her.

She stepped outside, waited for a bus to pass, then sprinted across the street. Here was the moment of truth: she turned around and—yes. Light. Lots of it. He was home. Thank God, he was safe, and he was home.

"But why don't you want to see me?" she said aloud, stamping her foot. "Why are you staying away?"

❦   ❦   ❦

The next day Madeline was on call. Six other temps were also on call; one by one their names were called, one by one they picked up their purses, briefcases, knapsacks, and left. By nine-thirty it was just Madeline, sitting in a cold plastic chair, trying to concentrate on *Time Must Have a Stop*.

"And then there was one."

Madeline looked up. The obnoxious receptionist was staring at her. "I beg your pardon?" Madeline asked.

"And then there was one. You know—it's an Agatha Christie book. Everyone staying at this big house gets killed one by one, and then only one person is left. So that's you."

"Yes, well…"

"Whatcha reading?"

"*Time Must Have a Stop*. It's by Aldous Huxley."

"Oh. I read *Brave New World* for school. I liked it."

"That's nice."

Please don't talk to me anymore, Madeline begged silently. You're not even particularly obnoxious today, but my nerves are stretched so tight I can hardly stop myself from running out of the room screaming. So please shut up. Or call a friend.

As if by magic the receptionist picked up the phone and dialed. "C.J.? Hi, what's up?...Really?...Really?...Oh God, that's unba*lee*vable! So did you call him or did he call you?"

Madeline sighed, and shut her book. She wouldn't be sent out today, that was certain, but she was obligated to stay here until eleven-thirty. And then? Go home and write? Go somewhere and eat sushi? Go to a hardware store, buy a rope and hang herself for being such a fool with Michael? She felt tears prick her eyes. Had he really stopped loving her? Was it really so unforgivable that she hadn't known what to say? If only she could talk to him, if only she could ask him to give her some time. Because maybe—*maybe*—with time and patience, maybe she would stop being so afraid.

But if he didn't come tonight? Or tomorrow night? A wave of despair ran through her. And then an idea, a sudden clear idea, popped up in her head: Why don't *you* see *him*? Today, at Columbia. But no; the last time she had done something like that had been with David, and she had nearly died in a public place. But Columbia—why not? She had to know for sure how he was feeling; she couldn't bear to sit through another evening unsure whether Michael would come. Better to know the worst.

She rose, walked to the receptionist's desk and mouthed "Bathroom," and in between "Really?" and "I told you so," the receptionist handed Madeline a key attached to a block of wood with the word LADIES in black letters. Madeline left Classic Temps and walked down the empty, echoing hall. It was an old-fashioned building next to Grand Central Station, and although Madeline had never set foot in the other offices, she felt that if she opened any door she would walk into the 1930s, complete with heavy black phones, men with watches tucked into their vests, and heavily rouged secretaries with pencils in their piled-up hair. But not only did she never open any doors, she never saw any open; it was a cold, lonely place, and Madeline couldn't wait for the day when she would walk into the elevator and never come back.

In the ladies room—a plain room with white tiles and two stalls—she combed her hair and took a good look at herself. She was wearing a dark purple jacket cut short, a white blouse, and a narrow cut grey and purple plaid skirt that buttoned in back. Ugh. Not that I want to make an impression on Michael, she told herself as she combed her hair, but it helps if you feel your best, or at least comfortable. But her hair was clean and shiny, she was well-rested, and—there it was, that change Michael had been talking about. Her lips were still well-shaped and slightly full, but there was a slight tug at each side—from sadness, she thought. Sadness, or experience. And her eyes were more open, less guarded, and there were definite lines spreading from the outer corners. I don't look like a teenager anymore, she thought with a shock. For years everyone always thought she was younger than she was, but now she looked absolutely resolutely twenty-seven. And she didn't mind. She peered at herself some more, and decided that no, she definitely didn't mind.

Back in the reception area, time dragged. From what Madeline could recall, Michael had a class from ten o'clock till eleven fifty, so if she took a taxi she could catch him before he went to lunch. The only hitch was, what if he had lunch plans with Robert? Well, she wasn't planning on staying long, just long enough to—what? To say, "I can imagine myself sitting on your lap and tweaking your nose"? Or, "Give me another three years and maybe then I'll be ready to have a relationship"? She didn't know what she would say; she would just go and see what happened. And if she did end up hyperventilating, at least she knew that all she had to do was cup her hands over her nose and mouth.

At eleven twenty-seven Madeline signed out. She walked across the reception area calmly enough, but once outside Classic Temps she ran down the empty halls, past the silent doors, and skidded to a stop at the elevator bank. She pressed the down button repeatedly, although it had lit up the first time she touched it. Hurry, hurry! she begged the elevator. A few moments later there was a "ding." She looked around wildly; there, at the end, one of the down arrows was lit. She ran over and stood in front of the door, hopping from one leg to the other. Hurry, hurry! The door opened; the elevator was full, but Madeline squeezed herself in. The elevator stopped at three different floors, and by the time it reached the lobby Madeline's hands were wet and she was ringing them desperately. Hurry, hurry!

She ran through the lobby to the street, dodging messengers and grey-suited commuters. Out on Lexington Avenue she stepped into the street and stuck out her hand for a taxi. Many passed, but they were all full; it had to be twenty of by now. She was so distraught she was practically crying, and when at last an empty taxi stopped in front of her, she wrenched open the door and fell in, practically shouting, "116th Street and Amsterdam. And hurry."

The white middle-aged driver gave her a disdainful look; Madeline perched her hands on the back of his seat and said beseechingly, "I'll give you five dollars above the fare if you get me there in ten minutes."

"Ten minutes!" he said as pulled out into the stream of traffic. "Make it fifteen and you got a deal."

"Okay. This is an emergency," she said by way of explanation.

"So I gathered. Boyfriend taking you to lunch?"

Madeline shot him a dirty look. "If it was just that it wouldn't be an emergency, would it?"

Lexington, Park, Madison. The driver was really making an effort; he ran through lights just as they turned red, he beeped, he cut people off—Madeline began to feel afraid they might crash. But her stomach was churning with excitement; in a little while she would see Michael, in just a few minutes he would be standing in front of her with those big green eyes and that calm, handsome face.

"I'm gonna cut over on 110th instead of through the park. That okay with you?"

"As long as you don't get us killed."

"What, and lose my five dollars?"

Fifteen minutes had passed by the time they reached Amsterdam and 110th Street, and it was seventeen minutes exactly when the driver screeched to a halt at 116th and Amsterdam. Madeline gave him $7 above the fare and ran off down the shady path that led to the heart of the Columbia campus. As she reached the Low Library steps she saw students pouring out of every building; classes were already out. Oh God, please don't let me miss him, please don't! She raced up the steps, turned right, and there it was, the East Asian Studies building, red brick with white marble trim like almost all Columbia buildings.

Madeline had been to Michael's office many times with Robert, so she knew exactly where she was going as she raced up the stairs to the fifth floor. A long hall, a few students, no sign of Michael. She ran into a rectangular room where a secretary was sitting and typing; Madeline stopped before the secretary's desk only to find she was so out of breath she could not speak. She put a hand on the desk and the other hand on her stomach, breathing heavily.

The secretary, a plump, middle-aged woman with black hair piled into a bun and adorned with two ivory sticks, regarded Madeline curiously. "Aren't you Robert Dellasandandrio's sister-in-law?"

Madeline nodded.

"I expect you're looking for Professor Eliot?"

Madeline nodded again.

"He'll be here in a moment. His class just got out."

"But—" Madeline pointed at the clock. "It's past twelve."

"Well, Professor Eliot always needs a little time to get his things together."

In other words, Madeline thought, Professor Eliot is *slow*.

"Why don't you have a seat and catch your breath. Would you like some water?"

"Please."

Madeline sat on a wooden couch with red cushions. Her left side was killing her, and she couldn't stop panting. The secretary rose and went to the water cooler in the corner, then came back with two small paper cups.

"I got you two; I think you could use them."

"Thanks."

Madeline drank the water quickly, and threw the empty cups in the garbage pail next to the couch. I must look a fright, she thought. Her cheeks always turned bright red when she ran, her hair was certainly a mess, and when she touched her face she felt sweat. What the fuck am I doing here? she thought as she took a comb out of her bookbag. Why did I run here like a crazy woman when all I had to do was wait until five o'clock when I could walk up one flight of stairs and see Michael then?

By ten after Madeline's pulse had dropped out of heart attack range, and she was just putting her comb in her bookbag when she heard the secretary say, "Here he is."

And there was Michael. In khakis, a white button-down shirt, an olive green corduroy jacket, carrying two books and a file folder under one arm. And when he saw Madeline his eyes widened, and an expression of joy filled his face—and in that moment Madeline knew there was no woman in Cambridge, and no change of heart. He loved her; thank God, he still loved her.

"Professor Eliot, this young woman has been waiting for you."

"Thank you, Grace," he said, his eyes staying on Madeline.

Oh no, Madeline thought as she stood and nervously wiped her hands on her skirt. What have I done? He still loves me, fine, but that's all I really wanted to know, and now that I know I can go home.

"Hello, Madeline," he said, walking towards her. "Why don't we go into my office?"

"Okay," she said weakly. She sent Grace a quick smile, and followed Michael to a door on the other side of the room. They passed other offices, some with open doors; Michael stopped at one and asked a short man with black hair if he wanted to borrow his copy of I Am a Cat. They moved down the room, and Michael stopped in front of a door with a small typewritten sign that said MICHAEL ELIOT and listed his office hours. Michael turned the handle, and they were in a decent-sized room lined with bookshelves; there was a large wooden desk, a wooden chair behind the desk and two more in front of it. The floor was covered by a beautiful rose carpet with an intricate design of gold and ivory around the edges.

Michael opened the large window, and the noise of campus gently filled the room. He put his books and folder on the desk, then he sat and looked up at her, smiling.

"It's nice to see you," he said.

She stood on the other side of the desk, running a finger along the wood. "I was on call," she said. "That's why I'm wearing these goofy clothes."

"You look nice."

She glanced at him, the floor, then smiled shyly.

"So," he said. "Are you hungry? I have a seminar at two, but if we leave now I should be able to make it."

"Okay."

"Shall we go to the Hungarian Pastry Shop?"

"That sounds good."

"Okay. Well—I'm ready."

"Okay."

He rose, and they walked back into the reception area.

"Grace, we're going to the Hungarian Pastry Shop. Would you like me to bring back something?"

"A Napoleon," Grace said without hesitation. "And a coffee. Let me get you some money," she said, reaching for her purse.

"Oh no—it's on me. You helped me so much this past week, it's the least I can do."

"How did she help you?" Madeline asked after they stepped into the hall.

"With my sutra. She made copies for me, typed letters—it was very generous of her."

"But isn't that her job?"

"Not technically," Michael said, reaching his arm out and opening the door to the stairwell. "Strictly speaking it's not departmental work."

"So you got the sutra to your editor on time?"

"Yes, I did. I'll tell you all about it at lunch."

He held the door for her, and they walked out onto campus. Columbia was such a pleasing sight with its red brick, white marble, and rich green lawns. Madeline had loved going to school here, had loved striding across the courtyards and up the marble steps on her way to classes. As busy as campus could be, there was always an air of stillness and stateliness, a dignified but very vivid energy. Thank God Bella met Robert, Madeline thought as she and Michael walked down the Low Library steps. Because if she hadn't I don't think I ever would have come here.

"Michael," she said suddenly. "Do you know that all the time I was at Barnard you were here?"

"I've thought about that."

"But I never met you. Maybe we passed each other on my way to Chinese Philosophy class."

"Maybe."

"What if I had taken a course with you?"

"Well," he said, smiling down at her. "I don't think we were meant to meet then."

"Oh." She wanted him to elaborate, but decided the topic was too close to the unmentionable topic of Michael being in love with her. "So you went to Cambridge this weekend."

"That's right."

"Did you have a good time?"

"Yes."

"Did you—did you see any old friends?"

"Yes."

They stepped onto Amsterdam Avenue and turned right. Madeline looked at Michael sharply. "What kind of old friends?"

"What kind?" He laughed. "I saw Paul—you know him, he's come to visit me a few times. And I happened to bump into a former classmate on Brattle Street."

"A former classmate?"

"Someone who was in my Ph.D. program. He wasn't a friend, exactly, but it was nice seeing him."

No women, she decided. Just as she had thought, but it didn't hurt to make sure.

"And you?" he asked. "Tell me what you've been doing."

So as they walked past St. Luke's Hospital and St. John the Divine she told him that she had sent off the Billy Ray Bonner story and was already well into the first draft of "The Virgin." "It's going to be a long short story," she told him. "Not quite a novella, but close. I thought about writing it from The Virgin's point of view, or maybe I'll switch to him at the end. I'm not sure. Changing the narrator in a short story is kind of tricky."

"It's not like a novel, is it, where you have so much space. There's a wonderful short story called 'The Blue Cup' where the narrator is switched at the end—I'll try to find it for you."

"Okay."

"And this weekend? Were you busy?"

"No," she said shyly. "I was bored. I finished *Antic Hay* and I started *Time Must Have a Stop*. And I went into The City with Bella and Robert; we saw two Hitchcock movies, *Frenzy* and *Psycho*."

"*Frenzy* is an amazing movie. I always remember that scene where he's in the back of the potato truck trying to get his diamond stickpin out of the dead girl's hand."

"That was so gruesome."

"My father met Hitchcock once."

"Did he really?"

They crossed One Hundred Eleventh Street and walked into the Hungarian Pastry Shop. The little restaurant was brimming with students; there didn't appear to be an empty table, but a harried waiter assured them there were two seats in back. They worked their way past gesturing smokers and knapsacks on the floor, and against the wall, squeezed between two other small tables, they saw an empty table covered with dirty dishes. Michael moved the table out slightly, and they squeezed into the chairs.

"Crowded," Madeline said as she stacked the dirty dishes.

"Very," Michael agreed. "You don't mind? I suppose it's not a very good place to talk."

Good, she thought, because I don't want to talk. "So your sutra," she said. "Tell me about it."

In between having the table cleaned, reading menus, ordering and eating brie sandwiches and minestrone soup, Michael told Madeline about typing until one in the morning each night and running to the library for last-minute checks on footnotes and having Grace make copies and meeting with his editor and the editor assuring him they would get back to him as soon as possible. As Michael spoke, Madeline felt relieved: everything was normal, it was just her and Michael talking as usual. He wasn't sending her moony glances, and he didn't seem at all interested in pressing her for a reply to his comment up at Stevens. He behaved as he always behaved: he was kind, gentle, respectful, soft-spoken, intelligent. That's how he is, Madeline thought, and that's how he'll always be. She watched him as he spoke, watched his large green eyes, his graceful hands, saw how he didn't get mad when the man next to him accidentally elbowed him. And he's so handsome, she thought, her eyes running along his high cheekbones and well-shaped mouth, and the way his sandy hair rested along his ears. And all those wrinkles by his eyes from his time in Nepal…

"Don't you agree?"

"What? Oh, I'm sorry, Michael; I was listening, but I guess I didn't hear you."

"I said that the food was good, and asked if you agreed."

"Good food," she said. "Really good food."

"Well." He looked at his watch. "It's only twenty after; we still have some time. You know," he said, looking her in the eye, "you can't imagine what a wonderful surprise it was to walk into the office and see you waiting for me."

A warm wave passed through her body. She blushed and looked at her hands. "Yes, well…"

"For a moment I thought you had come because of our pact."

"Our pact?"

"You know—if you ever got so angry you thought you might be violent? Remember, I told you to come see me at work."

"Oh no," she said. "I wasn't feeling violent. I was just—I was just in the neighborhood, you know, and I—"

She looked up at him. He was smiling, smiling at her so warmly; she felt all her resistance melt, and the warm wave came back and swept through her. But no! No, she couldn't do this; she wasn't ready. And she would tell him so. She sat up straight, hardened her expression and said, "Listen, Michael, I—"

"Professor Eliot?"

They looked up. A tall skinny student with a thick shock of black hair, pasty white skin, and a desperate look in his brown eyes stood next to their table.

"Hello," Michael said. "Stuart, right?"

"Right, from your Nirvana and Samsara seminar. I'm so, so sorry to interrupt your lunch but I've been working on my paper nonstop all weekend and it's just not done yet. I'm totally stuck, and I was hoping we could talk before class and then if you maybe could give me a two-day extension I swear to *God* I'll have it for you. I'm sorry," he said, looking at Madeline. "I see you're together, you're eating, but I've been living on Cheese Doodles and No Doze and if I don't get some help I'm going to totally freak out." He took a deep, shaky breath. "Your secretary told me where to find you. And she said not to forget her Napoleon."

"It's no problem about the extension," Michael said. "So don't worry about that. We can walk back to campus together and talk on the way. Okay?"

"Okay. I'm sorry," he said, again to Madeline. "I don't mean to drag him away from you."

"Madeline can walk with us," Michael said, smiling at her. "Would you like to?"

"Okay," she agreed.

As she stood by the cashier's watching Michael order Grace's food and pay the bill, Madeline smiled at Stuart reassuringly. Thank you, she told him silently. Thank you for coming at exactly the right moment. And if they could just go on like this, Madeline thought as she walked silently by Michael's side, listening as Stuart rambled on about the Four Noble Truths and the Three Jewels and the Eight Worldly Dharmas; if she and Michael could just go on being friends, and never ever have to discuss what he said at Stevens. But even as she thought all this, she felt herself melting. Watching Michael with Stuart, seeing how he treated Stuart with the same gentle respect that he treated her and, in fact, everyone; listening as Michael offered suggestions, soothed Stuart's nerves, reassured him about the extension, Madeline felt a desire to wrap her arms around him and bury her face in his neck. Michael is such a sweet person, she thought. He's so sweet and kind and good.

When they reached the Low Library steps, Michael stopped. Stuart stopped as well, then took a discreet step away.

"I have to go now," Michael said. "But I'll see you tonight?"

"You'll come for Scrabble?"

"I'd like to. If you want me to."

"I do," she said, blushing furiously.

"Thank you for coming today," he said. "As I said, it was a wonderful surprise. Well—" He looked over at Stuart, who was practically pawing the ground and snorting. "I have to go. I'll see you later." He reached out a hand and touched her hair, then turned to join Stuart.

Madeline turned abruptly and ran across campus towards Broadway. A few people turned their heads as she passed, wondering why that pretty blonde girl had such a peculiar expression on her face.

❦   ❦   ❦

When Madeline came home from Yoga for Women, she heard Bella talking as she opened the door.

"…dumped her. Just like that, out of nowhere. They were living together for years, they were practically engaged, and suddenly he tells her he met someone else and wants to leave. She's devastated, of course. Hi Maddy—my, aren't you sweaty."

"Hi. I am not." She stood in the doorway of the dining room, trying to hide her happy fluster at the sight of Michael sitting at the table with an open beer in his hand.

"Michael's back," Robert said. "So we can play Scrabble."

"Hello, Madeline," Michael said, smiling.

"Hi. Well—hmm. I better take a shower and change."

"You're not that sweaty," Bella called after her. "I was only kidding."

Madeline threw off her clothes, put on her bathrobe, and ran down the hall to the bathroom. After her shower she dressed in white cotton pants and a long sleeved blue and white striped T-shirt.

"What are you all dressed up for?" Robert asked as she took her seat.

"I'm not dressed up."

"You're not wearing sweatpants, which means you're dressed up."

"Give me the bag so I can pick my letters. Are we clockwise or counterclockwise tonight?"

"Let me check the notebook—clockwise."

"You know, I wouldn't even have to ask that ridiculous question every time if you'd just trust me."

"Madeline," Robert said, handing her the green velvet bag. "Any trust I might have had in you flew out the window the day you put down 'lepton.' Why don't you just confess—you looked at the dictionary."

"I did not! Michael," she said, turning to him and flushing, "do I use the dictionary when Robert's on the phone?"

"No," Michael said, looking at Robert. "She doesn't."

Robert raised an eyebrow. "Well, since Michael says so. But she's very sneaky, Michael—she might have been distracting you so you didn't even notice."

"I am not sneaky," Madeline said, "and I resent you saying that I am."

"Why don't we begin?" Michael said. "Madeline, pick a letter so we can see who goes first."

Madeline picked E, Michael B, Robert L, so Michael went first. He put down APACE, then Madeline put down CRUX; she was pleased at Robert's expression of despair—obviously she had spoiled his plans. The game went quickly, except for Michael, and Madeline felt calm and happy. It was so nice having Michael at her side again, nice to see him smiling at her, nice to feel his presence, hear his laugh. And during one of Michael's turns she studied him as he studied his letters; she remembered how he had touched her hair after lunch, and she suddenly felt something stir in her belly. The sensation of pleasure deepened as she looked at him; it was like warm gold filling the lower half of her body. She was overcome by an urge to throw herself in his lap, wrap her arms around him and kiss him. So I am sexually attracted to him, she thought. And—oh, Goddammit, why not?—I suppose I'm in love with him.

At last Michael had a word. As he picked up each letter with agonizing care, Madeline glanced at Robert and winked; Robert smiled and shook his head. Gradually Michael's word took shape: SEARING.

"Very good," Robert said, counting the points. "Too bad you couldn't use all your letters and get the fifty point bonus."

"Oh well," Michael said.

The piano music stopped suddenly. "Why'd you stop?" Robert asked Bella without turning to look at her.

"I have to call my friend Carolyn, the one who got dumped," Bella said, coming over and putting her hands on Robert's shoulders. "I need to give her some moral support."

"Carolyn's the assistant art director, right?"

"Right, you met her at the Christmas party. And you know," Bella said, wrapping her arms around Robert's neck, "I just had a great idea—why don't we give her two months to recuperate, then invite her to brunch to meet Michael?"

The back of Madeline's neck stiffened.

"Leave Michael alone, Bella," Robert said, his eyes never leaving his letters. "He doesn't want to get fixed up."

"She's really pretty," Bella said, smiling at Michael. "Long red hair, white skin—all the men in the office are crazy about her."

"Bella," Madeline said sharply. "Didn't you hear what Robert said? Leave Michael alone."

They all stared at her. "Madeline!" Bella cried. "You've never used that tone of voice with me!"

Madeline reddened. "I'm sorry, Bella. It's just that—I just can't sit through another brunch like the last one."

Robert snorted. "The problem with the last brunch, as I recall, had more to do with your date than Michael's. Not to mention Bella passing out."

Bella laughed. "Get it right, Robert—I threw up, then I passed out. One of my shining moments as a hostess. Anyway," she said, kissing Robert on the cheek. "I'm off." And a few minutes later bits of Bella's conversation flew into the dining room. "…better to cry it out…deceitful pig…worthless scumbag…"

Robert sighed. "It's a good thing Madeline's in our spare room or Bella would invite that woman to live with us. She loves taking in strays."

"Is that what I am?" Madeline laughed.

"You have exactly one minute left on the timer, Madeline—you have no time for conversation."

"Yes sir." She could not find a decent word, and in the end she put down LET.

"That is pathetic," Robert said. "And, gee—four points?"

"Robert," Madeline said menacingly. "Don't gloat. And don't you laugh either, Michael," she said, turning to him.

"I wasn't laughing."

"You were on the verge."

"Too bad I wasn't on the phone," Robert said. "You could have had a crack at the dictionary."

Robert put down CONFUSE, then set the timer for Michael's turn. Bella's loud and cheerful "Good-bye, Carolyn" rang through the apartment, and then a moment later the phone rang.

"Robert!" Bella called. "Itsa your motha ona the phone, and shes a wantin to talkin to yo-ou."

Robert sighed. "Do you think she covers the mouthpiece when she says things like that?"

"No," Madeline said.

"I didn't think so. Are you two ready for ice cream? Bella and I will be in the kitchen, we might as well get it now."

"Okay," Madeline said.

"That's fine," Michael agreed.

Robert went to take his call, and moments later streams of excited Italian filled the apartment.

"Must be a family crisis," Madeline said.

"Must be," Michael said.

She turned back to her letters. Now that she was alone with Michael the warm gold had started pulsating, and she felt so attracted to him, so in love with him. But I still don't know if I want to do this, she thought. And yet it was clear she had to do something: Michael was a dignified person, and he would not continue to come to the apartment if his position became humiliating. And she could not, would not, watch him being set up with someone. All she wanted to do was tell him one simple thing: she wanted to say "I love you, but I'm afraid." That was all. If she could just tell him that, she would feel better.

But the words wouldn't come. Robert and Bella were in the kitchen, she and Michael were alone, this was most definitely the moment that had to be seized, and yet her throat felt tight. If only he could read her mind! She glanced over at him; he was looking at his hands, and he looked a little sad. Oh no—that she could not bear.

And then she had an idea. She started grabbing letters from the Scrabble board and her wooden stand; she arranged the letters line by line, then moved them in front of Michael:

I

LOVE

YOU

BUT

IM

AFRAID

Michael read the words, and Madeline was charmed to see a faint blush spread over his cheekbones. In all the years she had known Michael, she had never once seen him blush.

Without looking at her, he started to collect letters for a reply. Oh, hurry! she thought, watching him. What if Robert came back before they finished? She clasped her hands tightly, looking from his moving hands to the doorway. At last he started putting letters in front of her.

IUN

She heard Robert hang up the phone and say something to Bella.

DERS

Hurry, Michael, hurry!

TAND
I understand.
Quickly she formed a reply, and slid the words in front of him:

CAN

WE

GO

SLOWLY

Michael read her message, then slid two letters in front of her: OK.

She raised her eyes. He was looking at her, his eyes huge, that faint blush still on his cheeks. She looked shyly at the table.

"Why did you stay away so long?" she asked, touching the OK with her fingertips. "I didn't see you for a whole week."

"I didn't want to crowd you," he said. "I knew you would need time to think, and I thought you could do that better if I wasn't always in your house. And I really did have to work on my sutra, and I really did need to go to Cambridge and give my father a copy."

"Well—I missed you. We see each other every day, you know; it doesn't feel right if you're not around."

"I'm glad to hear it."

He reached over and took her hand, and it was a moment she would always remember. When he touched her all her resistance dropped, and for the first time she let herself feel the connection that existed between them. She was so moved she could not speak; she lowered her face to his shoulder and closed her eyes.

"Finally," he said, bringing a hand to her head and stroking her hair. "Finally."

Laughter, a clash of dishes, then footsteps moving down the hall. Madeline raised her head, let go of Michael's hand; she had just finished mixing up their words when Robert walked into the room.

"Oh my God," Robert said. He put down the bowls of ice cream he was carrying, and stared at the looted Scrabble board. "I can't believe what I'm seeing. What is the meaning of this?" He pulled at his hair. "Have you two gone completely and totally insane?"

"It's my fault, Robert," Madeline said. "I wanted to show Michael something."

"Oh, you did. Well, couldn't you have waited until the game was over? Bella, come see what your sister has done."

Robert needed a good ten minutes to calm down, and was mollified only when Michael determined that since Robert had the highest score when the board was—as Robert said—vandalized, he had therefore won the game.

"Not that it's a real win, of course," Robert said, jabbing his spoon into his ice cream. "Tell me, Madeline, this isn't going to become a habit, is it?"

"No. I'm sorry, Robert—it was just a wild, uncontrollable impulse."

He stared at her. "You have utterly shaken the foundations of my trust. I know that you cheat, and I know you're not above taking help from Michael, but to willfully destroy the game—!"

"Robert," Bella said. "Would you shut up already? And tell me, what was your mother so upset about?"

Robert explained how one of his half-dozen younger sisters got pinched on the ass on the subway, and she pounded the man so hard his nose bled ("A true Dellasandandrio," Bella said proudly). Now *The Daily News* wanted to take her picture, and Mama Dellasandandrio was worried that the man would come after them. Madeline hardly heard a word; she ate her ice cream in a cloud of joy, sneaking looks at Michael, who still had that slight blush on his cheeks. And when Michael finally took his last bite of ice cream, Madeline said, "So Michael, can we go to your apartment now so I can get those books I wanted to borrow?"

Michael put his empty bowl on the table. "Of course."

Madeline stood. "See you guys later."

"I still haven't forgiven you," Robert said.

"You will. Bye."

Madeline ran to her room to get her keys, and as she came down the hall Michael was leaning against the door with his arms folded, watching her.

"Well," she said. "Let's go."

"All right."

She walked behind him up the stairs. So now Michael's going to kiss me, she thought. Kiss me, and maybe—? Well, she'd have to wait and see. She felt terribly excited, her body full of warm gold, but she also felt shy and nervous. But it was a delicious nervousness, and she almost wished Michael lived farther away so she could savor the feeling longer.

Michael opened the door and turned on the hall lights. The hall was lit by arcs of glass, giving the bookshelves and long dusky blue rug a hushed, peaceful feeling. Madeline expected him to pick her up and carry her to his bedroom, but instead he said, "Shall we go sit in my study?"

"Okay."

She followed him in and sat on the dark blue couch. He turned on the desk lamp, then asked her, "Would you like some tea?"

"No."

"Water?"

"No."

"You sure you don't want tea?"

"I'm sure."

He nodded, then sat on the couch. But instead of whisking her into his arms as she was eagerly expecting, he put his elbows on his knees, clasped his hands, and stared down at the rug as if he had never seen it before. Madeline was sitting perfectly straight, hands on knees, face turned to him. Well? she wanted to say. But he just continued sitting and staring at the floor, occasionally clearing his throat, occasionally rearranging his fingers, but otherwise—nothing.

Maybe I'm sitting too far away? Madeline wondered. She inched a little closer—he didn't even look at her. She cleared her throat. He didn't move. Bella's right, she realized; Michael is painfully shy. Didn't he know that she wanted him to kiss her? Come on, Michael, she coached him silently. Stop looking at the floor, turn around and take me in your arms.

But he didn't. She was sure he wanted to; he was blushing rather heavily now, and his breath was short and shallow. Nevertheless, he kept up his vigil with the rug. Well, Madeline thought. Quite obviously nothing is going to happen around here unless I make it happen. She inched closer to him, then she wrapped her hands around his upper arm, rose up a little and kissed him on the cheek.

He turned and looked at her. Sitting so close to him she could see his chest rising and falling rapidly.

"Michael," she said. "I want you to kiss me."

"You do?"

"Of course I do. So why don't you kiss me."

He unclasped his hands and put them on her shoulders. She closed her eyes and lifted her face and—oh, finally, his lips met hers and he kissed her. Slowly. He moved his face away and looked at her.

"Again," she said. "Kiss me again."

So he did, turning a little so he could wrap his arms around her. She moved her hands up to his neck and buried them in his hair. He kissed her again, softly; she pressed her chest against him and kissed him back. Gently she put her tongue on his lips and opened his mouth. He responded in kind, and the next minutes she was lost in pleasure, lost in the scent and touch of him, lost in the beautiful gold field that existed between them. Talk about Merger! she thought. She felt calm and happy, her body filled with pleasure as the warm gold moved up and down and all around her body.

Michael broke the kiss and moved back a little; he held her face in his hands and looked into her eyes. Love exuded from his eyes, and as she stared back at him she knew her eyes were doing the same. Then he began taking the pillows and putting them on the floor; the final pillow he propped at one end of the couch, then he gently maneuvered her so she was reclining with her head and shoulders resting against the lone pillow. She expected him to swing himself on top of her, but instead he sat at her side and leaned over to kiss her. And then slowly, unhurriedly, he kissed her again. His kisses were long and luxurious, soft and persistent, and in between kisses he explored her face, her ears, her neck. Touching, stroking, licking, gently biting; and anytime she reacted with a sound or by digging her hand deeper into his hair, he concentrated on that area, stroking, kissing, biting, until the pleasure was so intense she thought she might scream. Or have an orgasm, because by this time she felt a heartbeat ba-booming in her groin, and her underwear was wet against her skin.

Eventually he found the spot at the back of her neck, and the pleasure was almost more than she could bear; she closed her eyes and sank her nails into the pillow, murmuring his name over and over. He started by stroking the spot with his fingers, slowly tracing patterns, then he wet his fingers and pressed harder; then he took his tongue and slowly flicked it back and forth, back and forth, then he bit softly, small gentle bites—and then he did it all in reverse order, then started again from the beginning. Madeline had heard the expression "in a swoon," but this was the first time she really knew what it meant. And he hadn't even taken off any of her clothes. But one day, she thought, one day soon, he's going to do this to all of my body. *All* of it. My goodness, she thought. My-y goodness.

He gave the spot on her neck a final kiss, then turned her again so she was facing him.

"Michael?"

"Hmm?"

"How long have you been in love with me?"

"Since the first moment I saw you."

"Really?"

"Mmm hmm." He touched her lips with his fingertip. "After my ex-wife left me I was sure I would never love anyone again; I was really prepared to live the rest of my life alone. Then I met you. And the first time I looked at you, I saw our children in your eyes."

If any other man had said that to her, Madeline would have rolled her eyes and made a gagging gesture. But it was different coming from Michael.

"Really?" she asked shyly.

"Really. It's as if a voice inside me said, 'That's her.'"

"So why did you wait so long before you said anything?"

"Why?" He laughed. "Because you seemed to have the exact opposite reaction to me. I could tell you didn't like me, though I couldn't understand the reason. I tried to get close to you, but you were never very friendly. But then we talked about your writing, and you opened up to me, and then we started doing things together regularly. And playing Scrabble. And I saw that you were beginning to trust me, and I felt we were becoming good friends. Then you trusted me about all your religious experiences, and when you had those problems down the shore I was the one you turned to. So that gave me hope."

"That was a beautiful letter you wrote me. I guess I didn't see the full significance of it at the time."

"I wasn't sure if you would or not. And when you came back from the shore I was planning to tell you how I felt, I was just waiting for the right moment—but then you got involved with David, and I was kicking myself for having waited so long. But then you and he broke up, and I promised myself that the minute you were over him I'd tell you. So I did."

"And Patty?" she said, raising an eyebrow. "What about her?"

He sighed. "I still loved you, and although I still saw you almost every night it was really beginning to seem hopeless. So when Patty asked me out I thought, well, why not."

"Did you sleep with her?"

"No."

"Are you sure? Bella says Patty's a sex maniac; she says Patty even has a dildo collection."

"Well, she didn't show it to me. And yes, I'm sure I didn't sleep with her; I didn't even kiss her." He reached out a hand and ran his fingers through her hair. "But I'm sure you already know all that from Bella."

Madeline blushed. "Well...I guess I do. So who have you slept with since you met me?"

"No one."

"No one? Not even when you went to Cambridge to see your father? That was always Bella's theory; she was sure you had an old girlfriend up there."

"No, there was no one in Cambridge." He kissed her nose. "I've been waiting for you."

"But Michael—that's three years! Wasn't that difficult?"

"Sometimes. But I'm a very patient person. And except for David you never went out with anyone, so it wasn't as if I was being masochistic. And I didn't want to sleep with anyone else, Madeline—I only wanted you."

"David's the only one I've slept with since I met you."

"I know."

"We don't have to talk about him."

"I don't mind. You don't love him anymore."

"No." She kissed him. "Now I'm in love with you."

He kissed her again, kissed her long and deep, then moved his mouth to her ear and began teasing it with his teeth. Then back to her mouth, then the base of her throat, then to the spot on the back of her neck. She forgot herself entirely, then one moment she suddenly became aware of herself: she had her arms up behind her head, her back arched and her legs spread—and she remembered her cat Spike, how when Spike was in heat she would sit in the middle of the driveway with her ass raised, ready for anyone. Suddenly Madeline felt shy, a little ashamed; she brought her legs together and crossed her hands over her chest. Michael stopped kissing her; he moved his head back and cocked it to one side. "Don't be afraid," he murmured, and started in again with his kissing and stroking until without knowing it she had moved into the exact same position. Madeline had been kissed by many men in her life, but no one had ever kissed her like this. It was different because they loved each other, but it was something else—and she saw that it was different because Michael was so *slow*. No one had ever taken the time to explore her body like this, to gently probe every inch of her and see what she liked. And she saw that Bella was right: she should have known Michael would be like this, because if he touched glasses and flowers and Scrabble letters with such careful loving kindness, then of course he would touch her the same way.

A little later he moved away from her. "You should go downstairs now. It must be after ten."

She wrapped her arms around him. "Can't I stay here tonight?"

"I thought you wanted to go slowly."

"I do. I mean, I did, but I don't feel scared anymore."

"Well," he said, kissing her. "We're not in any hurry."

"I suppose not."

"Come on," he said, rising and taking her by the hand. "I'll walk you downstairs."

She let him pull her up, then the moment she was on her feet she wrapped her arms around his neck and started kissing him.

"If you don't leave now," he said after a few minutes, "I'm not going to be able to let you leave."

"I know."

"Oh, you do. Here's your keys," he said, picking them up from the desk.

"You're really rushing me out of here," she teased him.

"Actually, I'm exercising immense self-control. Come on," he said, and took her by the hand.

They walked downstairs holding hands, and when they were in front of the apartment door he took her in his arms.

"Are you temping tomorrow?"

"Mmm hmm."

"I'll be home by four."

"I'll be on call, but if I don't get a job I'll be here, so knock when you pass by."

"Can I take you out to dinner tomorrow? Sushi?"

"Okay. And after can we go back to your apartment so you can kiss me some more?"

"Anything you want."

"Michael?"

"Yes?"

"Is it okay if I tell Bella what happened?"

"Of course it's okay. We have nothing to hide."

They kissed again, then Madeline brought her mouth to his ear and told him how much she loved him, and how sorry she was that she had made him wait so long.

"Don't be sorry," he said. "There was never any hurry. Okay," he said, kissing her once more. "Good night. I'll see you tomorrow."

"See you tomorrow."

He kissed her again, then with an effort of will let her go, and moved down the hall. She watched as he walked up the stairs, and waited until she heard his apartment door open and close. Then she opened the apartment door and entered; there was a light in Bella and Robert's room, and a light in the kitchen. She ran down the hall to the kitchen, and saw Bella standing at the sink in her red bathrobe, drinking a glass of water.

"Bella!" she said, grabbing her sister's arm. "You'll never guess what I've been doing."

"What?"

"Kissing Michael."

"Kissing *Michael*?" Bella put down her glass and stared at Madeline. "Are you kidding me?"

"Nope. He's in love with me; he's been in love with me since he first saw me, and that's why he never went out with anyone."

Bella wrapped a hand around her neck. "I can't believe this! You mean all this time and we never knew! Oh my God—this is going to take some getting used to. Are you in love with him?"

Madeline nodded.

"Oh, Maddy," Bella said, taking Madeline in her arms. "This is wonderful! So tell me, what was it like kissing him?"

"Bella," Madeline said, laying a hand on Bella's arm. "It was *the* most erotic, *the* most sensual experience I've ever had in my whole entire life."

"I knew it, I just knew he'd be a good lover. So you didn't fuck?"

"No, we didn't fuck. We just kissed, that's all."

"Come on, let's go tell Robert."

The sisters went to the bedroom and flung open the door. Robert was sitting in bed wearing dark blue pajamas and reading volume two of George Eliot's letters. Bella and Madeline leapt on the bed, and Bella tore the book out of Robert's hands.

"What's going on?" Robert asked.

"Big news," Bella said. "And you'll never guess what it is: Michael's in love with Madeline."

"So," Robert said, folding his arms across his chest and looking from one sister to the other. "You finally figured it out."

"You mean you knew?"

"Of course I knew. I've known for years."

Madeline and Bella exchanged looks. "But how on earth did you know?" Madeline asked.

"It was obvious. The way he spoke to you, the way he looked at you—and then one day when we were going to work I asked him how he felt about you, and he admitted that he was in love with you."

Bella hit Robert's arm. "Why didn't you tell me? I could have helped them."

"They didn't need your help. So Madeline," Robert said, looking at her sternly. "How do you feel about Michael?"

"I'm in love with him."

"So you won't flake out on him? That would be pretty awkward, what with him living upstairs."

"I won't flake out on him."

"Well, I'm glad you two finally worked things out—now I don't have to play so much Scrabble."

"But Robert! You love Scrabble."

"I do, but not every night. I was just playing for you two."

"Oh my God," Bella said. "I just understood something—you two are going to get married, aren't you? I mean, not tomorrow or next week, but this is serious, isn't it?"

Madeline sighed. "With Michael how could it not be? But he said we could go slowly."

"Which won't be hard for Michael," Robert said, grinning. "Going slowly, that is."

"Now, Robert," Madeline said. "I'm beginning to be of the opinion that it's not so bad that Michael is slow. We'll have to stop teasing him about that."

"So Robert," Bella said. "Madeline says Michael's a great kisser. But they didn't fuck."

Robert sighed. "Don't tell me, because I don't want to know." He picked up his book. "Why don't you two go into the kitchen and discuss all the intimate details without me."

"Good idea. Come on, Maddy, I'll make us herb tea."

"Okay. Good night, Robert."

"Good night."

In the kitchen Madeline sat on a stool watching Bella put on the kettle and bustle around arranging tea bags and mugs, all the while chattering steadily.

"I mean, you did see a lot of each other, and you did do things in The City, but I always thought he thought of you like a kid sister or, I don't know, his little sidekick. I mean, I never imagined he was in *love* with you. He is such a sly dog, coming to our apartment all these years and never saying a word. And Robert! Don't think he's going to go unpunished for this! Imagine, keeping such a huge secret from me all this time. I wonder what else he hasn't told me..."

And when the tea was ready, Bella brought the mugs to the counter and hopped up on a stool.

"So Madeline," Bella said, eyes shining. "Tell me *everything.*"

Crete-Hoboken
1995–1996

About the Author

Florence Wetzel was born in 1962 in Brooklyn, NY. She grew up in Westfield, NJ, and attended Barnard College, where she studied with writer B.J. Chute. She is the author of the novels *Mrs. Papadakis and Aspasia,* and she is co-author (with Perry Robinson) of *Perry Robinson: The Traveler.* She has published fiction, journalism, memoir, and poetry in various publications, including the World Wide Web. Currently she lives in Hoboken, NJ.

0-595-27631-8

Printed in the United States
90686LV00004B/44/A